# Finding Their Omega

*Knot Her Pack #1*

Sadie Moss

For updates on new releases, promotions, and giveaways, sign up for my
MAILING LIST.

# Chapter 1

## *Ava*

The moment I enter the back area of the shelter, the dogs start howling.

I grin. "I know, babies, good morning! Good morning."

They say that animals can be soothed by a happy Omega's scent the same way humans can be, and I hope that's true as I walk among the cages greeting all of our animals. I've always wanted to help animals, so working at a shelter seemed perfect, but I have to admit it can really drain me.

There are so many animals brought to us too injured or sick to save. We always do our best—the vets here are saints—but it's the sad cycle of life. I've gone home crying quite a lot since working here.

But I'm not going to let the occasional loss stop me. I want to give every animal, even an animal on its last day, a bit of happiness and love. Even if that's only to comfort them in their last moments.

Luckily we have more happy endings than sad ones. It's my job to take care of the daily needs like grooming, nail clipping, walks, and feeding. I help the animals get ready for their forever homes by teaching them how to behave.

My friends joke that it's practice for when I'll have an unruly bunch of kids of my own. I'm not so sure about that. I'd like to be a mother someday, but right now I don't think it's in my future. Not after the way my last relationship ended...

One of the dogs, Roger, woofs at me, breaking me out of my depressing thoughts. I crouch down. "Hey there, buddy. You ready for your walk?"

Roger rattles his cage as he tries to jump up and down in excitement, his tail wagging. I wince. I'm not an expert, but I really feel like these cages for the dogs are too small.

Try telling that to Mr. Weems, though. He gives a new meaning to the term 'tightfisted.'

"I know, bud." I open the cage and think happy thoughts, making sure my body language stays easy and relaxed. "It's not fun being locked up. I get it."

I let Roger out of his cage, then clip on his leash and grab the poop baggies. "But right now we're going to get a lovely walk out in the sunshine! And then we'll brush your shiny coat so you look extra pretty. A family is going to take you home soon, I just know it."

"Ava!" My coworker Athena is at the front desk and smiles as I walk past with Roger. "I see you've got the good boy."

"He really is well-behaved. He'll be adopted in no time."

Athena is my most cheerful coworker, a Beta with strawberry-blonde hair and a big smile for everyone. Because of her name, sometimes customers get her mixed up with Bonnie, our goth Alpha who constantly stinks like burnt toast because she's got a permanent mental rain cloud over her head.

"It's always such a relief when they're like that," Athena

says. "The ones who are tougher... you worry about them. But you always work wonders."

"I just listen to them."

"It's more than that," Athena insists, but she lets me go with a laugh.

Of course, the moment that I get out onto the street, Roger starts pulling. It's the one thing I need to work on with him. He's good tempered, friendly, sweet, but the moment you take him out on a walk he can't help himself and he wants to run around and explore everything. He's a lab, so he's a big dog, but I'm determined not to let him win.

"Come on, Roger, work with me." I keep a firm grip on the leash. "I know it's not fun being in a cage all day, seriously, but you won't ever get adopted if your family can't control you on a walk."

Roger huffs at me as if to say what he thinks of *that*. I sigh. "Yeah, I get it, trust me. Maybe you're wondering if a family isn't all it's cracked up to be. I know I've wondered the same thing."

After all, there's a reason I'm on suppressants. My scent can still be detected by the animals, since their noses are simply far more sensitive than a human's. But to everyone else? I'm a Beta, as far as they can tell.

I have no intention of living in a cage. And if anyone finds out I'm an Omega, that's exactly what'll happen. They'll force me to bond with an Alpha or Alpha pack, and I refuse to give up my freedom. I'm just lucky I presented as an Omega late enough that I could hop on the suppressants in time.

Once you present, you're supposed to register with the ORD—the Omega Resources Division—so that they can help you find a suitable Alpha or Alphas to bond with. But most people present as teenagers, so everyone assumed I was a Beta for years, including me. Being a late bloomer meant I could get the blockers without too many questions, and I could keep living free as a Beta.

Nobody will ever control me. Especially not a damn Alpha. Or a pack of them.

"Oh fuck!"

"Oh my god!"

I'm so lost in thought and the effort of dealing with Roger as he tugs me along that I don't realize someone's in front of me until we run right into each other. I nearly fall over, and strong hands catch me.

When I look up, I have to crane my neck to meet his eyes. I'm only 5'2" and this guy is at least six feet. I practically bounced off him.

Then the scent hits me.

I inhale deeply, struggling to keep my body and my face under control. This man smells like bourbon, spicy cloves, and honey. It reminds me of warming myself on a cold winter morning, and my heart starts to race in a way it never has before.

Doesn't hurt that he's also handsome as hell, with biceps I couldn't even wrap both of my hands around. My throat goes dry and my skin feels too tight.

My fingers go lax as I just breathe in his intoxicating scent. The man's talking to me, but his words sound muffled, like he's speaking through water.

"Hello? Are you okay? Miss?"

I want to drop my mouth open to catch more of that smell. I want to bury my face in his neck and inhale the source. I want him to—

The leash drops from between my numb fingers, and Roger takes off running.

*Shit!*

"No, no, no!" I yell.

The man turns and watches the dog run. Now that my head's a little clearer, I'm focusing on his face and not just his scent and his muscles. He's definitely a few inches over six feet, towering over me by an entire foot, with slate-gray eyes and a jawline that looks like it's been carved from marble. Those eyes feel like they're looking right through me, down to my very core.

He runs a hand through his rich dark brown hair, glancing back at me. "I can go get him for you, if you want."

"No, I'm sorry, I couldn't possibly—"

"I don't mind at all. I'd be happy to do it."

"No, thank you, really, I'm going to—I have to—go—" I'm tripping over my tongue like I'm back in middle school and crushing on my English teacher. I have no idea why I'm acting like this, or what it could mean. I just know that it's a problem.

I rush after Roger, yelling his name, but my racing heart has nothing to do with chasing after the dog. "Roger! Roger, come here! Come on, boy!"

He heads right for the nearby park, naturally, and I'm able to corner him by the baseball field. Roger yips, his tail wagging, clearly thinking this was all a fun game. I groan and grab the leash again. "Bad boy, Roger. You need to stay with me!"

As I scratch behind his ears, I can't get the image—and the scent—of that man out of my head.

I haven't ever had that reaction to anyone. I don't know why it's happened now. But I'm on suppressants for my heat, and blockers for my scent. They should be working and they haven't ever failed me before, but...

5

I crouch down to pet Roger some more. "Maybe it's the brand?" I whisper to him.

I recently had to switch my black market supplier for suppressants and blockers because I couldn't afford the old ones anymore. Maybe these are less expensive because they're ineffective?

I just pray that these are still working and the man couldn't tell I'm an Omega. When I get home, I'll have to up my dose.

Nobody can know what I really am. Ever.

# Chapter 2

## *Dante*

Holy fuck, what a woman.

Betas don't usually do it for me. I'm an Omega guy, through and through. Call me a typical Alpha but I know what I want and I don't like to settle for anything.

Yet that woman... that Beta...

Her scent was enticing. Sweet lilac and warm vanilla, and something else that I couldn't manage to name before she took off. I want to know what it is. I *need* to know what it is.

It wasn't just her scent either. She's beautiful. Small, but the height difference doesn't bother me. It just means I could pick her up easily and carry her, press her against the wall to feel more of her soft, curvy body against mine.

Her eyes and hair are both a rich dark color, her hair tumbling down her back and framing her delicate face while her eyes are the highlight. Even though I only got a short look at her before she ran off, I know that I'm not going to forget that face. It's burned into my memory now.

I could go after her and ask for her number. My pack remains without an Omega, something that I know weighs on all of us even though we try to remain upbeat. We don't settle for anything less than the best. Call me a perfectionist, call me a romantic, but I want that spark. I want that Omega that will drive us all crazy and satisfy us in ways we couldn't even imagine. Until we find that Omega, we're not settling.

But I have had Betas in my bed. Just for a night, of course. Nothing wrong with having a little fun. It helps to ease my needs so I can focus on work without going crazy. Especially when heats hit.

I could get her number. I'm sure she felt something when we collided, from the way her eyes sparkled up at me. I've been told my scent's intoxicating even to Betas. And there was definitely something intoxicating about her.

*No.*

I shake my head, clearing that idea from my mind. I need to get work done, and I can't let myself be distracted.

When I get to the office for NexusTech Enterprises, I head right for the penthouse offices on the top floor. My pack mates and I built this company together, pioneering smart tech on devices like sunglasses and watches, and now we have the top floor all for ourselves.

It's the perfect situation for us to provide for an Omega, if we can ever find one.

"You look like you got hit by a bus," Ethan informs me.

"Oh, so how you usually look?" I tease him right back.

People have mistaken Ethan and me for brothers occasionally, since we have somewhat similar facial features, although my eyes are gray and his are green. But the sad truth is, Ethan was an only child who lost his parents young.

I know he wants an Omega, a *family*, more than any of us.

And I'm determined to give him one. I lead this pack and that means it's my job as top Alpha to look after my pack mates.

We haven't officially gone looking for an Omega yet, but that's okay. I know we'll find one when the time is right. I'm not going to settle for anything less than the best for myself and my pack mates.

Ethan grins and lobs a soft, squishy mini basketball at me. It's one of the ones we use to play with the mini net hanging over the back of the office door. I immediately catch it and pivot to toss it into the net.

"And the crowd goes wild," Ethan proclaims as I bow.

I see Garrett roll his eyes from over at his desk and I grin, sliding over to him. "What's ruffling your fur?"

"You," Garrett replies.

Something's always ruffling Garrett. He's gruff, but frankly, he's the guy I trust most in the world to have my back. He'll do anything to protect his pack. I think sometimes people don't appreciate him because they think he's too stereotypical for an Alpha, all bite and no bark, not great with words, just 'muscle.' But I know there's a soft heart and a deep protective streak.

"Guys," Caleb interjects, before I can get down to properly teasing Garrett. "This is due on Friday."

Ah, right. "Thanks, Caleb. Can you outline what our next steps are?"

We all sit down at the table in the center of the office as Caleb starts in. Caleb's quiet unless you want him to talk about something nerdy. Then he's the expert. He can talk for hours about tech. Ethan's more of our front guy, our best salesman, and I'm the CEO. I run the office. But Caleb is our techie.

Sometimes people make the mistake of thinking Caleb is insecure because he's so quiet. Garrett never has a problem speaking his mind, Ethan wouldn't know how to keep a thought to himself if you paid him, and I'm pretty damn opinionated myself. But Caleb's silence isn't a lack of confidence. Far from it. He just knows the value of waiting for just the right thing to say.

"I think that we need to do another round of testing," he begins. "I know that we had success..."

"You always do this," Garrett points out. "The watches work. It'll help keep Omegas so much safer if they can track—"

"We know what's at stake," I say calmly. "That's why Caleb wants us to be sure about everything."

Caleb shoots me a grateful smile. "Look, if we put this on the market and it turns out that there are some faults in the system, we're going to look like another one of those mumbo-jumbo assholes who want to take advantage of Omegas."

"Tracking heat cycles is notoriously difficult," Ethan chimes in. "Caleb's concerns are valid. I think it's worth taking another look to see how it can handle Omegas who've been on suppressants for a long time."

Heats can be miserable for an unmated Omega. The very idea that our own future Omega could be out there somewhere suffering through a heat when we could be taking care of her makes my Alpha blood boil and my skin itch.

While all Omegas are required to register with the ORD, it can take time to find them the right mate, and so many go on suppressants in the meantime to avoid unwanted attention from random Alphas or to avoid dealing with heats alone. There are even mated Omegas who might be on suppressants or blockers for health or job reasons.

"Not even doctors can tell you for sure how taking suppressants long-term can affect your heat cycle," Garrett replies gruffly. "How are we supposed to know?"

"I'm not saying we need to know the effects for certain," Caleb replies evenly. "But we do need to be able to have the watches know the *math*. It's about math. If we test them on Omegas who've been on suppressants for a certain number of years and are now off them, then we can teach the watch to calculate based on things like heart rate..."

He goes on, stuff that's way over my head. I'm no slouch, but I'm not nearly the tech genius that Caleb is.

The memory of that pretty Beta floats into my mind... her dark hair... what *was* that third part of her scent...?

"Dante?" Ethan snaps his fingers in front of my face. "Earth to Dante. Dante, it's Virgil calling!"

I blink and come back to myself. Fuck. I got distracted daydreaming about that Beta. "That joke wasn't funny the first time you told it."

"It's funny every time I tell it." Ethan winks at me and then gestures to the table, where I see Caleb's laying out schematics. "You care to join us?"

"Right. Of course." I focus back in on work and put that Beta out of my mind. She was lovely, but it was just a chance encounter. And I have a business to run.

Besides, it's time we found a proper Omega mate for our pack. I can't waste any more time on Beta hookups, no matter how pretty, or sweet-smelling, they might be.

# Chapter 3

## *Ava*

I up my dosage the moment I get home.

Call me paranoid, but I'd rather be safe than sorry. I still sometimes have nightmares about what might have happened if I'd presented as an Omega just a few weeks or months sooner than I did. What Marcus might have done. How I would still be trapped.

I'm never going to give an Alpha a chance to hurt me ever again. I have a life, and a fulfilling one. I don't need an Alpha, no matter what the media or convention says.

Even though I know I should be fine, I can't stop checking my scent wherever I go, just to be sure. Even at the shelter, where the scent of the animals can often obscure everything else, I keep discreetly double-checking.

I can't slip up. I can't be discovered.

I'm crouched down cleaning a cage out, and I lean into my armpit a bit, just to make sure. Even the dogs have stopped responding to my scent. That's how blocked it is, and yet here I am, still a ball of anxiety.

"Get it together, Ava," I mutter to myself.

Hands land on my shoulders and I scream in surprise, dropping the cleaning brush and nearly banging my head on the top of the cage.

"Sorry, sorry." Athena leaps back out of the way of my flailing limbs. "I didn't mean to startle you. Are you okay?"

"I'm fine. The only thing bruised is my dignity." I pull off my gloves and stand up. "Everything okay?"

"Everything's great." Athena beams at me. "It's just almost the end of the shift. We were wondering if you'd want to join us —it's Friday and all that—and we're headed to the club."

"Oh, I'd love to, but..."

"But, but, but. You always have an excuse." Athena tilts her head at me. "Are you okay? The last few days... you've been jumping at shadows. Is something wrong?"

Athena is a Beta, and so is everyone else who works here, except Bonnie, who's an Alpha. And Bonnie doesn't count, since she's a teenager who wears blockers for herself so she doesn't smell people and let her teen hormones take over. It's common practice for underage Alphas who present early, so that they don't get aggressive.

They're good people, all of them, and I like them. But even if they might not be Alphas, I don't know how they'd feel about me if they realized the truth that I'm an Omega—and a hidden one. They could report me to the ORD for dodging registration. I can't have that either.

"Are you guys going out to dinner first?" I hedge. "I could join you just for that."

"Ava, come on, you need to live a little. When was the last time you did anything social?" Before I can answer, Athena holds up a hand. "I'll tell you when. It was six months ago for my birthday when I took us all to that karaoke bar. You haven't been out doing anything social since."

"You know I'm here all the time."

"And we love you for it, really, we do." Athena smiles at me gently. "But we also love spending time with you, and this job can't be the only thing you have in your life. I know that you like spending time with us too, so come on. We're not *that* old yet. We can still kick it in the club."

I crack a smile. "Pretty sure nobody says 'kick it' anymore, dear."

Athena leans back and yells down the hall. "Bonnie? Do people still say 'kick it in the club'?"

"Nobody has *ever* said that," Bonnie deadpans from another room.

I descend into giggles. "Never change, Bonnie," I yell.

"That kid's got an attitude problem," Athena grumbles.

"She's hilarious. You just don't get her sense of humor." I sigh, knowing what I have to do. If I keep saying no to stuff, then Athena's going to keep pushing, and soon my other coworkers will join in.

And they might find out the truth.

I can't have that. I don't know how they'll react. I know they all mean well. It's not that I feel unsafe around them. But they might treat me differently, like I'm too delicate to do things. Or they'll pester me to find an Alpha.

It's a delicate balance that I have to walk: keeping myself distant enough that nobody figures out what I really am, but also not staying so aloof that I raise alarm bells or hurt feelings. It's exhausting, feeling like I'm always one small step away from disaster and losing everything.

"Okay," I say. "I'll go out with you guys, but I have an early shift tomorrow so I can't stay for too long, okay?"

Athena rolls her eyes, but she's smiling. "Fine, deal's a deal." She sticks her hand out for me to playfully shake. "See you at the end of the shift. I'll text you the address and time. We'll meet up around the corner to grab some food beforehand."

"Fine by me." She's clearly excited that I'm coming along. I love my coworkers and consider them friends, so I wish like hell that I could be just as excited.

I wish I wasn't filled with fear.

It takes me forever to pick out something to wear.

My bed is covered in my clothes. "Too slutty," I announce, throwing another dress onto the pile. "Too worn out." There goes another one. "Too frumpy." Another.

I'm not usually this anxious. I like to be friendly and social, and more carefree. But this thing with that Alpha the other day —I can't shake it. I haven't had that reaction to anyone before. A few seconds more and I might've been perfuming.

"Be honest," I tell myself, sorting through my clothes with increasing frustration. "You haven't been social, or carefree, in years. Not since you had to flee."

I was, once, with my friends in college. I wonder how they're doing. If they miss me, if they ever think about me and wonder why I disappeared off the face of the earth.

Finally, I settle on a little black dress. Classy, classic, nothing too crazy, but still sexy and fun. I won't look like I was dragged to the club against my will, but I also won't give the impression that I'm looking for someone to hook up with. This is a fun night with friends only.

By the time I'm ready to go, I'm almost late. My stomach is growling. "Just a quick top up."

I have to be careful. Better safe than sorry. I throw on another dose of blockers, and only then do I head out the door.

I make it just in time to the restaurant down the street from the club, where my six coworkers are already stationed at a booth in the corner. I slide into place, we order, and we eat. I have to basically force the food down.

Maybe it's just my anxiety, but I can't shake the feeling that this is a bad idea. That something is going to go wrong.

Everyone else is having fun. Relaxing, talking, making jokes. But sometimes I feel like one of them is sneaking a look at me. I wonder if it's just that they can pick up on my nerves, or if it's something more.

I really need to stop being so paranoid.

"Maybe I should go home," I tell Athena as we pay the bill.

"Nonsense, the evening's barely begun." She grabs my hand and leads me out the door with the others. "This will be a fun time, Ava. I promise."

There's a line outside the club, but we're all good-looking people, so we get in easily. Athena and I wink at the bouncer, and Athena even blows him a kiss, making me laugh. He ushers us in with an unimpressed raise of his eyebrow. He's wearing scent blockers on his nose so that Omegas can't entice him to let them in because of their scent, and Alphas can't intimidate him with theirs.

Once we're inside, the wall of scents and body heat hits me like I've run smack into it. I breathe carefully through my mouth. The club's already bouncing. I've clearly been out of the game too long. I don't remember clubs being quite this crowded.

That's probably the anxiety talking again.

"Here," another one of my coworkers says, managing to flag down the bartender. "Order!"

We have to yell over the crowd to tell the bartender what we want. I just stick to a basic Cosmopolitan. I'm only having one drink tonight, even though I'm not driving. In my state, I shouldn't be adding a ton of alcohol to the mix.

For a moment we just all sip our drinks, but then a song comes on that has my body moving along instinctively. Athena grins at me. "I love this song!" she yells over the music. "Come on!"

I down the rest of my drink and let her lead me through the twisting head of bodies and scents until we reach the middle of the dance floor. I can feel our other coworkers behind me like a conga line, until we're all bunched together and we can start dancing to the music.

Okay, I can admit—now that I'm in the middle of it, with a drink swimming in my veins, I can feel myself starting to have fun. Maybe Athena was right and this will be good for me.

I sway my hips, letting the bass of the song thump through my body, and I fall into a rhythm of dance. I'm not the best dancer, or at least not in my opinion, but I'm no slouch either. I like to have a good time.

I throw my head back, baring my teeth a little and letting the long waterfall of my hair fall free. My anxiety melts away as the song progresses, the music washing away everything else until it's just me and the melody.

All around me, people swirl—my friends mostly, but also

strangers. Everyone smells good. It's the smell of life and energy and joy.

After a few songs, I feel a body behind me. I push back a little, and find hands landing on my hips. I grin and dance along. The person behind me is an Alpha, I can tell by his scent, and it smells pretty good. He doesn't seem to be bad-looking either, at least from what I can tell with him standing behind me.

I dance with him, enjoying the feel of two bodies together, the playful, flirtatious rush. This is good, this is great, this is...

My thoughts all grind to a halt as the Alpha presses himself against me. I can feel the length of him against my ass, half-hard. Talk about a lack of etiquette.

But then his mouth presses against my throat and I feel him inhale sharply. His cheek rubs against my neck and my blood fills with ice. My heart stammers and then takes off running.

He's scenting me.

My world spins as my own scent filters through to me. Fuck, fuck, fuck. I'm perfuming. I don't know when I started, but somehow I got carried away in the music. I don't know how my scent overcame all the blockers I piled onto it. That should be impossible. And yet, it's happening.

The music is continuing to play, but around me, my friends have awkwardly paused and are looking around. I can see their nostrils flaring. They can tell an Omega is perfuming, but they haven't yet figured out it's me.

I want to burst into tears of humiliation.

Then the Alpha at my back tightens his grip, and I realize with a churn of my stomach that I'm in for more than just humiliation if I don't find a way to get out of this. This Alpha is trying to scent me and mark me as *his*.

He's trying to claim me.

Panic claws at my throat as I try to pull away. No Alpha is going to claim me, no Alpha is going to mark me. Not anyone ever, but especially not some stranger in a club, not like this—

"Holy shit. Ava?" Athena stares at me, her eyes wide with shock. "Is that... you?"

Around me, the crowd is shifting. There are a lot of Alphas in here and now they're all catching onto the scent of a perfuming Omega. Oh my god, I might be about to get stuck in the middle of an Alpha fight.

This is the kind of story that parents tell their little Omega kids about to warn them not to go around unmated. I'm going to become a cautionary tale, a story on the eleven o'clock news. Shit.

Eyes are starting to turn to me, and my friends seem to be in too much shock to say anything. I want to burst into tears. The Alpha still won't let go of me.

*I can't breathe, I can't—*

"There you are."

A hand lands on my shoulder and someone stands in front of me, blocking me from view of anyone else. My mouth drops open.

This is another Alpha, tall and muscular, with a devilish grin playing at the corners of his lips and mirth in his deep green eyes. The lights of the club dance off his messy brown hair as he dips his head a little, bronze highlights glinting among the strands.

"There you are," he repeats, smiling down at me. His eyes on mine are warm, but then his gaze flicks up to the Alpha who still has his hands on my hips, and those eyes sharpen. The mirth in them becomes something much harder.

My body reacts to him, to that handsome face, to the heat of

Sadie Moss

his firm body, to the protectiveness in his stance. I can only remember one other time I reacted so strongly to an Alpha, and it was the one I ran into the other day. My body starts to sway into him instinctively, my gaze locked on his as he returns his attention to me.

I can't seem to look away. It's like I'm under a spell. Whoever this Alpha is, with one simple, gentle touch, he has me more under his command than the Alpha who was just grabbing me and grinding against me.

"I was wondering where you'd got to," the Alpha continues. The green of his eyes is offset by the tiniest flecks of gold, and I want to sink into them like they're pools of cool, refreshing water in a forest. "Next time wait for me, okay?"

It strikes me in a sudden rush what he's doing. He's covering for me.

He's pretending that he's my Alpha.

He's *saving* me.

# Chapter 4

## *Ava*

I stare up at this new Alpha, trying not to look as shocked as I feel.

This could be some kind of trap—pretending to be the hero only to turn around and claim me just like this other Alpha at my back wants to do—but I have to take the risk. If people here think that I'm claimed, or at least in some kind of relationship with this Alpha, they'll back off.

Or at least, they should back off. The Alpha behind me might decide to challenge him for me. And that'll be a whole other mess.

But when this new Alpha tightens his grip on my shoulder and pulls me away, the first Alpha doesn't stop him. He growls, annoyed and huffing, but he doesn't try to keep me pressed against him.

I'm sure that has something to do with the glare of the new Alpha who's pulling me in. He looks like he could take on a whole crew of men by himself. No, not just like he can, but like he *will*, if anyone tries to step in and claim me instead.

*You need to sell this,* I think wildly, and I manage to get myself to put my hands on this new Alpha's chest.

Oh my god. It's like touching electricity. I immediately start to fall forward into him, my knees buckling. I've never had this reaction to someone before, unless you count the scent of that other Alpha earlier this week. Am I going to be like this around all Alphas now? Swooning constantly?

No. I panicked when that other Alpha tried scenting me. It's not every Alpha. What makes that last guy, and this one, different from the others?

My new Alpha bends down, and I can feel his muscles flex underneath his shirt. Fuck he's so hot. I've never been so close to trembling just from touching a man's chest.

"Let's get out of here," he murmurs. His lips brush against mine as he speaks and I almost whimper.

He smells *incredible.* His scent is a mix of cinnamon, freshly baked cookies, and just a hint of toasted marshmallows. I feel like I'm sipping hot cocoa and making s'mores around a campfire. I want him to tighten his arms around me and hug me with his body the way his scent feels like it's hugging me.

His hand strokes the small of my back, making me shiver, and I realize he's waiting for me to answer. "Yes," I whisper.

Part of me feels numb. I still can't believe this is actually happening to me, that I'm really caught out in a club with everyone staring at me. I'm the Omega you hear tragic stories about on the news.

Or the Omegas from romance movies who are rescued in just this kind of fashion. I don't want to be that Omega, though, or at least that's what I've always told myself. The Alpha might seem like a nice guy at first, all charm and sexual charisma, but underneath that, there's nothing but an obsessive need to control.

That's what the logical, fearful part of me is screaming, trying to get me to remember just how dangerous this can be. But the other part of me just wants to burrow closer into this Alpha, to inhale his scent, to let it flow through my body down between my legs...

I nearly jerk back on instinct and catch myself just in time. Holy shit, first that other Alpha and now this one. It's almost like I'm in heat.

The Alpha wraps his arm around me properly, tucking me securely against his side. He gives a cheeky wave to Athena and my other friends, who are still gaping. "Sorry to interrupt girls' night," he says, winking.

I tell myself it isn't charming, but I know I'm lying to myself.

The Alpha hustles me through the crowd, half bent over me, his voice low in my ear. "It's really not a good idea for an Omega who smells as delicious as you do to be in a club surrounded by Alphas."

"I know," I whisper back, and I can't hide the misery in my voice. I feel like a stupid child. Like a teenage Omega who snuck out of the house and is now being dragged home to her parents.

Not that my parents would've cared. They never cared about anything I did and I doubt that knowing I'm an Omega would've changed a thing.

"I would love to know what you're doing here, then," the Alpha continues. He sounds amused.

As we walk through the club, I see other Alphas sniffing the air, gazing at me with hunger in their eyes. But a sharp look or an intensifying of scent from my Alpha and they all back off. They know I'm his.

Or at least I'm pretending to be.

My heart races as we exit the club and get out onto the street. I have no idea what will happen now. Will this Alpha try to claim me as payment for his rescue? I find myself actually hoping that he will. Flashes of his body pressing mine up against the nearest wall fill my mind.

He's so much taller than I am, and while he's a bit slim it's the kind of slim that Olympic swimmers and runners have. Every inch of him is pure muscle. He'd feel so good between my legs, his body hovering over mine, dominating me as I run my fingers through his dark hair, his bronze highlights catching the light...

"Hello?" I hear his voice as if through a fog and I blink.

The Alpha smiles. "There you are. I said, I'm Ethan. What's your name?"

Panic floods me. I've never been so wildly attracted to an Alpha before. Never wanted one to dominate me and take me. Especially not in public where anyone could see. This is my ultimate nightmare.

I won't let this happen. He's not going to fool me with his hero schtick.

"Would you like a ride home?" Ethan asks me. His brow furrows with concern.

Oh, he's good. He's very good. I might almost believe he's genuine in his altruism if I didn't know better. But I do know better. He won't trap me in a car.

Even as more images flash in my mind of being pinned down in the backseat of the car, his sharp, muscular body thrusting into mine, his teeth at my throat as I scream in ecstasy—

*No.*

I turn and I take off running as fast as I can.

"Wh—what are you—hey!"

Oh no. He's chasing me.

I have to throw him off. I ditch my heels, running barefoot through the streets. He's not going to take me. He's not going to claim me. Nobody is.

My heart races and my mind screams in blind panic as I race through the dark city. It's late enough now that there aren't a lot of cars or people out which makes it easier for me to run, but harder for me to use a crowd or traffic to shake the following Alpha loose.

Adrenaline and fear give me an added boost and I dodge and weave through the streets. The only sound is my frantic, heaving beaths and the wild drumbeat of my heart in my ears.

Have I lost Ethan? Is he gone?

I keep running, refusing to stop, panicking that the moment I do, he'll be on me out of nowhere. *He could have genuinely been helping you,* something in me whispers, but I push that away and keep going. I can't trust that. I can't trust any Alpha.

I have no plan for where I'm headed, just that I need to get *away,* but at last I realize I don't hear feet behind me.

Up ahead, I see trees. A park. I veer to the left, toward it, and finally skid to a halt once I'm inside as if it's a kind of sanctuary.

My ears strain, trying to pick up any sound behind me. I sniff the air. No scent of cookies, marshmallows, or cinnamon.

Ethan's gone. I lost him.

For some reason, deep in my chest, I feel a twinge of disappointment.

There's a bench nearby, and I collapse onto it. I brace my elbows on my knees and put my face in my hands. My shoulders shake. I'm not crying, at least not yet. I'm still too high on adrenaline for that. But I feel like I'm going to cry at some point soon. Probably when I'm safe at home.

Oh, god, I have to get home. I don't even know where the hell I am. I need to figure that out, and get a ride share or something, and make it back to my apartment. I'll take a shower and douse myself in blockers and from there I can figure out what to do. Now that my coworkers know I'm an Omega, there's no way I can keep hiding it.

The snap of a twig interrupts my spiral of thoughts. My head shoots up.

At first, I hear nothing. See nothing.

Then, wafting on the breeze, the scents hit me. Multiple scents. They smell different, but the underlying thread is the same: arousal.

Oh no. Oh no, oh no, oh no, oh—

I leap to my feet but it's too late. Hands snatch me, two sets of them.

"What a delicious, pretty Omega," a voice purrs. "You shouldn't be out here all alone."

The tone sounds concerned and intoxicated at the same time, and most Omegas would probably be delighted to know an Alpha, more than one in fact, is so drawn in by their scent. I see two more Alphas in front of me. A pack for sure.

But I'm not most Omegas. I don't want my scent to be intoxicating and delicious. I don't want Alphas everywhere swooning over me like in the movies. When I hear the almost awed tone they use as they speak to me, all I can remember is how I was once tricked and manipulated.

*It's not real,* my mind whispers. *They don't really want to take care of you. They want to own you.*

One of the Alphas bends down and presses his face to my neck, trying to get more of my scent. Fear spikes through me, and I shriek at the top of my lungs, fury and terror mixing in me like a deadly cocktail.

A blur collides into the standing Alpha from the side, sending him flying to the ground. I get a strong whiff of a familiar scent: burnt marshmallows and cinnamon so strong it tickles my nostrils.

*Ethan.*

# Chapter 5

## *Ethan*

I could've kicked myself for losing the gorgeous Omega after I got her safely out of the club.

I've never smelled anyone so good. Ripe strawberries, the kind you want to sink your teeth into. Warm vanilla. And a bit of sweet lilac, refreshing and soothing.

It was easy enough to chase that scent through the city as she fled. I felt like I could follow her smell anywhere, blindfolded and with my hands tied. I've never reacted so strongly to an Omega's scent before.

I could hear Dante's voice in my head telling me that I shouldn't do something reckless, and yeah, okay, running through the dark city after a woman I've not even properly met is kind of reckless and dramatic. But I didn't care. I just knew that my instincts have never steered me wrong before, and they were telling me to find the Omega and protect her.

And it turns out, I was barely in time.

The Alpha I just tackled hits the earth hard underneath me, and I don't waste a second of my advantage. I grab him by the hair and swing with all my might, imagining punching through the back of the guy's skull. I strike him hard in the temple, and he's knocked cold.

One down, thank fuck. Now it's only three against one.

I leap to my feet and bare my teeth, snarling at the others. It's all the warning they get before I leap at another one.

One of his buddies tries to grab me, but I throw my elbow back and get him in the crotch. He stumbles back, wheezing and doubled over in pain. I punch the other guy I've got in the throat, and now there's only one left.

Of course the fucker pulls a knife. Just my luck. Somewhere, Garrett's rolling his eyes and doesn't know why.

There's no way I can let him get close. I quickly spin and roundhouse him with my foot, catching him on the temple and sending him sprawling. That'll leave a mark.

The beautiful Omega gapes up at me. Any other time, my heart would be racing over her beauty in the moonlight. She's got this perfect hourglass figure with soft curves, and her pale creamy skin practically shines in the light from the moonbeams. Sprawled out on the grass with her chocolate hair haloing her head, her dark eyes glittering, she looks like something out of my dreams.

But I don't have time to stare at her. We have to go before these guys recover.

"Come on." I pull her up to standing. "Let's go, gorgeous. Move, move, move."

I hustle her out of the park and down the street to my car, her hand securely held in mine. Behind us I can hear the yelps and howls of the four Alphas. They're going to come after us and I don't feel like getting my ass kicked in a brawl.

Ah, thank fuck, my car. I yank out my keys and unlock it. "Get in. Quick."

The Omega doesn't hesitate, although I see that flicker of fear in her gaze again. Thank god I don't have to argue with her and she doesn't try to run away this time. We slip into the car, I gun the engine, and we peel out.

Safe.

I glance over. The Omega hasn't even put on her seat belt. Instead, she's curled up into a ball, forehead pressed to her legs and shaking like a leaf. I reach out with my free hand, palm down. "It's okay. You're safe now. Here, sniff me. It's okay. I won't hurt you. See?"

The Omega tentatively raises her head and sniffs my hand. Her eyes are wide in the dark. She's practically feral right now. All I can smell is rotten strawberries and burnt vanilla. My whole car is doused in the scent of her fear.

It makes my heart ache. No Omega should have to be so upset, but especially not this one. I'd want to help out any Omega in distress. It's just what Alphas do. But I can't deny that there's something more about this one. Something that makes me want to rip the world apart until she's happy and her scent no longer stinks of fear.

My scent must be calm enough, because she doesn't bury her face in her knees again. She just watches me and shakes.

"I'm going to pet you, okay?" I say, keeping my voice low and calm. I reach out and gently stroke my fingers through her hair.

The Omega's eyes slip closed and tears slide down her face. After a moment of petting, she tentatively pushes her head farther into my hand, and uncurls a bit from her ball.

"That's a good girl," I praise. "Very good. It's okay. You're safe now. You're safe with me. I won't hurt you."

I try to keep my tone warm and praising without being

condescending. Omegas need comfort but they aren't children, and I have a feeling this Omega will be more upset than most, even in her state, if she feels that I'm treating her like she's anything less than an adult.

Her scent slowly calms, the delicious smell of strawberries, vanilla, and lilac coating the back of my tongue and sliding down my body, like it's burying itself into my very bones. I feel a little drunk, like I'd promise her the moon if she wanted it and find a way to get it out of the sky.

Which is... kind of ridiculous. I can't say I'm what you'd call a romantic. I like to flirt and have fun. Just ask Garrett, who's ruined more of my potential hookups than I can count. But this Omega has my blood singing.

She probably wouldn't appreciate it if I told her that, though. Way to come on too strong and sound like a damn stalker. She's scared, she doesn't need me acting like it was love at first sight. I need to get my stupid hormones under control.

"Let's start over, okay?" I say, trying to distract myself as much as her. "Why don't you give me your name this time. I'm Ethan."

"Ethan," she repeats, her voice soft. "I'm Ava."

"Ava. What a beautiful name."

The corner of her mouth twitches up at the praise. I finally slide my hand out of her hair and put it on the wheel so I can concentrate on driving. I've basically been moving in circles, but now I need to pick a proper destination.

"Ava, are you okay?"

"I—I'm better than I was." Her voice still shakes a little.

"Why'd you run from me?"

Ava's eyes sharpen. "I want to be free." Now her voice is full of anger and conviction.

She's still shaking a little, and she hasn't fully uncurled from her ball. She's still wary of me.

It makes me ache. I want nothing more than to soothe her.

"What happened back there at the club?" I ask. "You're unmated, that's clear. You taking blockers? Suppressants?"

"Both." Ava sighs and looks down, her lip quivering. "I even took extra before I left for the club. I don't know what happened."

I sigh. "You got them not-so-legally, I'm guessing? Since you're unmated?"

She nods, still staring at her knees. "The ones I had for years worked well but they got too expensive. I had to move to a cheaper brand. I've only been on it for a couple of weeks and now this has happened."

"Yeah, well, not to be too harsh about it, but I'm guessing you were taking placebos. Sugar pills. Nothing in them. Certainly nothing that would actually work to block your Omega scent or stop you from perfuming."

Ava wipes at her eyes. "I feel so stupid. I tried to—to make sure they were legitimate. I've never had a problem before with my old brand."

"There are a lot of shitty people out there. And they don't care that there are desperate Omegas like you. They don't care that they might be ruining lives. Getting people claimed by abusive Alphas and trapped forever. They just care about getting rich."

Ava hiccups, and buries her face in her knees. I can see her shoulders shaking as she silently cries.

I feel like I want to rip out my own heart and give it to her. Anything to make her feel better. "Hey. Listen. Your apartment probably isn't safe right now. If this has been going on for a couple of weeks... I'd say the first week you were fine with the old suppressants still in your system but this week? You're fucked. Your apartment will stink of unmated Omega and you'll be getting a lot of unwanted visitors. So how about I take you back to stay with my pack for a short bit?"

Ava's head shoots up, and I see the fear in her eyes. I keep myself calm. "No strings attached. I promise. It'll just be a safe place for you until you figure out your next move."

Usually, I'd offer to contact the ORD for her. I know some Omegas can present later in life, but that clearly isn't the case here. Seeing as she's still unmated, and has been on suppressants and blockers for years? Yeah, I'm willing to bet she won't want to be registering anywhere.

The people she was with—including the friend who glared at me—seemed a bit shocked. She's been hiding this whole time.

I'm kind of impressed, actually..

That makes this all more complicated and more dangerous. But I know that I can't leave her to fend for herself. I have to protect her.

I know that it's illegal. She has to be registered. If I take her in, my pack and I will be breaking the law the same as she is, and we could all get in major trouble. But when it comes to this Omega... something in me *growls* at the idea of abandoning her.

Fuck the law. Fuck the ORD. My pack and I will keep her safe. I feel it in my bones, I'd stand up to anyone to get that fearful look out of her eyes.

Ava chews on her bottom lip. I want to replace her teeth with my own and then lick inside her mouth.

It's going to be hard as hell for me to keep my hands off her while she stays with us, but I can control myself. She doesn't want a pack, she's made *that* much clear. Even without her behavior tonight, if you're an unmated Omega at her age, hiding your orientation with suppressants, it's a pretty good chance you don't want any Alphas claiming you.

*I bet you could convince her, change her mind*, a part of me whispers. The part of me that wants to spoil her, to see her nest in our home. To take care of her and make her part of our pack.

But I know that's just my old wishful thinking talking. I lost my parents young but I still remember how in love they were, and how safe and happy they made me feel. I've wanted an Omega for so damn long. That's all this is. It's just my stupid, silly, busted heart.

I'm not an animal. And as much as I'm instantly drawn to this woman, I know the difference between fantasy and reality. My priority right now isn't the start of some crazy romance. It's being a good Alpha and making sure this Omega feels safe.

"I promise," I say, my voice low, "nobody will lay a finger on you. We'll protect you. We'll keep you safe."

Ava swallows, staring out the windshield. Then she looks at me. "Okay," she whispers.

I try to ignore the surge of triumph in my veins. For one thing, this is not the same thing as an Omega coming home with me because she wants to bond with me. No matter what my instincts are screaming for or what my idle daydreams are made of.

For another, I know the others are going to have a hell of a lot to say about me bringing home an unregistered Omega. Especially Garrett.

Well, I'll cross that bridge when I get to it. I don't really care if they're upset or not. Ava needs my help, and I'm going to give it to her.

The others can just get over it.

# Chapter 6

## *Ava*

I can't stop smelling Ethan.

He smells so *good*. When he puts his hand in my hair, I almost melt and spread my legs, begging him to use those fingers other places.

I know that it's just my Omega instincts coming out after being suppressed for so long. I can't let my baser instincts win or dictate my actions. But oh my god. I want to climb into his lap and lick him all over, and grind against his cock until I come, until he pulls it out, until he—

I bury my face into my knees to hide my panting. I'm shaking with need, with desire for him. He smells so unbearably good and I know his knot would feel so very good inside of me. It would fill me and satisfy me like nothing else.

*Cut. It. Out.* I think fiercely to myself.

It makes sense that after so many years of suppressing my Omega side, now that it's out it's gone into overdrive. I'd probably be going this crazy for just about any Alpha.

*You didn't feel like this about the Alphas in the park, or the guy in the club.* I shove that thought away. Yes, based on my theory, I should've spread my legs and begged the Alphas in the park to claim me, every last one of them. But I didn't want them touching me.

I can still feel the ghost of their hands on me and it makes me want to throw up.

But Ethan... I have to keep my body pressed to the window to hold in the instinct to do something stupid like make him pull the car over and mount me.

I feel a little insane, to be honest.

The car is so full of his scent that even pressed against the opposite side of the vehicle, I can't escape it. He smells so very good. I can't remember ever feeling like this. I tell myself that it's just the hormones, but I could smell the other Alphas, and none of their scents even really registered to me beyond 'ew, no.'

Ethan, on the other hand? It's like his scent was instantly burned into my senses, into my brain.

He keeps up a string of soothing conversation. He doesn't seem to mind that I'm not responding. It hits me after a bit that he's talking just so that I keep hearing his voice. He's trying to soothe me. I must smell terrible right now, stinking of fear.

He talks about the weather, about his favorite food, about how often he goes to clubs and what clubs he thinks are best, about fashion, about movies he's seen lately. He tells me his favorite color is blue and that he loves Britney Spears' music.

It's sweet, actually. And charming.

I can't think of another Alpha I've ever met who would be so calm and casual with an unmated Omega who clearly doesn't want to be with them. Maybe I've just been around the wrong Alphas, but that's been my experience. Yet Ethan is so patient and cheerful.

Almost against my will, I find myself calming down and feeling soothed. Comforted.

Maybe... maybe I actually can be safe, with this Alpha. If only for a few days until I figure out what to do with my life now.

We get out of the city proper and into an upscale neighborhood. I find myself looking out the window in surprise. I don't think it's fair to call the homes here 'houses.' They're more like mansions.

And then they are, literally, mansions.

Ethan pulls into the gated drive of one of them and my jaw falls open. This mansion is gorgeous and huge, with a fountain out front. I'd been so focused on running for my life I had barely registered that Ethan's car is some fancy sports brand, but now it's all clicking into place.

Ethan's not just an Alpha with a thing for sports cars. He's a stinking rich Alpha. Wildly rich. Insanely rich. I can't afford to breathe in this neighborhood.

This is so far off from my own shitty apartment that we might as well be on the moon.

Ethan glances at me as he parks the car. There's an amused gleam in his eyes. "Like what you see?"

I'm too busy gaping to form a proper response.

Ethan opens the door for me and holds out a hand to help me to my feet. I uncurl slowly, feeling self-conscious in my little black dress and bare feet. My hair's a mess from running and then getting shoved into the grass. I must look so pathetic to him.

But Ethan doesn't say anything about my appearance as he takes my hand and leads me into the house. He keeps his grip light, like he knows I'm still seconds from bolting and doesn't want me to feel trapped.

The look in his eyes when I told him *I want to be free* was... something. I don't know what to call it. I just know it's like nothing I've seen on an Alpha's face before. Usually when I'm passing as a Beta and I talk about how glad I am, or how much I value my freedom, the Alphas around me look annoyed or even outright disapproving.

Marcus always looked outright disgusted.

The foyer that Ethan leads me into is two stories high, with a grand, sweeping staircase that curls around the back wall, and a shining chandelier hanging from the ceiling. The floors are elegant marble, and massive paintings hang from the walls. This foyer alone is bigger than my entire apartment.

"It's a bit late," Ethan says, a teasing note in his voice, "but I can still give you the grand tour if you want."

"Give who the grand tour?" someone says, and it's like lightning up my spine. I jolt.

I *know* that voice. I've heard it somewhere before, I'm sure of it.

From the top of the stairs descends a man. In the dim lighting of the foyer his body moves like a sleek predator, a wolf padding down to see what all the fuss is about. His gray eyes pierce through me, and then his scent hits.

Honey. Bourbon. Spicy clove.

Oh my god. It's the Alpha I ran into earlier this week.

When he reaches the landing, I see that he's just as tall, just as muscular, and just as handsome as I remember.

I can't believe this is happening to me. Any other Omega would probably feel lucky. I'm a little too busy feeling swept up in how good he looks... and smells.

Even from here, I can inhale his scent like a drug, and I nearly start panting. I want him to pull me into those powerful arms. His eyes seem to pin me in place, seeing right into the heart of me.

The way he stands exudes confidence. The kind that comes from a true Alpha. So many of them posture and swagger and it always said to me that they were secretly insecure. A truly confident Alpha doesn't need to make a scene or show off how strong he is. He just exists, and knows his worth.

That's what I'm getting from this Alpha standing on the stairs above me.

It makes me want to bare my throat in submission and it takes everything in me to hold that back and not give in. I'm not some silly teenage Omega. I'm not going to just swoon over the first confident Alpha I run into.

But it does tell me that this one is probably his pack leader.

I see the moment recognition enters his eyes. A small, warm smile tugs up the corner of his mouth. I kind of want to drown in it.

"Nice to see you again," he murmurs, walking down the rest of the steps.

"Ava, this is Dante, my pack leader," Ethan says. "Dante, this is Ava. She needs a place to stay. Her suppressants failed her."

Dante. I roll the name around in my mind. I like it. Strong, but a little dangerous in a fun way.

Maybe it's just from the fact that it's so late and he probably just rolled out of bed to see what's going on, but right now his rich dark brown hair is charmingly messy and he has a light shading of stubble on his chin. It makes him look disheveled, but naughty.

I swallow hard. I'm not going to think about that. I won't think about running my hands through that hair or how that stubble would feel on my skin. I'm stronger than that.

"Are you two related?" I ask.

Ethan chuckles as Dante answers me. "No, but we get that a lot. We're brothers in spirit only."

I nod, not sure what else to say. Dante's gaze on me is penetrating, and I see his eyes flick up and down my body, taking me in. His eyebrows rise a little as he realizes what a mess I look.

"What's the fucking ruckus for?" someone else growls as they enter. "Do any of you dumbasses know what time it is?"

"Garrett," Ethan says quickly. "We have a guest."

The Alpha who enters is wearing nothing but a pair of boxers, and I gulp, shivering inadvertently as I take in his broad-shouldered body and toned, well-defined muscles. He looks like he could pick me up with one hand and fuck me through a wall without breaking a sweat.

With his dark, almost black hair done in a short, rugged hairstyle and square jaw, he looks like the Alphas I've seen on romance novel covers. I've never wanted to be eaten alive so badly before.

The Alpha freezes, then squints at me. He moves closer, brown eyes narrowed, like he's not sure if I'm actually real. "An unmated Omega?"

His scent wafts over me as he draws closer and I have to lock my knees to keep them from buckling. He smells like freshly baked pie, like wood burning in a fireplace, and like a glass of sweet apple cider to wash it all down. Like pure, homespun safety.

The man Ethan referred to as Garrett stares at me. His scent mixes with Ethan's and Dante's until I feel like I'm going to pass out. I struggle to keep from panting and whining, every inch of my body on fire. I'm dizzy from their scents combining. I feel so turned on it's like I've been doused in flames and yet, I feel weirdly safe. Like I've been wrapped in a blanket to keep out the outside world.

"What are you doing?" Garrett asks me, his tone gruff. "Out there unmated? Do you have any idea how dangerous that is?"

"Yes, Garrett," Dante says, his tone tired but calm. "I think she does. You're safe here, Ava. It's all right."

Garrett mutters something under his breath. I can't quite catch what he says, but I glare at him anyway. Ethan smirks. "Careful, Garrett, she's a bit of a live wire."

"What's all..." Someone pauses to yawn. "The commotion...?"

A fourth Alpha enters, dressed in a white t-shirt and gray sweatpants, looking still half-asleep. His neatly trimmed blond hair is sticking up a little on one side, and it makes him look absolutely adorable. He's tall, with a muscular build that tells me he could also probably lift me with no effort. He has electric blue eyes and a strong jawline, but despite his chiseled features, there's something soft and kind about his face.

He blinks at me, then rubs at his eyes as if he's not quite believing what he's seeing.

"Nope," Ethan says cheerfully. "You're not dreaming."

"Caleb, this is Ava," Dante makes the introductions. "Ava, this is Caleb, the last member of our pack."

"Ava, hi." Caleb sticks out his hand for me to shake. *Oh my god. He's so cute I can hardly stand it.*

I find myself shaking his hand, blinking as his scent crashes over me like a wave. It's insanely comforting—rich dark chocolate, smooth caramel, and toasted hazelnuts.

*Yum.*

"Sorry, uh, I'm usually more awake than this." Caleb glances at the others. "What's going on?"

He's still holding my hand. I clear my throat.

Caleb lets go of me and steps back, taking most of his scent with him. I nearly whine at the loss.

Four pairs of bright eyes stare at me, then at each other.

"She needs a place to stay," Ethan repeats.

"She can't stay here," Garrett replies, his tone rough. "She's unmated and we don't have an Omega, do you have any idea what kind of problem that could be?"

"She's right here," I point out softly.

The thing is, I'm kind of in agreement with Garrett. I've never reacted like this to a single Alpha before, and now I've got four of them all vying for the attention of my body.

This is part of why I take suppressants. It's not just for protection, so that others don't judge me or try to take my life out of my hands. It's also because I hate what my Omega instincts do to me. I don't like being such a slave to my desires.

Yet here I am, wet and desperate with lust for these four Alphas that I've barely met. They make me feel safe, and I have to remind myself that it's the Omega hormones talking. No matter what my mind knows to be true, my body wants to be claimed and mated, pampered by a pack of gorgeous Alphas just like this one.

I can't let my body win. I feel so confused, torn between two completely different desires, but I know which one will win out. I just have to stay focused.

"We have a lot on our plates already," Garrett argues. "Are we sure we really have the time to take on an Omega and look after her? Especially if we're not going to bond with her? What about the PR mess if this gets out?"

"It will be fine," Dante says, in a low soothing tone that nonetheless makes it clear he's not going to be argued with.

"Do you really have nowhere else to go?" Caleb asks me.

I shake my head, swallowing hard. I could go back to my apartment, I guess, but I won't. I'd be too afraid of one of my neighbors scenting me and reporting me to the ORD office.

Caleb looks at Garrett. "Then I agree with Dante and Ethan. We should take care of her. We can't kick her out on her own like this."

Garrett sighs. "You're not registered with the ORD, are you?"

I shake my head again.

"Great. Just great. We're practically breaking the law." Garrett looks at the others, and then at me. "All right. Fine. You can stay." He points at the others. "But no shenanigans."

"That's my job to say," Dante points out quietly.

Garrett immediately ducks his head down in deference, which seems to be as much of an apology as anyone is going to get from me.

His obvious hesitance about having me here sets me on edge, but I remind myself that it's partly my own fear and exhaustion making me feel this way. I can't forget that these men are taking a risk letting me into their home and protecting me. Garrett has a point. An unregistered Omega could be a big problem for them if I'm discovered.

So instead, I say, "Thank you. I know that you don't owe me anything, and I really appreciate the kindness."

"Don't mention it," Dante says, his voice wrapping around me like a warm hug.

"Yeah, don't mention it," Garrett mutters.

I swallow hard, trying to calm my racing heart.

When I left my apartment earlier this evening, I never could've imagined that I'd end up spending the night in a mansion with four unnervingly gorgeous Alphas.

But here we are.

# Chapter 7

## *Ava*

"Now that that's settled," Ethan says, clapping his hands together, "why don't I give you the grand tour?"

"Ethan." Dante sighs. "Do you know what time it is?"

"Then you can go to bed," Ethan replies cheekily. I have to bite back a smile. His cheerfulness is infectious and puts me at ease. He offers me his arm. "This way m'lady."

"Oh my fucking god," Garrett mutters under his breath again, and he storms off.

I ignore him. *Yeah, grumpypants, I'm not exactly thrilled about any of this either.* But I follow Ethan as he leads me around the house, pointing out the various rooms.

It's. Huge.

I didn't realize people actually lived in houses this big. This pack is rich. Very rich. Garrett said something about a product and public relations. I wonder what kind of business they're in.

When you're rich like this, that has to come with some measure of being in the public spotlight. These men really are taking a risk by sheltering me here. I'm still wary, but I also feel warm with gratitude.

I genuinely don't know anyone else, Alpha or Beta, who would do the same.

Ethan shows me the home movie theater, and a large half-filled library where he explains Caleb's still working on building his book collection, and the home gym where he and the other three work out.

I try to banish from my mind the image of these four handsome Alphas working up a sweat lifting weights, their clothes sticking to them and showing off their muscles that much more. I'm not entirely successful.

Ethan doesn't take me out to the backyard, but he points out the massive, luxurious pool and hot tub, the tennis court, and the barbeque.

"Do you do a lot of entertaining?" I ask when he finishes showing me the downstairs.

"I love to hold a good party," Ethan admits with a grin. "But not as much as we'd really like. Work keeps us busy and then there's the whole..."

He trails off, and his eyes cut away like he's guilty.

"It's okay." I keep my voice gentle. "You can tell me."

"Well, it's a little awkward, seeing as you're an unmated Omega. But part of why we've been holding back a little on having people over is that we want to have an Omega for our pack."

He sounds incredibly earnest when he says it, and it startles me. The charming man who cracks jokes and seems to have a permanent smirk on his face isn't the kind of man I would expect to be so open and sincere, but Ethan is exactly that.

It makes me feel like I can relax around him. Like his jokes aren't a front or a way to charm pretty Betas and Omegas, but coming from somewhere deeper and more genuine.

"Anyway, let's see the upstairs." Ethan grins and leads me up the massive spiraling staircase. When I look down from the top to the marbled floor below, it feels like I'm in a fairytale about to make my grand entrance into the ball.

The upstairs has slightly less formal rooms. Downstairs had a library, a billiards room, a dining room, and enough others that I made a joke about the game *Clue*, which made Ethan laugh. But up here there don't seem to be strict designations for each room other than the bedrooms.

"We bought a house with children in mind," Ethan admits quietly, indicating some bedrooms that remain undecorated. "Dante likes to plan ahead even if it feels too far in advance. That's part of why he's our leader."

I've seen Alpha packs where there was a constant fight for dominance and who would be in charge. All four of these men clearly have strong personalities, but none of them seem to disrespect Dante. They all defer to him in the end. It's sweet and reassuring.

Ethan leads me to a room at the end of the hall. "This will be your room. We've used it as a guest room before, but don't worry, we had it deep cleaned, so it won't smell like any of our previous guests."

He's right. I can't smell any lingering scents. The walls are a soft cream color, and the room is fairly bare, clearly a guest room with the simple furniture. But the bed looks soft and comfortable, and suddenly my bones ache with exhaustion. I want to dive into this bed and let the pillows and blankets surround me.

"As long as you're living here, I hope you'll consider this your home too," Ethan tells me, his voice soft. "Anything you'd like to use, seriously. If you want to read a book, or watch a movie in the theater, or take a swim, it's all yours."

To my shock, tears spring into my eyes. I'm not usually this emotional. But then again, I'm also not normally flooded with Omega hormones after years of suppressing them. "Thank you. Really. It's very sweet, what you all are doing."

"Hey, of course. I'm sure it's a lot right now." Ethan smiles, and it's gentler than the playful smirks he's been giving so far. "I know you can't go back to your apartment, but in the morning just let us know what you want from there, and we'll go over and get it for you. Clothes, books, that kind of thing."

That does it. The tears slip free and I wipe at my face. "I miss my nest," I admit, a sob catching in my throat.

It wasn't much. I think my suppressants kept me from feeling the urge to nest as strongly as most Omegas do, but I still wanted to make my bed be full of lovely soft things that made me feel warm and safe. It was a place I could snuggle into at the end of the day and let the outside world fade away. A place that smelled like me, and was truly mine.

Now I have to sleep in a strange bed. It looks comfy, for sure, and I appreciate all the pillows. It's silly of me to cry over something like this. And yet, here I am. Missing my nest. Missing my home.

"Oh, gorgeous. Hey, come here." Ethan pulls me into him and hugs me tightly. I bury my face in his chest and inhale his scent, the toasted marshmallow undertone making me think of summer campfires and relaxed, happy times.

Ethan rubs my back. "You're going to be okay. And even if I hadn't been there, I'm sure your friends would've looked out for you. That one girl was glaring at me pretty hard as I led you out of the club."

I laugh a little. "That's Athena. She looks like a strawberry shortcake but she's got a strong personality. But they're my coworkers. We work at the shelter together." I pause. "They're all Betas," I add, quietly.

I don't know how Athena and the others will handle me now that they know I'm an Omega. I don't want them to treat me any differently.

"Well, that's nice. Probably how you got away with those placebos for so long."

"I just don't know if they'll judge me for hiding who I am. And being unmated. Not that it matters now, I suppose. I can't ever go back."

Ethan's body feels so warm and firm against mine. His scent envelops me, and I just want to crawl inside it. I shiver. I feel safe and protected, but I also can't entirely ignore the heat sliding up my spine.

Before I can stop myself, I press against him more, nuzzling into his chest. I feel Ethan's breathing kick up. A bulge grows against my hip, Ethan reacting to me, and my lips part as I start to pant. He wants me. He wants me, and he could take me right there on the bed. I bet it would feel so good, make me stop feeling so empty...

Ethan grabs my hips, like he's torn between pulling me closer and tearing me away. He clears his throat. "You, uh, you said you work at a shelter?"

I struggle to get my breathing under control. "Y-yes. Yes. An animal shelter, yes. That's where I work. A shelter." Oh my god, I sound like a complete idiot. Lust is making my head spin. "That's where I met Dante, actually," I blurt out.

Ethan looks down at me with a smile. "Oh? How'd that happen?"

"I was out walking one of the dogs. We need to do that, not just for exercise obviously, but also so they can get used to obeying a human. It helps prepare them for when they get adopted. This dog, Roger, he's on the big side, and so I was dealing with him and didn't see where I was going and literally bumped into Dante."

"And let me guess, you were smitten." Ethan mimes swooning.

"No," I protest, but I'm giggling.

"I think that's really great, that you work there. I think someone who dedicates their life to helping animals like that is a good person, and your coworkers are probably good people too, then. And I'm sure that means they know what a good person you are. If they're going to judge you for making the choice you thought was best for yourself, then they're not really worth your time."

He really had to go and be charming *and* sweet. I'm doomed. "I'll be honest I'm... I'm really not sure about still being there. I love the animals and the work, but the owner was a real tightwad. I don't think the animals are being treated as well as they should. Maybe this incident is a sign that it's time to move on and find another place to help out."

"Hey, maybe." Ethan curls his finger under my chin and tilts my head up. "My point is that you're okay, and nobody should judge you. It's all going to work out."

My breath catches in my throat. It's such a sweet gesture, but also one full of natural dominance. My throat is exposed but I don't feel scared. I feel vulnerable, but I like it. I've never liked it before.

The shadows play on Ethan's handsome face, but one of them seems darker than the rest. I reach up. "Did you get hurt?"

Ethan winces slightly as my fingers brush against the bruise. "Nothing I can't handle. And nothing that wasn't worth it."

My breath catches in my throat and I find my hand cupping his face, feeling the shape of it against my palm. Ethan shudders, and I feel him hard against me again. My mouth falls open and Ethan's arm comes around my waist, anchoring me against him. My legs spread just a little, just enough, that I can feel that hard outline of his cock between them, so close, so *very* close to where I want it... where I want *him*...

"Oh fuck," Ethan chokes out, and then he's pushing me away, the green of his eyes now thin rims around the large black of his hunger. He clears his throat and lets me go.

I stand in place, shivering. I want him so badly, but I also know it's just chemicals. That's it. My hormones are raging right now and Ethan's being very sweet and comforting, of course I'm going to react. It doesn't mean anything, and I won't let it mean anything.

I won't be claimed. Not by anyone.

Ethan smiles at me, his smile a little lopsided and self-deprecating. "I'll let you get your rest. You're probably exhausted. But don't hesitate to let us know if you need anything, okay?"

*I need you,* my body begs, but I ignore it. "Thank you, Ethan, I will."

He nods, then exits, closing the door softly behind him, leaving me alone with my out-of-control body and my conflicted thoughts.

# Chapter 8

## *Caleb*

I rifle through my closet for some suitable clothes, my nostrils still full of the scent of that sweet Omega.

Ava.

I can't believe we have an Omega in the house, and an unmated one at that. I thought I was dreaming when I first stumbled into the foyer and saw her, and I know that's not just because I was half asleep. Ava smells amazing, like no other Omega I've ever scented before.

I can already hear Dante telling me not to get my hopes up and Garrett storming away because he'd rather go brood than admit he wants a family, but... I can't help but wonder if maybe this is fate. We want an Omega. I know we do, even if some of us are reluctant to admit it.

Of course, my daydreams don't matter as much as getting Ava some proper clothes to sleep in. She's just in this cute little black dress and while it shows off her beautiful curves to the point of distraction, I think she'll want actual pajamas for going to bed.

And I guarantee Ethan didn't remember she doesn't have

anything to sleep in. I smile to myself as I select an old t-shirt and a pair of polka-dot boxers. Ethan's already head over heels for her, I can tell. It's sweet.

These might be a little big on her, but they're well-worn so they're comfy, and they'll have to do until we can get her some proper clothes in her size. Maybe we can stop by her apartment for her and get her something.

It's easy enough to figure out which room Ethan put her in. I just follow the trail of that intoxicating scent. The lilac is refreshing and stops the sweet strawberries and vanilla from being overwhelming. I've never smelled a combination of scents I like more.

I get to the door and knock. "Ava? May I come in?"

There's a pause. "Sure."

I enter and close the door behind me, offering out the shirt and boxers. "I thought you might want something to sleep in besides the dress."

Ava's on the bed, the covers and pillows partially rearranged. Fuck, she's beautiful. Her thick hair cascades down her back and I just want to bury my nose in her neck and run my fingers through her tresses over and over.

She sees the clothes and smiles tentatively. "Oh, thank you. I appreciate it."

I cross to her and hand them over. "I'm sorry they're just old clothes of mine."

"No, it's okay." She rubs her cheek against the fabric, burying her nose in them and inhaling deeply.

My chest swells with pride at the way her lashes flutter. She likes my scent.

Then Ava goes bright red and puts the clothes down. "Um. Yes. Thank you. Sorry about that."

I frown. "What are you apologizing for?"

"I don't know what came over me. Sniffing your clothes like that."

Ah. I sit down. "Ava... Ethan suggested you were unregistered. That's true, isn't it?"

Ava nods.

"That means you've never talked to anyone from ORD, right? You never took any classes or had a mentor?"

Ava shakes her head.

I dare to reach out and take her hand. "Do you have any Omegas in your life? Any at all who might've talked to you about what it's like?"

"No," Ava whispers. "All of my friends are Betas. I was worried if I had too many Omegas in my life something would go wrong. They'd sense I was one of them, or my body would react to them and override the blockers."

I nod. "Okay. So what do you know about Omegas?"

"I know that... we have heats." She grimaces. "I know that when we're in heat we crave, um, sex. Specifically. Well it's not just." Her face is bright pink.

"Think of it like you're in science class," I say. "That's what I do. Omegas in heat need penetration as much as or even more than orgasm."

She nods.

"Heats only last a few days, though. Don't worry."

Ava doesn't seem very reassured. I decide now's not the time to remind her that her first heat off of suppressants will be a doozy as her body makes up for all those years she didn't have one. She probably already knows, and that's a bridge to cross when we get to it.

I gesture at the bed. "I see you're trying to make a nest."

"I do have a nest at home. It just never felt so imperative before. Like I had to do it in order to feel safe and happy." Ava's face screws up but she can't stop a few tears from slipping free. "Everything just feels so much stronger now. My emotions, my desires, but also my anxiety."

I squeeze her hand. "That'll get better as you adjust to your hormones and you find ways to take care of your needs, like building a proper nest again."

"You know a lot more about Omegas than I do and you're not even one."

"Well, Omegas register with the ORD, and Betas and Alphas take a course on Omega needs so they can properly care for one. They were a little sterner with us Alphas than with the Betas," I add, trying for a joke. "Our job is to take care of an Omega, after all. To make sure our Omega is happy."

Ava frowns. "Then why don't you have an Omega? I mean... this house... you're clearly rich. And you're handsome, and strong."

I want to preen knowing that she thinks so highly of me and the rest of my pack as Alphas. "Thank you."

Ava blushes. "I just mean... you're considered quite a catch of Alphas, I'm sure. So... why don't you have an Omega yet? It can't be that nobody's wanted you."

I look away. I can feel my shoulders moving in, hunching, my body trying to close itself off. I struggle against it. I don't want her to think that she's done something wrong. I clear my throat.

"It just never happened. We run a very successful tech company, making lifestyle technology to help people in their daily lives. It was a startup and we've made a lot of money off of it, but it's been basically the four of us as the core team for most of those years. We haven't had time for mating."

That's a cop-out, and I know it is, and I think Ava suspects it is too. But I can't get into it right now. It's not something I want to talk about, not even with this beautiful, enticing Omega.

I smile, so she doesn't think I'm upset with her. "As a matter of fact, our latest product is designed to help Omegas track their heats. You might find it useful."

Ava giggles a little. "I don't suppose you have a device that tracks everything else about me too?"

"Our lives would be a lot easier if we could do that. Ethan told you about the library, right? You can use any of those books there. Most of them are mine. I've got a lot of different interests but because we were doing research for the watches, I'm pretty sure I've still got some books on Omega biology in there. Some of that could be helpful to you."

"Thank you, that would be helpful." Ava smiles at me. "You're all very sweet."

"We're just doing the best we can to help you out."

"I know. That's why it's sweet."

I've gotta get out of here before I do something stupid like actually run my fingers through her hair the way I want to. I stand up. "I'll let you sleep. And hey, sleep in as much as you want tomorrow, all right? You had a long night. None of us will bother you."

Ava nods, and I turn to go. I'm just at the door when I hear her voice.

"Caleb?"

I turn.

She's standing now, with her hands behind her back, wrestling with something. "I'm so sorry, but could you help me with this zipper? It's stuck. I think it got jammed or something when I was running earlier."

"Sure thing."

I walk over, swallowing hard as her scent hits me again. She's got her back to me, a sign of trust, with all that lovely hair pulled over her shoulder so it's out of the way. It exposes the back of her neck and shoulders, creamy skin that calls to me.

Breathing carefully, I reach up and fiddle with the zipper. Yeah, it's stuck. "I'm going to have to yank on this," I tell her. "And you're going to have to get the zipper replaced. It's definitely broken."

Ava sighs. "That's fine. Just do what you have to do."

I try to yank carefully so that I don't ruin the dress further by tearing it. It takes me a couple tries, but then I get it to budge, and I can peel the teeth of the zipper apart to get the dress off her.

Fuck. Inch after inch of her skin is revealed to me as the fabric of the dress is peeled away. My mouth waters. She smells so good, and her skin looks delicious. I can imagine trailing my tongue up the line of her spine...

I realize I've swayed into her, my nostrils flaring as I inhale her scent, like I'm trying to embed it into my bones. The heat of her, her soft skin, and her warm scent all call to me like nothing else I've ever felt before. It's like when I got drunk for the first time, my head swimming, drowning on dry land.

"Excuse me," I blurt out, my voice low and rough as I force myself to take a step back. My heart is pounding and I swear I can feel my blood pumping in my ears. I feel undone. "I'll let you get your rest."

"Right." Ava's clutching her dress to her and staring at me, her cheeks bright pink. "I—I should do that. Rest. Of course."

I practically stumble out of there like a drunk and make my way downstairs. Dammit. I've got to get a grip on myself. I can't go swooning over an Omega who clearly doesn't want to be bonded.

No matter how much I'd like to bond with her.

It's just our luck that the first Omega I feel such a pull to doesn't want to be mated and is willing and ready to go against the law to ensure it.

When I get downstairs, the others have gathered in the kitchen. Garrett's eating his feelings, which is typical. Ethan's pacing. Dante sits at the head of the table.

I go to make a pot of coffee. It'll fuck up my sleep schedule but it's been fucked already at this point. Might as well.

"Are we seriously going to keep this girl here?" Garrett asks.

"She's a woman, not a girl," Dante says. "A fully grown adult."

"Yeah, and an unmated Omega while she's at it," Garrett points out. "Her age only makes this ten times more dangerous. She's not eighteen. She's in her twenties. How the hell did she last this long without getting reported?"

"She had good suppressants," I find myself piping up. "If you—"

"Do *not* give me the medical lecture right now."

I put my hands up in a gesture of surrender.

"Do you think anyone else knows?" Ethan asks.

"Not until now," Dante says. "I doubt she confided in anyone. Too big of a risk."

"So, what, we help her register?" Garrett asks. "They're going to question us pretty damn closely to make sure we didn't know this whole time."

Ethan and I are already shaking our heads. "She won't register," Ethan says.

Garrett gapes at us. "You gotta be fuckin' kidding me."

"What, you thought she was hiding her status all this time for shits and giggles?" Ethan snaps. "And that she'd just, what, throw in the towel and say, oh well, I had a good run, guess I'd better register now?"

"You need to know when you can't fight anymore," Garrett points out.

Ethan scoffs. "Now that's rich, coming from you."

"The rules are there for a reason. To protect Omegas."

"Clearly she doesn't feel that way," Dante interjects quietly.

We all fall silent, as we do whenever Dante talks. I look at my leader. Dante looks pretty damn tired. I wonder what he's thinking.

The coffee machine *dings*, shattering the silence. I turn and grab a mug, then go ahead and grab three for the others too. Garrett takes his black, Dante takes a touch of milk and one sugar, I take two sugars, and Ethan takes... well, let's just say no coffee beans were harmed in the making of his drink.

Dante nods at me in thanks as I hand him his coffee. "We don't know when she presented, but most of us present as our second gender when we're in high school. She could've been doing this for an entire decade for all we know. And you have to be pretty desperate to try the black market. I assume that's where she got the pills."

"Yeah. She had a reliable source, but it got too expensive so she tried another. I'll bet you anything they're just placebos."

A low growl starts up in the back of Garrett's throat. "Fuckers. Taking advantage of the desperate."

"That's what our work is for," Dante reminds him. "To help

with this kind of thing. So Omegas have technology that will actually take care of them."

"Yeah, but will it help her?" Garrett snaps. "We don't have time to make some fancy new gadget. She's off suppressants and desperate *now*."

"And her friends at the club know she's an Omega," Ethan murmurs.

Dante scrubs a hand over his face.

"We can't turn her out," I say. "What kind of Alphas would we be if we did that?"

"Nobody's turning her out," Dante says. "We just need a plan."

"I don't know that we can think of one at..." Ethan checks his watch. "Four in the morning."

"We should ask her what she thinks too," Dante says.

"But we'll shelter her?" Garrett asks. "The longer we do that the more trouble we're going to get into."

"She deserves a safe place to figure out her next move. She'll probably have to rearrange her entire life. Maybe even skip town. She'll need to plan and we can't turn her out."

Relief spreads through me to hear Dante's words. I know that Garrett wouldn't ever turn a desperate Omega out, but his crankiness masks it. He's just asking the tough questions we need to be asked as we figure this out. Because this is a risk. It's a big one, for all of us.

But we're Alphas. We protect Omegas. It's what we do. We can't betray our nature. Especially not for an Omega like Ava. I know I'd want to help no matter who the Omega was, but there's something about her... something *more*.

"She needs to figure it out quickly," Garrett says. "Because it's all of our asses on the line."

"I know," Dante promises.

I finally sit down, feeling relief flood my veins. Ava's going to stay with us. "I'm glad, Dante."

Garrett gives me a sharp look. "She's not staying for good, Caleb."

I sip my coffee so I don't say something I regret. I know that. I know we can't really keep her.

But that doesn't mean I need the reminder.

# Chapter 9

## *Ava*

I wake up with my nose buried in heaven.

I moan a little, my body online before my brain, as my nose is flooded with a cacophony of delicious scents. It's over-whelming in the best way, and at first I can't even pick out or name any individual scent, I just know that it's all around me and in me and it smells *amazing*.

My hips grind down against the mattress as my mind comes back to itself. I begin to identify the various scents: spicy clove, cinnamon, sweet apple cider, and smooth caramel.

Dante, Ethan, Garrett, and Caleb.

Their four scents mixing together into the perfect cocktail. It's homey and intoxicating at the same time. I feel completely, utterly safe for the first time in years, possibly my entire life.

But I also feel wildly hot all over.

I blink and push myself up a little, looking around. Last night comes flooding back to me and I wince with humiliation. I have no idea what my friends and everyone else at the club think of me now but I don't think it's anything flattering.

And now here I am, in the house, no, the *mansion* of four

Alphas. Four gorgeous Alphas. Four gorgeous Alphas who smell *amazing*.

I look down. I'm wearing Caleb's shirt and boxers, that must be part of why the scent is so strong. And the sheets too. Even though they washed them and this is one of their guest rooms, the scent of this pack is in the entire house. It can't truly be erased from anywhere.

Now it's enveloping me. Tempting me. Calling to me.

I know that I shouldn't give in to it, but I press my face back into the pillow and inhale deeply. My toes curl and my body shudders with heat as I spread my legs and picture them sliding into bed with me.

My hand moves down between my legs, under the boxers, and I whimper into the pillow. Oh, god, it'd be so perfect... they smell so *good*...

I'm still half-asleep, and my eyelids drift closed as I drag my fingertips slowly over my clit. It's already swollen and throbbing, more sensitive than usual, just from the way I'm thinking about the four gorgeous Alphas who live in this house. I bite down on my lower lip, letting the soft flesh slide between my teeth as I slip my fingers downward a bit more, sliding them between my folds to gather my wetness.

Ethan's incredible scent of cinnamon and toasted marshmallow still lingers in my nostrils, and as I start to breathe harder, it's as if I'm inhaling more of him. My mouth is practically watering, and my legs move restlessly beneath the blankets as I find the little nub of my clit again. My fingers slide easily over the sensitive bundle of nerves, and I whimper softly, scrunching up my face as I recall the solidness of Ethan's body as he held me against him last night.

He was so strong, so tall, so purely *masculine*.

The breathtaking tilt of his lips as he smiled down at me filters through my mind, and I move my fingers faster, imagining him pressing those lips to mine.

*How would he kiss me? Would it be flirty and teasing, the same way he talks? Or would it be hard and ravenous?*

Maybe he'd switch back and forth between the two, teasing us both until he couldn't hold back any longer, and then sliding his tongue into my mouth like he wanted to fuck me with it.

*How would he fuck me?*

That thought rises up above the others, and before I can stop myself, I'm lost in a fantasy of him crawling up to hover over me on the bed, his lean hips settling between my legs.

I can imagine the slick glide of his cock through my folds, and I shudder in response, circling my clit faster as I arch against my hand.

*And his knot...*

*Fuck. What would that feel like?*

The heat in my veins rises up even higher, and I suck in a gasping breath as I alternate between sliding my fingers into myself and working my clit. My toes curl against the sheets, my free hand reaching up to squeeze my breast through the borrowed shirt I'm wearing.

The shirt that smells like Caleb.

Rich chocolate, smooth caramel, and toasted hazelnuts join the spicy and sweet scents that make me think of Ethan, and suddenly, there are three people in my fantasy instead of just two.

"Oh my god," I whisper softly, licking my lips.

My imagination is going haywire, full of too many enticing thoughts to sort through them all. In my mind's eye, I see Ethan pull out of me, his cock slick and glistening with my arousal. He looks over at Caleb and grins, then moves to one side to make room for his pack mate.

Caleb is the one I imagine sliding into me this time, and I clench my thighs hard around the hand that's buried between my legs, the same way I'd squeeze them around his waist as he buried himself to the hilt inside me. I think of the way he looked at me last night, the softness and warmth in his gorgeous blue eyes, and something sweet spreads through me, radiating out from my chest and heightening every sensation.

*He would kiss me slow and deep, I bet. So deep that I could drown in it, that I could lose myself in it entirely.*

A muffled whine escapes my throat, and I press my lips together to keep myself from getting too loud.

The hand between my legs isn't enough anymore.

I've gotten used to taking care of my own needs, since I haven't dated anyone or even kissed anyone since my Omega status revealed itself. Usually, I can get myself off in just a minute or two, a perfunctory kind of thing that keeps me from going mad from lack of sexual release.

I know exactly how to touch myself to make myself come... but this morning, my body isn't satisfied with any of my usual tricks. It's desperate for more, so I give my nipple one sharp pinch through the shirt, then slide that hand down to join the one between my legs. Keeping up the pressure on my clit, I slide two fingers into my wet pussy, curling them a little to find the perfect spot.

*There. Oh god, there...*

The scents of bourbon, honey, and clove linger in the air, along with the scents of a burning fireplace and sweet apple cider that practically made me want to climb Garrett when I got a whiff of him last night. I can smell all four of the men as if they've imprinted themselves on my skin from the limited contact we had last night, and I drag in a deep breath through my nose, wanting more of it.

*Four Alphas. If they all decided to claim me at once, how would that even work?*

Once again, my imagination is only too happy to fill in the answer to that question. I increase the pressure on my clit as I imagine Caleb moving aside to allow Dante to have a turn.

*Dante would take the lead,* I think. *Dominant and powerful.*

I imagine him hitching my leg up toward my chest, opening me up more for him, holding me in place so that he can give me his cock in just the way I need it. I imagine the muscles in his neck straining as he fucks me into the mattress.

I'm so wet by now that I can feel it trickling over my hand as I slide my fingers in and out of my core, and I can hear the sounds of each movement in the quiet room.

*I'm close. Fuck, I need to come so bad.*

Everything else has faded from my mind, banished by the arousal that blazes through me like a forest fire. I've forgotten where I am, forgotten everything that happened last night. In the fantasy playing out in my mind, there's nothing but me and the four Alphas who smell like sex and comfort. Their scents surround me like a blanket as I imagine Dante nodding sharply to Garrett.

The burly, rugged man with hair so dark it's almost black moves toward me in my mind—and unlike last night, this version of him doesn't seem to have any doubts at all about having me here. The desire that burns in his rich brown eyes is hot enough that it feels like it could scorch me, and I imagine the way he might slide his own fingers into me to make sure I was ready to take him.

My hands are working at a fever pitch now, my breath coming in choppy inhales and exhales, and I moan quietly as I imagine Garrett impaling me with a single, smooth stroke.

"Fuck!" I hiss, my hips bucking upward.

That last image was too much for my needy, sensitive body to take, and it pushes me over the crest of my orgasm. My body shakes as pleasure bursts through me, my clit throbbing beneath my fingertips as my inner walls clench around the intrusion of my fingers.

I work myself through it, filthy thoughts of the men decorating me with their cum running through my mind.

My body slowly relaxes, melting into the mattress as the rapid thud of my heart peaks and then starts to slow. My chest rises with a slow breath, and I slide my fingers out from beneath the waistband of the boxers. I blink my eyes open, staring up at the ceiling of this unfamiliar room.

But as the afterglow of pleasure fades, all of my fears return, and horror hits me like a cold splash of water.

*I can't believe I just did that.* I'm not supposed to be giving in to my instincts like this and letting them rule me. I'm not one of those Omegas. I can control myself.

This was just a small slip-up, I tell myself. I'll be fine. This is fine. I'm going to have some self-control and not do it again. I was half-asleep. I had a stressful night last night. It's all fine.

Getting out of bed takes forever. The little pocket of warmth under the blankets feels like a haven, and I'm terrified of what's going to happen today. These men gave me a safe place to sleep but are they really going to let me stay? I don't know, and I have no backup plan.

There are also the more long-term concerns. Even if this pack is willing to hide me, it can't be forever. I can't go back to work. Athena and the others know the truth of what I am now and they must know I'm not registered. If they don't, they'll figure it out quickly.

Ethan covered for me by acting like my Alpha, but I don't know if anyone who works with me will actually buy it. I keep to myself to protect anyone from figuring out the truth. I've never had any coworkers over to my apartment in case they saw my nest of a bed or caught my real scent. It could be enough for them to buy that I'm just private about my personal life. Or it could make them even more suspicious and sure that I'm hiding something.

I don't know, and that not-knowing could spell doom for me.

*Well, you'll never figure out a plan if you don't go downstairs and talk to them,* I tell myself. I stay wearing the clothes I had on, since my dress needs to be repaired in the zipper, and try not to feel exposed as I head down to the kitchen.

My brain is screaming at me that I'm wearing Caleb's clothes and that I smell like all four Alphas from the bed. I probably look like I'm doing the walk of shame. It makes heat crawl up my neck.

When I get to the kitchen, delicious food fills my nostrils with its scent and I nearly collapse in joy as hunger smacks me in the face. I hadn't realized just how *hungry* I am.

I enter, to find all four Alphas there. Dante's at the stove, cooking sausages and eggs. Garrett's sipping coffee and staring out the window like the morning sunlight has personally insulted him. Ethan's futzing with the fanciest espresso machine I've seen in my life, and Caleb is eating quietly at the table.

All four of them freeze as I enter, their heads shooting up to look at me. I can see their nostrils flaring and I know they're smelling me.

A sly look slides into Ethan's eyes. Dante looks triumphant. Caleb's blushing as he stares down resolutely at his food.

Garrett's not even looking at me, after that first quick instinctive glance. But I know he can smell it too, because just like all the others, he's purring with satisfaction.

I can see heat burning in their faces, every last one of them. Their scents change too, becoming sharper, headier. I feel dizzy with it. My body responds, heating up, and I know that they can sense the change in my scent as well.

They know what I just did in bed. They know I touched myself.

My breathing comes in little pants. I want them to pick me up and press me between them. I want to be pinned by their broad, muscular bodies. I want them to lick into my mouth and between my legs until I'm screaming pleasure, and then I want them to fill me...

Something sizzles in the pan and Dante yelps as hot oil gets on him. Ethan bursts out laughing and Caleb snorts into the back of his hand. Even Garrett's smirking as he turns his face away, trying to hide it for either his dignity or Dante's.

The tension breaks, and Dante waves his hand at the food on the stove. "You want some?"

"Yes, please," I say meekly.

They're still purring as Ethan gets me a plate and Dante loads it up with sausages, eggs, and toast. Ethan pours me a coffee. "Sugar? Milk?"

"Two sugars and two splashes, please, thank you."

"So polite," Caleb says from the table, grinning at me.

I take my food and sit down. I take my first bite. "Holy fuck."

This is better than anything I've ever eaten before. This is gourmet. I sip the coffee and moan a little. Oh my god. I'm scarfing the food down like a maniac. I've never had anything this good.

Dante's purrs get a little louder, his satisfaction in feeding me well obvious to everyone in the room. Caleb watches me with a soft smile on his face. "Good?"

I nod, my mouth full of food. I swallow. "Sorry, I feel like a toddler, where are my manners—it's just really, really delicious. Holy crap."

Ethan chuckles and refills my coffee. "We're the kind of guys who like only the best, and luckily we can afford it. And we like to take good care of each other."

"Like all packs *should*," Garrett mutters, continuing to stare out the window.

"Ignore him, he's grumpy in the mornings."

"You say that like he's *only* grumpy in the mornings," Caleb points out.

"Well, he's grumpier than usual."

"He wouldn't be," Dante says, still over by the stove, "if he would eat breakfast."

"I said I'm not..."

"Hungry," the other three men all say at once.

"But you'll feel better once you do," Dante adds while Ethan simultaneously silently imitates exactly what he's saying.

I laugh. "I'm guessing this is an everyday kind of argument?"

"It's not an argument, it's them being wrong."

"Sorry, so this is an everyday them being wrong?"

Garrett points at me. "She thinks she's funny."

"I know I'm funny. I'm hilarious." I bat my eyes at him.

Ethan and Caleb struggle to muffle their chuckles in their coffee.

Dante loads my plate up with some fluffy blueberry pancakes and then pours some syrup over them, and gives me a side of bacon. I feel like a princess. I haven't been spoiled like this in... well, ever, actually.

"So, Dante cooks," I say. "Who else does what?"

"Caleb does the laundry," Ethan volunteers.

"Only because you turned all our clothes pink."

"It was one time!"

"He bleached my shirt," Garrett adds.

"You told me you wanted that stain out, so I got the stain out."

"With *bleach*."

I grin as I tuck into my pancakes. They're all smiling as they banter with each other, lighthearted, the arguments clearly well-worn and lacking any real sting. They're a family. A real family, one that cares about each other and supports each other, one that's actually there instead of being constantly checked-out and distant.

Something in my chest howls with yearning for that.

"Seriously," Caleb says, changing the subject, "we're going to have to keep feeding you if you're this impressed."

"Hey, at least she's impressed." Ethan grins. "Some people are just critics."

"Some people," Garrett says mildly, "didn't grow up thinking pizza for breakfast was gourmet."

"And *some* people were born with silver spoons up their asses."

"Garrett likes my cooking," Dante says. His tone is mild but Ethan and Garrett both shut their mouths with an audible *click*.

I have to admit it's pretty sexy, seeing Dante do that. These men are all so in sync. I wonder if I could ever—

Nope. I shut down that train of thought. There's no reason for me to be thinking like this. I don't *want* that, and I haven't fought against the Omega fate for so many years to give up now. I'll have to do something drastic like move across the country if I want to stay unregistered, and that'll mean I don't get to stay in touch with these men.

And that's fine. It's how it should be.

Caleb's watch goes off. "Time to go." He gets up.

Dante nods and gestures at Ethan, who starts to clean up the various dishes. Seems he gets clean up duty.

"Where are you going?"

"We have to go into the office," Caleb explains. "We're launching a product soon and that means it's all hands on deck."

Dante nods in agreement. Caleb presses his hand to my shoulder, squeezing gently. His scent fills me again, and I feel calm and safe. "We won't be gone long, though. And Ethan and Garrett will be here to look after you."

I glance at Dante, wanting reassurance from him too, even though I hate to admit it. I don't say anything out loud, just smile and nod at him. "Thanks for the breakfast."

Dante nods back at me, serious, focused, and then gestures for Caleb to follow him out of the room.

Odd. Garrett's at least consistent in his gruff manner. Ethan and Caleb seem happy to have me here. Dante feels... more hot and cold. I can't get a read on him.

I stand up to help Ethan with the dishes but he waves me away. "You keep eating. I'll take care of this."

I settle back down and do as I'm told. I'm not fond of the idea of someone else doing all the work while I sit here and be pampered. Ethan seems to sense this, because he waggles his eyebrows at me as he starts up the sink. "Not used to being lazy, hmm?"

"Not used to someone else taking care of things."

"You've been on your own for a long time."

I nod.

Garrett finishes his own food. Even though he protested, he wolfs it down like he hasn't eaten in days. He deposits his stuff in the sink and walks out without a word.

"Don't worry about him," Ethan says. "Garrett's rough around the edges but he's got a big heart, trust me. I've known the guy for a decade."

"You all have been without an Omega for that long?" It startles me. But then I want to clap my hand over my face. "I'm sorry, that was a rude question."

"No, you're fine. It's natural you'd wonder about it. We all have our reasons why we haven't really been ready to find an Omega."

Ethan doesn't elaborate, and I don't pry. I don't want to press them on anything they're not willing to talk about, especially when there's no need. I won't be here long. The less we get intimate, the better.

I finish eating, give my dishes to Ethan and thank him, then I'm left with literally nothing to do. I work at the shelter all the time. It's my entire life. Now that I actually have a day off but can't leave the house—or rather, the mansion—I'm at a loss.

Finally, I settle on watching a movie in the home theater. It's fine, like having a total movie theater all to myself, and it keeps me out of the way of Ethan and Garrett. I don't want to step on anyone's toes.

The credits are just rolling when I hear my name being called. "Ava?"

I emerge. "Ethan?"

He's at the front door, grinning over a pile of boxes. "So... don't be upset."

"Why would I be upset?"

"I decided it would be too risky to go back to your apartment. Maybe I can go back there to get some keepsakes of yours, but I figure, for your clothes, it's best to just get you some new ones so that you don't have to worry about someone following me back here and finding you." Ethan gestures at the various boxes. "So I went shopping for you."

He went shopping for me. Normally I'd worry about a man trying to pick out my clothes, but Ethan sounds confident, and the clothes he's currently sporting look great on him: a dark blue cashmere sweater with the sleeves rolled up, and a pair of black jeans that hug his legs in all the right ways, showing off how muscled he is.

"Here." Ethan hefts up a box like it's nothing. "I'll carry them upstairs for you."

I'm not about to be outdone by an Alpha. I pick up a box myself and follow Ethan. I can't let myself get used to someone being around to do things for me. This isn't going to last. As soon as I can get out of here and out of the city, I'm gone for good.

We get my clothes up to the room I'm staying in, and I start unpacking them. My jaw drops open and I can feel my eyes going wide.

"Ethan. I can't possibly accept these." I pick up a purse. It's Bulgari. This has to be at least three thousand dollars. "This is all designer."

"You're not putting us out, I promise."

I pull out a silky blouse that looks like it costs more than my entire month's expenses. Everything in here is beautiful, and in colors that compliment my dark hair and curvy body. And there are multiple boxes of them. I've never owned this many clothes in my life, and I have no idea how I'm going to pack them all up again and get them to my new place when I leave.

"This is..." My voice trails off as I look at him. "Ethan, really."

"Hey, you're going to be starting over." Ethan shrugs. "Figure now you have one less thing to worry about. Hell, go ahead and sell them for extra cash if you want, when the time comes."

Tears prick at my eyes and I sit down on the bed, still holding the silky blouse. This really is the end of my old life. I can't go back. My job, my friends, my apartment... it's all gone now.

"Hey." Ethan sits next to me. "It's okay."

"Is it?" I whisper. "Some asshole decides that Omegas don't matter, and now my whole life is turned upside down."

"Trust me," Ethan mutters. "If we ever get a hold of the person who made those placebos, we're going to make sure they regret being born."

Ethan's so cheerful and charming that his fury takes me aback. But unlike when Marcus would be angry, I don't feel threatened. Ethan's angry on my behalf. He's being protective.

It makes me feel safe.

Ethan's hand lands on my back. His touch is tentative at first, like he's not sure if I'll be okay with it, but when I don't move, he rubs my back in slow circles. "You're clearly someone who values her independence," he murmurs. "It takes a lot of inner strength to go it alone the way you have. Whatever happens, I believe that you'll be able to find the life you want for yourself."

I wipe at my eyes. "That means a lot."

"Well, I truly mean it." He stands with a gentle smile. "I'll let you have some time to yourself."

Part of me wants to beg him to stay, but I also feel embarrassed crying in front of a near-stranger, even if it's one that's been so kind to me.

So I just nod. "Thank you."

Ethan leaves me alone, and I turn my attention to the unpacking.

Some of the clothes he bought me are so soft that they feel like clouds against my skin. I tug off the clothes Caleb lent me last night and pull on a pair of pants, a bra, and a nice top, then put the rest of the things away in the closet and drawers.

Everything is well-made and luxurious, and I almost want to make a pile and roll around in it. Which is an odd thought, actually, now that I think about it. I've never wanted to just roll around in clothes bef—

"Ah!"

I double over as a wave of heat rushes through me, and a cramp punches me right in my lower gut. I grab on to a box and try to steady myself. I feel like I can't move, like even breathing is going to bring me more pain if I'm not careful about it.

What—what's happening? Why—

I breathe in deeply and carefully. I'm not sure exactly what's going on, but I suspect...

This might be the start of my first-ever heat.

# Chapter 10

## *Garrett*

I thought hitting the gym would help. I was wrong.

I thought taking a shower would help. I was wrong.

Now here I am, trying to get work done, on the other side of the fucking house from her, and I still can't concentrate.

Goddammit.

I scroll through work documents on my computer, but the screen's blurry in front of my gaze. I'm not really paying attention to anything in front of me.

It's that Omega. Ava.

She's gorgeous, and she smells like no other Omega has ever smelled to me. Just our damn luck that the Omega we're all drawn to is one that doesn't want to even get registered, never mind bond with a pack. We're all asking for heartache with this one.

Well, maybe the other three are asking for it, but I'm sure as hell not. I know better. I'll just stay out of her way and she'll stay out of mine until—

Was that a cry?

I'm standing before I even realize I want to leave my chair, sniffing hard. I can't quite get a whiff from here, but I'm sure I heard some kind of distressed noise.

"Ah!"

There it is again. I'm sure I heard it this time.

I hurry through the house and up the stairs. Maybe the suppressants she was given weren't placebos after all but had some kind of chemical, something she's allergic to or something that's harmful in large doses.

*What if she's hurt?*

I nearly collide with Ethan as we hit the landing outside the room at the same time. I nod at him, and Ethan opens the door.

The scent hits me immediately. Not just her scent, but the *way* it smells. Ripe strawberries and so much sweet cream I feel dizzy. I stumble a little, heat flooding my body. It reminds me of how she smelled when she entered the kitchen and I knew, even without turning my head, that she'd touched herself.

She'd smelled like all four of us too. I'd been unable to stop myself from purring. I have got to get a damn grip.

I blink and shake my head, trying to clear it even as my body screams at me to give in to my need, and I realize that the reason I'm feeling this way is she's in heat.

There, curled up on the floor, lies Ava. She's whimpering, tears in her eyes and clinging to her pretty lashes. Not the full heat yet, but the beginnings of it.

"Shit," Ethen murmurs. "I don't know if she's had one before."

If she's been on suppressants the whole time? Probably not. I cross to her. "Ava."

Her eyes open and she focuses on me. "Garrett?"

"Come here." I scoop her up and carefully lay her on the bed while Ethan arranges the pillows so that she's comfortable.

Ava moans and clutches at me. "I know," I soothe her. "We'll get you something to help with the cramps."

There's got to be a tea or something we've got around the house that'll help.

Ava shakes her head. "No, I... I need... I *want*..."

Her eyes are a bit glassy and while I've never experienced this myself, I know about it from the classes on caring for your Omega that they had us take in college. She's only in the beginning of her heat, but it's starting.

She needs comfort. She needs touch. She needs scent.

And she needs an Alpha's knot.

I swallow hard but press my hands to her neck and shoulders so she can feel soothed. It's where a bite would go and it gives her my scent, so I hope the pressure and smell helps.

"Breathe," I tell her. Ethan hovers behind me, looking nervous. Not wanting to overstep. "Deep breaths. You're okay."

"No," Ava whimpers, and it breaks my damn heart. "No, I need *more*. More, please..."

I curl myself around her and hold on to her. She buries her nose in my neck to scent me and clings to me. "There you go. Shh. It's okay."

"It's not okay," she sobs. "I need more. Please, I need it to feel better. I need..."

She's babbling, but I know what she needs even if she doesn't. She needs an Alpha knot. Or at the very least an orgasm.

I look at Ethan. He holds his hands out, palms up, in a gesture of helplessness. I know how he feels, but we have to do something. We can't let her just lie here miserable.

Knotting her would be going too far. But I know what else I can do.

"It's all right, little Omega," I murmur gruffly. "We've got you."

She sniffles, her small, delicate frame shuddering against mine. My body responds instantly, my cock pulsing against the constraints of my pants. Fuck, I've never scented an Omega who smells as tantalizing as this beautiful, dark-haired woman does.

Threading my fingers through her silken hair, I palm the back of her head and kiss her. She kisses me back instantly, her soft lips pressing hungrily against mine as she arches against me. A quiet mewling noise spills from her mouth into mine, and I swallow it up, my tongue dancing with hers as I ease her gently onto her back, hovering over her as I brace myself on one elbow.

She whimpers suddenly, grabbing on to my shoulder as her breath hitches.

This isn't enough. I know that.

*She needs to come.*

Continuing to kiss her, I release my hold on the back of her head and slide my hand down her body instead, kneading her breasts when I reach them and making her moan against my lips. My hand travels lower, and I swear I can feel the warmth radiating from her pussy before I even reach it. My fingers quickly undo the fastenings on her pants, and I delve my hand inside as she lifts her hips, seeking more of my touch.

"Do you want this?" I ask, my voice hoarse. "You want Ethan and me to take care of you?"

"Yes," she whispers, still kissing me like she might die if she stops. "Yes, yes. Please. *Yes.*"

"Then spread your legs a little," I command, sliding my finger through the slickness of her folds.

She does it immediately, her scent filling the air even more strongly, wrapping around me and making me feel dizzy.

Tangy strawberries. Sweet lilac. Just a hint of the most addictive, pure vanilla.

I have to look at her, so I break the kiss and pull back just enough to gaze down at her face, grazing my fingers over her clit as I do. Her eyes fly wide open, the rich brown of her irises blending with the jet black of her pupils. Her cheeks are already flushed from arousal, and her nostrils are flaring with every exhale.

A line appears between her eyebrows, her lips turning downward in a frown, and I know it's because she's not getting enough of what she needs.

"Help me," I tell Ethan, not even bothering to glance his way as I speak to him. I couldn't look away from the stunning little Omega beneath me if a meteor were hurtling toward this room. Not even if my life depended on it. "She needs more stimulation."

"Fuck," Ethan groans, sounding almost as wrecked as I feel.

If Ava were in her full heat, I'm not sure either of us would be able to resist knotting her, but even though this is just the beginning of her heat, she's perfuming hard enough to make both of us purr deeply.

The mattress shifts as he crawls up onto it, sandwiching her between the two of us as he settles on her other side.

"What do you need?" he asks, gazing down at Ava's delicate features. "What can I do?"

"Kiss me," she gasps, reaching for him and pulling him down.

He gives her just what she needs, his mouth slanting over hers. From my vantage point, I'm only inches away from both of their faces, and the sight of him kissing her turns me on more than I ever would've thought.

We've never shared a woman before, but somehow, it doesn't bother me at all to see my pack mate kissing Ava. In fact, it makes a kind of satisfaction rise inside me, because I can see the way her body responds to him. He's easing her discomfort, giving her pleasure, and I like that a lot.

Making Ava feel good feels... *right.*

Keeping my gaze locked on their faces, I work her clit harder, circling it and sliding my fingertips over it as I try to gauge what movements make her respond the most strongly. She shifts her hips, lifting them off the mattress to chase my touch whenever I back off, and I take that as a sign that she can handle more.

Slipping two fingers inside her, I grind the heel of my hand against her clit, and she responds by crying out into Ethan's mouth.

"God, you taste so good," he growls, breathing hard as he lifts his head.

"More. Ethan, *more.*"

Ava reaches for him again, and he catches her hand in his own, pressing his lips to each of her fingertips as a purr rumbles in his chest.

"You want more?" he murmurs, and there's a teasing tone I recognize in his voice. "You want me to kiss you again?"

"Yes," she breathes, nodding emphatically. Her eyes are still a bit glassy, but it's from pleasure now and not from pain. I can tell that what we're doing is working. "Kiss me. Please."

Ethan grins. But instead of dropping his head to press his lips to hers, he moves downward, dropping a kiss to her collarbone.

Ava moans, writhing a little on the mattress. "I meant kiss my mouth."

"Did you?" His eyes darken as he shoots her a look, pushing up her shirt to expose the bra that covers her breasts. His lips close around one breast, sucking on her nipple and dampening the fabric, and she hisses out a breath. "Does that mean you don't want me to kiss you here?"

"No, no, you can..." Her eyes almost roll back as I press my fingers deeper inside her. "You can keep doing that. It feels so good."

"Glad you like it. What about this?"

He moves lower, trailing his lips and tongue over her stomach, and my cock pulses as I feel Ava clench around me, her pussy gripping my fingers so tight that it's like she's trying to drag them deeper inside her.

"That feels... oh god. Oh fuck."

She tosses her head back and forth, her dark hair fanning out on the pillow beneath her, and as Ethan presses open-mouthed kisses to her lower belly and then moves down even farther, I adjust the position of my hand to make room for him. Keeping my fingers buried inside her wet heat, I work her pants and panties down a bit more. Then I slide my fingers in and out in short strokes as Ethan's tongue makes contact with her clit.

Ava's back arches, a breathy whine spilling from her lips, and the scent of her arousal spikes even higher. Ethan groans, and the vibrations of the sound must do something for her, because she cries out. Her body starts to shake, and I work in tandem with my pack mate, moving my fingers faster as his tongue flicks back and forth over her clit.

"Come for us, little Omega," I growl softly. "That's right. Just like that."

Her luminous eyes lock on mine, and before I know it, I'm kissing her again, tasting the sweetness of her tongue and her lips as her orgasm hits her. She shudders from head to toe, her hands flailing as if searching for something to hold on to. One of them lands in my hair, her fingers curling into the strands, and the slight sting in my scalp as she grips my dark locks tightly makes my cock throb.

"That's a good girl," I murmur between kisses, showering her with praise as Ethan and I keep working her clit and her pussy, wanting to draw out her climax as long as possible. "Such a good fucking girl. So perfect."

The sexiest little noises I've ever heard spill from her lips, and she's breathing like she just ran a marathon. She keeps kissing me as the orgasm rolls through her, and when it finally starts to subside, she unclenches her fingers, releasing her tight grip on my hair.

"Fuck, you taste good when you come," Ethan murmurs. When I withdraw my fingers from her pussy, he doesn't waste a second, using his tongue to clean up the mess of arousal that soaks her entrance.

Unable to resist, I bring my fingers to my mouth to see for myself.

Tangy sweetness that reminds me of her unique scent hits my tongue, and I groan, licking each finger clean.

"He's right," I tell the beautiful Omega sprawled out between us. "I've never tasted anything so delicious."

"Thank you."

Ava's smile is somehow both shy and sultry at the same time, and it makes my balls tighten with another flare of arousal. Her tongue darts out to wet her pillowy lips as she melts into the bed, all loose limbs and sated sighs, and I ache everywhere.

I want her so fucking badly that my cock is aching and leaking into my pants. But I won't do anything. It's too soon and someone needs to have self-control. She's not our Omega. I'm not going to cross that line.

Instead, I pet her hair, taking in the relaxed look of bliss on her face. It soothes something inside me.

For a moment, there's nothing but peace.

And then Ava bursts into tears.

# Chapter 11

## *Ava*

For a moment, in the aftermath of my orgasm, I feel nothing but pleasure and bliss.

That was amazing. I've never had an orgasm like that before. I tell myself it's only because it's been so long since I had sex or felt the touch of another person like that, but... the way that they *smelled*, the way they looked at me and touched me...

It's unlike anything I've felt before. And while I try to deny it in my mind, my body knows the truth.

Almost better than the pleasure is the erasure of my pain. It was the worst cramping pain I'd ever been in, like fire in my belly, and now it's abated. I can stretch my limbs out. I feel such relief.

But as that all fades, something else wells up in me instead: a sob.

Tears spring into my eyes and pour down my cheeks. I don't even know entirely why. I just had an amazing orgasm, and my pain is gone. I should be relaxed and happy. Instead, I just feel so small and overwhelmed.

I sob hard and curl up into a ball. Ethan and Garrett exchange alarmed looks.

This is so embarrassing. No, worse than that, it's humiliating. I can't believe this is happening to me.

"S-sorry," I choke out, stumbling to my feet and pulling my pants back up. "E-excuse me."

I dash to the bathroom and slam the door behind me. My knees give out, and I slide to the floor, my back pressed to the now closed door. I hide my face in my knees.

My body is shaking, and each sob makes me heave. I don't understand. I feel like I'm floating apart, like my body isn't fully tied to the earth anymore.

"Ava?" Ethan calls. "Are you okay?"

Pounding starts on the door. "Ava." Garrett's voice is a low growl, but it doesn't make me scared. He doesn't sound angry, just concerned. "Ava, open up."

I should stay hidden in here. When I get upset, I just want to be left alone. At least usually. But right now, I have this unending need for a hug. I want to be held. I haven't been held in a long, long time.

"What's wrong?" Ethan says. He sounds pleading. "Ava, please tell us what's wrong."

"Ava, open the door."

Before I can even truly decide, I find myself standing and opening the door.

I'm crying even harder as arms pull me in. I recognize it's Ethan by his scent, and I burrow into him as I inhale his warm, loving campfire smell.

He carries me to the bed and sits down on it, keeping me in his lap. He rocks back and forth a little, just a bit, and rubs my back.

"Did we hurt you?" Garrett asks. He sounds stricken.

I already suspected that Garrett's not nearly as hard-hearted as he likes to act. He didn't have to help me out just now with that orgasm and he wasn't aggressive or possessive as he did it. He was truly helping me out. I worry most Alphas would've knotted me without a second thought, but Garrett made it all about me.

Now, I have confirmation of his soft heart. He's looking at me like he's going to tear his own hand off if I say that he hurt me.

I shake my head. "You did nothing wrong." My words come out as hiccups, I'm crying so hard.

My stomach curls in shame. I'm good at hiding my emotions and dealing with things on my own at least most of the time, and now here I am, crying uncontrollably. I feel like a child.

"It's okay," Ethan soothes. "You're okay. Just cry it out. We're here for you."

"What's wrong?" Garrett asks again. I can tell he wants a solution. He wants to fix things and make it all better, and it comforts me. But there's really nothing he can do in this situation. He can't fix my heart.

"I'm..." I pause. Am I really about to tell this story?

Nobody knows about Marcus and what happened. I haven't gotten close enough to anyone to think I could trust them with this. But now that I'm such an absolute mess, maybe it's time for me to share this.

They deserve to know why I'm so scared, after all. Since it's not really their fault.

"I'm..."

"Deep breaths," Ethan gently reminds me.

I do as he tells me. His smell and presence are grounding. "I didn't present until I was already in college. I know that's late for people. My parents are both Betas, so I thought I was a Beta too."

Garrett nods. He crouches down in front of us so that we're eye to eye, his gaze on me intense but kind.

I take another deep breath and continue. "Before I knew I was an Omega, I had a boyfriend. Named Marcus.

"In movies they always... you know. Show abusive people as so loud and violent. You think, how could someone possibly date that person? Don't they know this person is bad news? It's obvious that the guy is a jerk."

"You were abused?" Ethan asks.

Garrett's already growling low in the back of his throat.

"Not physically. Or... I worry it might have gotten to that point, honestly. I wouldn't put it past him."

Garrett's growling grows louder.

I've never had an Alpha growl over me in a protective way. Marcus would growl, but it was *at* me. It was to put me in my place. Garrett looks like he's going to track Marcus down and rip his throat out.

"He started out so nice." I want them to understand. I need them to understand. "He was so *charming*."

My head falls to Ethan's shoulder and I stare down at my hands as I talk, unable to meet their gazes anymore. Ethan tightens his hold on me slightly and keeps rocking me.

"He was so popular. I never understood why he was interested in me. I suppose maybe that was part of it. I wasn't popular. I was quiet. I kept to myself. He saw someone he could manipulate easily that way."

Garrett snorts, not at me, but like he thinks that's bullshit. I try to smile, but it doesn't quite fit on my face.

"And I thought I was a Beta, so I had my expectations... tempered, I guess you could say. I knew he'd probably want to find an Omega someday, so I was all right if it wasn't too serious. But he would do all these romantic gestures for me, so I started to think that maybe it could be something more."

My face burns with embarrassment. Marcus drew me in with his charm, and it still stings to think about it, especially considering how bad things got once he showed his true colors.

"But then he started... commenting on things," I whisper. "How I ate. What I ate. How much I ate. How I did my hair. What clothes I wore. And I was young and hadn't ever had anyone paying attention to me like that before, so I would follow his suggestions because I wanted to make him happy. I thought it was a sign that he cared about me, that he would talk about these things."

As I talk, it's almost as if I'm back there. I can remember his scent in the back of my mind, and I can see his face when he would get angry. I can hear his voice when he would snarl and growl at me, and the horrible things he'd tell me.

"The compliments stopped coming. He would talk down to me all the time. And he would say things like '*I know you can do so much better. Why are you being like this?*' As if all of the insults he lobbed at me were actually my fault, and not his. I was a failure. I wasn't being a good enough girlfriend."

Ethan keeps rubbing my back. I close my eyes and let the tears slide down my face.

"It was terrifying. I had always thought of myself as independent." And now I'm sharing even more.

"My parents weren't very close to me. They never really showed me affection. I thought that meant I knew how to be on my own but I guess it made me more vulnerable than I thought because I just lapped up his charisma."

"Hey, I get it," Ethan says softly. "I lost my parents young. It doesn't make you weak."

I laugh bitterly. "I loved his Alpha nature, how strong and confident he was. But then when I was dependent on his love, he used it against me."

Garrett growls again. I keep plowing forward. If I don't get it all out now, I don't know if I ever will.

"It kept getting worse. He would tell me when I could and couldn't go out with friends. He wouldn't let me leave the apartment. He would pick me up and carry me places like it was nothing. The next thing I knew, he controlled every aspect of my life."

I wipe at my eyes. "And I know that it wasn't all at once. It was gradual. But it felt like it was all at once. One moment I was independent and free and had friends. The next moment, I blink, and I'm... I have no friends, and I'm alone, and my grades are slipping, and I can't even leave the house without this man's permission."

Ethan strokes my hair. And then, tentative, like he's not sure if he should do it, I feel Garrett's hand on my knee.

Usually, if a man put his hand on my knee, I expect him to be flirting with me. But Garrett's touch is soothing. Grounding. Like he wants to hold me but isn't sure if he can.

"I've never been so scared in my life. I knew I had to get out. After class one day, I didn't go home. I was able to get away and get help. I had to transfer to another college in the end."

I sigh, remembering the entire life I had to leave behind. "I'm still not sure that my old friends know what happened. I've never contacted them. I've been too scared."

That's something I regret. But I also know I couldn't have done it any differently.

"A bit after I left him, I presented as an Omega. I had just finished my degree, and was in a transition period in my life, so it was easy for me to hide the truth. I just knew that if I'd presented as an Omega when I was dating this guy that he never would've let me go. I would've been trapped with him forever."

I'm sure that Ethan and Garrett can smell my fear on me. I can still remember that day like it's just happened. The sensations sweeping through me, and then the horror. The fear.

It's a fear that I've lived with ever since, if I'm being honest with myself. To the point where I don't remember what it's like to live without it.

"I never want to be trapped like that again. Not ever. I'm never going to let someone control me and my life that way. So I found someone who knew someone, and I went on suppressants and blockers, and I never told anybody the truth."

Someone passes me a tissue to blow my nose. I look up.

Dante and Caleb now stand behind Garrett. Caleb's the one with the tissues. All three of them look concerned.

"I guess you two heard all of that?" I whisper.

On the one hand, I'm glad. It means I don't have to explain anything all over again. On the other hand, it means four people now know the truth about me and my pain.

Now that it's out in the open, it feels even more real than before. This really happened to me. And now I'm outed as an Omega, at least to some people, and I have to uproot my life and change everything all over again.

Dante nods. Caleb helps me throw away the tissues. "Do you want us to track him down?" he asks. "Because we can do that. I have some tech..."

"We can rip his throat out," Garrett growls.

I find myself laughing through my tears as I wipe my eyes. It's just so sweet of them. "No, it's okay."

"Hey, you know that you should be proud of yourself, right?" Ethan murmurs. "It's not easy to get out of a situation like that. You're a very strong woman, Ava."

"I don't feel very strong right now," I admit in a murmur. "I'm crying over everything."

"This is something worth crying about," Caleb points out. "Have you ever talked about this before?"

I shake my head. "Not with anyone. I considered a therapist, but I worried that my Omega status would come up so I didn't want to take the chance."

"You've been alone this whole time," Dante says, his voice rich and low. "You haven't ever talked about this out loud before. That's a lot. Of course you're going to have emotions about it. We're not judging you."

"Fuck anyone who does," Garrett adds vehemently.

I smile. They really are sweet men. "Thank you."

"You know that... we won't ever do that, right?" Caleb asks. He sounds heartbroken that I might think otherwise. "Your life is yours. We would never, ever control you like that."

Garrett growls. "Fuckers like that are the kind of Alphas who give all of us a bad name. They should be..."

Dante gives him a firm look, probably sensing I don't want to have a lot of anger around me right now.

"I know you're not our Omega," Dante says. "But that doesn't matter. You're still a person. We'll protect you, bonded or not. We're going to figure this out. As long as you're with us, we'll take care of you."

"You don't owe us anything," Ethan adds, as if he can sense

my lingering concerns. "This isn't a transaction. You deserve, all Omegas deserve, to be taken care of like this and to make their own choices in life."

"Just because you're bonded or in a relationship with someone doesn't mean that you should give up your freedom or be controlled," Caleb adds.

I nod. "That's why I never registered. I didn't want to end up with an Alpha like him. I wanted to keep myself safe and stay in control of my life."

"You deserve that," Dante tells me seriously.

The other three nod in agreement.

It warms my heart. With most other Alphas, I'm not sure I would trust it. I would be wary and wondering if they were just saying these things to placate me and lure me into a false sense of security. Marcus really messed with my head, and I'm only now realizing just how deep my trust issues run.

But I don't feel that way with these four men. I feel like they're telling me the truth. I feel safe. They look at me with their eyes alight with earnestness, like they really would go to the ends of the earth to help me feel okay.

I told my story. I told the truth about Marcus. And the world didn't fall down. It's kind of amazing, and mostly a relief.

"Thank you," I tell them, and I mean it.

# Chapter 12

## *Ava*

Over the next couple of days, I start to get more comfortable.

None of the four men were disrespectful about my space to begin with, but I notice after I confess everything about Marcus that they start to ask me if they can touch me, or to telegraph when they need to touch me or be near me.

It's sweet that they're being so careful.

I try to treat this place as my own, as Ethan told me, but it's hard to shake the feeling that I'm a guest in this house. On the third day, I grab some of the workout clothes that Ethan got for me. I've been feeling full of restless energy, and it's not just the fact that I'm cooped up in this house. It's more than that.

I've got to work some of it off.

Once I put the clothes on, I head down to the large indoor gym the men have set up. I've never used a gym before, preferring to go for runs outside and do yoga in the park, but that's not really an option right now, so I'll take what I can get.

Like the rest of the house, the gym's amazing. I have no shortage of equipment to use here. But the moment I walk in, all hopes of a workout are dashed.

Dante's there, lifting weights.

His muscles gleam and his shirt sticks to him, showing off his toned body. I swallow hard. He really is a handsome man.

But he's also a man who I'm not sure has entirely warmed to me. At this point I feel like I know where I stand with all of the others, even Garrett, but Dante is still a mystery to me.

Dante puts down his weights and looks up, spotting me. I wonder if he could smell me. Probably. The thought makes me flush.

"Sorry," I blurt out. "I'll go."

I turn, but Dante's voice stops me. "No, no. Don't worry about it."

His voice is softer than I expect. I turn back to look at him. "Are you sure?"

He nods.

Okay, then.

I start up the treadmill while Dante goes back to the weights. At first, I try to ignore him, wishing that I'd brought my earbuds so that I could listen to music and tune him out. But then once I start glancing over at him, I can't stop.

He's moving these huge weights around, but his movements are fluid, like water. Like these weights are nothing. I can't help but wonder what it would be like to have him pick me up. He'd move me just as easily, I'm sure...

I trip on the damn treadmill and yelp, falling forward.

Strong arms wrap around me to keep me upright and I gasp, heat shooting through me as Dante's scent and the heat of his body hit me like a wave. His hands fall to my hips as I get upright again and turn off the treadmill.

"Thanks," I blurt out. I twist a little to look at him.

We're both breathing hard, even though there's not really any reason for us to be. Up close, I feel dizzy staring into his slate eyes. The sweat makes his hair darker, almost dark enough to match Garrett's, and his stubble stands out.

He looks completely disheveled. I want to lick the sweat off his throat and drag him into the shower with me...

Dante clears his throat and steps back. "No problem."

He goes to another weight machine. I watch him, taking in his laser-like focus. "I'm going to be honest... most rich people don't seem as compassionate as the four of you."

Dante smirks a little. "Well, maybe that's because out of the three of us, Garrett was the only one born rich."

"Really?"

He nods. He's not looking at me. I feel like it would be dangerous if he did. "We all met in college when we were studying computer science and engineering."

That gets a laugh out of me. "Sorry. You don't look like your typical nerds, that's all."

"I know, and only Caleb really acts the part." Dante grins at me, and it makes my heart flutter. "We bonded pretty quickly. Ethan is the best with marketing and sales, even though I swear he'd be good at anything he puts his mind to. Caleb is a whiz with tech, and Garrett's best with finances. Comes from his background handling a lot of money from a young age. He's the one who provided the initial capital that allowed us to succeed and get our company off the ground."

Dante's face hardens briefly before relaxing again as he adds, "It cost him a lot with his family. They didn't like the fact that he was using his inheritance this way instead of joining in the family business. But Garrett isn't one to be intimidated."

"I've noticed."

He chuckles. "Most people do. Anyway, Caleb and I were there on scholarships. I wouldn't have been able to afford to go otherwise. And we're lucky that we worked things out financially so that Ethan could pay back his student loans."

I get out a mat and start doing my yoga poses, keeping one eye on Dante. He sets the weights down, watching me as I move through them fluidly. I tell myself I'm imagining the gleam in his eye, but my heart races anyway.

Out of all the men, Dante is the one I'm least sure about. Maybe he wants me, maybe he doesn't. And my own heart and body are a mess. I need to hold on to my self-control.

Or what remains of it.

"Sounds like you really worked your way up," I say, going into downward dog and trying not to feel like I'm presenting my ass.

Too late. I can just barely see Dante from this angle, upside down, and he's staring at me like he wants to devour me. My heart kicks into high gear. His scent fills my nostrils and I want to whimper.

"We did. I can't lie, having Garrett's money helped. We all make a great team and none of us would've made it without the others. We only succeed together."

"I like that," I whisper softly, going out of downward dog and moving into a plank. "You're a real family, huh?"

"People mistake Ethan and I for brothers," Dante says slowly. "But I don't think it's just a matter of... looking alike. I think people can feel how close all four of us are. They can tell. Honestly, I feel like they're my brothers in every way that matters.

"I was good at making friends growing up. I can be pretty damn charming." He waggles his eyebrows at me. "But I didn't really know what friendship was. Or what family was, actually. Not until I bonded with these guys."

Envy slides through me and I move out of plank to sit and look at Dante. I've never had that. "Sounds really nice. My parents weren't ever... they were distant. And I haven't had many friends, what with the whole starting my life over twice thing."

"Well, you have friends now," Dante points out. "You have us."

That warms me all over. Although, I'm not sure you're supposed to want your friend to pin you to your yoga mat and fuck you until you scream. "I gotta say... I'm impressed. I thought you kind of just came from wealth."

"I think most people do." Dante sighs. "On the one hand, I appreciate that people see me and think I'm sophisticated. Especially when we deal with higher-end clients and investors. But I don't want to ever take what I have for granted, and I don't want anyone else to think I do either."

I feel a bit ashamed, assuming that this man just had everything handed to him. But on the other hand, I feel really inspired. Maybe someday I can achieve my dreams too.

"You don't strike me as someone who takes his life for granted," I tell him softly.

Dante moves closer, holding out a hand. I take it and let him help me to my feet, nearly swaying right into him. This close to him, his scent completely envelopes me. I feel drunk on the bourbon scent he gives off.

He has to be able to smell me too. I watch as his eyes darken.

There's no doubt in my mind now that he wants me, and god do I want him. I inhale sharply. I know I probably shouldn't, but I'm seconds away from begging him to fuck me. That heat crawls up my skin again, and settles between my legs...

A low purr starts up in the back of Dante's throat. "Do you have any idea what your scent does to me?"

I swallow hard. "Why don't you show me?" I whisper.

Dante shifts closer, his hips pressing against mine and... *oh fuck.* He's hard and thick, straining against the fabric of his pants. My body responds instantly to the realization, arousal rushing through me.

The door bursts open, startling us both.

I whirl around, my face feeling like it's on fire. I probably shouldn't be embarrassed, given what passed between Garrett and I in front of Ethan the other day, but I still feel like I should cover myself up or something.

Except it's Ethan coming in now, and he doesn't look like he's here for a workout. His eyes are wide and dark with worry, and he's breathing hard. He keeps clenching and unclenching his jaw. "You'd better come up. Now."

I glance at Dante, who's also glancing at me. He looks back at Ethan and nods.

We head up from the gym to the foyer, Ethan leading the way. When we arrive, I see Garrett practically toe to toe with a man in a suit, while Caleb stands in the doorway to the dining room, watching, his entire body tense.

There's a second person in a suit, this one a woman. Her gaze lands on me and her nostrils flare, taking in my scent. There's absolutely no hiding what I am right now. Especially now with how I've just been working out.

"You must be the Omega," she says.

Garrett starts growling.

"Stand down," Dante murmurs to him. He walks up to the woman. "Who are you, and what are you doing in our house?"

Garrett stops growling, but he absolutely does not stand down.

The woman holds out a badge and my heart drops to the floor. "We're from the Omega Resources Division. I'm sure you can guess why we're here."

My vision blurs, and I realize I'm hyperventilating. Ethan puts his hands on my shoulders in an attempt to ground me. Caleb hurries across the room to stand next to me, like he's going to wrap himself around me if he needs to.

"I can guess next week's lottery numbers," Dante says with a smile, his tone so smooth that butter wouldn't melt in his mouth. "Doesn't mean they're accurate."

The woman gives him a tight, unimpressed smile in return. I'm guessing from her scent that she's a Beta. So is her partner, the one who's currently in a staring contest with Garrett. It makes sense. If they sent an Alpha to pick up an Omega and go against another Alpha in the process it could get very messy, very quickly.

"We're here because someone reported you as harboring an unregistered Omega," the woman informs us. "We're here to take her to the local facility and process her in the system."

"Like *hell* you are," Garrett snarls.

Dante takes a step to the side, which now puts him directly between the woman and me. She can't even see me now. His shoulders are raised and his weight drops a little. The beginnings of a fight stance.

Caleb grabs my wrist and Ethan keeps his hands on my shoulders. I breathe in their scents, trying to calm myself.

"Once she's processed," the woman says, "then you can officially make a bid to court her, if that's what you want. But we can't allow her to keep living with you unregistered. Even if you're bonded."

She pauses, then looks us all up and down. "I certainly hope you're not illegally bonded."

"Why?" Garrett says mockingly. Challenging her.

"Because the paperwork's a fucking headache," the man mutters.

Garrett goes back to glaring at him.

My stomach feels like it's uncoiling in my belly. My knees buckle, and I realize I'm crying. I clutch at Ethan and Caleb. I want to scream, I want to cry, I want to beg them not to let me be taken by these people.

I can't be a registered Omega. I can't. I'll be trapped. I'll be controlled by someone like Marcus.

Caleb guides me into deep breathing. My vision clears a little, and I look over at Garrett. He looks like he's literally ready to hold these agents off and tell me to run for it, and I can feel how tense Ethan is, like he's going to do the same.

Dante isn't as obviously ready to fight as Garrett is, but I can tell he's about to launch himself forward with his fists flying. He's just more subtle about it.

"She doesn't want to go," he says, his voice low and tense.

"The last time I checked, it wasn't about what people did and didn't want to do when it came to the law. If people could just do what they wanted regardless, it wouldn't be a law, now would it?"

"So you're going to drag an unwilling Omega from her

*home.*" Dante's lips curl up into a parody of a smile. "Good to know. Fine, upstanding public servants, you are."

He calls this place my home. My heart swells with joy in the midst of my fear and despair.

And I think that's what makes me do it. That's what decides it for me.

I look at the agents again. I could beg the men not to let me be taken in, and I know somehow, deep in my chest, that they would do it if I asked. They'd fight these agents off and give me time to run.

But what would that really accomplish? I'd be completely on the run, and I'd have doomed all four of them to legal trouble for breaking the law. It could ruin their company, their reputations, their entire lives.

I can't do that to them. I won't.

They're ready to put it all on the line for me and I have to return the favor. I *want* to return the favor. They're willing to protect me. I want to protect them too.

And there's only one way to do that right now.

I take a deep breath. "Okay," I say, and I'm impressed that my voice doesn't waver. "I'll go with you."

Garrett looks like he wants to tear someone's head off.

Ethan lets me go reluctantly. Caleb squeezes my hand, giving me a reassuring smile before letting go as well. Dante looks at me for a long moment, and I think maybe he won't move, but then he takes a small step aside to let me pass by him and go to the agent.

"If they give you any trouble," Garrett calls as the agents lead me out, "I'll rip their throats out."

"Promises, promises," the male agent mutters, sounding exhausted.

My heart pounds harder with every step I take, and the intense, comforting scents of the four Alphas fades as I'm ushered into a car and we start to drive away. I already miss their aromas and their steady presence, and I twist my hands together on my lap, staring out the window.

*Will I ever see them again?*

# Chapter 13

## *Ava*

The drive feels like it takes forever, but that might just be because I spend the entire time wanting to throw up.

Neither agent speaks to me. I can't tell if it's because they don't care, or because they can sense that I'm not going to want to talk to them.

My stomach is in knots by the time we arrive. The ORD offices are located in a sleek, modern building, all chrome and clean lines. When I get inside, everything is bright and spacious, well-organized. There's this overwhelming sense of efficiency, from both the space and the people.

The two agents lead me through the offices to a small room, where they leave me alone. I kind of expected an interrogation room like at a police station, but instead, it has a sleek white couch to match the walls, and a kitchenette.

I wouldn't call it homey, but it's better than I thought it would be.

After a few moments alone, the door opens again. It's not the agents.

This time it's an older woman, middle-aged, her auburn hair

getting a few streaks of gray in it. Her face is still fresh, though, and she carries herself well. She's probably just graying a bit early, or is letting it go gray when most people would start dyeing it.

Then I see the folder in her hands, and I snap back to the reality of my situation. She's flipping through it as she comes to sit down. She glances up at me, surprised I'm still standing. "Please, Ava—may I call you Ava?"

I nod.

"Ava, feel free to sit down."

I fold my arms and stay standing.

The woman doesn't seem perturbed. "I'm Cary. I've just been looking over your file here. We had to conduct interviews with your coworkers, speak to your neighbors, make sure that we weren't making a mistake. We like to be thorough."

The idea of these strangers going through my life and investigating everything about me has my throat closing up in panic.

"You wouldn't believe the tricks some people try," Cary murmurs, as if to herself. "Reporting people thinking they'll just get them in trouble and bring them in here, no questions asked. As if we won't make sure first that the person isn't a Beta or Alpha, or that they aren't already registered and bonded. Ridiculous."

She closes the file and smiles up at me. "I was very impressed by how long you've been under our radar. You're quite a determined girl. I can understand. It's a scary process. I saw in your file that your parents were both Betas, so they probably didn't prepare you very well for what the process is actually like."

I still don't say anything. I don't want to give this woman

anything if I can help it. Besides, she's already got all the information she needs, clearly. What's the point in me talking to her?

Cary sets the file aside. "I know that you're scared." She pats the seat beside her. "Please, come sit down and let me hold your hand. It'll help you feel calmer."

I hate that her motherly tone works on me. Tears spring into my eyes and I sit down. Cary takes my hand and squeezes it gently. It's not as good as if Dante or one of the other men took my hand but it's still reassuring.

"There we go. Omegas need lots of physical touch. I should know." Cary laughs lightly. "I am one."

"And you're working for *these* people," I mutter before I can stop myself.

Cary squeezes my hand again, not at all put out. "I know. You're scared and confused. But having Omegas on our teams here is very important to us. Who knows better how to take care of Omegas than other Omegas?"

She reaches into her pocket and pulls out a little packet of tissues, handing them to me. "We think of our Omegas as clients. We want to provide our clients, just as any business does, with the best possible experience. We want to take care of them. That's why we offer support and information, and give Omegas a place to stay if they need it until they find an Alpha or pack to bond with. Does that make sense?"

I wipe at my eyes and blow my nose. "I suppose," I say reluctantly.

"Now, you've been on suppressants for a long time, I'm guessing?"

I nod. "Years."

"Yes. That means your heat will be coming on soon. We're still figuring out what the effects of long-term suppressants are, but we do know that when you're off them, heats can be very miserable if you don't have an Alpha pack, or even just one Alpha, to take care of you." Cary smiles. "I know it might seem scary, but this is for your benefit, so that your needs can be met."

"And I can be *owned*, you mean," I shoot back. "So you can use my biology against me to have some Alpha control me."

"See, I thought that too, when I was young. I was younger than you are, I was only nineteen, but I was furious. I hated my parents for giving me to ORD." Cary shakes her head at the memory. "But then I was with people who understood me for the first time in my life. They ran tests to make sure they knew everything about me that would be important for my health and long-term care. And they worked tirelessly with me to find me the right Alpha pack."

"And did they?" I ask, my curiosity getting the better of me.

"They did. It took a long time. I'm a very stubborn woman." She laughs lightly. "I rejected so many Alphas and packs! I think my representatives were tearing their hair out toward the end. But they kept working with me until I finally found Jeff and Andy."

She pulls out her phone. "Would you like to see some pictures?"

I don't want to be rude, so I nod. "Um, sure."

Cary opens her phone and pulls up some photos of herself and two men about the same age. The two men are on a fishing trip, holding up large trout and smiling. There's another picture of the three of them sitting around a campfire together, roasting marshmallows.

"One reason I was so stubborn," Cary admits softly, "is that I'm infertile. We run tests for that so Omegas can know right away how fertile they are. I was scared no Alpha would want an Omega who couldn't give him children."

She swipes through, showing me some more photos, these ones of Jeff, Andy, and Cary with various children.

"But Jeff and Andy are foster parents and work with the local hospital to take in kids from bad homes. They were already doing it before they met me, and they were so happy to welcome me in. Once I was there, we looked into adopting."

"You have five?" I ask.

"Yes. Some of them are off to college by now." Cary beams down at her children, clearly full of pride. "It never mattered to my mates whether the children were adopted or biological, just that I would love them as well as they did, and so it worked out."

She puts her phone away. "We're going to work with you every step of the way to make sure that you are with Alphas who will truly love all of you and take care of your needs, whatever those needs might be, Ava."

It sounds tempting. Like I might actually be able to find someone who won't make me give up my life, or try to control me. I wipe at my eyes again as fresh tears fall.

"But what... what if my body takes over?" I whisper.

Cary tilts her head. "What do you mean?"

"The Alphas who helped to hide me. They're good people. But they smell... no Alphas have smelled like this to me before. They smell so *good*. I can pick up their scents like I never have before. All I want to do when I'm around them is..."

I cut myself off and bite down hard on my bottom lip. I don't want to say it out loud, it feels so embarrassing.

Cary pats my knee. "I know what you mean. Part of it could be that you're off your suppressants. Everything's going to feel a little intense for you for a bit. But it's perfectly normal for Alphas to smell good to you, especially since you're unmated."

She gestures to my body. "Right now, no matter how fertile you might actually be, your body is screaming that this is the prime time for you to mate. Not all Alphas will smell amazing to you. Some might even smell bad. But your body is tuned to Alphas. Desiring an Alpha and being turned on by their scents is perfectly normal."

"So how does this whole..." I wave my hand in the air. "Process, work?"

"Well, first, we run various tests. We want to determine your status and fertility. Then we'll add your information to the ORD database."

"So you can keep track of me."

"Not for the reasons you think. Eligible Alphas like to search the database so they can find Omegas that might be a good match for them. But it also allows us to check up on Omegas if we suspect they're being mistreated, or to quickly dismiss a case if someone's claiming an Omega is unmated when they're actually already bonded."

"And then what? Once you've gotten all this information."

"We present you in a public showcase, along with other Omegas. There the Alpha packs will get to meet you in person, and see if they want to put in a bid for you."

A shiver runs down my spine. Cary must notice, because she smiles again reassuringly. "Don't worry. You get to reject any Alpha bid you don't want. And if you do accept an Alpha or Alpha pack and we begin the courting process, we'll be checking in with you to make sure that you're truly comfortable."

She squeezes my hand again. "You can back out at any time during the courting. I *promise*."

I swallow hard. Maybe I should be more suspicious, but when Cary says that, I believe her. She sounds so earnest and genuine. And she seems happy in those photos with her family.

"Okay," I say quietly. It's not like I have much of a choice now. But knowing that this worked out for one Omega gives me hope that maybe, this will work out for me too."

"I'm glad." Cary stands up. "Now, let's take you to get your tests out of the way. Shall we?"

I accept her hand to help me stand up, and then I follow her into the unknown.

# Chapter 14

## *Ethan*

None of us are happy about this fucking situation.

I thought Garrett would rip that Beta male's throat out at one point. Not that I would've stopped him. I would've been too busy getting Ava out of the house.

Even now, we're all restless. I can't stop pacing. Garrett's over by the window again, and Dante looks thunderous. Caleb's quiet, on the sofa, but I know that he's just trying to do it for our sakes so that at least one of us isn't about ready to claw the walls down.

Our living room feels too damn small. My skin itches. I want Ava back *now*.

"You know what we need to do," I say firmly. The others all look at me in confusion, so I add, "We have to court her. Put in a bid for her."

"What?" Garrett growls. "Are you fucking serious?"

"Do I sound like I'm joking?"

"You think we should court her." Dante speaks slowly.

"I know that you all felt it too. That pull toward her."

"Ethan, I know you want a family..."

112

"This isn't about that. I mean, of course it is. Of course I want an Omega and a family." The things I didn't get as a child. "But I'm not doing this because of any Omega. You know me."

"I know that when an Omega's in heat…"

"No, don't you try to dismiss it as just sex pheromones or whatever you're going to say. Who scored best on the tests, huh? You or me? I know what I'm talking about, I know when it's just pheromones and perfuming, and this isn't it."

"You rescued her from the club," Dante points out. "You feel an obligation toward her. I get it. You're protective. But that doesn't mean she's the one for us."

"You heard her," Garrett adds. "She was pretty damn clear about not wanting to be in a pack or to have any Alpha in her life again."

"Can you blame her, after the last one?" Caleb says quietly. "She's been hurt. I know that we all have in our own way. But she's in the system now. Someone's going to take her, if not us."

The idea of another Alpha having Ava makes me want to rip something to pieces. Preferably that other Alpha. "None of you like that idea. I can see it in your faces."

"It's just sex," Dante protests.

"Oh? So you've fucked her then?"

"No, I haven't fucked her."

"So it's not just sex."

"But what if it *is*?"

"We're not going to know that until we try!" I point out, jabbing at the ground. "Dante, you can't give up on something before it's even started. If you felt something, then why don't we pursue it? That's the whole point of courting! If it doesn't work, we report it, and some other Alpha gets a shot."

"I want to try it," Caleb says. "I know what I felt. What I feel. I know all of us feel it too."

"Nobody wants to see an Omega get hurt," I add. "But you can't tell me that what happened back there just now was just normal Alpha instincts. I was ready to run with her. And Garrett, I know you were ready to kill for her."

Dante groans and sinks into a chair. "We have a big launch coming up. Is now really the time to be courting an Omega?"

"Life's never going to wait around for when we have free time in our schedules," I point out. "Ava's public presentation will be happening soon."

Dante says nothing, just stares down at his hands. I think he's wavering, though, which just leaves Garrett.

I look over at Garrett, who's refusing to meet my gaze. "Come on, man."

"Don't you come on me," Garrett mutters. "You know why this could spell doom for all of us."

"We won't let her distract us from our work. Our job is to protect our Omega. To provide for her, to care for her. We can't do that with a failing company, now can we?"

"This isn't just about that."

There are a lot of things I could say, but I don't. I don't want to be hurtful, no matter how annoyed I am. I can't say what I would do in Garrett's situation.

On the one hand, he's kind of got what I always wanted. On the other hand, I'm not a guy known for following rules.

But would I really be able to go against my parents, if they were still alive? If I still got to have them instead of losing them when I did?

I don't know.

I look back at Dante. "I think we'll regret it forever if we don't at least give it a shot. What can we possibly lose?"

"And," Caleb adds, "what could we possibly gain?"

"You talk about how it could not work out. But what if it does?" I gesture at the house around us. "We didn't earn this, any of it, by playing it safe. We took risks, and it paid off. Don't you think she's worth the risk?"

"You can't tell me it didn't rip your heart in half to see her go earlier," Caleb adds, still quiet. "I know it ripped mine. I didn't want her to go."

I nod in agreement. "We were willing to put it all on the line for her earlier. What's changed since then, really? Nothing. This will just be doing it in a different way."

"A way that won't end with us in jail," Caleb mutters.

Dante looks back and forth from me to Caleb and back again, then groans and sinks back into the couch. "All right. All right. We'll put a bid on her. Even though she's probably going to break my damn heart."

I grin in triumph, then look over at Garrett. "It's three to one, Garrett. What do you say?"

Garrett looks over at me. I hold my breath, and wait for his answer. Hoping that he'll choose to say yes.

*Please, please say yes.*

# Chapter 15

## *Ava*

I'm absolutely terrified.

The last several days have been better than I feared. Cary's been my handler every step of the way. I've done my various tests, been registered, all of it.

Now, I'm being put into a dress and dolled up for the Omega presentation, and I kind of want to throw up.

Cary watches as I'm laced into the corset of the dress.

"You have such beautiful natural curves," the Beta in charge of wardrobe tells me. "We want to use the corset to emphasize them and draw attention to them."

"If a single person says anything about child-bearing hips," I mutter, "I'm going to start biting."

Cary just laughs. She's taken every bit of my grumpiness in stride. Not like she's dismissing me. More like she understands.

That's the one thing reassuring me. That, and the moments when I imagine I can smell the four men I left behind. Nothing soothes me like their scents did, and although imagining it isn't really the same thing at all, it's all that I've got—and that's better than nothing.

I take a deep breath, close my eyes, and let the memory of those scents soothe me once again.

"There," the woman lacing me up says, breaking my concentration. "You're all set."

"You look beautiful," Cary tells me.

I open my eyes and look into the mirror. "Thank you."

"We were right to go with the sweetheart neckline and bare shoulders. Your hair really deserves to be shown off."

The dress I'm wearing is several shades of blue, the layers of tulle underneath a shining midnight and then going lighter and lighter until the top layers are a soft baby blue. The corset top is baby blue satin, but luckily they listened to me when I begged them to keep it simple.

With my arms and shoulders exposed, they curled my hair and are letting it fall around me, except for braiding and pinning back some strands around the crown of my head so that nothing gets in my face.

I have to admit, looking at myself in the mirror... I do look pretty. I like how I look.

Cary puts her hands on my shoulders and smiles, meeting my eyes in the mirror. "Take deep breaths. You look beautiful. And you scored well on the tests. There are going to be a lot of prominent Alpha packs who will be dying to meet you."

I swallow. Maybe those words would make other Omegas preen, but I don't care if I'm extra fertile, or have good genetics. I don't care how 'desirable' I am.

"I can still say no to all of them if I want to, right?" I ask.

Cary squeezes my shoulders and nods. "Yes. And I'll be in the room if you ever need me, keeping an eye on things. No Alpha is going to just steal you away."

I take deep breaths, as she told me. There are security

guards. Cary and the other handlers are here too. Nobody's going to just steal me and take away my freedom. This is my choice.

I hope.

The event is taking place in the ballroom at the nicest hotel in the city, the kind of hotel that's been around for a hundred years and still has all the décor from the Gilded Age, everything gold and shining, not a single detail overlooked.

I'm not the only Omega here at the event, but I'm the last. I take my place in line, listening to the other Omegas laugh and talk amongst themselves.

Judging by their looks, they're all a few years younger than I am. Some are out of college, some look like they're only nineteen, but they've probably known who they were since they were in high school.

They all seem excited. Not nervous, like I am.

"Allison!" one of the handlers calls, and the Omega in question goes up the steps and walks down the runway to reach the podium at the end, giving the Alphas in the room a good look at her.

The walls hide the room from me. I have no idea who's out there, can't get any kind of sneak peek at what kind of men might be bidding on me.

My heart races as one by one, each Omega is called up for her turn. Each Omega says a little something about themselves and what they're looking for in a relationship when they get to the end.

The ORD handler assigned to them sometimes says something too, and then each Omega ends with a reminder from the ORD that there is also a brochure about each Omega that the Alphas can peruse.

I'm guessing that's where they put the less-flattering information like, "impatient," or "doesn't like to do the dishes," or, in my case, "will put up a fight and possibly bite your ear off if you try any shenanigans."

Finally, it's my turn.

I take a deep breath and walk up the steps as my name is called. The bright lights blind me at first and I have to blink and walk carefully so I don't fall and embarrass myself.

Once my eyes adjust, I still can't see past the lights to who might be in the crowd watching me. I get to the end of the podium, and turn in a slow circle so that everyone can get a good look at me.

"Ava here is one of our most special Omegas," Cary says, speaking on my behalf. "She's amazing with animals and would like to have children someday, but isn't in a rush. I will say, gentlemen, that while Ava is sweet and kind, this is not an Omega who is going to stay home and do the housekeeping. She's got dreams and aspirations of her own, and she values her independence."

My nerves calm a little at hearing Cary speak up for me, letting the Alphas know what they're in for.

"I'd warn against bidding on her if you're in it to tame her spirit or if you want a stay-at-home Omega. But for the Alpha who can appreciate her personality and will give her the support and comfort she deserves, you won't find a more loyal or sweet mate than Ava."

I still can't see anyone's faces, but I can feel the attitude in the room, and as I stand there and show myself off, I feel... admiration. I don't feel awkward. I toss a bit of my long dark hair behind my shoulder, and I feel as if I can hear the Alphas thinking *she looks beautiful.*

I have to admit, it is kind of fun. Intoxicating, even. To know that people think I'm desirable.

But then—the Alphas in here might not be the kind I want. The kind I need. I swallow my hopes back down and turn one last time before heading back down the walkway.

Cary meets me when I get back down, taking my hands so I don't fall over as I adjust back to the regular lighting. "You did wonderfully."

"Now what happens?"

"Now," she says, leading me to a chair, "the Alphas will put in their bids for the different Omegas they want to meet. Then the Alphas and the Omegas get to mingle so you get a glimpse of each other's personalities for yourself."

"Wouldn't you want to put a bid in *after* that happens?"

"An Alpha can always put a bid in for an Omega after meeting one, if they didn't put a bid in for that Omega originally. But attraction is important. Scent is very important. Every Alpha got a bit of your scent and got to see what you look like, and that's a strong start. You want to be attracted to your mates and for your scents to be compatible."

I nod. "What about if *I* don't like how they look or how they smell?"

"Then you'll tell me. I want you to actually put in the effort, Ava." Cary's voice gets a little stern with me. "I don't want you to just dismiss everyone out of hand. There are some lovely Alphas out there who have the potential to make you happy. I don't want you to dismiss them before giving it real thought."

I take a deep breath and blow it out slowly. I don't want to be dismissed for being an Omega. It's unfair of me to dismiss everyone just for being an Alpha. "Okay."

Cary smiles. "Great. Now go and mingle. At the end of it,

we'll go over the Alphas who've put in a bid for you. You can reject any of the ones you don't want, all right? You can stay with us in the facility until you find Alphas you're comfortable having court you."

I try to believe her, but I can't quite shake the nerves as I step out into the ballroom again. This time, it's through a side door, and I can hear the voices of everyone chatting with each other like a hum of bees.

The moment I enter the room, though, conversation stops around me.

Everyone's staring at me.

*You can do this,* I tell myself. It'll be okay. Cary won't let anything happen to me.

"Hi, Ava." A man walks up to me with dark skin and a wide smile. "I'm Jason. My pack and I put in a bid for you, we're hoping you'd like to chat with us?"

I nod and let him take my hand to lead me to two other men. They all have a spicy undertone to their scent, one with sweetness mixed in like jalapeños, another making me want to sneeze with how intense it is. Jason is sweet and friendly, and I don't feel unsafe at all with the three men, but I don't feel drawn to their scent either.

After Jason and his two other Alphas in his pack, I'm introduced to Blake, a lone Alpha who's looking for an Omega. Blake is funny, and makes me laugh, but he doesn't feel grounded in the way that I want, and I can't always tell when he's being serious.

Also, his scent makes my nose itch. I'm just not a fan of sandalwood.

Cary's there throughout, appearing when she can sense I'm not feeling it and guiding me to the next group, or bringing a new Alpha to me. I have to admit I do feel desired, and pretty, with Alphas complimenting me. I could be crazy, but it feels like there are more Alphas coming to me than to the other Omegas.

"Ava." Cary gently touches my elbow, distracting me from my conversation with a five-Alpha pack. Their scents are all wildly different, it's hard for my nose. I feel a bit dizzy and confused. "I'd like to you meet Dante and his pack."

My jaw drops open.

All four men are there, in sleek suits. Caleb's is a sleek charcoal gray, while Ethan is wearing a striking blue suit, clearly wanting to light up the room and charm everyone. Dante's and Garrett's are both dark, almost black, well-tailored and sophisticated.

Their scents make my knees want to buckle.

"You're here," I blurt out. "You put a bid in on me."

"As if we were going to pass up the chance." Ethan grins at me and then winks at Cary, who might be happily bonded but still blushes. I don't blame her.

Dante takes my hand, his thumb gently rubbing back and forth over my knuckles. "You look breathtaking."

Garrett glowers at some other Alphas who are looking our way. I have to bite back a laugh.

"How are you?" Caleb asks. "Are you doing okay? Are they taking care of you?"

"They are," I promise him. "Cary here has been looking out for me."

My breath catches in my throat as Dante raises my hand up to kiss my knuckles. "Good," he murmurs.

Unlike the other Alpha packs, I already know these men, so I'm not sure what to say to make conversation. But my body thrills with excitement, knowing they're here to try to court me.

"I'm glad you're here," I admit. I don't want them to think they did all this for nothing.

"Good." Dante finally lets go of my hand. I flex my fingers, my skin feeling cold now that he's no longer touching me. He's still looking into my eyes, like he can't look away. I feel caught, but for once, I don't mind it.

"I love what they did with your hair," Caleb adds. He steps in close, his fingers sliding through the strands as he picks up a lock of my hair and twirls it around his finger.

So close to them, their scents intensify and I feel like I'm going to swoon, in a good way, not in a panicked way.

"You sure the dress isn't too much?" I ask. "I asked them to keep it simple, but they still wanted to go the ballgown route."

"You're stunning," Ethan tells me. "The belle of the ball."

"Maybe don't say that so loudly the other Omegas hear you?" I laugh. I don't want anyone else to feel insulted.

"Let them," Garrett says, sounding a bit smug. I blush harder.

"You know that if anything's wrong you can tell us, right?" Dante murmurs, stepping in a little closer so that he can talk to me without Cary overhearing. The other three are around me too, blocking anyone else from seeing me, keeping me in a little bubble.

I should probably feel caged, but I don't. I feel the opposite. I feel shielded. Safe.

"Perhaps we should finish meeting the other Alphas?" Cary says politely, cutting in.

Garrett's already staring at the others in the room like he's going to eat them for breakfast. I don't want to leave them. Even though we haven't said much, just being in their presence calms me down.

But Cary's right. I need to give the other Alphas a fair shot. Even if I already suspect that I know who I want to court me.

The very fact that they're here for me has my stomach erupting with the kind of butterflies I thought were just fake, the ones that I thought weren't actually ever going to happen to me. I feel like I'm in high school again, and the football captain that everyone had a crush on just asked me to prom.

"I really should go and finish meeting everyone," I say. I try to sound firm, but my voice comes out far too soft instead. Perhaps even longing. "I have to be fair to everybody."

The men all exchange a look of reluctance, but take steps back away from me. Cary takes me by the elbow and gently leads me away.

I can feel the men's eyes on me as I leave them, and it kindles the warmth in my chest again. I know that they care about me and that they want me. If I had doubts that they'd stick with me after I was taken to the ORD facility, those are gone now.

It seems like this pack really wants a chance with me. Do I want to give it to them?

Cary leads me through the crowd to speak to a few other Alpha packs before our time is up. I notice that while some Alphas I've spoken to are also speaking to other Omegas, a few aren't. They talk to me and then they leave.

Was more than one pack really only interested in me? I'm not sure how I feel about that, if I'm flattered or if it just makes me more nervous.

But at the end of the party, I'm not sure it really matters, because there's only one pack I care about. And they came specifically to see me. Not because they liked Cary's spiel or because they think I'm beautiful, or even because they like my scent, but because they know me.

I try to give the other Alphas a chance. At the end of it, Cary gives me a list so that I can flip through the Alphas and remind myself of the people I met. But when I close my eyes and try to picture any of them, I either don't remember at all, or I immediately wrinkle my nose at the unpleasant scent memory.

None of the Alphas affected me the way Dante's pack does.

Cary and the other ORD representatives shuffle the Alphas out, and the room is quiet as the various Omegas are given chairs. We sit down and review the Alphas we spoke with, to mark whoever we would like to actually try courting.

I scan every entry and try to be fair. I ask myself, what about finances? What about professions? What do they think about kids? How would they feel if I had a demanding career outside of the home?

I want to run my own animal shelter someday, and I know that won't happen right away, but whether I'm an employee or the manager or the owner, I'm going to have to put in a lot of hours to take care of these animals. I need an Alpha pack who would be okay with that. And I need Alphas who will be able to provide for me financially, and feel happy in their careers.

But even as I ask myself these questions and try to be objective, my mind keeps flitting back to Dante and his pack.

They smell so good. They've already proven they can and want to take care of me. They sought me out after I was taken from them. I'm still sure that they would've physically fought the ORD agents who came to their doorstep for me if I hadn't said something and chosen to go without a fight.

My heart is set on them.

I tell myself that it's for practical reasons as well. They're certainly financially stable, confident, established. I trust them, seeing as they had me alone in their home and never took advantage of me. I like them, I like their personalities.

They also happen to drive me insane with desire, making my body hum with a kind of arousal I didn't even know I could feel before I met them.

I'm not making this choice because it's practical or logical. I'm making it because it's what I want. Full stop.

Cary walks over to me. "Have you made a decision?"

She sounds a little knowing, like she already suspects what I'm going to say. "Do you know about how I got to the facility?"

She nods. "Yes. And I know that's who those Alphas were. I want you to know, I checked them out. I couldn't stop them from applying for you, of course. But I wanted to make sure they hadn't been holding you hostage in any way."

She really is looking out for me. "I appreciate it. But they really were keeping me safe. I didn't know what to do after what happened at the club. I'm sure I'd be a lot worse off if it wasn't for them."

"And you want them to court you?" Cary asks. She's not quite smiling, but she has a gleam in her eye that suggests she's amused.

I nod. "I want to accept their bid."

Cary smiles and takes the brochure from me. "All right then. I'm going to save this, in case the courting doesn't work out, we can look at this again and find another pack to try. All right?"

I nod again. As Cary walks away, I know that I'm about to change my life forever.

Part of me is terrified. This is still the thing that I knew for years I didn't want, the thing that I was scared of because it could take away everything I wanted to do with my life.

But the other part of me is thrilled. Excited. I want to see the men again, to be surrounded by their scents and to feel the comfort and safety they gave me.

I feel like I'm sitting on a rollercoaster that's about to take off, my stomach mixing with fear and exhilaration in equal measure.

*Am I really ready to make this permanent?* I ask myself. It's one thing to be drawn to someone. It's another to bond with them forever.

But I guess there's only one way to find out.

# Chapter 16

## *Ava*

After I accept the bid from Dante and his pack, the process of officially registering the courtship begins.

I'm grateful for it, in an ideological sense. It means that there's less of a chance that some crappy Alpha will be able to sneak in through the system and get any Omega they want. I know that this is all for the safety of the Omegas, and I appreciate it.

On the other hand, it's driving me nuts with impatience.

Getting a few moments with Dante and his pack has made me miss them even more. I long for their scents, their touch, their warm looks my way. I want to be surrounded by them again. And while I know this paperwork is important, I feel like I'm going to start clawing the walls if I don't get to see them soon.

I'm kept away from the Alphas, in fact from any Alpha at all, only interacting with Betas and other Omegas. Cary explains that Dante and the others are going through paperwork on their end and are only interacting with fellow Alphas and Betas.

"The Alpha and Omega instincts can be heightened right now," she warns me during one of our sessions as I fill out more paperwork. I swear, the pile of papers I need to sign is never ending. "We don't want to risk you going into heat fully and bonding with the nearest Alpha out of desperation."

I think about how I felt when I was with the men, the mood swings, how heightened everything was and how scared it made me feel. "What's heat like?"

Cary takes a deep breath and thinks for a moment. "I know that books and movies like to romanticize it a bit..."

I shudder. Heat has never felt romantic to me. The idea that I'd be so desperate for sex that I would beg literally any Alpha in front of me for it is terrifying. I could end up bonded to someone who was awful, all because I was a slave to my body's desires. That's not very romantic to me.

"But heats can actually feel more like discomfort than anything else," Cary continues. She might be oblivious to my anxiety, but she might also simply be ignoring it and pushing through it the way she's done before. "If you don't receive sexual satisfaction, it can feel like physical pain."

"And I need a knot," I add dully.

That's the problem. Omegas who aren't mated, or are too young to mate, can get artificial knots and hole up on their own, but I hear it's not the same thing. But just rubbing one off won't do. You need the feeling of being full that only a knot can give you.

"Mostly. You actually also need to feel the Alpha's release, and your own orgasms. The knot is only one part of it. I know that's the part that tends to get focused on and I understand why." Cary smiles. "But your pleasure is important as well for the heat to be gone."

"Is that why artificial knots don't work as well? There's no... Alpha release?"

Cary nods. "Yes. An artificial knot does help, since between that and the orgasms you have two out of three. But the release really does add that extra bit. It's better if you're an Omega to have someone else helping you through the heat since it'll be hard for you to concentrate."

Cary taps some paperwork. "This is why we have Alpha packs a lot of the time. Helping an Omega through a heat can be a lot for just one person."

I read through the paperwork. It's explaining the science behind heats. "Nesting gets worse?"

"Yes. You'll have a compulsion to nest, as well as experience some mood swings that are stronger than usual. That's all entirely normal. If you feel yourself wanting to cry, that's okay. That's why we'll have an ORD representative check in with you." Cary takes my hand. "We want to make sure if you are having mood swings or crying it's because of your hormones, not because you're being mistreated."

"Thank you." I take a deep breath. "So... the bond?"

"Ah. Yes." Cary slides her hand away. "It's important that you understand how powerful heats are. They can make you beg for a bonding bite even if you wouldn't normally want it, so we need to make sure that you have Alphas who will not give in to temptation and understand when it's the heat talking."

I nod. Cary stays relaxed. "I know that you're already starting to experience symptoms. I know that it can be scary, since you've been on suppressants for a long time. But don't worry. I'm sure that your Alphas will take care of you. That's what they're there for, and it'll be a good time to see if you're as compatible as you all hope."

I hope that we are too. None of the other Alphas made me feel the way that Dante's pack does. The way my body reacted, and how much I keep thinking about them... none of the others measured up.

Cary watches me finish signing the paperwork. "Wonderful. That should be the last of it. And remember, we'll be checking up on you. If you change your mind, or want to back out, we'll come and get you no matter what."

"Thank you." I mean that with all of my heart. Cary was really good to me this whole time. I don't know if I would've felt nearly as comfortable with any of this if she hadn't been there the whole time, metaphorically—and sometimes literally—holding my hand.

But now, it's time.

I left the house with nothing, and so I don't have anything with me when Cary brings me out to meet the men again. They're all waiting outside the facility. Ethan's pacing and Garrett's once again glaring into the distance. It reminds me of when I first saw them at breakfast, their unique energies and personalities so defined to me.

Caleb sees me and smiles. "Ava!" he calls.

Ethan stops pacing and Garrett looks over his shoulder at me, but Dante immediately moves to come up and take me by the hand. "You okay?" he asks again. As if something might have changed in the last few days.

"I'm doing better now," I tell him honestly, feeling a sense of safety and relief now that I can breathe in his scent again.

"I'll get the car," Garrett says, sounding a little gruff. Like maybe he's choked up.

The car itself is the same one Ethan picked me up and rescued me in, what feels like a lifetime ago. I know it wasn't really that long, but it feels like a whole other life, a whole other Ava who experienced that.

The air is thick with anticipation. I can smell all four of them again and I just want to bask in it. I'm not even aware that I'm perfuming at first until I see Caleb shifting in his seat and Ethan inhaling hard through his nose.

I shiver. I know it's logistically impossible in this cramped space, but my mind is suddenly filled with the ways I want them to touch me right here, right now...

Cary said days of sex. Days. Days of being touched... being *fucked*...

Wait.

"I might go into heat," I point out. "That's going to be days of your focus. You've got a business to run, is that going to be a problem? I don't want to be a distraction, I know how important your work is to you."

"You won't be," Dante says empathetically. He puts his hand on my knee reassuringly. "The four of us can do more work from home instead while you're here. We've worked hard to build up our company, and that means we can reap the rewards too."

His voice drops down into an Alpha purr. "Like taking the time to be there for our Omega."

I shiver, my body flooding with heat and my heart with gratitude. The purr in his voice promises exactly what I'll get when we arrive at their mansion, and I can feel myself starting to get a little wet already.

When we get there, Ethan helps me out of the car. "All of your clothes are still in the bedroom. We can talk décor, if you want. I know you'll want to nest."

He leads me up to the second floor, my hand securely in his. Talking décor already? They're serious about me.

It warms me to know that this isn't just an attraction to them. They're serious about this relationship, about courting me.

"Your scent has been lingering in this bedroom since you left," Ethan tells me as he opens the door to the bedroom. "It made me miss you even more every time I walked by it. I'm glad you're back."

He steps closer, his hands falling to my hips. He looks so handsome in his suit, and my body feels like it's on fire just from this small contact between us.

"I'm..." I swallow. "I'm glad to be back too."

"We'll prove to you that we're good for you, gorgeous," he murmurs.

His hand comes up to gently curl under my chin and lift my head. I whimper. My body clenches. I want his scent, his body, everywhere.

Ethan groans slightly. "Are you getting wet, my pretty Omega?"

I nod. My hands slide up his chest, feeling the soft fabric of his suit. "You look good. All of you."

"You have no idea what it was like to see you on the podium looking like this." He toys with the strands of my hair, letting them flow over his fingers. "I was tempted to leap on stage and declare you mine in front of everyone. You were the most beautiful Omega there, and everyone knew it."

I can feel myself blushing. "You're biased."

"Maybe a little, but I'm not lying when I say you were the most popular Omega tonight." Ethan leans in, his lips brushing against the sensitive skin just behind my ear. "But while you do look beautiful in this gown…"

His fingers trail down my exposed back, playing with the buttons at the back of the dress. "I think you look just as good with a bare face and wearing those soft gray sweats you seem so fond of."

I press myself against him, laughing, but it turns into a moan as I feel his body against mine. He's so fucking hot, all firm muscle, and suddenly it feels like I'm going to burn up if I don't have him inside of me.

My fingers clench around his suit jacket. "Ethan…"

He tilts my jaw up again, and then, he's kissing me.

I melt into it, whimpering. I want this dress off of me ten minutes ago. I want his suit off of him. I want bare skin, and his scent, and I want… I want…

"My beautiful Omega," Ethan murmurs, a purr in his voice. "Do you need me to take care of you?"

I *do* need him. I'm tired of holding myself back. There's only one thing that will tame the fire building inside of me, and I know that's Ethan.

"Yes," I whisper. "Please."

# Chapter 17

## *Ava*

A grin breaks out across Ethan's devilishly handsome face, as if he was hoping I would say that. He presses one more kiss to my lips, then moves in a flash, scooping me up into his arms bridal style.

I wrap my arms around his neck instinctively, leaning into his lean, muscled chest as he carries me into the bathroom attached to my bedroom.

After the time I spent in the ORD facilities, the massive bathroom feels even more luxurious. It's not as if I had time to truly get used to it before I was taken away, but somehow, being back here feels a little like coming home—in a way that both excites and terrifies me.

Ethan sets me down beside the wide, deep bathtub, and as I glance around, I realize that the room has changed since I was here last. In the time when I was away, they filled the room with decadent looking bath products, everything from bath bombs to body wash to fluffy looking loofahs and candles.

"This..." I blink, swallowing around the sudden lump in my throat. "Did you do this for me?"

"Of course." Ethan shucks his jacket and rolls his sleeves up, then kneels by the tub to turn on the water, glancing up at me over his shoulder. "I picked most of it out, although it was a group effort between the four of us. I just have better taste in bath products than Garrett or Dante do."

"But how did you know I'd accept your bid?" My heart thuds heavily, and I glance between the array of bath products and Ethan as my stomach flutters. "How did you know I'd be back here?"

"We didn't know," he answers simply, pouring something into the bath that makes bubbles start to froth up. Then he rises to his feet, taking a step closer so that we're less than a foot apart. "But we hoped. None of us have ever felt this way about an Omega before. We knew we wanted you, and we hoped like hell that you'd be willing to give us a chance to prove ourselves."

The butterflies in my stomach start flapping even more wildly as the arousal I was feeling in the bedroom mixes with something else. Something warmer and deeper that settles in my chest and makes my pulse pick up.

I can practically feel the flush on my cheeks as I whisper, "Well, you're doing a pretty good job of proving yourself right now."

His crooked smile is one of the sexiest things I've ever seen. He moves even closer, his hand settling at my waist as he drops his head and presses a kiss to my lips.

"I got scents that complement the way you smell to me," he murmurs, his voice dropping a little, turning low and husky. "Citrus to go with the vanilla and strawberry, and something like fresh rain to go with the lilac."

I bite my lip, touched by the gesture. Not only did he and his pack mates buy things to make the bathroom seem cozy and welcoming, but he already knows my scent well enough to pick products that are uniquely suited to complement me.

And the scents rising from the bathtub along with the curling steam truly do smell divine... although nothing could smell quite as good as Ethan does in this moment.

As if he can read my thoughts, his beautiful green eyes darken. I'm aware of the distinct bulge at the front of his pants, and it makes heat stir low in my belly.

"Um, maybe I don't need a bath after all," I murmur. "I mean, it smells so good, and it means so much to me. But I'd rather—"

My voice breaks off before I can finish the thought. *I'd rather have you fuck me senseless. I'd rather feel you knot me and make me come so many times I forget my own name.*

It doesn't matter though. Even though I don't speak the words, Ethan seems to be able to pluck those thoughts right out of my head too. His grin widens, and he trails his fingertips down the side of my face, making my nipples harden as goose-bumps break out across my skin.

"Don't worry, gorgeous," he says quietly. "You can have a bath and an orgasm at the same time. I'll make sure of it."

I blink as I process that, my chest heaving a little behind the constraints of my dress as the air in the room suddenly seems to thicken.

"Okay," I whisper. "That sounds... nice."

"I hope you'll call it more than nice after I'm done with you." Ethan gives me a heated look, his spicy scent tickling my nostrils. "Now turn around so I can get this dress off."

I follow his command, and his dexterous fingers brush over my skin before tugging on the corset strings at the back of my dress. I'm not wearing a bra beneath it, and as the fabric falls away from my body, I'm intensely aware of the cool air hitting my bare skin.

"So fucking beautiful," Ethan murmurs behind me. He undoes the corset lacings the rest of the way, and the dress slides down my body to pool around my feet. "Step out."

I lift one foot and then the other, and he gathers up the dress and drapes it over the small towel caddy set against one wall. I turn around just as his gaze returns to me, and he freezes, his throat visibly moving as he swallows.

"Damn, you're a vision right now," he whispers, his voice strained.

I can't help glancing down at myself. All I have left on is a pair of panties and the heels I wore under the dress, and I can practically feel Ethan's gaze roaming over me. It feels incredibly intimate to be looked at by him this way, but surprisingly, I don't feel unnerved by it. Despite the fact that I trust him, I would've expected my old habits and fears to make me resist being vulnerable in front of any Alpha, but with Ethan, it feels almost... natural.

Dragging my bottom lip between my teeth, I reach down and slide my panties over my hips, allowing them to fall to the floor too. I step out of my heels, and Ethan clears his throat as he grabs the faucet and turns the water off.

"Let me know if the temperature is okay, yeah?" he says, holding out his hand.

I take it, and he helps me carefully into the tub. Warm water caresses my legs, scented steam rising up to mix with the scent of Alpha and arousal that lingers in the air, and an involuntary sigh falls from my lips. I settle into the tub, leaning against one side of it as my entire body is submerged in warm, soapy water up to my shoulders.

Part of me is expecting Ethan to strip down and join me, and an even bigger part of me really hopes that he will. But instead, he kneels beside the large bathtub, scooping up some water to wet my hair.

"Were you nervous tonight?" he asks quietly, grabbing a bottle of heavenly smelling shampoo and pouring a bit onto his palm.

"Yeah." I nod, breathing out a little laugh. "So nervous."

"It didn't show," he assures me. "You were the most beautiful Omega in the room. Every single Alpha pack in the place had their eyes on you. I swear Garrett almost busted a blood vessel glaring at all of them."

He starts to work the shampoo into my hair, his strong fingers massaging my scalp and sending little tingles of pleasure sliding down my spine. I moan softly, squeezing my thighs together.

Never in my entire life have I been pampered like this—certainly never by Marcus—and my body feels like it's melting, bones and all. The simple enjoyment of having my hair washed mingles with the arousal that burns through me from Ethan's touch, and my body can barely distinguish between all the different kinds of pleasure it's experiencing right now.

All it knows is that it wants more.

"Ethan," I gasp out, shifting my hips. "Please..."

"I've got you." His nostrils flare. "Lean back a little, gorgeous."

I do, and he supports the back of my neck, letting the hot water around me rinse the shampoo out of my hair. Then he rests my head against the edge of the tub, and finally, his hands start to wander lower.

His palms skate over my breasts, and a plaintive whimper

bursts from my lips as my sensitive nipples respond to the touch. When one of his hands slides between my legs, my thighs spread automatically, desperate to give him more access to the place where I want him most.

"Fuck. You're wet," he groans, slipping a finger inside me.

"Of course I am." I try to smile teasingly at him, but it's hard when my eyes are about to roll back in my head. "I'm in the bath."

Ethan chuckles, the sound rich and low. He leans closer, sliding his finger in and out of me as he drops his head and grazes his nose over my neck.

I can feel him scenting me, pulling in long drags of my scent, and it makes my pulse skyrocket. Before I can stop it, slick arousal gushes from me, coating his fingers beneath the surface of the water.

Ethan stiffens, his finger stilling for a moment.

Then he pulls back, grinning at me hungrily. "*Now* you're really fucking wet, and it has nothing to do with the bath, gorgeous."

I can't even argue, and I definitely can't find the brain power to joke with him right now. Instead, I grab the back of his head and pull him closer, crushing my lips to his. It's been way too long since the last time he made me come, and my body feels like it's on fire, yearning for him in a way I can't even articulate.

"More, Ethan," I mumble against his lips, not even caring how bossy I sound. "*More.*"

"Anything my pretty Omega wants."

His finger moves faster, and he starts to play with my clit, rolling his thumb over it as he adds a second finger in my pussy. Water sloshes in the tub as I roll my hips to meet each thrust of his fingers, and my desperate gasps and whimpers bounce off the walls of the bathroom. The entire room smells like our combined scents of arousal now, the thick steam wafting up from the bath full of it.

It smells fucking *divine*.

In fact, the only thing that could make it better would be if the other Alpha's scents were mixed into it too.

That thought hits me at the exact same moment my orgasm does, and I quake against Ethan's touch, sending water spilling over the edge of the bathtub and onto the floor. He deepens our kiss, swallowing up the noises I'm making as if he's savoring each one.

Almost immediately in the wake of my orgasm, a fierce need builds up inside me all over again, and as if he can sense it, Ethan doesn't let up the motion of his fingers. He keeps up the deliberate pressure on my clit, driving me straight from one climax into another.

"I love the way you sound when you come," he whispers hoarsely. "From the first moment I heard it, I knew I wanted to listen to you make those sexy little noises over and over."

Since he said he liked it so much, I moan again, melting against the hard porcelain of the bathtub. The warm water is as soothing as a blanket, and I feel like I could easily curl up and fall asleep right here.

But there's something else I want more than that right now.

I sit up straighter, and Ethan leans back to give me room. Frothy white bubbles cling to my bare breasts, and when his gaze drifts downward, his pupils expand as a heated look crosses his face.

"Stand up," I tell him.

Everything Cary told me about Omegas and their heats is filtering through my mind on overdrive.

141

I know I'm not fully in heat yet. If I was at the height of my heat cycle, two orgasms would barely be enough to sate me, and I would probably be begging to have all four of the Alphas here to help take care of me.

When I spoke with Cary, I was anxious about everything heat would entail, including the idea of craving an Alpha in a raw, primal way. It scared me to think of giving up that much power.

But in this quiet, steamy bathroom with Ethan, I don't feel like I've given up any power at all.

Instead, I feel more powerful than I ever have before as Ethan slowly rises to his feet, staring down at me with awe and desire on his face.

The bulge in his pants is thick and large, and I rise up onto my knees in the tub. My lower half is still submerged in water, but my upper body is bare and wet, making my nipples peak. When I reach for the button of his pants and flick it open, Ethan's chest heaves with a deep inhale. I work his pants down, hooking his boxers too, and his cock springs free.

It's even bigger than it looked like when it was hidden by his pants.

I whimper, and the sound makes Ethan smile.

Unable to help myself, I wrap my fingers around his length, feeling the silky, warm skin beneath my palm. I lean forward, my tongue darting out, then pause and look up at him with a question in my eyes.

"You want to taste, gorgeous?" Warmth gleams in his eyes. "Go ahead."

A flush rises up my cheeks, but he's right. I *do* want to taste. This man smells so good that his scent is almost enough to make me come, and I want to find out if he tastes anywhere near as amazing as he smells.

I drag my tongue up his shaft, and when I get to the tip, I lap at the little slit, licking away the precum there.

"Oh god," I whimper, my thighs clenching as a shudder runs through me.

It's better than I imagined. Sweet and just a little salty, like a dessert you can't stop eating. I wrap my lips around him, swirling my tongue and sucking lightly, as if I'm trying to draw out more of the incredible flavor.

"Fuck, that's good." Ethan's strong fingers stroke my damp hair, smoothing it away from my face, tender and careful. His eyes are half-lidded as he gazes down at me. "You look so stunning right now."

His praise does something to me, making warmth and pride swell inside me. I keep going, sucking and licking and using my hand to stroke him in time with my mouth. His cock pulses against my tongue, and the grunts and groans that spill from him are like gasoline on a fire, lighting me up from the inside out.

When his cock starts to thicken near the base, I gasp and pull away with a wet pop, watching as his knot swells beneath my hand. The sight of it is thrilling and terrifying, and even as part of me wonders how that will ever fit inside me, my pussy clenches in anticipation.

"Have you ever seen a knot up close?" Ethan asks.

"No." I shake my head. "Marcus never knotted me. It's... big."

"Don't worry, you don't have to take it tonight," Ethan assures me. His fingers smooth over my hair again, gentle and soothing. "But you can touch it all you want."

Curiosity urges me on, and I give a tentative squeeze around the thick bulge. Ethan groans, his hand spasming a little on top of my head, like he's trying to keep himself from gripping my hair. My stomach flutters at the thought of what it would feel like to have him fist my hair, to have him control my movements as I suck him and to feel the sting in my scalp as he guides me up and down his cock.

I'm on the verge of begging him to do that, but this is all so new for me. He and his pack have earned my trust, but I'm in uncharted territory here, and the last thing I want to do is cry after this like I did after he and Garrett gave me the most incredible orgasms of my life.

So I just keep exploring his knot on my own, teasing and fondling it, then leaning closer to slide my tongue over it.

Ethan lets me do whatever I want for a few moments, but when I start to suck on his tip again while squeezing his knot tightly, he lets out a choked noise, his upper body bowing over me a little.

"If you keep doing that, I'm gonna come," he grunts. "Feels so... fucking... good."

I keep going, pumping his shaft and squeezing his knot, my heart pounding rapidly in my chest. When he explodes inside my mouth, I swallow it all, moaning around his thick length as the sweet, salty liquid coats my tongue. I keep suckling at his cock, hungry for more, even as it slowly starts to soften, his knot deflating.

"Fuck. That's all I can take, gorgeous," he groans, finally pulling me away from his cock. I lean forward, swiping the tip one last time with my tongue, and he laughs. "You're insatiable."

A blush rises in my cheeks, and I run my fingertips over my lips, which are still tingling from being stretched around his cock.

"I never was before," I whisper. "You make me that way. You and your pack."

It's a big admission, but it's not a lie.

My instinct is to hide my feelings, to try to hold people at a distance and maintain my independence at all times. But even though I spent years trying to avoid everything related to my Omega status, I'm not so sure that was the right choice anymore.

Some part of me that's always felt cold and empty doesn't feel that way anymore, and I know it's because of these four Alphas whose lives I crashed into.

And I want to give this courtship between us a real chance.

A half smile curves Ethan's lips, and he tucks himself away, then grabs a fluffy towel from beside the tub. He lifts me out as if I weigh nothing, then wraps the towel around me, touching me like I'm something precious.

"I'm glad you were at the club that night," I whisper.

His smile widens, soft and sweet. "I am too, gorgeous. I went there to blow off a little steam after a long day of work, but I had no idea I'd find our perfect Omega."

He dries me off methodically, making sure my hair is taken care of, then wraps me up in another towel so I'm nice and dry. He scoops me up, my head against his shoulder.

I'm already feeling sleepy, my limbs heavy and sated.

Ethan carries me to bed and gently lays me down. I think he lies down with me, but I'm already falling asleep as my head hits the pillow.

All I know is that I feel cared for, and cozy, and safe.

# Chapter 18

## *Ava*

I'm not sure how most Alphas court, but this pack definitely doesn't do things halfway.

Over the next few days, I'm pampered like I've never been pampered before. Ethan takes me to look at cars so that I can buy one for myself, and tells me not to bother looking at the price tag.

Part of me wants to protest, since I'm not used to being gifted things or spoiled, but having a car would be really nice. I've had to use the local transportation system to get around town and it takes twice or sometimes three times as long for me as it would if I had a car.

We end up going with a pale blue VW bug. I think it's adorable.

Dante cooks for me, asking me what my favorite foods are and making it all fresh. Gnocchi, pork tamales, butter chicken with garlic naan bread, crepes... I feel like I'm dining out at a fancy restaurant every day, and I can't get enough of it.

"You're going to fatten me up," I tease him at one point. I

like watching him cook. Dante narrates what he does while he's doing it, and I kind of want to ask him to teach me.

But I don't want him thinking that I don't enjoy him cooking for me. I also just like watching him and seeing it all come together.

"I'm going to make sure my Omega has three meals a day," Dante counters. "How many times did you forget breakfast or skip lunch working at the shelter?"

He's got a point. "You know, a girl could get used to this."

"Good. That's the plan." He smiles possessively at me over the stove.

It's not just meals that he makes for us throughout the day, though. He preps meals ahead of time and puts them in the fridge so that they'll be ready to heat up when my heat strikes and they'll need to look after me even more.

Caleb's helping me decorate my room, so that I can make it a proper nest. Cary was right about my nesting kicking into high gear. I care about the exact position of furniture, and I want to have a ton of soft things like throw blankets and pillows. I even want to put wallpaper on the ceiling so that it's interesting to stare up at when I'm in bed.

I've always cared a bit about my home, and made my bed into a nest, but it's never been like this. Caleb buys me literally whatever I want, and once again tells me that price is no concern.

Caleb's fondness and commitment to helping me makes me feel validated. Like I'm not some silly Omega he's putting up with, some rich Alpha who just hands over his credit card while rolling his eyes at his friends going, *women, am I right?*

All of them do a good job of making me feel like they care. Although I'm not quite as sure how Garrett's doing.

He helps me move the furniture around in the other rooms without complaint and will quietly ask me if I need anything. If I ever need to leave the house, he accompanies me as a silent bodyguard.

He's not really one for words much, that's clear, or at least not the easy tenderness and affection that the other three are showing me. But I know that he cares. I just wish I could find a way to get through to him.

But I never doubt that I'm safe with him. That he'll take good care of me.

Through it all, I do my best not to interfere with their work too much. I know that they're taking time off to court me, especially with my heat inevitable. That's going to put them out of commission for a few days and I don't want their work to suffer for it.

I think I'm doing a good job of keeping myself out of the way, but then, I walk into the kitchen and find I've stumbled upon Dante in a business meeting.

He's wearing a button-up shirt and a tie, and even the pants to match, like he's refusing to cheat by being business only from the waist-up. He's sitting at the head of the table looking at his computer and nodding along with whatever's being said.

I freeze.

"Sorry," I mouth silently as Dante looks up.

But Dante just smiles at me and then looks back at the laptop. "I think we're good for now. Let's stay on schedule and double-check everything, I don't want any surprises whatsoever. Let's have another meeting tomorrow morning, eight sharp, to discuss the rest of the day's progress. We're almost there, every-one, great work."

If his coworkers are surprised by him ending the meeting

early, none of them say anything as Dante ends the meeting and gestures for me to come closer. I walk over and he immediately pulls me into his lap.

Snuggling onto his lap, I feel immediately safer, and also definitely warmer. Dante nuzzles into my neck and I tip my head back, melting against his chest. "I don't want to interrupt your work..."

"Work can wait," Dante promises, his voice a low rumble against my throat. "Trust us. We know when we can take breaks. Besides, you're our priority now. What's the point of our success if we can't use it to take care of our Omega?"

I shiver, heat sliding down my spine and pooling between my legs. As I adjust myself more comfortably in his lap, wiggling my ass against him to tease him, I can see his laptop screen is filled with schematics and data, and I sit up a little, pausing.

"Is this what you're working on?"

Dante looks up from where he's kissing my neck. "Hmm? Oh, yeah." He grins at me. "I think you'll like this one. We've been working on it for a bit, Ethan and Caleb were running themselves ragged for months."

He keeps one arm securely around me as he leans forward to tap away at the laptop. "It's a smart watch. We've created something similar before, but this one is specifically for Omegas."

"It looks kind of like a cuff."

"Yeah, we redesigned it so that it'll press closer to the skin, better to monitor things like your pulse." Dante tilts the laptop so I can see better. "We want Omegas to be able to monitor their heats, fertility levels, all of that much better than they can now. Right now we have way too many Omegas with irregular heats getting caught by surprise."

"And so this will help them to know when it's coming?"

"Exactly. Especially for Omegas who've been on suppressants at one point or another. Or Omegas who might have complications that make their heats harder to predict." Dante kisses my neck. "Obviously this isn't a substitute for medicine or consulting a doctor."

"But," I say slowly, the pieces falling into place, "it can take time to work through various medications to find out what works for you, or to wean yourself off suppressants."

Dante nods. "So while Omegas work with a doctor, or even if there's not really any medical solution, this device will be able to tell them when a heat's coming, when they're most fertile... it'll help them keep track of themselves."

"There are apps."

"Apps aren't actually monitoring your body. We wanted this to be a health device first, and a smart device second."

Dante taps the screen to show me some lists. "We want you to be able to do things like tell the time, make phone calls, sync it to your headphones to listen to music. But we made sure those things come secondary. They're a bonus."

"This is... Dante, this is amazing," I tell him. I mean it.

"I hope so." Dante rubs his temples. "We want it to be perfect. I won't let them put the product out just to meet the deadline, only to have things go wrong. But pushing the deadline will be a problem for the shareholders and could also make us look like we can't deliver."

I reach up and massage his shoulders. I want to help him relax, and words alone feel like they'd just be empty platitudes.

Dante purrs, his eyes falling closed for a moment. When he opens them again, the black is starting to overtake the gray. "I want to help Omegas."

I hum, nodding.

"But it means even more now that we have you." His voice is soft. "I want to help *you*."

It's incredibly sweet, and more than I ever thought I would get from an Alpha. Selfless caring.

I don't know which one of us leans in first, if it's him or me, but it doesn't matter once we're kissing. I whimper, heat sliding through me. His hands on me are large and steady, and so very warm, and he kisses me with a casual confidence that would have my knees buckling if I were standing.

He kisses me deep and slow until I'm squirming on his lap. I'm sure he can smell how slick I am. How desperate I am for him to touch me more.

Dante's hand slides up my leg, right up to my thigh, and he starts kissing down my neck. I moan. I want him, I want him, I want...

I reach down and palm his cock. Oh fuck, he's hard, I can feel the bulge of it.

"You want it so badly don't you?" Dante murmurs. He massages my thigh, but doesn't reach up any farther, doesn't dip his fingers in the slick he's sure to find between my legs. "You want cock. Not just any cock, though, hmm?"

"N-no," I admit, my voice cracking. "Not just... not just any... *Dante*..."

His hand slides up my shirt, sending a thrill up my spine as his hands meet more of my bare skin. "You want my Alpha cock. You want my *knot*."

I nod. I'm past words at this point, practically panting.

He nips at my throat. "You want to have me fill you up? Give you that sensation your body's craving so desperately? The stretch of it, pressing up on all the places that make you orgasm over and over while that hot liquid pumps inside you? *Claiming you?*"

I'm no longer massaging his shoulders. More like clawing at them. "*Please.*"

I want him to set me on the table, or readjust me in his lap, and fuck me here and now. I want it so badly I can taste it in the back of my throat. My body is alight with electricity, so much I'm shivering with it.

But then Dante's hand slides back down to my knee. His hand moves out from under my shirt. His kisses on my neck become gentler.

I understand why he and the others are holding off. I appreciate that they want to respect my previous bad experiences and they don't want to push me too hard, too fast. It's very sweet and respectful of them.

But also... I really am ready for them to fuck me already.

Despite the buzzing in my body, it's clear that Dante's not going to break that barrier today. Already his touches have turned reassuring, soothing, and his kisses have gentled. I know he doesn't want to push me, and if he can't tell how ready I am, then I don't want to push him.

Reluctantly, I get off his lap. "I'll stop distracting you. Sorry."

Dante grins at me. "You can distract me anytime."

I laugh, but I do leave the room, my entire body buzzing. I feel like now, it's only a matter of time. Just a matter of time until we actually do cross that line.

# Chapter 19

## *Ava*

A major sign of my impending heat is my restlessness.

I'm one who likes routine, usually. It's helpful when you work with animals, since they rely on us and on that routine for their mental well-being. But right now, I can't seem to sit still. I want something, and I can't seem to stop moving around until I get it. I'm buzzing with energy.

I need a distraction. I need something. I'll take just about anything at this point.

I have no idea what I'm looking for as I go into the living room, just that I'll know it when I find it, and I'm so tunnel visioned and scatterbrained at the same time that I don't see anyone else is there until I hear Garrett say,

"Where's the fire?"

"Oh my god!" I blurt out, literally jumping a bit off the ground.

"Fuck, I'm sorry." Garrett's stretched out on the couch, and fuck, I'm sure he didn't plan this when he sat down this way but it really shows off his body.

He's so firm and muscled, with a stocky build and long legs to give him the height to loom over me.

"I didn't mean to startle you."

"No, you're fine, I'm just... jumpy." That's not the right word. "On edge," I correct.

"Jumpy, huh?" Garrett gives me a slow once-over that has me shivering. It feels like all it takes is just one look from him or the other members of the pack and I'm filled with an uncontrollable fire. "Let's see what we can do about that."

He shifts and pats the couch. I walk over, unsure of what he's going to do. I sit down, and Garrett reaches over... and starts to massage my head.

I go stiff with surprise, but then quickly relax into it. Garrett's gruff, but when it comes to the physical, he's gentle and looks after me. I close my eyes, relaxing more and more bit by bit until I feel like I'm a puddle against the couch.

For a moment, there's just silence. The two of us being in the same space, Garrett touching me in a way that is intimate, but not sexual.

I've wondered about this, because I've had my suspicions, but I haven't wanted to ask so far for fear of offending. But I figure... now's as good a time as any. And I want answers, so that I can move forward properly instead of questioning.

"How much convincing did Caleb and Ethan have to do?"

Garrett doesn't pause in his massaging. I suppose he expected me to ask him. "I thought you might have figured out I was reluctant."

"I wasn't sure. I didn't want to be unfair to you."

"You're not. I was the most on the fence about having you live with us."

I'd nod, normally, except I can't really when my head is being massaged like this. "I see."

Garrett gives an amused chuckle. "I don't know that you do. It wasn't because of you. You didn't do anything wrong."

"Is this the... it's not you, it's me?" I tease him gently.

"Kind of. But not in the way you think. It's not that I didn't want you." Garrett growls a little in the back of his throat. "It's because of my family."

"Your family?"

"They've always had particular expectations for how I would live my life. One of those things was that I would have a particular kind of Omega as my mate."

I frown. "What kind?"

"The kind with..." Garrett pauses. "Breeding."

It's such an crude way of saying it, but I know what he means. He's not saying it for himself. He's quoting whatever his parents said. Whatever they tried to put on him.

"They wanted me to pick someone wealthy and connected. My parents don't seem to care about anything except wealth and connections." Garrett's tone is low and rough, a bit disgusted, but his hands are still gentle and firm as they massage my scalp.

"Sounds like you don't agree."

"You got that right. I had a lot of fights with them. I don't subscribe to how they see the bond between Alpha and Omega. We barely speak anymore."

There's a pause, and then he adds, "I know that my family money is how I was able to help us jumpstart this company. But I don't ever want to rely on something like that to make my way. I made my own way, with my own pack. And I'm going to pick my own Omega."

"Even an Omega who grew up poor?" I whisper.

I can't see him with my eyes closed or with my head at this angle, but I can feel his surprise. "You don't..."

"No, I want to share." It's not just that it feels fair. It's also that I want him to see all of who I am. "I had two Beta parents. They really didn't teach me anything. They weren't around much. And I try to forgive them for it because they were both working so hard to make ends meet. We never had a lot. And they thought I was a Beta. I also thought I was a Beta. So... they had no idea there were things to teach me."

"Do you talk to them?"

"No. Not since I went to college. Sometimes I think that's how Marcus could get to me. I didn't have anybody to fall back on. No parents to care about me. I was an easy target."

"How your parents treated you isn't your fault. They should've been there for you."

"I know. Or. In my head, I know." I shrug. "Sometimes it's hard to tell my heart that."

"Well, we'll have to keep working to change your heart's mind until you really know it."

His hands slide away from my head and down my neck. I arch up, urging them farther down. I want his hands all over my body. Heat is simmering just under my skin. I know we're talking about something serious, but at the same time, his hands on me are melting me into a puddle, and I don't want to resist it.

"I know I'm not what most people see on paper as the ideal Omega," I whisper, staring up at him. Garret's hands massage farther down my body, making my breath hitch. "I'm independent. I don't want to just be a homemaker. I like my freedom. I have no family connections."

"You're the ideal Omega for us," Garrett replies. His hands

massage my breasts, and I whimper, arching into his touch. My legs spread, wanting, *presenting*. "We want you for who you are. We cherish you."

His head bends down so that his lips are right at my ear. "We *adore* you."

Garrett's gruff. I would dare say that a lot of the time, he's cranky. But his voice right now is filled with nothing but sincerity.

Suddenly, just having his hands on me isn't enough.

I push myself up, take his face into my hands, and kiss him.

# Chapter 20

## *Ava*

Garrett's mouth is hungry against mine, and he kisses me like he seems to do everything else—with a firm command and total control. His sweet apple cider scent mixes with the scent of a roaring fire, and I swear I can almost feel the heat of the flames.

*God, I would gladly let that fire burn me down.*

The restlessness I felt earlier rises up again, urging me on as I climb onto his lap and wrap my arms around his broad, muscled shoulders. The feel of his hands on me, even just massaging my scalp, eased the discomfort earlier, but now that the dam has broken, I need more than that.

I don't just need an orgasm either. I need a cock.

*His* cock.

That thought sends a shot of heat through me, so intense that it's like being struck by lightning, and I practically climb his body as I grind against him.

"Garrett," I gasp out in between heated kisses. "Please. I need... I need..."

"I know what you need, little one," he rasps. "I can smell it. You're practically coating me in your scent right now."

"Then fuck me," I demand, past the point of worrying if I'm being too demanding. All I know is that I need to feel him inside me. I need to feel the strength and power of his body as he moves. Need to wrap my legs around him so that we're touching everywhere.

Garrett's purr is a deep rumble in his chest, vibrating against me as he lifts me off his lap in one smooth motion. He sets me on my feet and stands in front of me, then tugs my shirt off. I mirror his action, grabbing the hem of his shirt and pulling it upward. He's so much bigger than me that he has to help me get it over his head, then he tosses it aside, the muscles of his bare chest flexing.

My hands go to his pecs, drawn to the solid slabs of muscle, which are warm beneath my palms.

His purr grows louder, and he drops his head to kiss me as he works my pants and panties down. I'm already working to kick off my shoes, and by the time I'm naked, we're both breathing hard.

Garrett shoves his own pants and boxers off, discarding them like he resents them for ever separating us, and the second they're gone, he takes my wrist and brings my hand to his cock, which is rock hard and so thick that I'm not sure I can even wrap my fingers all the way around it.

"Do you want this?" he asks, his voice deep and gruff. "You want my cock inside you?"

"Y-yes," I breathe, my voice shaking a little as I stroke him.

He groans, his body stiffening, as if he's struggling to stay still. He lets me drag my hand up and down his length two more times, his dark brown eyes locked on my face the entire time. And then it's like something in him snaps. He scoops me up into

159

his arms, his hands gripping the backs of my thighs and wrapping my legs around him.

He strides away from the couch, and at first I think he's going to carry me upstairs like this—but we don't make it that far. Instead of heading for the stairs that lead to the second story, Garrett presses me up against a wall next to the large open doorway that connects the living room to the foyer.

My back hits the cool plaster, and Garrett rolls his hips, sliding his cock through my folds. I'm so wet for him already that his shaft glides easily, and every time the broad, rounded head hits my clit, I whimper.

"Give me your cock," I beg, feeling like I might die if that thick shaft doesn't split me open in the next two seconds. "Please, Garrett. *Please.*"

"You don't have to beg, little one," he assures me, adjusting his grip on my thighs as his cock notches at my entrance. "You just have to hold on."

With that, he presses his hips forward, sliding into me. And I wasn't wrong when I had my hand wrapped around him—he's fucking *huge.* Bigger than Ethan, which is saying something.

My fingers dig into his shoulders, and I hook my legs together above his ass, biting my lip as I tense up a little against the intrusion.

Garrett stops immediately, although I can feel the effort it takes him to go still. "You all right?" he asks, dropping his head to find my eyes.

"Yes," I gasp. Even though it's a lot, it's everything my body has been craving, and along with the pinch of discomfort, there's a burning pleasure radiating through me.

"Breathe," he reminds me gently. "Relax, little one. I'm not in any hurry here. I'd fuck you all day if I could, so we can take our time."

"Right." I laugh softly, touched by the way he's so invested in taking care of me—and by the fact that he wants me so badly. "Okay."

Leaning in, he kisses me deeply, his tongue delving into my mouth as his fireside and apple cider scent fills my nostrils. The kiss is so all-consuming that it makes all other thoughts scatter from my head, and when our lips break apart, he gives my ass a squeeze.

"There you go," he murmurs encouragingly, pressing his cock a few inches deeper inside. "Just breathe and let me in. You feel so fucking amazing."

He pulls out a little and then slides back in, working his way a little deeper with each thrust. At first, it's hard to keep myself from tensing up again, but with every kiss, every roll of his hips, my body adjusts even more.

Some part of me, some primal and instinctive part, knows how *right* this is. My body knows it can take him, and when he's finally rooted all the way inside me, we both go still, catching our breath as we cling to each other.

"Is that good?" he murmurs, his breath stirring my hair.

"So good." My heels dig into his ass, and I clench around him. "You can move more now. I can take it. I *need* it."

"Such a good girl." He sounds almost delirious, and he draws back and then pitches his hips forward, fucking me less gently than he did when he was working his way in.

The feel of his thick cock stretching me pulls a gasp from my lips, and I whimper plaintively as he keeps going.

"Yes," I whisper. "Yes, yes, yes."

I'm soaking his shaft with every thrust, my body providing

all the slickness he needs to fuck me hard and deep. I'm already getting close, every nerve ending in my body screaming with the pleasure of having an Alpha's cock inside me like this. It's almost more than I can take, almost too good for my brain to process, and I bury my face against Garrett's shoulder, holding on just like he told me to as he pounds into me again and again.

The sound of our bodies slapping together fills the room, mixed with his deep grunts and my soft mewls, and my legs tighten around his waist as a climax builds inside me.

"Oh fuck," I whimper. "Keep going. Keep going, you're gonna make me—"

The word breaks off on a loud cry as my orgasm explodes like a bomb, detonating and sending pleasure shooting through my limbs. I lift my head from Garrett's shoulder, and as I do... my gaze locks with Ethan's burning green eyes.

The shock of surprise mixes with the euphoria of the orgasm, and I keep coming, feeling like I might shake apart as I cling to Garrett, overwhelmed by the surge of pleasure. Ethan never looks away from me. He doesn't even blink, and I can't seem to pull my gaze away from him either.

*What do I look like right now? What does he see?*

That thought makes me moan, and Ethan's full lips quirk up in a smile as Garrett stills inside me, having realized that we're not alone.

"Don't stop because of me," Ethan drawls, cocking an eyebrow. "I'm enjoying the hell out of this little show." His voice drops to a lower register as he adds, "And I know you've got another one in you, gorgeous. I want to hear Garrett make you scream at least two more times."

Garrett chuckles. He pulls back a little, his hard features softened with desire as he looks down at me. "What do you say, little one? Should we show him how good I can make you feel? Should we let him see how you're soaking my cock?"

"Yes," I breathe, feeling like I've died and gone to Omega heaven.

The idea of Ethan watching Garrett fuck me makes me flush from head to toe, but it's not from embarrassment. The Omega in me recognizes that all of the Alphas in this house could be mine if I choose to bond with them, and the idea of being shared between them satisfies something inside me that I can't even put into words.

Garrett grins, the expression making him look less severe than usual. He pulls me away from the wall, holding me up with a firm grip on my thighs, his cock still buried inside me. Instead of using the wall to brace me as he fucks into me, he lifts and lowers me smoothly, sliding me up and down his thick shaft.

I know that from this angle, Ethan can see so much more. He can probably see the way my pussy swallows up Garrett's cock, and he can see the way my breasts bounce each time Garrett pulls me down.

"Maybe..." I bite my lip, hissing out a breath as Garrett hits a new spot inside me that makes sparks dance across my vision. "Maybe Ethan can... do more than just watch."

Ethan and Garrett both purr loudly in response to that, and I can hear Ethan's footsteps as he crosses the room toward us. The warmth of his body seeps into mine as he steps up behind me, and when he presses a kiss to my neck, I whimper and clench tightly around Garrett.

"Are you gonna come for us again?" Ethan murmurs.

I nod, because it's not even really a question at this point. I can already feel the tingling rush of pleasure building in my core, ready to be unleashed.

"Fuck, you smell good when you're turned on like this." Ethan's nose trails up the line of my neck, and then he steps closer, his chest pressing against my back as he encloses me between him and Garrett.

"Hold her up. Keep her steady," Garrett says.

"I've got her. Come here, gorgeous."

Ethan unwinds my arms from around Garrett's neck, draping them around his own neck instead. My upper body rests against his chest, and I have the most thrilling feeling of weightlessness as I realize that the two of them have me balanced between them. That they'll hold me up no matter what.

With my upper body leaning against Ethan, we both have a perfect view of the way my pussy stretches around Garrett's cock. Ethan presses a kiss to my temple, reaching down to palm one of my breasts.

"So fucking beautiful. You want more?"

"Yeah."

The word is a breathy sigh, and Ethan and Garrett share a look before Garrett starts to fuck me again. I'm suspended between the two of them, my arms around Ethan's shoulders and my legs wrapped around Garrett's waist, and as Garrett's fingers dig into the flesh of my thighs and Ethan rolls my nipple between his finger and thumb, I can't hold back anymore.

Another orgasm hits me like a wrecking ball, making me writhe and buck between them as I scream just like Ethan said he wanted.

Garrett starts to thrust again, working me through it, his firm grip keeping my hips right where he wants them as his massive cock drives into me.

"One more," Ethan murmurs roughly. "Give us one more."

While one skilled hand continues to work my breast, he reaches down and finds my clit, sliding his fingers over it as Garrett keeps fucking me. I feel dizzy, my entire body tingling as if there's an actual electric current running through me.

I tilt my head a little, silently begging for Ethan's mouth on mine, and he gives me exactly what I want.

His kiss is pure, raw Alpha hunger. His tongue slides into my mouth as if he's trying to get me off with it before Garrett can make me come on his cock again. But honestly, between the fingers on my clit, the thick cock filling me to the brim, and the way Ethan is kissing me like he never wants to stop, I'm already a goner.

"Ethan!" I tighten my grip around his neck, my back arching as pleasure lights me up. "Garrett!"

"Oh shit. Oh *fuck*. You're squeezing me so tight, little one."

Garrett's thrusts lose their steady rhythm, and the knot at the base of his cock swells. There's a feeling of intense pressure as he drives into me one more time, his knot slipping inside me, and I can feel the flood of heat as his cum spills inside me.

I can also feel the way his knot locks us together, keeping him from pulling out, and my pulse quickens. It's nothing like I expected it to be, more pleasurable and more overwhelming all at once.

"Does that feel good, gorgeous?" Ethan murmurs, stepping closer to Garrett so that I'm pinned firmly between them. Garrett's cock is still lodged inside me, and behind me, I can feel the branding heat of Ethan's hard-on through his pants.

"Uh huh."

I whimper softly as a wave of emotions rise up in me. It's not panic or the need to cry like last time, but it still hits me like a ton of bricks. I crane my neck awkwardly to kiss Ethan again, needing to feel his mouth on mine, and when we break apart, I unwrap my arms from behind his neck and wrap them around Garrett's shoulders, melting against the big, gruff Alpha.

"Don't let go," I whisper. "Don't leave me. Please."

I'm barely aware of what I'm saying. All I know is that I want this feeling to last. This feeling of closeness. This connection.

"Couldn't even if I wanted to," Garrett murmurs gruffly. "And I don't fucking want to."

I don't know if he's talking about this moment, with his knot inside me, or in a larger sense. My heart thrills a little at the idea that he might be attached to me enough to not want to let me go at all, but instead of getting lost in those thoughts, I tighten my grip on him, burrowing my face against his chest.

I feel small and fragile, protected and cherished, and I'm so damn grateful that neither of the men is telling me that I'm being too emotional. They just hold me between them, neither of them seeming to care at all that Garrett is naked.

Finally, Garrett takes a step back, bringing me with him. He shares a look with Ethan over my shoulder, and the handsome, flirtatious Alpha trails his fingers down the curve of my spine.

"Garrett's got you, gorgeous," he murmurs. "He'll take good care of you."

With that, Garrett turns and carries me upstairs. His cock pulses inside me slightly as he brings me to my bedroom, settling me on the bed. He rolls us both onto our sides, his knot still keeping us linked together as his strong arms pull me against his chest.

"Are you... cuddling me?" I ask, as I snuggle deeper into his embrace.

He chuckles. "Yes. How am I doing? I've never actually cuddled before."

The admission from this gruff, stoic Alpha makes me grin, and I press a kiss to the warm skin of his chest. "You're doing great."

As usual, words fail me when I need them most. Because the truth is, he's doing better than great. He strokes his hand down my back, burying his face in my hair and breathing in deeply to absorb my scent, and it's just...

*Perfect.*

# Chapter 21

## *Ava*

My night with Garrett was amazing. I wake up feeling refreshed, feeling warm and safe... no, feeling more than all of that.

I feel content.

But once I get up and start my day, the feeling fades.

Everything's irritating me. It's too cold, then it's too hot. Nothing tastes good. I'm hungry, but I'm not hungry, and I don't want to eat. I can't find anything I want to do. I prowl around the house like a ghost or a restless cat.

Finally, I start rearranging my room.

I know that I put things in a particular place, in a particular way, already. Caleb helped me. But now none of it looks right. It doesn't *feel* right.

I move furniture around and rearrange pillows. I'm not sure I like the wall color anymore. The rug needs to be in a different spot, but I'm not sure what spot.

"Fucking curtains," I mutter. I reach up to try to take them down, tugging, tugging, tugging...

"You need a stool?" Caleb asks.

I jump, nearly tearing the curtains. "They're not *right*." My voice hitches into something close to a sob.

Behind Caleb, I see the other three Alphas at the doorway. All four of them have worry in their eyes.

I tug at the curtain again. I know that this isn't how you take a curtain down, and yet, I can't seem to stop myself.

"Here." Caleb gently uncurls my fingers from the curtain. Ethan walks over and reaches up to undo them from their hooks. "We'll take it down for you."

"I don't understand, they were fine the other day." Tears start to stream down my face and there's a hiccup in my voice. "I don't... but they're not right anymore. I hate them. I want to burn them."

"We can burn them," Garrett says, sounding perhaps a little too eager about it.

"Ava." Dante steps forward. "Would you like different curtains?"

I nod. "I... I don't know why they just don't work anymore."

"You're nesting," Caleb says gently. "That's all. It means your heat is coming on."

That's probably supposed to soothe me, but instead, it makes me burst into tears.

Ethan's still undoing the curtain and taking it down, but he deftly moves out of the way at the same time so that Caleb can scoop me up and take me to the bed. Once I'm inside the literal nest of blankets and pillows, I feel a bit better.

Being cradled by one of my Alphas helps too.

Garrett climbs into the bed on my other side, the two of them curled around me like they're shielding me from an attack. They purr, not out of pleasure, but to soothe me.

"I'm sorry," I sob. "I know it's not a big deal, I know that I should just be fine."

"Don't apologize," Garrett growls. "We're not mad at you, are we?"

I shake my head. I can tell they're not upset. Marcus used to play games with me, but that's not what's happening here. I can smell my Alphas' scents and there's nothing there but concern.

"Ava." Dante crouches down in front of the bed to get eye-level with me. "Would you like me to take you shopping? We'll find the perfect pair of curtains. I promise."

"Are you sure?" I don't want to interrupt his day. This is silly, I should be fine. I already picked out these curtains. I know that I should still like them, in theory. But I'm just so upset about it. I can't make myself calm down.

"Of course I'm sure." Dante reaches out and takes my hand. "Come on. It'll be great to get out and get some fresh air. Stretch your legs."

I wipe at my eyes and nod. Dante pulls me to my feet, then keeps me going, until I'm in his arms and held against his chest.

I breathe in his scent. It soothes me and helps me stop crying.

I'm so glad that I have these four men. I don't know what I'd do without them. My heat isn't even properly here yet and I'm already so upset about such little things. I feel irrational and out of control. I can't imagine how bad it would be if I didn't have these men and their scents to soothe me and take care of me.

"Thank you," I say, still sniffling a bit even if I'm no longer fully crying. "You're all so kind and understanding."

"We love taking care of you," Caleb points out. "Don't forget that."

Ethan finally finishes getting the curtains down. "There we go. You're all set for when you come back with new ones."

"This is what we like to do," Dante says softly. "We're going to take care of you no matter what."

With the four of them around me, enveloped in their scents, I believe him.

# Chapter 22

## *Ava*

Dante takes me to the nicest, most expensive shopping area I've ever been to. It's a far fancier mall than anyplace I've dared to shop in before, outdoors with a beautiful tree-lined cobblestone street for people to walk in, shops and restaurants on either side, and a large indoor area at the end, all glass and designer stores.

I couldn't even afford to breathe at a place like this before, on my salary, but when we park, Dante just hands me his black American Express card.

"Dante..."

He waves it lightly through the air. "Go on, take it. You're our Omega. What's ours is yours."

I take the card, still feeling a bit unsure, but he smiles warmly.

"Why do you think we're so successful?" he asks. "Just for ourselves? We want to spend our wealth on our Omega. This is your pack now, and your money too. Spending this money on you makes me, and makes all of us, happy."

I might burst into tears again, I'm filled with such warmth and gratefulness. I nod, and he helps me out of the car.

The shops aren't too busy at this time of day, but as we walk, I have to admit that a few of the people we pass smell sour to me. I keep wrinkling my nose.

Dante finally chuckles. "You smell something?"

I lower my voice so nobody around us overhears and gets offended. "I don't like how people smell."

"What about me?"

I inhale deeply and shudder. "You smell amazing."

Dante nods. "That's what I thought. As you approach your heat, if you've started to bond with an Alpha or a pack already, other people's scents will start to sour."

My heart picks up, but not from anxiety. That's a good thing. That means even if something bad happens and I'm separated from Dante when my heat hits, I won't be as mindless as I thought. Anyone else who tries anything will smell sour to me. I won't want them.

It's like having back a piece of the autonomy I feared I'd lost.

Dante steers me into a shop with a hand on the small of my back, and I start searching for the perfect fabric for the curtains.

"I want something pastel," I mutter as I search.

Dante nods along, listening attentively. He's very patient as I shop, which is good, because I'm being wildly picky.

"Maybe you could find some other things that will also go with the curtains," he suggests after I've rejected what feels like the fiftieth curtain selection. "That way you'll start building your color scheme for the space."

I nod. I like that idea.

Dante doesn't stick too close by me, letting me wander. While I appreciate his presence and his scent, it's nice that he's not hovering. I'm not some prize he has to keep under lock and key. I'm my own person, and he's letting me be that.

And buying things for the home is *nice*. It soothes that itch in my chest. I look for things that I can put around the house, not just in my room. Some little touches here and there to make the entire place feel like I live there too. Like I'm not just a guest with one little corner for myself.

I catch Marcus's scent before I see or hear him.

The first notes that hit me are the first that always would: a spicy scent like cologne. Then after is the scent of expensive leather. But underneath both, the scent I used to dismiss, is the bitter smell of sweat.

It tastes like fear and anger on the back of my tongue.

I know that scent. I don't know if the bitterness was always there, or if it just feels this way to me now, but I do know that this scent always confused and unsettled me. I used to tell myself it didn't matter as much. I was a Beta, so of course maybe an Alpha smell would unsettle me.

Love, I would say to myself, is not about scents.

But now maybe I wonder if it was my Omega instincts telling me to save myself. Trying to warn me of danger in a way I didn't yet know how to understand.

My hands shake. Even before I turn around, I'm absolutely certain that the man behind me is my ex-boyfriend.

I clench my hands into fists so he can't tell I'm upset.

My head raises, and I lock eyes with Dante who's across the store. He starts heading for me immediately, reading my fear in my face even if he's too far right now to catch my scent.

"Ava?"

I turn around and take a deep breath. "Marcus."

And there he is. In the flesh. The man who terrified and terrorized me.

Marcus is tall and imposing, with broad shoulders and a

muscular build. I have a type, I guess. But where Garrett exudes solid strength and Dante incites heat, Marcus's six feet of muscle just makes me feel fear. I hate knowing how much smaller I am than him.

His hair is a dark, ash blond, darker than Caleb's. I once thought that his blue eyes sparkled with charm and charisma, the way Ethan's do. But now they seem cold and threatening.

His mouth has the same hard set to it that I remember. It makes him seem unapproachable. Once upon a time, that made me feel like he was just aloof and private. It made me feel special when he approached me and wanted me.

Now I know it's just because he's judging everyone around him.

"So, it is you." Marcus looks me up and down and his nostrils flare. "I thought so, but then I thought... that's not possible. Not *my* Ava. *My* Ava is a Beta."

Suddenly his scent is pushed out of my nose by the arrival of Dante's warm, welcoming scent. All spice and heat and safety. I inhale it like it's a drug.

Dante puts his arm around me and draws me close into his side. Marcus's eyebrows fly up. "Dante?"

"Marcus." Dante's tone is very carefully polite. "What's the CEO of Prodigy Crop doing here? Don't you have lackeys who can run your errands for you?"

Marcus smiles, the dark smile that I remember so well. It used to haunt my nightmares. "Not all of us have a triplet of frat boys to follow our every command."

I bristle. He's referring to Ethan, Caleb, and Garrett. I know it, and I'm not about to let him talk shit about them.

Dante squeezes my shoulders comfortingly. "Well, I'm sure

you've had a nice talk with Ava. Why don't you head on out? We have purchases to make."

"I'll leave when I'm ready. I'm not done here yet." Marcus drops his gaze to me again. "You never told me you were an Omega."

"I..." I hate how small and shaky my voice is. "I didn't know. Until after."

"And you never contacted me? I should've been told about your presentation ceremony so I could put in my bid."

A growl starts up in the back of Dante's throat. "Unfortunate that she's decided to let my pack court her instead. Which she would have decided on even if you *had* known about the presentation and put a bid in. The Omega gets the last word on who she wants to court her, remember?"

He draws himself up, and I hear him dipping into his Alpha voice. "Or maybe you've never been able to garner any Omega's interest, so you don't know how it works?"

Marcus's eyes blaze and I shrink. I remember how he would get when his eyes were like that. "You..."

"I am her *Alpha*." Dante's voice is low, so that we don't cause a scene, but the protectiveness and possessiveness could not be clearer. "You will *back off* from *my Omega*."

He's definitely dipping into that voice now, the voice that will give me a command and I'll obey, that voice that means it's time to fight.

Marcus darts his gaze back and forth between us. He doesn't seem to know which way he wants to go.

To help him along in the decision, Dante takes a small step forward, pushing me behind him at the same time. His body is completely blocking me from Marcus now.

I cling to Dante's shirt and press my nose to the firm muscles of his back, inhaling his scent. My hands are shaking again. If they ever stopped.

"Fine." Marcus's own voice is garbled, like he's also dipping into that Alpha range and is trying to hold it back.

He takes a step away, but also to the side, so that I'm in his line of sight once more. The look he gives me is hungry and makes me want to scream. "I'll see you later, Ava."

He glares at Dante once more, then turns and stalks off.

# Chapter 23

## *Ava*

My legs give out.

The shaking isn't just in my hands now. It's everywhere. I feel cold all over, except for my face, which feels flushed. I can't stop shaking.

Dante whips around, crouching just a bit and pulling me into his arms, letting me bury my nose in his neck where his scent is the strongest.

"What a strong Omega," he purrs. "*My* strong Omega. You were so brave. It's okay. I've got you. I'll protect you. I'll rip his damn throat out if he tries anything, I don't care who's watching or where we are. You were so brave. You're safe. I'll keep you safe."

Tears slip free and I nod frantically, but I still can't stop shaking.

Dante gently picks me up, keeping his arms around me, and nods for a clerk. The woman rushes up, looking concerned. "Sir?"

"I'm afraid my Omega's had a bit of a bad shock." Dante's tone is apologetic, but not embarrassed. "Would you mind taking these items and arranging to have them sent to our residence?"

He takes care of everything with the clerk, his calm voice washing over me. You'd think that he was arranging this so I wouldn't have to carry too many bags, and not because I'm having a panic attack.

It really does make me feel safe, to know that he's so calm. Dante will handle this. Dante will protect me.

He gets me out of the shop and back to the car, where he sets me down on the hood. I keep my arms and legs wrapped around him, and he rocks me, purring, rubbing my back.

I don't know how much time passes until I'm feeling less like I'll fall apart, but Dante doesn't complain. Whether it's five minutes or an hour, he's patient, and he just keeps reassuring me, holding me.

He pulls back just enough to take my face into his hands. "Are you okay if I drive?"

I nod.

We get into the car. I'm still shaking a bit, but it's not as bad as before. Dante drives one-handed, his other hand on my leg to help calm me down.

It works. I feel secure, with him touching me.

We pull up to the mansion and get out, but the moment we open the door, the Alphas must sense something's wrong because all three of them descend.

"Ava?" Caleb's there first. "You smell..."

He kneels in front of me and buries his face in my stomach, wrapping his arms around me like a supplicant. I run my fingers through his hair and brace my other hand on his shoulder. He smells so lovely. So comforting.

"What happened?" Garrett growls, a threat in his voice. "Did someone touch her? Did someone hurt her?"

Ethan's fidgeting, clearly wanting to help, but not sure what to do.

"I think we should move to the living room," Dante says, ever the leader.

Caleb picks me up and gets to his feet in the same instant, carrying me to the living room couch. All four of them crowd around me, giving me their soothing scents.

"We ran into her ex while we were shopping," Dante says, keeping his voice quiet so he doesn't upset me.

Ethan strokes my hair while I lean my head on Caleb's shoulder. "Marcus," I whisper.

"He seems to think he has a prior claim on Ava, because he dated her before she knew she was an Omega. He was upset that Ava hadn't arranged for him to be notified so he could be at her presentation ceremony."

"If that's the case," Garrett mutters, "the girl I kissed in fifth grade should've invited me to her goddamn ceremony too."

"I hate this," I whisper. "I hate how upset he makes me feel."

"Ava." Ethan's voice is gentle. "He abused you. That's going to upset anyone."

"I hate that I fell for it. How charming and sweet he could be."

"He can certainly present a false face to the world," Dante growls. He glances at me, his lips pulling to one side. "When you talked about a man named Marcus before, I didn't realize that it was Marcus Travers. He's a competitor of ours."

"Wait. You know him?" I ask.

"Unfortunately." He glances at his pack mates. "It's not just any Marcus. It's our favorite guy to hate."

"What? The fucking Prodigy asshole?" Garrett snarls. "Oh, he's asking for it. He knows he's asking for it. I told that guy last time..."

"I'm sorry," I blurt out. "I'm sorry. This is my fault. If I'd just... I shouldn't have given in. I was drawn to that Alpha energy, but I should've known..."

"There's no 'should' here," Caleb murmurs.

Dante nods firmly. "He gave you every reason to be scared of Alphas, after what he did to you. I know you feel your instincts steered you wrong, but baby girl, nothing that happened to you was your fault. And we will protect you. No matter what."

The other three men all add murmurs of agreement.

"We'll keep you safe from him," Garrett promises. "He won't ever fucking touch you again."

"That's our vow to you," Ethan adds. "Even if you decide you don't want to be our Omega and don't want to bond with us. Nobody should have to be at the mercy of an asshole like that."

"You have our word." Caleb kisses the top of my head. "We're going to take care of you."

"That man," Dante growls, "is against everything an Alpha should be. There's no way we'll let him get to you. We'll make sure he never has any claim on you."

I'm touched by their defense of me, their protectiveness, their compassion. But no matter how much it means to me, I can't fully erase the part of me that is still terrified of Marcus.

I wonder if I ever will.

# Chapter 24

## *Caleb*

The moment Ava entered the house, I smelled her and knew something was wrong.

I think we're all able to pick up on her scent more strongly, and more instinctively, than we could at first. It's a part of how the bond is made. Already whenever I leave the house and I go out in public, any other Omega I run into smells sour to me. Too cloying, like an overly sweet cheap grocery store cake.

Which sounds absolutely insulting, so I'd never say it out loud to any Omega. But I know it's the growing bond between me, between all of us, and Ava as we continue to court her.

I'm so upset about this Marcus guy I could take a swing at him myself, which isn't my usual style. But Ava's approaching her heat. She was already unhappy and upset when Dante took her shopping.

Then they came back, and she smelled so *afraid*.

Even a few hours later, I can still catch whiffs of it.

She feels better. I can tell that, which is better than nothing. I want her to feel better. But I'm more in tune with her than the others, aware of her emotions, and I can tell she's still on edge.

I can't blame her. She must be feeling really raw after all of that. When she confided in us the first time about her abusive ex, it was clearly upsetting to her, but she'd felt it was all in the past.

Now that past is back to haunt her.

I wish I could snap my fingers and fix it easily. I'm good at that, at work, at our company. I'm good with people, and oftentimes, the solution we're looking for is a simple one. But this is one of those things you can't fix with just a few magic words or an email to another department.

However, I think I have some ideas of what can help.

The rest of the pack likes to lovingly tease me for being a nerd, but I think research is important. You can never be too careful, and it's something I remind them about as we put the finishing touches on this Omega smart watch project.

Once Ava got here, I stepped up that reading, brushing up on everything I've ever read about Omegas—but not just biology, like the research I did for the watch. Now I've been reading about Omega *behavior* during heat. What they need. How they feel. How they'll act.

And now, I'm ready to pamper her.

I head upstairs to her bedroom. Her nest, rather. If she chooses to bond with us and be our mate, this room will be the one she considers her own for her heats, but it probably won't be the place she sleeps every night.

Right now, though, it's her domain. And she wants to nest and fix it up so it's perfect.

As I walk up the stairs, I can catch a whiff of her scent. She's much calmer now. The things she bought from the shop arrived about an hour ago and so now she's redecorating, hanging up the curtains, all of that.

We asked if she wanted help, but Ava politely declined. I think she wanted some time to be alone after everything. I get that, but I think it's time she had a break.

I know she won't take one when she should. She's determined to be independent and not give in to her instincts. I understand. But giving in isn't a bad thing. Not when we're here to catch her.

"Ava?" I call, so she can hear me coming. "Can I come in?"

I get up to her door and knock. "Ava?"

"Sure thing! Come on in!" She sounds like she's yelling, but it's muffled.

As I enter the room, I immediately realize why. She's got the coverlet over her head as she's trying to completely redo the sheets on the bed.

I can't quite hide my chuckle. "You look like the world's frilliest ghost."

Ava wrestles with the bedding until her head pops out, her dark hair all around her face. She's so adorable I want to devour her. I know she's still making up her mind, and none of us will ever push her, but I know what I feel. My heart aches to make her our Omega for good.

I can see how lighthearted she's trying to be, but the stress around the corners of her mouth and eyes give it away.

She needs a break.

"How's it going?" I ask, sauntering over.

"I think you can tell how it's going," she shoots back, laughing and pushing her hair out of her face.

"Honestly, I think it's going great." I look around. She's added more décor and redone the curtains. "I really like the art you chose."

"You're sweet."

"I'm honest. People are just used to honesty only when it's mean." I hold out my hand. "Come on, I have a surprise for you."

She takes my hand, smiling up at me. I can sense that she's secretly relieved to have an excuse for a break, even if there's a part of her that's still a bit anxious, frantically telling her she needs to make this perfect.

That's okay. I know how to quell that part.

Her hand is warm and trusting in mine as I lead her downstairs to the home theater we have set up. I've already gotten out all the treats: the popcorn maker and cotton candy machine, the soda, the ice cream.

Ava laughs as I lead her in. "Caleb. You didn't have to do all this for me."

"Of course I did." I sit her down and get her some treats. "You're our Omega. You deserve to be pampered. And I'm guessing it's been a while since you ate."

"I am craving junk food," Ava admits.

I wink at her and get going on the treats. I'm not surprised she's craving junk food. She needs extra energy for the next few days and her body's preparing for a possible pregnancy, but definitely for a long few days of sex.

Ava smiles up at me as I bring her the food, her eyes full of wonder like she can't believe I'm doing this for her. As if my doing this for her is some kind of chore and not a pleasure, an honor. It brings me joy to give her joy and to take care of her, that's what Alphas do.

"The others are out. I think Dante went to talk to our lawyers." Probably investigating if there was anything we could do about Marcus. "Garrett went for a run with Ethan."

I don't add that the two of them needed to work off some

steam. Garrett's our fighter and Ethan's always restless. After what happened with Ava, knowing they can't go and just beat the shit out of this guy like they want... yeah I don't blame them for needing to work off the energy some other way.

Ava gives me a shrewd look, and I'm sure she's read between the lines. I might understand her, but she understands me too.

She doesn't press, though, she just takes the food and lets me snuggle down next to her. "I have a whole lineup planned."

"Oh?"

I grin down at her. "Now, I could have asked you what you like to watch, but, I think it's more fun if I guess."

"Okay." Ava laughs. "Go ahead, then, what's up first?"

I use the remote to get the movie started, and Ava's eyes go round and wide when the Disney animated *101 Dalmatians* starts playing.

"How'd you know?" she looks over at me. "Who told you?"

"Well, I wasn't sure how much you liked it, but I figured you must have a little bit, since you love dogs so much."

"This was my favorite when I was little. I watched it so many times, I practically had it memorized. I can probably still quote scenes from it." Ava smiles at the screen. "I used to do the whole bit with Lucky when I was cold." She imitates Lucy's voice. "My ears are froze, and my nose is froze, and my toes are froze!"

I grin down at her. "You are so fucking adorable, did you know that?"

Ava blushes and ducks her head down, but I can tell from her sweet scent how pleased she is. "You're not too bad yourself."

I put my arm around her shoulders as the movie starts. "What was your favorite?" she asks. "Growing up?"

"Peter Pan. I really liked Wendy. Not that I had a crush on her, that was Tinkerbell. But I liked how she became okay with growing up at the end and she realized... how it was all about balance."

"You've always been very mature, haven't you?" Ava asks. "Very observant."

"I suppose so. Although mostly I think it translates to 'nerdy.' Just ask the others."

Ava leans her head on my shoulder. "I like that."

We watch the movie, occasionally whispering through it to talk about things like Disney, and animals, and then when it finishes I start the next film on the list.

Ava laughs. "Okay, you're wrong about this one. I've never seen it."

"You've never seen *You've Got Mail?*"

"I'm not a huge fan of rom-coms."

"You'll like this one."

"Oh yeah?" Ava looks at me playfully. "Why is that?"

"Because it's about an Alpha and an Omega who fall for each other through a computer screen. No scents, no heats or ruts. Nothing. They fall for who the other one truly is. And when they meet in person, and don't know they're pen pals, they don't like each other. It's about two people coming together because they're right for each other. Not just because of biology."

Ava stares at me with a soft, awed expression on her face.

"What is it?" I whisper.

She smiles. "It's just... you get me. You really get me."

My chest fills with so much warmth that I feel like it might burst as I reach over to rest my hand lightly on her leg. "I try."

# Chapter 25

## *Ava*

I squirm a little on the comfy, padded seat, feeling like a kid who can't stay still, intensely aware of the warmth of Caleb's hand on my thigh.

The best and worst part of my growing connection with this Alpha pack is how much I crave them—and how *constant* that craving is. I don't think there's been a single moment since I came into this house when I haven't been aroused at some level.

And being in this small dark room with Caleb, laughing with him and learning more about him, has only fanned the ever-present flame of desire that sits low in my belly.

We lapse into silence as the movie continues to play, and I squeeze my thighs together a little, trying to relieve the ache between them. I have some vague notion that I'm being subtle, but that thought gets blown to bits when Caleb starts to purr beside me, a deep vibration in his chest that's matched by a surge of his chocolate, hazelnut, and caramel scent in the air.

*Oh god. He definitely knows.*

Since the jig is most definitely up, I stop trying to hide what I'm doing, reaching down between my legs to slide my fingers over my clit. The rush of relief and pleasure is instantaneous, but before I can repeat the motion, Caleb's hand leaves my leg so that his long, masculine fingers can wrap around my wrist.

I glance over at him, a guilty flush rising in my cheeks—but he's smiling at me, clearly not upset.

"That's my job," he tells me, his voice hushed as the characters on the screen continue to talk. "There are four Alphas in this house whose only goal is to take care of you, sweetheart. Whenever you need it. *However* you need it."

He releases my wrist as he finishes speaking, then slips his hand between my legs to replace mine. His fingers move confidently as he finds my clit through the fabric of my pants, and I moan, opening my legs wider to give him room to maneuver.

Even though this is a private movie theatre inside their house, it feels illicit and thrilling to be doing this here and now. Caleb and I both keep our eyes on the screen in front of us, but I don't think either of us are really paying attention to it anymore —at least, I know I'm not. All I can focus on is the delicious pressure on my clit and the way Caleb's scent fills my nostrils every time I suck in a deep breath.

"I can feel how wet you are," he whispers. It's barely audible over the sounds of the movie, but it makes me shiver anyway. He sounds so hungry, as if just knowing that I'm soaked has him turned on beyond belief.

"I am," I whimper, undulating my hips against his hand. "I can't help it. Oh god, Caleb."

His fingers pull away from my clit, but only long enough for his hand to snake down beneath the waistband of my pants. With nothing between us, I'm acutely aware of the warmth of his skin as his fingers find my clit again. I'm so wet that he doesn't even have to slide them inside me to coat them. They glide easily over my slippery flesh, and with each circle, he increases the pressure and speed.

My hands clench around the armrests of my chair, my thigh muscles tensing as the pleasure inside me breaks with the suddenness of a rubber band snapping. My mouth drops open on a breathy moan as I ride it out, shuddering and shaking through my climax.

I'm panting in the aftermath, and Caleb slowly drags his fingers away from my clit.

"I need to taste you," he groans. "You smell so sweet."

He withdraws his hand from my pants, and I can't help but turn toward him to watch as he raises his fingers to his lips. He sticks them in his mouth and sucks on them, and my whole body reacts to the sight—not just the way his cheeks hollow around his fingers, but the way his bright blue eyes gleam with lust as he samples my arousal.

Before I know what I'm doing, I'm crawling out of my chair and onto his, straddling his lap. He pulls his fingers from his mouth, and half a second later, our lips crash together.

I can taste myself on him.

It tastes fucking amazing, especially mixed with his heady, sweet Alpha scent, and I lick into his mouth, trying to get more of it. He kisses me back with the same fervor, and the two of us work together to tug off my shirt and get rid of my pants and panties.

It takes a bit of maneuvering, which is made a lot more difficult by the fact that neither of us seem willing to stop kissing long enough to undress. In between heated kisses, I drag his shirt over his head, and he undoes his pants and shoves them down.

His cock juts out from his body, and I can't resist teasing my fingers along his length, making him groan as he palms the back of my head to kiss me again.

"Put me inside you," he murmurs, nipping my lower lip.

"We'll make a mess," I warn. I'm already dripping. I can feel it sliding down my inner thighs, smearing over his lap where I'm straddling him. "Are you sure? These are nice seats."

He pulls back a little, his gentle features shifting into heated amusement. "Seats can be cleaned. And even if they couldn't, I wouldn't care at all if you make a mess. In fact, I hope you do."

As if to prove his point, he grabs my hips and moves me against him, making more of my arousal drip down between us. I decide to take him at his word—partly because I'm sure he and his pack can afford to replace or clean the chair, and partly because I need this too bad to stop, no matter what kind of mess we make.

I lift my hips a little, fisting his cock and guiding him to my entrance. But before I can sink down on him, Caleb stops me, his grip tightening on my hips.

"Wait," he whispers.

I freeze.

*Did he change his mind? Decide he'd rather not risk messing up the seat?*

As if in answer to my silent question, Caleb lifts me up. But instead of depositing me on my feet, he turns me around and then settles me back on his lap, my legs draped over his and my back resting against his chest.

His breath tickles my ear as he murmurs, "I don't want you to miss the movie. This is a good part."

I'm about to tell him that *this*—the feel of his cock pressed against my ass, hard and throbbing—is the good part, but before

I can, he shifts my position a little so that the head of his shaft finds my entrance.

He slides inside, using his hold on my hips to pull my body tight against his, and the only words I can manage to utter are, "Oh. *Ohhh.*"

"Fuck, you feel so good. Keep your eyes on the screen, sweetheart," Caleb instructs as his hands start to roam over me.

He plays with my breasts, tugging lightly at my nipples before massaging the soft mounds of flesh with his hands. He can't thrust very hard from this position, but he rolls his hips, sliding partway in and out, and the feel of it makes me melt against him even more.

The hand that was between my legs when we were sitting side by side finds my clit again, and the feel of him working the sensitive little nub while he's buried inside me is so much better than it was before. My inner walls clench around him as my body responds to his touch, and he groans, his fingers moving faster.

It's like a current flowing through both of us, each of us feeding the other's pleasure, and even though I'm looking toward the front of the little movie theater, I might as well be watching a blank screen.

My head rests on Caleb's shoulder, and the flickering light from the big screen on the wall in front of us plays over my pale skin as he fucks me. It feels incredible, slow and deep and perfect, and I can't help looking down to watch his cock slide in and out of my pussy. His shaft is thick and veiny, and it glistens with arousal every time he pulls out. I can feel my slick dripping down between us, and I know there will be a wet spot on the chair when we finish.

"So sweet," Caleb murmurs, dragging his nose along the

curve of my neck. "I never knew an Omega could smell this good until we met you. I can't get enough of you, sweetheart. I think about you all the fucking time."

I shiver against him, reaching up to loop one arm around the back of his neck. "I think about you too. I never knew Alphas could be like this. That you could make me feel... protected. Safe. Cherished."

I don't mention the other Alpha who once made me feel the opposite of all those things. I don't want to speak Marcus's name again, and I've already spent too much time today thinking about him. I can tell that Caleb picks up on the words I'm not saying, though, because the kisses he's pressing to my neck become even more gentle and tender, as if he's trying to make up for all the hurt I've ever endured in the past.

"You'll always be safe with us," he murmurs roughly. "I promise."

That declaration affects me almost as much as his fingers on my clit do. For maybe the first time in my life, I let go entirely, trusting that he'll take care of me. I didn't even realize that some part of me was still unconsciously trying to hold back, to keep some walls up around my heart, but as those walls drop, the pleasurable sensations rushing through me seem to multiply. It hits me like a tidal wave crashing down over a beach, and I arch against Caleb, one hand latching on to his wrist while the other slides through his thick blond hair.

"Oh fuck!" I whimper, the movie completely forgotten by now. "Fuck. Fuck. *Fuck*. I need your knot. Please, Caleb. Oh god, I need it. Fill me up."

He groans, his hands settling on my hips to give him more leverage as he works me up and down on his cock in time to his thrusts. "Goddamn, Ava. You ready for this?"

"Yes," I whine. "I want to feel you knot me. I need your cum inside me. I want all of it."

I'm not the only one shaking from the intensity of the need and pleasure I'm feeling. Caleb's body shudders beneath mine, and when the knot at the base of his cock starts to swell, I know what to expect this time. Not only that, but my Omega instincts crave it even more strongly than before. When he brings me down to meet his next stroke, I slam myself onto his knot, letting out a keening wail as it lodges itself inside me, locking us together.

"*Fuck.*" His curse sounds like it's torn from somewhere deep inside him as he floods me with his release, making heat spread through my lower body. He pulses against me, like he's still trying to thrust a little but can't because of his knot, and his fingers keep playing with my clit, sending me hurtling into another climax.

This time, I turn my head in time to bury my face in his neck as I come, muffling my whimpers and moans against his deliciously warm skin.

"That... that was..."

I can't get my mouth to work. Or at least, I can't get it to form full sentences, so I give up on trying and just kiss his neck instead, letting his scent and taste overwhelm my senses.

"I hope you were going to say 'good.'" Caleb chuckles, his voice low and warm. "Because I've never felt anything so perfect."

"Perfect is a... good way to describe it," I pant quietly, still trying to get my breath back.

With his knot buried inside me, Caleb slows the movements of his fingers on my clit, but he doesn't stop altogether. It's not enough to push me toward another climax yet, but it keeps a soft hum of pleasure buzzing through my veins.

"I'm glad," he murmurs, his purr caressing my ears. "Because we'll be here for a little while, and I intend to make you come at least twice more while I've got you knotted. The movie may be done, but I'm not."

I laugh, looking up at the screen to realize that the credits are rolling. Somewhere in the middle of all of that, the movie ended, and I didn't even notice.

"That sounds good to me." I crane my neck to look up at him, clenching around his knot. "And I was thinking... maybe movie nights could become a regular thing. If you want."

Caleb beams at me, looking so pleased by my suggestion that it makes my heart race.

"I think that's a great idea," he murmurs, dropping his head to kiss me as his fingers start working me up toward my third orgasm of the night. "I'd love to."

I know there would be no chance of containing my smile, so I don't even try.

# Chapter 26

## *Ava*

It's a few days later that I overhear them arguing.

In my whole time here, I've never heard a disagreement between any of the pack. They tease each other, and I know that they have strong personalities and need to talk things through sometimes, but they never fight.

Except for now.

I'm not sure I'd call it a proper fight, but it's an argument for sure. I'm heading down the stairs and pause on the landing, not sure at first if I've heard correctly. Maybe someone was just watching television.

But then I hear more voices, and I know for sure it's them. Garrett is snarling something, too low for me to hear the words. Dante replied, his tone terse.

My stomach twists into a knot of concern and I head for the sound. As I get closer, I can smell the agitation in their scent. They're in the formal dining room, one I don't think they've been in before, at least not that I've seen. We all eat more informally at the table in the kitchen with the big bay window overlooking the front yard.

When I open the door, I see that they're really in the middle of it. I think Dante called them here to sit around the table in a more formal discussion, but that's done for. Now Ethan is pacing again and Garrett's up on his feet, hands in fists, and Dante's up too. Only Caleb is still seated.

"What's going on?"

They all go stiff and look over at me.

"Ava," Dante says. He sounds tired. "We... have something we need to tell you."

"Marcus is being a—" Garrett starts, but Caleb stomps on his foot.

"Marcus isn't letting things go," Dante explains, a growl lurking in his voice. "His rival company, Prodigy Corp, has just announced a new product."

"A smart watch for Omegas," Ethan says tensely.

I blink rapidly. "But... how?"

This can't be a coincidence that he's announcing the launch of the very same product that my Alphas have been working on all this time.

"He's trying to undercut us," Garrett says. "So that he ruins us. He wants to sabotage the company and release his product before ours."

"Because you haven't announced your product yet," I say, remembering what Caleb and Dante have told me about their research and how careful they want to be to make sure the product is the best it can be. "So how is he able to launch a copycat?"

"People talk. He's probably started digging stuff up on us starting the moment he left the shop so that he could find a way to attack us."

My eyes sting. I know my hormones are making me more

emotional, but I think this would move me to tears anyway. I'm so upset. "This is my fault. I'm so sorry."

All four of them look at me with alarm in their eyes.

"If Marcus wasn't trying to punish me, he never would have done this to you. He's attacking you to get at me. I'm so sorry, this is on me."

"No." Dante walks over to me and hugs me tightly. "This isn't on you at all. This is on him. And you're our Omega, remember?"

"If he attacks one of us, he attacks all of us," Ethan says. "That's how it works. We're here for you and we're not going to back down."

"But now your company could be in jeopardy."

"You didn't make him do this. And if Marcus wants a fight? We'll give him one."

"You're worth it," Caleb chimes in. "We won't let an asshole push us around, or let anyone abuse an Omega. But especially not *our* Omega. Not a member of our pack."

"He won't get away with this," Garrett adds. "Besides, he might not even be able to successfully release his product. He might be bluffing, or only be partway through the process and rushing it."

"A product like ours, we've kept it top secret," Ethan says, "but it's the kind of product that's been needed by the community for years. It's not impossible that someone else would have a similar idea. He's probably just modifying it into a watch to get at us."

"And even if he does actually have a product to release," Garrett continues, "we'll just have to make sure our product is better. More successful. First released doesn't equal best."

I know that he's right. I've seen it happen with products

myself. One person rushes something out, and it's incomplete. Or a product is released, and another company pays attention to the reviews, takes notes, and releases their own, better product based on that feedback and the other company's missteps.

But despite their reassurances, I can't adopt their confidence. I can't help but worry what Marcus's actions will do to the Alphas, and to their company. They worked so hard to build it from the ground up and to make it a success. To have Marcus do something that could tear it all down... and because of me...

It makes me feel like throwing up. I can't let them be hurt because of me. I can't.

I just wish I knew what to do to make it right.

# Chapter 27

## *Garrett*

I can't say that this isn't a problem. But I *can* say that we've had our problems before, and we've always gotten through them and come out on top.

And like hell am I going to let this be the one time it goes the other way.

It's not like we haven't weathered other storms before. My family being one of those storms. But it means more to me this time than it ever has before, because this time? It's my Omega at stake.

Ava isn't sure if she's our Omega yet or not. I respect that. My entire being wants to officially bond with her, to make her our Omega in every possible way. But this is her choice, and whether she chooses us or not, I'm going to do every damn thing I can to make sure that she's safe and taken care of.

That bastard's not going to get the best of any of us. And he certainly won't get Ava.

I work day and night on our project to make sure that it'll not only be better than Marcus's, but that it'll premiere first. I won't let him get one over on us in any way. I know that our company will find a way to bounce back no matter what, but will Ava's spirit be able to after something like this?

She needs a win against her ex. She needs to know that she's okay and safe now. And beating Marcus with this smart watch is the best way to do that.

Ava's quiet over the next few days while we work. I know that Caleb is with her a lot, the two of them just being quiet together, watching a movie or even just reading with her curled up at his side. Ethan takes her on walks, makes her laugh.

I focus on my work. Ava takes the rough edges of me and smooths them out. Whenever she's near, I feel something in my chest melting. I feel like I know where she is, always, even if I can't see her. She's a constant presence in the back of my mind.

Normally this might be a distraction, but instead, it's a way for me to focus. I never lose sight of what's important or why I'm doing this.

I'm working when Dante passes by. "You need to eat."

"I'm fine."

"When was the last time you slept?"

I pause just a little too long before answering. Even though I don't look up from the computer, I can feel his smirk. "That's what I thought. Go eat. There's food in the kitchen for you."

He'll just keep pestering me until I do it, and in the end, taking one slightly longer interruption to eat will be less frustrating than a bunch of little interruptions with Dante nagging me.

I get up and head into the kitchen. Sure enough, there's soup simmering on the stove, kept warm for me, and what looks like a panini in the oven for me.

Ava enters through the other door, and I glance over at her.

"You want something to eat?" I ask.

She smiles. "Yes, please."

She looks tired, and it immediately ignites my protective instincts—the impulse to care for her and make sure she's healthy and safe.

I pull the panini for me out of the oven but go to make a fresh one for her. Ava perches herself on the counter to watch. She's in a yellow sundress, one that shows off her legs and her shoulders, her breasts pushing up against the fabric.

She's fucking beautiful, and heat stirs in my gut the way it always does when I'm around her. I want to get my hands and mouth all over her, and help her relax and forget about Marcus in the most primal way possible.

I make myself focus on lunch first. Ava's gaze is heavy on me, and I can tell that she knows what I'm thinking about. She knows I'm turned on by her, that I want her. But we need to eat.

"You look tired," she says quietly as I finish the panini and give it to her. "Thank you."

"No problem. And I'm fine."

"You're the type to just keep bulldozing through everything, huh?" She smiles. "The kind of guy who never met a fight he couldn't win with a good old Alpha showdown."

"It's gotten me pretty far." I grab my own food, but I don't suggest we sit at the table. I step between her legs instead, the two of us up close together, her ankle hooked around my calf as we share bites.

She's such a darling little thing. I can't stop wanting to devour her. But I also want to take care of her, and taking care of her right now means eating and getting back to work.

"You're our priority." I say. "We're not going to stop until this is taken care of and you're safe. Don't think I haven't noticed you won't go anywhere outside alone."

Ava bites her lip and shrugs, flushing a little out of embarrassment. "I know it's silly. But I can't help how... paranoid I feel."

"Abuse does that to you. It's not a bad thing. You're not silly or paranoid. This jackass has given you every reason to feel afraid. But you won't have to be soon. We'll take care of him. Then you can go and do whatever you want to do with your life."

"Thank you." Ava puts her hand on my chest. "Really. I mean it."

It would be so fucking easy to pull her in and kiss her, grind against her, whisper in her ear and fuck her right here on the counter until she's stuffed full of my knot and coming with my name on her lips.

I need a goddamn distraction. "And we mean it when we say that you shouldn't worry about us. We're happy to take care of you and look after you. It's what any Alpha should do for their Omega."

"Yes. I know that." She smiles softly. "But I also know how much this company means to you. Dante told me about how you all made it together and I would hate to be the reason that you lose something that's so important to all of you. I can't be the reason that you four are unhappy."

"I hate to break it to you, but you're our Omega," I point out gently.

Most of the time, I don't know how to be gentle. It doesn't come naturally to me. But when I'm faced with Ava, it's like all the roughness drains out of me, and I'm left with nothing but a desire to hold her close and keep her safe.

"We protect our Omega. Our company is important to us,

but it's just a company. We can rebuild or pivot. People are irreplaceable."

"But it's your dream. I wouldn't want to ruin that."

"Spoken like someone who has a dream of their own," I point out, still keeping my tone gentle.

She nods.

"What is it?"

Ava smiles shyly, like she's not used to talking about it. Maybe she's not. She seems to have not really had a lot of friends, pretending to be a Beta all this time, and it makes my heart ache for her. She deserves to have friends and people she can confide in.

"I'd like to open my own animal shelter. I want to provide a home for animals in need."

"That's great."

Ava sighs. "Yeah, but it's a money trap. I was working at this one shelter before, and I know it's a crappy place. The guy was pinching pennies constantly, and it wasn't good for the animals. But at the same time, I sort of get it. I don't agree with it, but I understand, because there's just no way to really make money running a shelter. He was trying to not go bankrupt."

"But you want to do it anyway."

She nods, her eyes lighting up. "I love animals. I always have. I couldn't really get close to people when I was pretending to be a Beta, but animals don't care about what I am. They didn't care if I was Beta or Omega. If they scented me, it didn't matter. They still treated me the same."

"That's great." I find myself smiling a little. "I gotta admit, I was always a fan of animals myself. They're not complicated like people are."

"You remind me a bit of a dog, sometimes," Ava admits.

"The loyalty, I mean."

"Oh, it wasn't all the growling?"

She laughs. "Maybe that too, a little bit. I just didn't mean... you aren't some dumb asshole, that's not what I meant."

"I know that's not what you meant." I wink at her. "So, an animal shelter, huh? Did you ever give any thought to how you might start your own shelter?"

"I figured I would have to get good at convincing rich people to donate money." Ava laughs. "But I just... there are so many animals that need a home. Our cities are filled with stray cat colonies and they're living barely five years, killing off local wildlife, hungry and sick..."

I love the way her eyes blaze when she's passionate about something. I try to keep my face serious while listening because I don't want her to think I'm not taking her seriously. Usually, this isn't a problem. Ethan has joked that I should be a bouncer at a club, or a bodyguard for a mafia don.

But around Ava? I can't seem to stop smiling. It's a challenge. And right now, in spite of myself, I know the corners of my mouth are curving upward fondly.

"And there are so many dogs that people buy from breeders and they could be adopting. But people think that adopted dogs, shelter dogs, are poorly behaved. And maybe they are, but it's just because the shelters don't have the resources to train them properly. So I'd want to have a place like that," Ava continues. "And..."

She pauses. "Why are you smiling like that?"

Caught. I shrug. "You're wonderful, that's all."

Ava blushes. "I mean. I'm in good company. You guys are making a watch that will help Omegas track their heats, things like that. That's amazing."

"Ava, you literally want to help animals. That's your dream in life. You want to give them homes and save them from the street. Maybe you should take a look in the mirror sometime."

She blushes harder. "I don't know that most Alphas would like it."

She puts her hand on my chest, but instead of it being a flirtatious move, she uses the gesture to push me back so that she can hop down from the counter and put her plate in the dishwasher.

"Well, we're not most Alphas."

"Are you sure?" She turns back to face me. "Running a shelter is a full-time job. More than that, actually. It's an overtime job. Think sixty to eighty hours a week, not forty."

"Sounds exhausting. You'll need a few Alphas to make sure you're being taken care of properly."

"Very smooth." She's smiling, but I can sense that there's still tension from the tightness in the corners of her mouth.

"Ava. The shelter will demand that much of your time at first. We understand that. When we first started our company, I don't think any of us slept for months. It was an around-the-clock project. Things like this are to begin with."

"But now you're at home, with me."

"Exactly." I step into her and take her hands, pulling her to me. "Ava, once you get it settled and you have managers and volunteers you can count on, you'll be able to live a balanced life. Just like we do now. And I know I speak for the others when I say we'll give you whatever financial support, whatever time, whatever—any kind of support you need. It's yours."

"Most Alphas don't like the idea of their Omega working outside of the home so much like that," she whispers.

"Traditionally, no," I agree. "But times are changing. And I don't care what most Alphas are like anyway. I care that I'm a good Alpha for *you* and what *you* need."

"You don't think it's silly?" She waves a hand in the air, not really able to look me in the eye. "The silly Omega trying to save all the animals? I sound like a Disney cliché."

"No, you don't." I gently catch her chin in my hand and tilt her face up so that she has to look at me. "Ava, it's not silly. It's admirable. Nobody will ever make a change in this world if we all decide it's too fucking silly to attempt. Maybe you can't save every animal, but you'll save a lot, and that's worth something."

She smiles at me, her eyes brimming with relief and gratitude. Fuck. She really is special.

It hits me that while I already thought of this woman as my Omega, it's only now that I'm realizing just how lucky I am to have her in my life. And how much I'll do to keep her safe and happy.

I pick her up and set her on the counter again, burying my nose into her neck so that I can nuzzle her, inhale that sweet scent. "Your big heart is one of the things I love most about you."

Ava's fingers run through my hair. I know she's not ready for the bite yet, but she lets me scent her, mixing our two scents together so that people can smell her on me, and me on her. A purr rumbles in the pit of my chest.

For a long moment, we stay just like that. Holding each other.

I already wanted to protect her, but now it's like a fire in my blood, even stronger than before. She will never have to fear Marcus again. The other Alphas and I will make sure of it.

Even though we haven't given her our claiming bites yet, I can feel it. This is our Omega. Ava is ours. And nobody is going to hurt her. Not on my watch.

# Chapter 28

## *Ava*

I can't seem to sit still.

And I can't seem to be calm.

All I can think about is how Marcus could hurt my Alphas. And then there's the fact that I'm calling them 'my Alphas.' I know that we haven't bonded yet, that we're still in the early stages of courtship, but no matter what happens, I don't want Marcus to hurt them.

I don't want him to hurt anyone, especially not because of me—and especially not these four men.

They took me in and kept me safe. They're courting me with so much gentle affection and care. They make me feel safe and valued.

These are good men, damn it, and they're trying to do good work with their company. Specifically, good work for Omegas. And this is what happens as a reward for all of their kindness and good deeds? An asshole abusive Alpha trying to punish them for it?

Marcus isn't even really trying to punish them so much as

he's trying to punish me. This is my fault. He wouldn't be coming after them so hard if it wasn't for me.

It's my fault, and I don't know what to do to fix it.

There doesn't seem to be anything *to* do. I'm completely helpless.

I'm desperate to feel control over something, and I can't seem to stop being irritated by everything. I'm hungry but I don't know what I want to eat. The bedroom isn't right, and nothing can satisfy me. The position of the pillows can't even seem to be comfortable.

Honestly, it feels kind of like I'm going insane. I keep reminding myself that this is because of all the hormonal changes in my body, that I'm just dealing with a lot right now. But even if I repeat that logical mantra all day long, it doesn't stop or change how I'm feeling.

I can't seem to get comfortable, no matter what I do. And maybe it is irrational, but at the same time, I feel like it's not. I have a reason to be upset and anxious with Marcus coming after my Alphas and me like this.

I'm still trying to rearrange my room when Dante enters.

"Hey, do you want some lunch?" His voice is soft, which for some reason only irks me more.

"No, I'm fine."

"When was the last time you ate?"

I roll my eyes as I fluff pillows. "Doesn't matter. I'm not hungry."

"Spoken by someone who hasn't eaten in far too long. Come on, I've made..."

"I'm not made of glass," I blurt, whirling around. "You can stop talking to me like that."

Dante blinks at me in surprise. His face flashes with

emotions that are going by too quickly for me to identify, and then he settles into a neutral expression.

"No, you're not made of glass, baby girl. As a matter of fact, you're one of the strongest and most courageous people I've ever met."

"You don't have to placate me," I mutter, rubbing at my chest. Something inside me just feels... *off*, and I can't seem to fix it. I feel like crying, and I don't even know why.

A crease appears between Dante's eyes, his dark gray eyes scanning me as if he's trying to figure out what to say that won't set me off. I wish I could tell him, but since I don't even know what's got me so agitated, I have no idea what would make the feeling go away.

"I don't need any food," I say tightly. "I'll come down later and eat something. You can just go."

I turn away before he can see the tears threatening in my eyes, holding myself stiffly. I can feel his presence lingering in the doorway for a long moment, and then his soft voice reaches my ears.

"All right. Come down whenever you're ready."

He leaves, closing the door behind him, and I press the heels of my hands to my eyes.

*God, Ava, what is wrong with you?*

I go back to trying to arrange my room in just the right way, moving pillows around, fluffing things out, fixing blankets—but nothing is working.

My chest aches, and I can feel myself spiraling into a full-blown breakdown, but I feel powerless to stop it. I don't understand this. I lived on my own for years before I met these alphas. I lived in a crappy little apartment without any of these expensive, luxurious amenities. So why am I falling to pieces over not being able to get this room set up right?

Part of me wants to open the door and call for Dante, to beg him to come back. But what could he do? He can't fix this. He can't fix *me*.

Maybe I'm broken. I spent so many years suppressing my Omega side, and maybe this is the result. Is something inside me permanently damaged from messing with my hormones for so long?

Feeling more and more miserable, I finally give up on trying to rearrange things for the millionth time and crawl into bed, slipping under the covers and pulling them over my head. I curl up into a ball, wrapping my arms around myself like I'm trying to keep myself from flying apart into pieces.

I don't know how much time passes. My mind is racing so fast that it's hard to gauge the actual passing of seconds and minutes, anxiety rising inside me as I imagine dozens of different scenarios in which everything falls apart. In which the Alphas realize I'm not a good enough Omega for them. In which I try to go back to my old life, only to realize it no longer fits me, like an old outfit I've outgrown.

What if I lose it all?

What would I do then?

A warm scent fills my nose, but I'm so lost in my thoughts that it takes me a moment to register it. Tears are falling down my cheeks, and as I sniffle, the scent grows stronger. It's a mix of dark chocolate, hazelnuts, caramel, and something I can't identify, but that somehow evokes a feeling of *understanding*.

"Oh, Ava." Caleb burrows under the covers with me and pulls me into his chest, curling around me and cuddling me like he's trying to shield me from the world.

I sob into his chest, something settling in my chest as I inhale his scent and feel his strong arms around me. I try to speak, to explain myself and how fucked up I feel, but I can't get the words out.

"Shh." Caleb rubs my back. "I've got you. I've got you. I know, sweetheart, I know."

I feel, when he says that, that he really does know. That he can see into my mind and knows exactly what I'm so upset about, what I'm so afraid of.

Caleb holds me in his lap and gently brings us up to sitting, letting the blankets fall away so I can see into the room again. Garrett is standing behind Ethan, who's crouched next to the mattress, both men staring at me in deep concern.

"Oh, gorgeous, it's okay." Ethan strokes my hair and leans in so that I can tuck my face into his neck and get his scent. "What happened?"

"Nothing." I whisper, then shake my head. "I snapped at Dante, and then he left, and I... I..."

I don't know how to explain that I'm worried I pushed him away and that he'll never want to come back. That I'm afraid he'll get sick of my wild mood swings and decide he and his pack would be better off without me.

"Shit," Ethan mutters. He cranes his neck to look at Garrett over my head. "Get Dante. Right now. She needs him."

Garrett turns on his heel and leaves immediately, the sound of his footsteps disappearing down the hall. Less than a minute later, he returns, and Dante is with him this time.

The second the pack leader gets a look at my face, his own features crumple into an expression of raw pain.

"Baby girl," he breathes. "I didn't know. Fuck, I should never have left you alone."

"It wasn't you. It was me." Tears blur my vision, and I give another little shake of my head. I'm the one who told him to leave. I'm the one who pushed him away.

*Fuck.* I've been alone so long, it's like I don't know how to be any other way. Is it too late for me to learn to let people in? To trust?

A little sob spills from my lips at the thought, and Dante winces at the sound.

"Fix it," Garrett tells Dante quietly, so low that I don't think he means for me to hear.

Determination fills Dante's face, and he steps past Garrett and comes over to me.

"Ava..."

His voice is warm and concerned, and he sits on the bed next to Caleb, who transfers me to him. Dante pulls me in, tucking my face into his neck so that I can scent him and smell for myself how much like *home* he is. I can't detect any trace of anger or negative emotion in his scent. Just concern.

"It's not your fault, baby girl," he whispers.

"Yes, it is," I insist through my tears. "I'm the one who was being so unreasonable. Why did I tell you to go when I just wanted you to stay? When I just needed... needed..."

"Because you were scared." He purrs, rocking me slightly. "And sometimes we don't ask for what we need when we're scared. I meant what I said before. You *are* strong, Ava. I hope you know that none of us ever doubt that. But you had to be so strong all by yourself for so long—and you don't have to do that anymore. It's okay to ask for help when you need it."

Dante keeps purring and stroking my hair, and I slowly melt against his body, letting him take all my weight. Giving myself over to the reassuring feeling of being held in his arms.

"Thank you," I whisper. "I'm sorry if I'm a lot to handle sometimes. I'm still learning how to... how to do all of this. Sometimes I get scared of how much I need you all. Not because it feels bad to lean on you, but because it makes me scared that I wouldn't know how to function without you if I lost you."

"You won't lose us," he says gruffly. "Ever. There's nothing you could do to make us want you less. I promise you that."

His voice rumbles in his chest, vibrating through me, and I wipe at my eyes as the messy knot of emotions in my chest slowly begins to untangle.

"We just want to do what's right for you," Ethan adds quietly. "This is our first time taking care of an Omega, so there might be a learning curve as we figure out what you need."

"But never think that we don't want you," Dante murmurs. "We always want you. All we want is to be near you."

Now that they're all around me, Dante's scent the strongest, I can feel that sensation of *safety* and *home* settling into my bones again. My wildly swinging emotions feel more settled, and it's easier to see that all of my fears were based on my emotions, the rollercoaster that's in my head right now, not reality.

None of them say anything more, the other three sitting close around us while Dante purrs and rocks me. My tears slowly die away and my breathing evens out as time passes, and I continue to be held. None of them complain or say anything. They just keep holding me and keeping me safe.

My hand presses lightly against Dante's chest, his heartbeat a heavy thud beneath my palm. As I listen to it, I realize that even though it's terrifying to allow these Alphas to see so much of me, to allow them past the defenses I've kept up for years, there's something amazing about it too.

If I give them my heart, I'll be giving them the power to hurt me. But I'll also be giving them the chance to love me in a way I've never been loved before in my life.

And as scary as it is, I think I want to take that risk.

# Chapter 29

## *Ava*

The next morning, I come down to breakfast and find Dante cooking breakfast in a nice suit. The other Alphas are all dressed in their usual work-from-home attire, which consists of slightly more casual business wear.

"What's the occasion?" I ask, my brows pulling together.

"I'm going into the office today." Dante smiles at me and prepares me a plate. "I thought you might like to come with me."

The idea of getting out of the house is nice, and I want to stay close to Dante after yesterday. I want to stay close to all four men if possible, but Dante is the one I felt the most unstable with yesterday, even though things are better now.

"That sounds great." I take the plate from him. "I'll just get changed after breakfast."

"I think you look just fine now," Ethan says flirtatiously, winking at me from the table.

I'm wearing an oversized shirt that Caleb gave me, and the boxers he gave me when I was first here, since after yesterday I hadn't wanted to smell anything except them. "Yes, I'm sure that would be a hoot at the office."

"It would be an event, that's for sure," Garrett mutters.

I grin at him and devour my breakfast. I didn't eat anything for most of yesterday and now I feel starving, and Dante is quick to pile my plate up with a second helping.

The food is delicious, as always, and I feel like I'm going to burst by the time I finish my third helping, but I know what I'm eating is nothing compared to what the men wolf down as Alphas.

"You need a lot of carbs," Caleb explained to me at one point, when I expressed feeling self-conscious and confused about just how much food I've been eating, far more than usual. "When your heat hits, you'll be burning a fuck-ton of carbs during the sex, and your body will want it so badly it'll be hard to convince you to take a break to eat. So your body wants you to load up on the front end so you don't die or pass out from hunger."

It's times like these when I understand why Omegas traditionally live with Alpha packs. If we didn't have multiple people taking care of us, feeding us beforehand, fucking us during, keeping us safe, how would we as Omegas have survived long enough to create civilization?

When I finish eating, I head upstairs to get changed into something cute. I want to show myself off a little for Dante, and I also want to look nice for being in the office.

This is the first time I'm going to meet anyone who's important to Dante and the pack. Their company is the most important thing to them and they care about their employees. I want to make a good impression.

There are plenty of cute clothes for me to choose from, but I settle on a soft pink skirt and a cream blouse to go with it, with some pink heels. Nothing too crazy, just an inch and a half, so I look a little sophisticated without looking like some kind of sugar baby.

I do my hair and put on a bit of light makeup, and when I'm satisfied with my appearance, I head downstairs. Dante is standing by the door, and I can tell the moment he sees me, because his honey and bourbon scent turns rich and hungry. When I get closer, I see his eyes are dark, the gray of his irises almost swallowed by the black.

"You look good," he says quietly.

"Thank you." I do a little twirl, grinning.

Dante's nostrils flare. "We should get going."

I want to tease him a bit more and see how long he can control himself, but I don't want to actually distract him from necessary work.

Now that Marcus is trying to get at us by releasing an identical product ahead of Dante's company, I don't think they can afford to be distracted.

When my heat finally arrives, they'll have to drop everything for a few days, so I know it's important for them to get as much done before that as possible. If my flirting keeps Dante from focusing, and they fail in their product launch as a result, I'll never forgive myself.

Dante offers me his arm and I take it, smiling as I press against his side. Having his scent around me, knowing that I make him happy and proud, feels like the best thing I could ever hope for.

We're touching in some small way for the entire drive over. Nothing crazy, but Dante has his hand on my thigh, and I have my hand over his. Just a constant place of connection. It helps me to feel grounded.

"I think I've learned my lesson about keeping myself locked away from you all," I admit quietly as we drive over to the office.

"Oh?" Dante's voice is gentle, not smug or amused.

"I feel so much better being close to at least one of you. The moment you touch me it all feels better." I pause. "I'm surprised that it's not scaring me."

"Well... I don't know what it's like to be an Omega. But I know how scared I got when I realized I wanted to make a proper pack with the other three."

It's hard to imagine the confident Dante being nervous about anything, never mind *scared*. Even when he was up against Marcus in the store, he wasn't scared. He was upset because he was angry on my behalf. I was the one who was scared.

"It's scary when you think that you want someone to be in your life forever and you want to make a commitment to them. Whether that's a business partner, or a spouse, or even wanting a child... you're not going to be the same person anymore, by committing to them."

"Once you do that, someone has the power to hurt you," I admit.

Dante nods. "And I can't say that it wasn't scary at first, agreeing to move in together. To being not just business partners but a *pack*. Discussing getting an Omega, sharing our secrets, opening up. It was a lot."

"And did you ever stop being scared?"

Dante nods. "I don't know when it was. There was just one day when I woke up, and I realized that I wasn't worried anymore about one of them saying he couldn't do this, or one of them taking the money and running. I actually trusted them and felt safe with them."

"Isn't it scary how not scared you are?"

"Sometimes, yes, but I think that's just how it is with every relationship. That moment when you realize that you're feeling safe and okay? That's a good thing. Relationships are supposed to make you feel better. If we make you feel better, then we're doing something right. That's not supposed to be scary."

I nod. It reassures me, to know that this is natural. That whether I originally looked for it or not, my Omega experience is turning out okay.

We get to the office that houses the company, and park in Dante's designated spot. My stomach twists and it hits me like a punch to the gut that Dante and the other three *own* this place.

It's kind of how I felt when Ethan took me home and I saw the mansion for the first time, as Dante takes me up to the offices.

My four Alphas are rich and powerful. I've become used to just thinking of them as the sweet men who take care of me. But they're more than just good men. They're powerful men. They have a high social status.

As we walk in and all eyes turn to us, my heart races, and I find myself hoping that I'll live up to everyone's expectations of me.

I'm sure that Dante's employees won't be surprised if he has an Omega mate. They're probably wondering why he hasn't found one already, as handsome and popular as he is. But as everyone waves to Dante and greets him enthusiastically, clearly happy to see him, I worry that I'm not going to measure up.

They must want their beloved boss to have someone sophisticated and wonderful. It's clear, as Dante speaks to everyone, that he's liked and admired. More than any other boss or company owner I've met.

The fear sinks into my stomach that I won't be everything they want for Dante.

But then Dante puts his arm around me and nuzzles into my neck, scenting me. "And this is Ava," he says proudly to one of the IT guys, the floor manager, and a receptionist.

All three people look at me, and I know they can smell me. In fact, they can probably smell that I'm near my heat. But I don't mind as much now, because Dante's made it clear that I'm his, and that he's happy to have me here.

I smile and hold out my hand. "It's so nice to meet you all. Dante's been telling me all about the company and how much it means to him."

"It's a pleasure to work for him," the IT guy says. "And it's great to meet you."

"We knew something was going on when Dante and the others were working from home all of a sudden," the receptionist gushes, sounding excited. "But an Omega! That's so great! Congratulations."

My face flushes hot. "Well, we're... we're not mated just yet."

I feel like crap the moment I say it, because I worry that makes it sound like I'm denying my connection with Dante, when I just don't want anyone to have a false impression.

"We've only just started courting," Dante says. "We're trying to do the steps in the right order. Call me old-fashioned."

"I'm sure the next step is coming up soon," the floor manager says, winking.

I struggle not to glare at him. I'm sure they can all tell my heat's coming up but I'm still embarrassed to have it mentioned.

"Yes." Dante squeezes me. "I've got to go and check on some things in my office, but I'm glad everyone's getting to meet Ava."

Everyone does, in fact, seem happy to see me. "I didn't think they'd be so welcoming," I admit as we make our way through the office. I'm still tucked under Dante's arm, and he squeezes me gently.

I can smell how proud of me he is, how pleased he is to show me off. It makes me happy, and I hope that he can tell how pleased I am to be shown off like this.

"Everyone needs to know that you're my Omega," Dante murmurs. "I'm going to show you off to everybody."

Back in the old days, Omegas that were courted by an Alpha or Alpha pack would be shown off to the various members of the Alpha's society like their family and friends. It was a big deal, and kind of like a coming out party for debutantes, or the way women in Regency periods were presented in court when they were ready to get married.

Now, it's a lot more informal. But it's still important that as the Omega, I'm introduced to all the people in the lives of my pack who are important to my Alphas.

I'd introduce the men to my friends and family too, except I don't really have any. I haven't seen my parents in a decade, and I don't want to, and I'm not sure what to do about my former coworkers.

Dante shows me around the building. "The other three and I have offices on the top floor, but we like to wander around the other departments to make sure that we're available to everyone."

"Sure it's not your way of micromanaging?" I tease him, leaning into his side.

"Hey, I'm not a micromanager. That's Caleb." Dante smirks

at me. "In all seriousness, Caleb spends a lot of time in the tech area with Ethan, since that's their specialty. I can show you if you want."

"I'd love that, actually." I'm not sure how well I'll understand everything, but I want to see all the aspects of the business.

"We try to keep our team small."

"You mean, you four workaholics would do all the work yourselves if you could."

"Maybe." Dante grins. "But that's part of why we're glad you're here. It means that we can have something in our lives that isn't work."

I understand what he means. Dante knows every inch of this office, knows the name of every employee, and that's fantastic. But everyone's also surprised that he and the others haven't been in the office, and I know a thing or two about flinging yourself into your work.

"It's almost like I make you happy," I tease him, not realizing how it sounds until the words are flying out of my mouth.

"You do," Dante says seriously. "You make me very happy. For most of my adult life, our work with this company, building it up, has been the most important thing to us. But now that's changing, and I think that's a good thing."

I don't know what to say to that, so I just nuzzle into him instead.

At the tech section, I do get to see some of the prototypes for the watch and try them on. "Are they comfortable?" Dante asks.

I nod, turning my wrist this way and that. I'm still worried about Marcus, but I'm feeling better as I try on this watch. It's comfortable, smooth, and has a pretty design in lots of different colors for people to choose from.

"This will change so many lives," I murmur.

I'm used to how wonderful my Alphas are, that it kind of... slips my mind, just how much they're doing for Omegas. And it's not because they met me. This isn't just for me. That's just the kind of people they are.

Dante grins at me. "That's the plan."

Dante leads me to his office, a huge room that has large glass windows with remote-control shades that he presses a button to lower.

"Usually I like to keep the windows open," he says, closing the door behind him. "I want people to feel like I'm approach-able and like they can talk to me if there's a problem. I want them to easily see if I'm busy and in a meeting, or if I'm avail-able to chat about something."

I nod, but for some reason, I can't hear his voice very well. It sounds almost... muffled? That can't be right.

Come to think of it I couldn't really hear the other voices before as well as usual either. I kind of zoned out during the conversation. I didn't think about it, figuring it was just my nerves.

Except now, Dante's voice sounds muffled. I feel like I'm struggling to hear him.

My heart is pounding in my ears, and my body feels hot all over. Not just hot either. It feels... aching. *Empty.*

My breaths come in rapidly and I stumble forward to brace my hands on the desk. "Dante."

The word comes out as a moan.

I look at him, and all I can think, all I can possibly want, is Dante's Alpha knot.

"Please," I manage to get out. It's a whimper.

Dante grabs me to keep me from sinking to the floor. "Ava. Baby girl, you're... you're perfuming all over the place. *Fuck.*"

On that last word, his voice drops down into an Alpha growl. I whimper again, my panties immediately ruined with my slick as I shiver with heat.

I'm glad that he closed the door to his office, because there's no way that anyone would be able to avoid smelling me otherwise. This is far worse than the club, I can already tell.

"My heat," I blurt out in realization, the last word turning into a moan. "My heat has started."

It's here, for real this time. There's no way to stop it or get control of myself.

And we're in Dante's office.

# Chapter 30

## *Dante*

Ava lets out another plaintive moan, and my Alpha instincts go into overdrive.

She's in heat.

*Full* heat.

And it's clearly taking her body by storm. She's perfuming so strongly that my cock is instantly rock hard, straining against my pants. My pulse races, and I feel like I'm going mad as the beautiful Omega before me mewls softly.

She steps closer, rubbing her body against mine like she's trying to bathe in my scent. Like she's trying to mark herself with my essence.

"Please," she whispers, wrapping her arms around me and nearly climbing my body as she grinds against me. "It's too much, I can't take it. I need you, Dante. I need your cock. I need your knot."

I clench my jaw, my chest heaving as more of her sweet scent floods my nostrils. I'm on the verge of losing all control and going into a rut right here in my office, but I'm trying to hold myself back. I need to get Ava home, so that she can have her nest and the other three Alphas in my pack. She'll need that safety and security as her heat goes on, and she'll need all four of us to see to her needs during the height of it.

"I know, baby girl," I whisper roughly, threading my fingers through the hair at the back of her head and grazing my cheek against hers, letting her feel the slight rasp of my stubble. "I'll take you home, and my pack and I will take care of you. You just need to hold on, okay?"

I start walking toward the door as I speak, prepared to carry her out of the building. I'm not sure she's capable of walking on her own at this point, too lost in the torrent of sensations and emotions brought on by her heat. But as I open my office door to leave, Ava reaches out with one hand to grip the doorframe, clinging to it even as she keeps her other arm wrapped around my shoulders.

"No!" Her voice is high and desperate. "No, I can't wait. I can't. It *hurts*, Dante. It hurts so much. Please."

My heart cracks open at the pain and pleading in her voice. I already hurt her once without meaning to, making her feel neglected and abandoned when I was trying to give her space. That's what led to me asking her to accompany me to the office today. I want to show her how important she is to me, how I always want her around... and how I'll always take care of her.

She's sobbing softly in my arms now, and a sudden certainty fills me.

I have to give my Omega what she needs.

Nothing—*nothing*—is more important than that.

With a low growl, I palm the back of her head and crush my lips to hers, kissing her fiercely and hungrily. Her hitched sob breaks off in a gasp, and her delicate tongue slides against mine as she kisses me back.

I can feel her body respond immediately, her scent changing in the air as her arousal grows, and I take a step backward so that we're fully inside my office again. She releases the door frame to wrap both of her arms around me, and I close the thick wooden door with a heavy thud.

As soon as the door closes, I press her up against it, pinning her against the smooth surface as I devour her mouth. Every instinct I was trying to suppress so that I could get her home comes roaring to the surface, wild and unrestrained. My cock is so hard it's almost painful, but I know it's only a fraction of the pain Ava must've been feeling as her body screams for something it's being denied.

*But I won't deny her.*

"Is this what you need, baby girl?" I ask, breaking our kiss and pulsing my hips against hers to let her feel how hard I am for her. "You need me to split you open with my cock right here in this office? To make you scream so loud that everyone in the building will know you're being fucked senseless?"

Her pupils dilate, making her soft brown eyes look hazy with lust, and she nods, licking her lips. "Yes. That's what I need. Fuck me. Make me scream."

The raw desire on her face is matched by something else that makes my heart clench—trust. She trusts me to take care of her in this moment, to give her what she needs. I feel as if I already let her down once, and I'll be damned if I ever do it again.

Keeping my gaze locked on her face, I slowly set her down. The second I start to move away from her, she lets out a soft wail of frustration, but I don't give her any time to doubt my intentions. I grip her hips and spin her around to face the door, purring loudly as her palms slap against the dark wood.

The sound goes straight to my cock, as does the way she immediately bends over, presenting her ass in that tight little skirt like the most perfect gift on earth.

"That's right," I murmur, feeling nearly delirious myself. "So fucking good for me."

My hands gather up the fabric of her skirt as I speak, bunching it up and dragging the hem upward. I shove the entire thing up to her waist, leaving her bare except for the pair of light blue cotton panties she's wearing.

"Fuck." I groan softly. "There are entire shops dedicated to expensive lingerie, but they're all wasting their time. Because nothing will ever be as sexy as this. You've soaked through your panties, baby girl, and it smells so fucking good."

With the way she's bent over, her cloth-covered pussy peeks out from between her legs, and I can see the way the fabric has turned darker where it's wet. Driven by an urge too powerful to resist, I drop to my knees behind her and drag my nose along the damp fabric, inhaling her scent until I'm lightheaded from it.

"Dante..."

She whimpers, but it's not the same kind of whimper I heard her make earlier. There's no pain in this sound, only desire.

"Say that again," I tell her. "I want to hear my name on your lips while you come on my face."

Her legs shake, and I can tell she's already close. Her body is so primed and ready for sex that I can practically taste her need on the air.

Hooking her panties with my fingers, I drag them down her legs until they fall to the floor between her high-heel clad feet.

"Step out. Then move your feet apart," I murmur. "Spread your legs for me."

She whimpers again, following my directions immediately, and my cock feels like it could punch a hole in my pants as I gaze at her wet, swollen folds.

"So pretty and pink," I growl. Gripping her ass cheeks to hold them apart, I drag my tongue up the line of her slit, a purr building deep in my chest. "So fucking delicious."

Now that I've had a taste of her, I can't resist taking more. She bumps her hips back against me in a silent plea, and I respond by lapping and sucking and nipping at her like a man possessed.

"Dante," she mewls. "Make me come. Right there, right there... oh god."

I stiffen my tongue and spear it into her, eating her out like she's my last meal as one hand slides around to find her clit. I circle it fast and hard, knowing she doesn't need me to drag this out any more than I already have. Her noises rise in pitch and volume, and each time she cries out my name, it goes straight to my cock, which is weeping precum that soaks into the front of my pants.

"Dante, Dante, Dante," she chants, her head dropping between her arms as she keeps her hands braced on the door. "Dante!"

The last word is a muffled scream, and her legs buckle as she comes on my tongue. I grab her hips quickly, never letting up with my mouth as I hold her up and work her through the orgasm. It passes through her in waves, and with each wave, a fresh surge of arousal gushes from her to coat my tongue. After a long moment, she finally goes still, the shuddering of her legs easing off a bit.

But the sated relaxation only lasts for a second.

She makes a small, pained sound in the back of her throat,

her dark hair shifting around her face as she shakes her head. "*More.*"

I'm not surprised that one orgasm was hardly enough to take the edge off. This isn't like the past several days when her heat was looming on the horizon. It's here, and it will take days of near constant sex for her to finally be satisfied.

Keeping one hand on her hip to make sure she stays steady and upright, I rise smoothly to my feet behind her. My other hand shakes slightly as I quickly work my button and fly open. My cock is so sensitive that I hiss out a breath as I wrap my hand around it, and I drag it through the wetness of her crease as my heart pounds heavily in my chest.

"Wait..." Ava sounds like it pains her to say the word, but she lifts her head and peers at me over her shoulder. Her cheeks are flushed, her gorgeous brown eyes glazed, and I can see the light redness of teeth marks where she had her bottom lip tucked between her teeth.

"What is it, baby girl?" I rasp. "What do you need?"

"You don't have to do this here," she whispers, her eyes shining. "This is your office. Everyone who works for you is out there. I tried to stay quiet before, but Dante... if you fuck me, I won't be able to be quiet. I know it."

A hungry smile tugs at my lips. "I don't give a fuck. Let every single person out there hear you scream, baby girl. Let them know what you sound like when your Alpha takes care of you."

Her jaw drops, heat flashing through her expression. To show her exactly how much I mean the words I just spoke, I press the tip of my cock inside her, and when she nods, I shove myself the rest of the way inside. Her body is tight and so

231

fucking wet, stretching around me and squeezing me in a way that makes my balls draw up tight.

"So good," I groan. "You feel so fucking good."

"So..." She arches her back a little, her fingers clawing at the wood of the door. "So do you."

The curve of her spine is devastatingly sexy, even hidden beneath the fabric of her top, and when I draw out and slam back inside, she arches even more.

"Yes!" she screams, and I *know* everyone outside my office heard that.

*Good.*

I meant it when I said I didn't give a fuck who hears us. Everyone in this office is well acquainted with what an Omega's heat cycle means, so they'll understand that she needed to be taken care of. And if I'm being honest with myself, the most primal part of my Alpha side loves the idea that everyone in this office will hear my beautiful, sweet Omega scream for me.

I fuck her harder and deeper, rutting into her body as I lose myself in the sheer perfection of the feeling. It's a good thing she's wearing heels, since it erases some of the difference in our heights, but I still have to bend my knees a little to get right where I need to be.

"So good," I repeat, my fingers buried in the soft flesh of her hips. "You're taking me so well. You're so perfect."

Her response isn't any kind of recognizable words, just a soft, needy sound that I know I'll never forget as long as I live. She clenches around my cock, her inner walls tightening like a vise, and my hips slap against her ass as I bare my teeth and keep fucking her.

"Oh god, I'm... I'm..."

She wails, throwing her head back as her orgasm hits. I let

go of her hip with one hand, reaching up to wrap her hair around my fist as I keep driving into her. Her mouth drops open as she screams again, and I can feel my knot swelling at the base of my cock.

I thrust into her one more time, forcing my knot as deep as it will go, and then empty myself inside her, my cock pulsing with each spurt of my release.

Ava is panting hard, and I wrap both of my arms around her waist, palming one breast and splaying the fingers of my other hand over her stomach as I drape my upper body over hers. We both breathe heavily into the sudden silence of the room, and although I know my knot will go down more quickly than usual in response to the pheromones she's emitting due to her heat, I almost wish we could stay like this forever. She'll need to be knotted again soon, though.

"I love hearing you scream my name, baby girl," I whisper, nuzzling at her hair. "Almost as much as I love feeling you take my knot."

She makes a soft, contented sound, turning her head so that her lips can find mine. We stay like that for a long while, kissing and breathing each other in as I whisper words of praise and adoration, telling her how perfect she is, how sweet she is, how grateful I am that she came into our lives.

After some time, my knot begins to deflate. When I finally pull out, a mixture of our cum slides down her leg, and we both groan at the separation. I gather up the mess with two fingers and shove it back inside her, then pull her panties back up her legs. Then I pull her skirt down and help her straighten before turning her around.

Her cheeks are an alluring rose pink, flushed from the exertion of the sex and the orgasms, and I press my lips to her forehead, eyes, nose, cheekbones, and jaw before finding her lips. She tilts her head up, and one of my hands slides into the hair at the back of her head as our kiss deepens. Then I pull back, resting my forehead against hers.

"Do you think you can make it home?" I ask quietly. "Garrett, Caleb, and Ethan will want to be with you for your heat. But if you can't make it, I'll have them come here. We can bring your whole nest here if you want. I'll kick everyone out of the office for a week if we have to. Whatever you need."

Her soft sigh brushes against my lips as she murmurs, "Take me home."

Hearing her refer to the huge house I've shared with my pack for the past several years as *home* makes something warm expand inside my chest. I kiss her again, then scoop her up in my arms before I can lose myself in the plush pillows of her lips. She squeaks and wraps her arms around my neck, and I chuckle as I open the door and stride from the room.

Ava buries her face against my chest as I carry her toward the elevator, probably not quite ready to meet everyone's gaze after they heard the sounds of her falling apart on my cock.

I hold her closer, possessiveness rising in me as I lift my chin and meet the eyes of those around us as a few people look up to see us pass. No one's gaze lingers on Ava. They can clearly read the protective aura radiating from me, and they know I don't want them ogling my Omega as she goes into heat.

The elevator ride down to the garage seems to take forever, and I can feel Ava starting to shift restlessly in my arms as we descend, her body already growing hungry for more. When we reach my car, I open the passenger door and settle her on the front seat, then reach over her to buckle her seatbelt. She lifts her head to smell my neck, and I clench my jaw at the feel of her scenting me like this.

"I'll get you home quick," I promise her. "Just hang tight, baby girl."

"Thank you," she whispers, and I can't resist kissing her hard before drawing back and closing the door.

I slide in behind the wheel, and as I pull out of the garage, Ava lets out a shuddery breath.

"I feel..." She drags her bottom lip between her teeth.

"What? What do you feel?"

"Empty. Too empty."

She squeezes her legs together as she speaks, as if she's trying to relieve the ache all on her own. I was already acutely aware of her scent—that delicious lilac, strawberry, and vanilla mixed with the sweetness of her arousal—but in the confined interior of the car, it's even more potent.

Keeping my eyes on the road, I grip the wheel with one hand and reach over to slip the other between her legs. Pushing the wet crotch of her panties aside, I slide two fingers into her, filling her up the best way I can right now.

"Ride my fingers," I tell her gruffly. "Get yourself off on my hand. It will help."

Ava nods, reaching down to wrap her delicate fingers around my forearm. She rolls her hips, fucking herself on my fingers, and I clench my jaw so hard that the muscles in my cheeks ache. She keeps going, using her grip on my forearm to guide my fingers in and out of her slick pussy, and I flick my thumb back and forth over her clit to increase the sensations.

For just a second, I chance taking my gaze off the road and flick a glance in her direction. Her eyes are closed, her mouth partway open, her head tipped back against the headrest as she works toward a climax.

"There you go. We're almost back," I tell her, my spent cock already hardening again. "Make yourself come."

Following her urging, I fuck her faster with my fingers, never letting up on her clit. She comes just as I'm making the turn onto our driveway to pull into the garage, and the sound she makes is so fucking sexy that I almost crash the car into the side of the house. I course correct and roll into the garage, then flick the ignition off and turn toward Ava.

She's shuddering softly with the last aftershocks of the climax, and I slide my fingers out of her and out from beneath her skirt. They're covered with my cum and her sweet arousal, and I hold them up to her lips.

"Taste yourself," I tell her. "Taste us. Can you taste how much I want you? How wild you make me?"

Her eyes pop open, and she lunges forward, wrapping her lips around my fingers and practically deep-throating them in her eagerness. I groan as she swirls her tongue around them, letting her lick away every drop before I finally slide them out from between her lips.

Then I'm out of the car in a heartbeat, striding around the front and wrenching her door open. I unbuckle her and pull her back into my arms, heat filling me at the way her arms and legs wrap around me. Her skirt rides up, and I know her soaked panties and ass must be on full display—but the only people who will be able to see her now are my fellow pack mates, so I don't care.

She presses open-mouthed kisses along my neck, making the urge to rut her rise up inside me all over again as I stalk into the house with the delicate Omega wrapped in my arms.

Garrett is in the living room, and he looks up as soon as we step inside. He's on his feet a half second later, his nostrils flaring as Ava's scent hits him full on.

"What—" He starts toward us.

"Ava's heat has started," I say curtly, knowing he won't need to hear more than that. "We need to get her to her nest."

He nods immediately, and we head for the stairs.

Caleb and Ethan are halfway down by the time we reach the bottom of the steps, probably drawn by Ava's scent, but they both reverse direction as soon as they see us, leading the way up to the second floor and toward Ava's room.

Our Omega needs us.

And now all four of us can take care of her.

# Chapter 31

## *Ava*

I'm barely aware that we're moving up the stairs and down the wide hallway toward my room. All I can really focus on is the way Dante's skin tastes beneath my lips. I keep darting my tongue out, practically licking him, and all around us, the scents of cinnamon and cookies, rich dark chocolate, caramel, apple cider, and a roaring fire fill the air.

It's intoxicating, and even though my body is already screaming for more, unsatisfied with the three orgasms I've already had since my heat set in at the NexusTech office, a sense of comfort and peace fills me too.

*I'm home.*

That thought still scares me a little, but only because of how *right* it feels. The little apartment I lived in for years was fine, but it was nothing compared to this house—and not because of the luxury that surrounds me here in the mansion with the four Alphas.

It's because of them.

Dante, Caleb, Ethan, and Garrett.

They fill this place up with their laughter and deep voices,

238

with their intoxicating scents, and with their unique personalities. They treat each other like family, and now that I'm here, they treat me like family too.

I've never had that before.

I've never been treasured and protected. I've never been desired so wholly, both physically and emotionally, and I'm overwhelmed by how much I desire them right back.

Dante strides into my bedroom, his large hands gripping my thighs to hold me up as I keep my arms and legs wrapped around him. The other three Alphas are right behind us, but when Dante starts to head toward my bed, I make a little noise of protest in my throat. He stops immediately, smoothing one hand down my messy hair.

"Where do you want to be, baby girl?"

I finally drag my lips away from his neck, glancing around the room. I've been arranging and re-arranging the space for days now, trying to get it just right, and I point to a corner where I've got several throw pillows stacked against each other. "Over there. But it needs more blankets. The fluffy ones. And more pillows."

"On it." Caleb nods, reading my mind the way he seems to do so often. He crosses the room and opens the closet, pulling out several more blankets and pillows that I hadn't decided what to do with yet.

He brings them over, laying out one of the pillows on the floor and setting the pillows down nearby as he jerks his chin at Ethan.

"There are a few more in the closet," he tells his pack mate. "And even more in that walk-in closet down the hall. I got extras and backups of everything in case Ava needed more."

I'm touched by how far out of his way he went to make sure

I'd have everything I would need, and I'm grateful when Ethan disappears into the hall to get more. I've never felt such a strong need for a nest before in my life. I want to be surrounded by soft, fluffy things, to feel perfectly safe and secure. The way they're all so attentive to my needs makes it hard to feel worried about what the rest of my heat will be like, but I know instinctively that having a nest where I feel safe will allow me to give myself over to the heat and let my Alphas take care of me without holding anything back.

As if my thoughts have reminded my body of everything it needs, a spasm runs through me, my core clenching tightly and my lower belly seeming to melt with heat.

"I need... one of you inside me," I gasp out, grinding against Dante until I'm practically dry humping his stomach.

"We've got you, baby girl," he purrs.

Garrett and Caleb lay down one more blanket, and as Ethan returns with more stuff from the closet, Dante sets me down, laying me back on the soft blanket. Ethan lowers the lights a little, and when he closes the door behind him, I swear their scents all spike in the air.

Dante leans back, kneeling between my legs with Garrett and Caleb on either side of him, and Ethan lays out the new blankets and pillows he got as Garrett reaches up with one hand and shucks his shirt, tugging it over his head. He hooks the backs of my knees and tugs me toward him, angling my body so that he's the one between my legs instead of Dante. My skirt is bunched up so high it's practically around my waist now, and Garrett's chest heaves as he looks down at the apex of my thighs.

"Are you this wet for us?" he groans. "Is that all your slick?"

"Some of it is Dante's cum," I whisper, reaching down to slide a finger into myself beneath my panties as if to be sure.

Garrett's gaze flicks to Dante, a slight bit of jealousy lighting in his eyes, but it snuffs itself out when Dante says, "She was in pain. Her heat hit her suddenly, and she needed a knot before things got any worse. So I took care of her, helping to take the edge off before I brought her back here."

"To be with all of you," I add, and when Garrett's eyes dart back to me, warmth reflects in their dark brown depths.

"I'm glad Dante was there to help," he murmurs, letting go of my knees and working quickly to get rid of his pants.

His cock springs free, and he fists himself as he watches Ethan join Dante and Caleb as they undress me. My soaked panties are the last thing to go, and instead of pulling them down my legs, Dante just rips them at the seam, tugging them away from my body and tossing them away.

"Me too," I say breathlessly. "But now it's your turn."

Reaching for Garrett, I pull him closer to me, feeling small and fragile beneath his massive body, but somehow also protected and shielded. The thick head of his cock brushes against my stomach, leaving a trail of precum as he shifts his hips downward and notches himself at my entrance.

"Gonna fill you up," he growls hoarsely. Then he pitches his hips forward, driving into me.

I gasp, every nerve ending in my body doing a joyful dance at the feeling of being stretched and claimed by this gruff, handsome, stoic Alpha. He draws back until just the tip is still buried inside me, then plunges in again, fucking me in such long strokes that I think the friction of it might drive me mad with pleasure.

Lifting my hips to meet each of his thrusts, I wrap my legs around him and press my heels into his firm, muscled ass, urging him to go harder and deeper. He does, his deep grunts filling the air as he bottoms out over and over. The other three Alphas surround me, their hands all over my body—massaging my breasts, toying with my nipples, even reaching down to play with my clit—until I feel like I'm being swept up in some sort of never-ending current of pleasure.

It doesn't take long for me to come, and when I do, I stiffen beneath Garrett, my legs clamping around his waist as my eyelids flutter. He leans down and kisses me, stilling inside me as his tongue delves into my mouth... but his knot doesn't swell. I make a noise into our kiss, and he draws back to gaze down at me, his dark eyes blazing.

"Not yet," he says soothingly. "You'll get a knot soon enough, little Omega. But first, all three of my pack mates are going to fuck you and make you come. All right?"

That sounds like heaven to me, so I nod emphatically, my head bobbing up and down as my entire body aches for more stimulation.

"Good girl." He gives me another kiss, running his fingers through my hair.

When he pulls out of me, he fists the base of his cock, which is glistening with slick and cum. I don't know where he found the self-control to keep from knotting me right this minute, but as much as I crave his knot, I'm glad he did. Because I need all of these men inside me. I need to feel their cocks stretching me, impaling me, *claiming* me. And even though Cary told me that Alphas' knots deflate faster during their Omega's heat, I'm not sure I could stand to wait that long to have each of them fuck me.

I need them all *now*.

"You look so beautiful like this," Caleb murmurs quietly, moving between my legs as Garrett shifts out of the way to make room for him. Sometime while I was preoccupied by Garrett, the other three men undressed, and they're all fully naked now too. "Your hair spread out around you, your nipples hard, and your breasts flushed. You look fucked out and perfect. I can't believe you're here with us right now. I'm so glad we get to be the ones to help you through your first heat."

His voice is full of warmth and conviction, and tears blur my vision for a second as a rush of emotions surges up to join the arousal coursing through me. My entire body is extra sensitive right now, and it feels as if my heart is too. I slide my fingers through the silky blond hair at the nape of his neck and pull him down to kiss me, and as our lips meet, his cock slides into my waiting core. I'm messy and so wet, and he groans at the feel of it as my body welcomes him inside.

"I want you to come again for me," he whispers in between kisses. "I know you need it. Chase what feels good, sweetheart. Take whatever you need."

He starts to fuck me in steady strokes, and I *do* take what I need. When licks of fire start to sweep through my veins, I press against his chest, urging him to roll over. He does, pulling me with him so that our positions are reversed. I end up on top of him, and his hands settle at my waist as I start to ride him. I've never particularly loved this position before, too self-conscious to really enjoy it.

But there's no room for embarrassment right now.

Not with him looking up at me with awe and desire in his eyes.

Not with the other three Alphas running their hands over my body, worshipping me like I'm everything they could ever want.

I let my head tip back and close my eyes, the muscles in my

thighs burning as I slide up and down Caleb's thick cock, fucking myself on it as hard and deep as I want. When fingertips graze over my clit, I don't even bother to look to see who it is, trusting all four of these Alphas to take care of me.

The fingers move faster, and someone wraps their lips around my nipple, teasing it with their teeth as I ride Caleb. The feel of it, combined with the hungry, appreciative groans that fill my ears, pushes me over the edge into another hard climax. I slam down on Caleb's cock one more time and stay there, rolling my hips in tiny movements as I grind against him, trying to bring him deeper... just a little deeper.

"Fuck." His voice is choked. "If you keep doing that, I'm going to knot you right now. I won't be able to wait."

The desperation and desire in his voice go right to my head. It takes all my self-control to stop, but I want what Garrett offered too much to keep going. I want all four of these Alphas to make me come on their cocks.

Still, I can't keep myself from squeezing around Caleb's shaft, sending another rush of pleasure tearing through me as the pulsing of my inner walls sets off another orgasm. Caleb sits up suddenly, closing his mouth around one of my breasts and sucking hard. It's intense and sharp, a sensation unlike anything I've ever felt before, and I can feel myself gush all over his cock as I shiver, my hands clutching at his head.

Bracing one hand on my back, he carefully reverses our positions again, depositing me on the soft blanket before slowly dragging his still-hard cock out of my sopping pussy.

Dante is next, and even though I still have remnants of his cum inside me and smeared all over my inner thighs, my body feels just as hungry for him now as it did back in his office.

"Thank you for getting me through the first part," I tell him softly. "And for bringing me back here afterward. I know you meant it when you said you'd bring my entire nest to your office, but this is better. So much better."

"I'm glad. I'd do anything for you, baby girl. I hope you know that. I never want you to think that I—"

He breaks off, clearing his throat, and I know he's thinking of how he made me cry the other day. Rationally, I know it was silly, but I couldn't help the way I felt in the moment. But more than the feeling of sadness and hurt, I remember the relief I felt when he came back and held me in his arms. I remember the way his voice rumbled in my ear as he spoke, and the way he cradled me against his body.

"I know," I whisper. "And I don't think that. I know I matter to you. And you... you matter to me too, Dante."

His steel-gray eyes seem to melt, his irises gleaming like molten metal, and he holds my gaze as he starts to fuck me for the second time today. It feels even more incredible than it did when he bent me over in his office, because this time, I'm surrounded by the three other Alphas who are slowly claiming my heart. They all watch me and Dante move together, reaching out to touch me or kiss me as I gasp and writhe beneath him.

When I come on his cock, Dante makes the sexiest groan, wrapping his arms around me and sitting back on his heels as he pulls me into his lap. One arm stays looped around me as the other catches my chin, and he watches every expression that passes over my face as I come, devouring them with his gaze.

"You're so fucking beautiful when you come," he murmurs gruffly. "I can't wait to watch you do that a hundred more times."

My stomach flutters at the implication in his words, and I gasp out, "A hundred times? That's a lot."

"That's not even scratching the surface, baby girl," he promises. "The things I want to do to you..."

He kisses me again, slow and deep and possessive, his scent and the other Alphas' scents wrapping around me like the most perfect blanket. When he finally lifts me off his cock and settles me back onto the blankets, I know I should be exhausted. I can feel the strain in my muscles from coming so hard so many times, but my Omega instincts aren't satisfied yet. They won't be satisfied until I get the one thing I still need.

*Ethan.*

The handsome, devilishly charming man flashes me a grin as he moves in to fill the space vacated by his pack mate when Dante steps aside. He slides his hands along my inner thighs, the warmth of his palms searing my skin and making my breath catch. He uses his thumbs to spread my pussy lips, opening me up to his greedy gaze as his tongue slides over his lower lip.

"I've been thinking about this for so long," he murmurs in a husky voice. "Since the night I first met you, honestly. But this? It's better than anything my imagination could ever have dreamed up. You're a fucking vision, gorgeous."

I whimper as his thumbs slide up to pinch my clit between them, and when a gush of slick seeps from me, Ethan groans. He drags his fingers through the wetness and uses it to coat his cock, stroking himself even as he lines up the smooth head with my entrance.

He presses inside, and I can't help but look down to watch as his shaft disappears inside me, my stomach fluttering at the sight. The vein on top of his cock pulses as he pulls out and glides back in with agonizing slowness, and I feel like I could come just from the sight of him fucking me like this.

"Watching you watch me fuck you is my new favorite thing in the entire world," he says, a chuckle in his voice. When my gaze darts back up to his face, he's grinning down at me. "Don't stop now, gorgeous. Keep watching your body take my cock. Keep watching the way you swallow me up."

Licking my lips, I let my gaze drift back down, and as he starts to move in a steady rhythm, I moan with every thrust. The other three Alphas are a constant presence around us, and at one point, as pleasure starts to build so high that it threatens to overwhelm me, I reach for all of them. Garrett and Dante grip my hands as Ethan holds my legs under the knees, keeping me steady and lifting my ass up to meet his thrusts. Caleb's hands are on my breasts, plucking at my nipples and rolling them between his fingers in a way that sends little darts of sensation shooting through me.

"Fuck yes," I whine. "Don't stop. Please, just, all of you... keep going. Don't let go. Don't stop. Don't—oh god!"

I break off with a sharp cry as another orgasm rips through me like a tornado, tearing me apart and putting me back together all in one fell swoop. I toss my head back and forth, my back arching as I clamp down around Ethan just in time to feel his knot swell. He thrusts hard and deep, burying it inside me, and our bodies lock together as he shouts out his own release, pumping me full of his cum.

"Fuck, Ava. Oh *fuck!*"

He's breathing just as hard as I am as he looks down at the place where his cock disappears inside my pussy, and he releases his hold on one of my legs to slide his fingers around my opening, grazing my clit and making me jump as pleasure spikes again.

"Holy shit, that's so incredible," he breathes. His eyes are dark as his gaze travels back up to my face. "Does that feel good?"

"So good," I murmur on a sigh. "I feel so full. I can feel your cum inside me, and it…"

I trail off, not sure how to describe or explain why the feel of this Alpha's cum coating my womb feels both erotic and comforting at the same time. Instead, I just reach down to tangle my fingers with his, guiding his fingertip back to my clit and using both of our hands to tip myself over into another orgasm. A full body shudder passes through me as I come for the… honestly, I've lost count of how many times it's been at this point.

Unlinking my fingers from Ethan's, I look at the three Alphas gathered around us. They all look like they're on the verge of exploding just from watching me climax, and I suddenly want to see that more than anything in the world.

"Come on me," I whisper. "While Ethan is knotted inside me. I want to be marked by all of you on the outside and the inside."

"Fucking hell."

Garrett's voice is like sandpaper, and his fist is already flying over his cock as he shuffles a little closer on his knees. Dante and Caleb follow his lead, moving toward me as they stroke themselves. My gaze darts back and forth, wanting to see everything, ravenous at the sight of these three powerful Alphas jerking off above me.

It's like a domino effect. Garrett comes first, white ropes of cum spilling over his fingers and splattering across my lower belly. Dante grunts and comes on my breasts, painting them with his release, and Caleb finishes on my upper chest and neck. Some of his cum lands on my lower lip, and I draw it into my mouth, sucking up the taste of him.

Ethan grins at me. Bracing one hand near my head, he leans over me and drags his other hand in a slow trail up my stomach, between my breasts, and along the line of my neck, gathering a mixture of his friends' cum on his fingers. When he reaches my mouth, he offers it to me, and all four of the men let out deep purrs of satisfaction as I wrap my lips around his thick fingers.

"Such a good girl," he whispers, adoration shining in his eyes. "Our perfect girl."

I smile, his words of praise making fuzzy warmth expand inside me. My limbs feel heavy, and for the first time since my heat struck, I actually feel mostly sated. Now that the desperate need to be knotted and claimed has been satisfied, exhaustion is creeping in, making my eyelids droop a little.

Ethan slips his finger from my mouth, his thumb dragging along my lower lip. With his knot still inside me, I know he won't be going anywhere, and the other three Alphas settle in around me, making it clear that they have no plans to leave my side either.

With that knowledge resting lightly in my chest, I let my eyes close all the way as I fall into a doze.

# Chapter 32

## *Ava*

I wake up several hours later, feeling wrung out like a rag.

It's not a bad worn out. But wow, I've never been this tired in my life before. I have no idea how long I've been asleep, but the light coming in through the windows and the shadows spilling across the floor tell me that it's been several hours.

All around me, the men are sprawled out like a bunch of puppies, dead to the world. I smile fondly, observing them for a moment. Watching how they sleep.

That was far more satisfying than I ever realized sex could be. My desperation was matched by their enthusiasm and skill, and I swore if my body wasn't so exhausted, I'd still be humming with pleasure.

Ethan's at my back, and when I roll over to check on him, I find myself nose-to-nose with him. Unlike the others, his green eyes are open.

He smiles at me, slow and sly. "How're you feeling?" he murmurs.

"Exhausted," I reply. "But... good. It's a good tired."

The arm he has draped over my waist allows him to press

his hand to my back and trace his fingers up and down my skin in nonsense patterns. It's soothing, and I let my eyes slip closed again, drifting.

"You should eat something," Ethan whispers, still keeping his voice low not to wake the others.

I don't want the others to wake up either. They gave it their all taking care of me. We had another round of sex, and I honestly lost track of how many orgasms I had. It was all just a blur of sex and skin.

It's amazing, but I'm sure it's tired them out. And it's only a matter of time until my body demands another knot and more orgasms. We have to take advantage of the break while it lasts and let them rest.

"Yeah," I agree quietly. I didn't notice it before, but now that Ethan's mentioned food, I feel starving. Like I haven't eaten in days.

This is why I was loading up on all those carbs the last couple weeks. I really did need them.

"I'll be right back," Ethan promises. He nuzzles into me, scenting me again and letting me scent him, as if he can read my mind and knows how important this is to me right now.

It's weird, in this heat haze, how much I instinctively know about myself. I know that right now, I'm content and happy, being touched by my Alphas and surrounded by the smell of them. But I'm also aware of how quickly that will morph into panic if I don't have their scents, or their touch. It's important to keep reaffirming that.

Ethan kisses me on the forehead and slips away, making no noise as he pads out of the room like a wolf on the prowl. I laugh a little realizing he didn't grab any clothes on his way out. It's not the most scandalous thing we've ever done, given all the crazy sex we just had, but it still amuses me anyway.

I cuddle back into the other three Alphas while I wait and ignore my rumbling stomach. They're heavy and warm, completely passed out, and I like watching how they breathe and sleep differently.

Caleb's curled up a bit, almost but not quite the fetal position, while Garrett is splayed out like a starfish, which is hilarious. Dante's on his back, hands resting lightly on his stomach, like he read somewhere that it's good for your back and trained himself into it. It wouldn't surprise me, honestly. It would fit him perfectly to do something like that.

I snuggle against them, letting myself drift in and out of a doze. A few moments later, I hear the door open softly. I sit up, still in the middle of a tangle of limbs, to see Ethan entering with a tray of food.

My mouth waters as the smells hit me. I hate to leave my puppy pile, but I also don't want to spill hot food on someone's skin or stain the sheets. Those are already on their way to being ruined anyway. No need to make it worse.

I climb carefully over the men to sit on the floor, on the deliciously soft rug that I picked out. Now that my heat is in full swing, all the little things that had me anxious and fretting about my room don't bother me anymore. In fact I feel pleased with myself, proud of my choices and my nest.

Ethan kneels and sets the tray down in my lap, then sits next to me, draping his arm over my shoulders. I'm practically drooling over the food.

Dante truly made a lot of food in advance for this, more food than I think we can actually eat during my heat, but I think he would rather be prepared than risk me being even the slightest bit hungry.

In front of me is delicious tomato bisque with rice, one of my favorite comfort foods growing up. I remember I told Dante about it when he was asking me what my favorite meals are.

"My parents worked multiple jobs," I tell him. "I usually had to fend for myself for meals. And it was easy to warm up a couple cans of Campbell's tomato soup and cook some rice in a steamer."

Ethan also took one of the pre-made sandwiches that Dante made, this one cheese, tomato, and bacon, and put it in the panini maker, and the freshly made sandwich makes my mouth water. The cheese is perfectly melty, the bread is crispy, and the bacon is sizzling.

I scarf down the food hungrily, struggling not to choke or burn my tongue as I eat.

Ethan watches me fondly, arching a brow when I take too big of a bite. "Careful there, gorgeous. You can slow down and enjoy it."

"I *am* enjoying it," I point out, and I'm not lying. It really does taste absolutely amazing. Dante's a fantastic cook and this truly does make me feel the way that I'd always hoped it would when I was a kid. I hadn't had parents to comfort me and make me food after the long cold walk home from school in winter, so I did it for myself.

"Dante said he made some of your favorites," Ethan says. "What makes this one of them?"

"You know how I said my parents weren't really... close with me?"

He nods.

"You know, growing up, people would say that was just how

Betas are. But I've met plenty of wonderful, nurturing Betas who love their kids. They aren't naturally distant." I sigh. "Is it mean of me to say that I think my parents were just... kind of assholes?"

Ethan claps a hand over his mouth to muffle his outburst of laughter. I can feel his body shake since he's pressed up against my side. "No, I think that's understandable."

"They weren't abusive," I add quickly. "They just weren't there. If I'd done sports, they never would've shown up to a game."

Ethan nods, understanding in his eyes.

"I had to fend for myself a lot," I say quietly. I continue to eat my food, and it continues to be delicious, but there's now a bit of a lump in my throat. "They never made meals, they were always working. I packed my own lunch for school, ate cereal every morning, and learned how to make myself dinner."

"Boxed mac n' cheese?"

"And Chef Boyardee," I add.

Ethan chuckles.

"I remember one time, it was snowing out, and I was sad having to come home to a cold, empty house. And my friend was excited because she knew when she got home, her dad would have made her tomato soup with rice, and a grilled cheese sandwich."

Ethan nods, and I shrug. "It's a simple meal for a parent to make. I think every family has their own version, some easy comfort meal for their kids on a cold day. But it stuck in my mind, because even if it wasn't a big deal to that dad... it was to me. The idea of someone loving you enough to make you a nice hot meal."

"Dante doesn't talk about it much," Ethan says. "You know

how he is. But I know he loves us, every time he cooks for us. Every morning I get downstairs and he's making breakfast. He packs us food. When we eat out or order delivery it's usually to give him a break."

That makes me chuckle. I can easily see how it would take some cajoling to get Dante to admit he needs a night off.

Then I sober up.

"Every time I made myself that meal," I whisper, "I was trying to comfort myself. Trying to love myself, because my parents didn't." I sigh. "Okay, maybe that's harsh. They took care of me financially. As best they could. I know they had to work so much to make ends meet. But even when they were around..."

"It was like they weren't there," Ethan finishes.

I nod.

Ethan leans back against the bed. "I get it. Kind of. My situation was a little different. I literally didn't have parents."

I inhale sharply. Ethan gives me a rueful smile, one corner of his mouth turning up. It's like a bittersweet version of his usual smirk. "Yeah. They died when I was a teenager. And I was on my own, pretty much. Bounced from place to place."

I take his hand and squeeze it, resting my head on his shoulder so that he can feel me.

"For a long time I craved a pack, so when I found these guys... I was ecstatic." Ethan shakes his head at himself. "I couldn't quite believe it was real. Actually having pack mates? People who would have my back no matter what? It felt like a miracle."

I smile fondly. Ethan sounds so happy and delighted with his pack, and I can't blame him. These four men make me happy too, happier than I could've ever imagined. But it's sweet and reassuring to see the wonder I feel reflected in Ethan's face.

"But even while I... I got confident in our pack, I didn't really expect us to find an Omega."

That surprises me. My eyebrows fly up. "But you're all amazing," I blurt out. "Why wouldn't any Omega want to be with you?"

Ethan, for the first time since I've met him, looks bashful. Bashful is more Caleb's realm, but Ethan's blushing and ducking his eyes down. It's adorable.

"Garrett told you about his family."

I nod.

"And, well, we've been so focused on the company. And it wasn't so much that we thought no Omega would want us. But... I think we wanted to meet an Omega the old-fashioned way. We didn't want to go to what felt like an auction. Like we were bidding on pieces of art."

Ethan smirks. "Although..." He tucks a lock of my hair behind my ear, his fingertips trailing down the curve of my jaw. "You are beautiful enough to be a piece of art."

I can feel my face heating up. "You're not so bad yourself."

He pulls away and gestures for me to finish eating. I do, knowing that I won't have much time left before the heat takes over again.

"I wanted an Omega so badly," Ethan admits, his voice serious in a way that he rarely gets. "I was scared of how much I wanted it, honestly. More than any of the others. And I worried that we'd never find someone who would be a match for us. The others worried about it too, I know, but I think they used to talk about it when I wasn't around so that they wouldn't upset me."

"I understand."

"They like to look out for me. Just like I want to look out for them."

I finish eating and set the tray aside. That food was amazing. I'm sure that everything else Dante's prepared ahead of time for me will be just as delicious. I feel so well cared-for in a way that I didn't think was possible even in my wildest dreams.

"I know what you mean." I gesture to the empty tray I just set aside. "I hope that I'll be able to take care of you four the way you're taking care of me."

Ethan kisses me gently. "I'm sure you will."

"And I hope you know... I'm not... *that* special..."

"Yes, you are." His voice is fierce. "Maybe your parents didn't make you feel that way, but that's their loss. We are lucky to have you, gorgeous. You're a wonderful Omega. You're the missing piece that I didn't even know we needed. I wanted an Omega. Of course I did. But I had no idea what you could bring to us, how you could complete us."

I nuzzle into him, lying back and pulling him down with me to lie beside me so that we can cuddle properly, our legs tangled together. My heart breaks to know that he lost his family so young, even as it rejoices that he found the other Alphas to make a new family with.

But I'm also grateful and blown away by how much he cares about me. I hadn't dreamed that we'd have so much in common when I first met him at the club. Even after he rescued me, Ethan gave me the impression of this confident, devil-may-care kind of man.

Even as I've gotten to know him better, I didn't know that out of all of them, he was the one who wanted an Omega the most.

I love that he's letting me see this vulnerable side of him.

That I'm really getting to know every part of him, and of the other three.

"For years I was hiding who I was," I whisper. "So I couldn't get close to anyone. I was too scared. I left my parents behind, but I didn't get a chance to replace them, to find that new family the way you did."

Tears spring into my eyes, and Ethan gently wipes them away. "Until now," I add.

And I mean it.

All of my fear is gone. There's nothing but trust and love. I feel so very loved. I didn't know it was possible to be like this, and for the first time, I'm grateful that everything happened the way it did. If fate hadn't played its tricks, I wouldn't have these wonderful Alphas becoming my new home.

Heat and warmth bloom in Ethan's eyes, and he kisses me. Desire blooms in my chest again, sliding down my spine and settling between my legs, and I smile against his lips as he seems to read my unspoken thoughts.

*I think we're done talking for now.*

# Chapter 33

## *Ava*

Ethan goes up onto one elbow, leaning over me as he keeps kissing me. I'm messy with cum and sweat and slick, and the entire room smells like sex, but he doesn't seem to mind any of that. Honestly, if the way he's purring is any indication, he likes it a lot.

So do I.

I never quite understood the nesting instinct that would occasionally rise up in me despite the black-market heat suppressors I took, but now I do. Because this room, with its dim lighting, fuzzy blankets and pillows, and hazy atmosphere of sex and desire, has created a perfect haven that nothing outside can penetrate. In here, nothing else matters but me and these four Alphas and the growing connection between us.

I was already starting to grow much closer to all of them, but here in this room, speaking in low voices in between rounds of sex, I feel like all of our facades are being stripped away. I'm seeing the truest and most real versions of them, and they're seeing the same in me.

And none of them are running.

259

When Ethan draws back to look at me, his green eyes lock with mine, and there's so much warmth and happiness in their depths that it makes my heart skip a beat.

I whimper, the spike in my emotions making the desire in my veins surge higher too, and he chuckles, dropping his head to kiss me again as his fingers trail down the front of my body. He finds my pussy and fucks me slowly and steadily with two fingers, working me up with slow deliberateness until I'm writhing and moaning into his mouth.

"Do you want to come on my fingers or my cock?" he murmurs against my lips.

"Both!" I gasp, clutching at his arm as I try to grind harder against his touch.

He laughs quietly, his toasted marshmallow and cinnamon scent surrounding me like a warm hug. "Good answer. I can do that."

I expect him to start fucking me faster with those long, talented fingers, but he keeps up the torturous pace, waiting until I'm mewling and writhing beneath him before he finally presses firmly on my clit with his thumb. This time, he doesn't tease me or drag it out, and my orgasm cracks through me like a bolt of lightning as the pad of his thumb slides over my sensitive bud.

I'm still shaking in the aftermath, the muscles of my inner thighs clenching as I squeeze my legs together, when Ethan grabs my hand and brings it to his cock, wrapping my fingers around his length. He's hard and hot against my palm, and I bite my bottom lip as he drags my hand up and down his length.

"You feel what you do to me?" he whispers roughly.

"But I've barely done anything."

"You exist. That's enough."

My gaze flies up to meet his, and I blink away the emotional tears that sting my eyes.

*Oh my god, these Alphas.* I don't know how they always know the right thing to say, how they've managed to work their way into my heart in such a short time, but I'm starting to realize that it doesn't matter. It doesn't matter if it's logical. It doesn't matter if I'm falling headfirst into something I never thought I wanted.

All that matters is the way I feel, and the way I can tell they feel.

Lifting my head a little, I find Ethan's mouth with mine, kissing him deeply. He settles between my legs, and I keep my fingers wrapped around his cock as I guide him to my entrance. We both sigh contentedly as he sinks inside me, and I'm grateful for the amount of slick my body has produced, because although I'm a little sore, it mostly just feels amazing to be filled up again.

"You feel so fucking incredible. So tight," Ethan groans. "Like you were made for me."

His hands burrow into the hair on either side of my head, and he cradles my jaw as he starts to move, dipping his head to sample my lips between thrusts. It's slow and easy at first, nowhere near as frantic and desperate as the first time he and his pack mates claimed me after Dante brought me home. But although the heat builds slowly, it's no less scorching, and after several minutes, I'm gasping with each deep thrust. His movements become sharper and harder, his hips snapping forward to bury his cock inside me over and over again as I rock beneath him.

My breasts bounce with each thrusts, and his gaze drops to them, his pupils expanding.

"So pretty," he murmurs. "God, you're addicting."

"She truly is."

The sleepy, raspy voice from beside us draws my attention, and I turn to look at Garrett, who's watching his pack mate fuck me with hooded eyes. My stomach clenches with a rush of need, and my pussy must tighten around Ethan's cock, because the man above me lets out a choked grunt.

"I love how turned on you get by all of us," he says, never breaking the pace of his strokes. "You want Garrett to watch me fuck you? Or do you want him to join us?"

One thing I've started to notice about all four of these Alphas is how often they follow my lead. Unlike Marcus, who was always forceful and demanding, these men ask me what I want all the time—and are usually more than happy to give it to me, whatever it may be.

And this time, there's not even a moment's hesitation before I answer.

"I want him to join us," I say, my voice coming out in choppy gasps as Ethan keeps fucking me. "I want you both inside me."

Ethan's hips stutter, and he bottoms out inside me and then goes still. "You mean... you want him in your mouth?"

I shake my head, squirming against Ethan to try to get more of that incredible friction I was feeling. "No."

"Then where, gorgeous? Use your words. I want to hear you say it, and I'm damn positive that Garrett wants to hear it."

"I want him in my ass," I whimper. "While you're in my pussy. I need both of you. I want you to knot me at the same time."

Garrett lets out a low, hungry purr that goes right to my clit. He curses under his breath, and I'm aware of him and Ethan exchanging a look above me. Then, in one smooth move, Ethan flips our positions, shifting onto his back and pulling me with him so that I'm on top.

"Relax on top of me," he commands, tugging me down so that my upper body is draped over his. He feels perfectly deep in this position, his cock throbbing inside me, and I shiver at the sensation. "There you go. Good girl. Garrett's gonna get you all ready and open you up."

As he speaks, Ethan grabs my hips, working me up and down gently on his shaft. At the same time, Garrett slides into position behind me. Large, calloused hands grip and massage my ass cheeks, and when he spreads them wide open, baring my back hole to his view, I mewl and grind harder against Ethan.

"You're so fucking wet already," Garrett growls. "You're a mess, little one. You've been dripping all over Ethan's cock, haven't you?"

I nod, burying my face against Ethan's chest, kissing and nipping at his firm pecs.

"But you could still be wetter," Garrett continues. "I'll help with that."

Before I can ask him what he means, I hear him spit. Something warm and wet lands right on my puckered hole, and I inhale sharply, my toes curling at the sensation. He spits again before releasing his grip on one of my ass cheeks to slide a finger inside me, and I'm practically crawling out of my skin from how good it feels.

"More," I plead as he starts to thrust his finger in and out. "I can take more. Two fingers. Three. Please!"

"So greedy," he chuckles. "Is it really my fingers that you want? Or is it my cock?"

But he does what I ask even as he teases me, sliding a second finger inside me and spreading them apart to stretch me out.

The feeling of fullness is so intense that it sends me crashing headlong into an orgasm I didn't even see coming.

"Fuck! Oh god!" I cry out raggedly.

Ethan fists my hair as I come, tilting his head down to kiss me, and Garrett fucks me through it, his breathing harsh behind me. When I finally go lax in the aftermath of the climax, he uses the opportunity to work a third finger inside me, making my ass burn from the intrusion.

"Too much?" he rasps.

"No!" I shake my head, my heart hammering hard in my chest. "Keep going."

He does, and I lose track of how much time passes as they work me into a state of bliss between them, Garrett's fingers in my ass and Ethan's cock in my pussy. When Garrett finally pulls out at some point, I make a frustrated sound, but he just leans down to press a kiss to my temple.

"Don't worry, little one," he promises in a low voice. "You won't be empty for long. I'm gonna give you my cock now, just like you want."

The smooth head of his dick presses against my back hole, and although I've never done this before, my body doesn't protest. He's clearly done a good job preparing me—although my body is so hungry for him that I'm not sure I'd even care if he hadn't. The small amount of discomfort is completely overshadowed by the rush of intense pleasure as his cock slowly enters my ass.

"Breathe," Ethan murmurs, and I blink, sucking in a gulp of air. I didn't realize I'd stopped breathing until he pointed it out.

"You too," I whisper back, and he laughs softly. My hands are braced on his chest, and I feel it move beneath my palms as he inhales. He looks almost as close to falling apart as I feel, and

I know it's got to be taking all of his restraint to keep from fucking up into me as Garrett works his way inside.

Finally, Garrett's hips are flush with my ass, his cock buried entirely inside me. I squirm between them, impaled completely and so full that my eyes are rolling back in my head. My tongue feels frozen in my mouth, my mind like mush as I struggle to remember how to speak well enough to tell them what I need now.

"Move. Please!"

The words burst out of me, and I can hear the desperation in my voice. My Omega scent perfumes the air, and both Ethan and Garrett respond immediately. They were gentle as they worked me up to this, but now they don't hold anything back. Garrett pulls back and then thrusts hard into my ass, and when he pulls back again, Ethan punches his hips upward so that his cock sinks deeper inside me than I think I've ever felt it before.

"Yes. Fuck, yes!"

My fingers curl against Ethan's chest, and I brace myself as well as I can, my arms trembling from the effort of staying upright. I feel like I'm about to float out of my body, a buzzing kind of euphoria filling my veins until I'm almost electric with it. Garrett's rough grunts and Ethan's muttered curses mix with my gasps and whimpers, the perfect soundtrack to the wild, primal way they're fucking me.

Their thrusts get harder and deeper, making me cry out each time one of them bottoms out, and it suddenly strikes me that there are other noises in the room—hungry, masculine sounds that aren't coming from either Garrett or Ethan.

I blink, forcing my eyes to focus as I look over and see that both Dante and Caleb have woken up and are watching us.

They're both murmuring appreciatively, their gazes tracking every movement as I rock between their pack mates.

Their scents hit my nose, stronger and more potent now that they're awake and so fucking turned on, and I feel like I'm bathing in the delicious smells of bourbon, dark chocolate, cinnamon, sweet cider, and sex.

"Oh god, I'm gonna come," I breathe, the sudden rush of sensation stealing my breath. "I'm gonna... oh... oh... *ohhhh....*"

It hits me like a thousand pound wrecking ball, knocking the remaining breath from my lungs. Ethan holds my hips, keeping me in place as he and Garrett pound into me, and when their knots inflate at nearly the same time, I let out a full-throated scream.

"Fuck, you're so damn *tight*," Ethan bites out, his temple gleaming with sweat as he drives himself upward one last time, lodging his knot inside me.

The warm rush of his cum fills my womb as Garrett grunts something unintelligible behind me. The knot in my ass feels more foreign than the one in my pussy, and with both men buried to the hilt, I can practically feel their knots rubbing together through the thin barrier that separates them.

It's so much, so *intense*, that it takes me several long moments to sort through the flood of sensations. The men give me time, running their hands over me, soothing me with their touch, and whispering words of praise. At first, it's just Garrett and Ethan touching me, but as the full body shudders of my orgasm start to subside, Caleb and Dante move closer, their strong hands joining the others until I feel like I'm being touched everywhere.

"You're doing so well, baby girl," Dante whispers, dropping his head to press a kiss to my temple. "Such a perfect, strong, beautiful Omega. No one could take their knots like this. No one but you."

His words make me shiver again, my ass and pussy clenching hard, and Garrett and Ethan both groan.

"You feel that?" Caleb catches my chin, turning my face to look at him. "You're ruining my brothers. Right here. Right now. You're ruining them for anyone else."

He moves closer, his lips meeting mine, and at the same time he kisses me, Dante works a hand between me and Ethan, finding my clit with the pads of his fingers. He applies just enough pressure to end up on the pleasure side of the pleasure/pain divide, and I moan into Caleb's mouth.

A sudden urge rises up in me, and I lift one hand from Ethan's chest and wrap it around Dante's cock. Garrett seems to read my mind, because he loops an arm around my torso to hold me up as I reach for Caleb with my other hand. I'm truly encapsulated by the four of them like this, and my hands slide over Caleb's and Dante's shafts as Caleb slips a hand down to help his pack leader work my clit.

I've never felt as connected to the four Alphas as I do in this moment, and I don't hold any part of myself back, trusting Garrett to hold me up as I give myself over to it all.

My hands move a little jerkily, and I'm sure I've given better hand jobs—but I'd never know it from the way Dante and Caleb react, their nostrils flaring with heavy breaths as they pulse against my palms.

"So good," I whisper, dragging my bottom lip between my teeth. "So fucking good. Make me come again. I'm so close."

"So am I," Caleb admits, his voice strained.

"Fuck. Me too." Dante presses his lips together, and both men's fingers move faster on my clit, circling it and pinching it.

Suddenly, the gathering tension inside me bursts in a haze of bright white light, blocking out everything else. Garrett tightens his grip on me, keeping me steady as my body jerks and stiffens. I'm coming and coming, a wave that feels like it'll never stop, but I fight through the haze as I drop my head and lean to one side to wrap my lips around Dante's cock.

"Ava..."

He purrs my name, the sound pouring over me like liquid sex, and I suck his tip, swirling my tongue around it as he strokes himself to climax. His release hits my tongue, and I moan hungrily, swallowing each jet of cum. On my other side, Caleb's breathing has grown harsh and choppy, and I release Dante with a wet pop and turn toward Caleb next. He moves closer, shifting his stance a little to give me easier access, and I take him into my mouth too. It only takes a second for him to explode, his taste mingling with Dante's on my taste buds.

I'm mewling like a kitten, sated and starving at the same time, and I slide my tongue over his velvety mushroom head, somehow unable to convince myself to release his cock from my mouth. It's hard to describe exactly *why*, but I need it here. I keep suckling on his length even as he slowly softens, the small knot that formed as he came deflating.

"You need to rest, sweetheart," he murmurs softly, stroking my hair.

I whine, shaking my head as well as I can with his cock still in my mouth. He chuckles, and I'm vaguely aware of him sharing a look with the other Alphas. Then he grips my chin and draws back, sliding his shaft out from between my lips. I make a pitiful, frustrated sound, and he chuckles, dropping his head to kiss me and seeming unbothered that I have the taste of Dante still on my lips.

"Don't worry," he whispers. "We've got you. We know what you need."

He lies down beside Ethan, settling into the nest of blankets and pillows, and Dante's strong hands grip my shoulders, guiding me down gently so that I'm half draped over Ethan and half draped over Caleb, with Garrett still behind me. My face is right at Caleb's crotch level, and warmth swells in my chest as I realize they really are giving me what I need.

Leaning closer, I draw Caleb into my mouth again, sucking softly on his half hard cock. He groans, tangling a hand in my hair, and my eyelids droop closed. It feels so good, so comforting, to have him inside me like this, a complement to the way Ethan and Garrett are filling me up. I draw him in a little deeper, humming contentedly around his length, and Dante lifts one of my hands in his, kissing my knuckles.

"Rest, baby girl," he says in his deep voice. "We'll be right here with you."

So I do.

# Chapter 34

## *Caleb*

Two days later, I wake up smelling strawberries and cream.

Stretching a little, I blink my eyes open and see Ava curled up in my arms.

She didn't fall asleep with my cock in her mouth this time, although I wouldn't have had any complaints if she had. Watching her suckle my half hard cock like that was one of the most incredible experiences of my life—not just because it felt amazing, but because of the way it seemed to soothe her so completely.

She's still dead asleep herself, curled into me, her dark hair spilling out around her. It's almost like a reverse halo, one of sweet rich darkness instead of light.

She's beautiful. She's perfection.

I reach out and trace the shape of her face with the tip of my finger, drawing down between her brows, to the top of her nose, and along her cheekbones. It amazes me that we got so lucky with this beautiful, wonderful Omega. There are still moments where I can't quite believe we actually have her.

I nose in closer, breathing in her scent. It's absolutely addicting. But I know it's more than that. It's not just that she's beautiful or that she smells good. Plenty of women are beautiful, and plenty of Omegas smell good. This is something more.

Every bit of time I've spent with her has made me more certain that this is the woman for us. This is the Omega that I need.

I prop myself up and look at the other three men. All of them are passed out too, dead to the world, which I suppose isn't surprising. We've all been in a haze of sex the past few days, snatching sleep and food when we can and basically helping to fuck Ava in shifts.

Even though we're all exhausted, the look that I see on the faces of my pack are full of a relaxation I've never seen before.

Ethan is usually going a hundred miles a minute. And Dante is our leader. He's stressed all the time because he feels he has to take care of us as well as our company. Garrett is basically the human personification of a clenched fist.

But now, with Ava... I've seen them all relax and open up. Soften. It makes me happy in a way that I didn't think I could be.

I always knew we needed an Omega. I need an Omega. But I wasn't sure how to picture what that would look like for us. And I never expected how happy it would make me not only to have an Omega of my own, but to see the other three most important people in my life be happy.

It feels like a miracle.

I know the others have pushed the thoughts away, but I've had a lot of time to think about this. I've watched them all go through their own struggles. Dante is a protector at heart, and I know he's wanted an Omega to take care of.

Garrett cut ties with his family, and we watched it make

him gruff and closed off, distrusting, wounded in a way he didn't like to talk about. Now with Ava, I see him opening up. She gives him a reason to soften.

As for Ethan, it's obvious they were kindred spirits from the start. One look at each other and they're both grinning helplessly. That guy was gone for her the moment he saw her at the club, and I wish I'd been there so I could've seen the look on his face.

I'm so glad that he followed his instincts and brought her home that night. I know Ethan would do anything to protect any panicked, upset Omega, it's just who he is, but he could've put her in a hotel, or called the ORD, or any other number of things to help her.

Instead, he brought her to us. And I'm forever grateful.

I know what to call this, even though the other three might not be ready to say it out loud yet. I'm falling in love with her.

I want to claim her fully and cement our bond. It's not time yet. We'll follow Ava's lead on this and I think we need to focus on getting her through her heat, anyway. Romances love to show the Omega getting the claiming bite during a heat, it's framed as super romantic and sexy, but honestly, in heat your hormones are taking over.

Yeah, I've done a lot of research on this too. Just like they say not to trust it if someone blurts out they love you right after sex, don't trust an Omega who begs to be bitten during a heat. Sure, they're not trying to manipulate you. They don't even realize that they're lying. The brain is flooded with so many endorphins in the moments of heat and orgasm that you really do believe you want what you're asking for.

But when the smoke clears, you might realize that you didn't mean it, and now you're stuck.

So no, this isn't a conversation for right now. We need to get through the heat first. But I know that this is for me, in my heart. There's no doubt in my mind.

I go to lie back down and find Ava's eyes open and dark, staring at me with hunger. She whimpers and stretches, and I can smell the slick on her. She's wet and wanting again, and I know that I'm not even going to try to resist her. Why would I?

Ava leans up, whimpering, and I know what she needs.

So I give it to her.

My fingers slide through her gorgeous dark locks, and I savor the feeling of the silky strands against my skin. When I guide her lips to mine, she comes eagerly, her small tongue sliding into my mouth as she makes the sexiest little noise in her throat.

*Fuck, her noises.*

I can't even bear to think about this thing between all of us not working out. Even without the bond, I'm so attached to this beautiful Omega that I feel like it would kill me to lose her. But if for some reason she changed her mind and walked out of our lives forever, I know in my soul that I would never forget those noises. Her little gasps and whimpers, her moans and sighs. They'll live rent-free in my head forever, and I truly wouldn't want it any other way.

"You're so beautiful like this," I murmur between kisses, sliding my tongue over her plush lips.

She draws back just a little, her brown eyes hooded and dark with desire. "Like what? Fucked into oblivion by you and your pack?"

I can't help the smile that tugs at my lips. I've never been one to joke or tease much—that's more Ethan's thing than mine

—but it feels as natural as breathing to banter with this beautiful, feisty, sweet woman.

"Yes, like that," I confirm. "Just like that. Although I don't think you've quite reached the point of 'oblivion' yet. Maybe I need to try a little harder."

"Good call."

She grins against my mouth, reaching up to slide her hands over my shoulders and back. She palms my ass, pulling me closer as she rolls onto her back. I settle between her legs, my cock already hard and pulsing against her cum-slicked pussy. She whimpers when the tip of my dick grazes her clit, her nipples hardening.

"I know you'll have other heats," I murmur roughly, going up onto my knees and sliding my hands down the insides of her thighs. "But I'll always remember this one. I'll remember every minute of it, sweetheart. The way you sound. The way you smell." My gaze drops to her pussy, which is swollen and flushed. "The way you look."

"Me too," she breathes. "I'll never forget any of this."

"Then watch," I tell her, my voice taking on an edge of Alpha command. I don't speak in this register as often as Garrett or Dante do, but being around Ava brings it out in me. "Watch your body take my cock."

She sucks in a breath, her gaze lingering on my face for a moment before it trails downward to the place where I'm lining myself up with her entrance. The head of my shaft disappears inside her, and both of us watch as I slowly press all the way inside. It's an incredible sight, filthy and beautiful all at once. She stretches around me, her body swallowing me up like it was made for this, and I grip her legs under the knees, lifting her to meet my thrust as I draw out and shove back in.

Her hands come up to squeeze her breasts, her fingers toying with her nipples as she stares at my cock sliding in and out of her.

"Caleb," she breathes. "You feel so... so good. Never want to... stop fucking you."

I can't help the smile that tugs at my lips at that. "I don't want to either, sweetheart. I've found a new definition of heaven, and it's being inside you."

My fingers tighten around her legs, and I spread her wider for me, holding her just where I want her as a familiar pressure builds at the base of my spine, my balls tightening. I've fucked her enough times by now to be learning her body, and I put that knowledge to good use, tilting her hips up a bit more angling my thrusts to hit her g-spot. She shakes her head back and forth, her breath coming in quick gasps, and although her eyelids drop closed for a moment, she forces them open again a moment later —as if she doesn't want to miss a second of this.

*That makes two of us.*

I'm close to coming, and from the way her body is responding to me, I think I could get her over the edge in just a few more strokes too. But instead of going harder to chase that pleasure, I slow down, drawing it out and leaving both of us on a plateau of pleasure, so close to the finish line but just short of crossing it.

"Tell me when you can't take it anymore," I whisper, lifting my gaze briefly to meet Ava's gorgeous brown eyes.

She nods, understanding my meaning. I would never torture my beautiful Omega by denying her an orgasm—or at least, I'd never torture her beyond what I think she'll enjoy.

And selfishly, I'm not ready for this to be over yet. Even knowing that she'll likely need to be claimed again by me and my pack before long, I want to hold on to this moment with just the two of us moving in sync. I don't begrudge sharing her with them at all, but right now, I want her all to myself.

"You're so good," I praise her, warmth infusing my voice. "So good for me. So sweet. So fucking sexy."

She nods, her eyes turning glassy. Her prefect breasts rise and fall faster as she pants, still cupped in her delicate hands. I can feel the way she tightens around me, her inner walls rippling and gripping my cock, and although it takes almost more self-control than I have, I slow my strokes, pulling out almost entirely to give her a chance to drift back down from the edge.

"Beautiful. Just like that," I murmur when she relaxes a little.

Keeping my gaze locked on her, I slide back in. The incredible sensation of being wrapped in her slick, soft heat hits me all over again, and I pause for a second to get my own shit back under control before I resume my slow, steady thrusts.

I lose track of time as I fuck her like that, pausing before either of us come, pulling back every time we get close. The room is quiet except for our soft noises and the sounds of our bodies joining together, and I feel more at peace in this moment than I have in a long time—maybe ever.

Finally, small tremors start to wrack Ava's small frame. She moans as I slide into her, her mouth dropping open, and her gaze flies up to meet mine.

"I can't," she whispers hoarsely. "Caleb, I can't hold it off any more. I need... oh fuck, I need to come."

"Do it," I tell her, my own muscles straining as pleasure builds inside me like a wild animal trapped inside a cage. I can't hold back any longer either. "Come for me, sweetheart. Let yourself fall apart. I've got you. I've always got you."

With those words, I let go of her legs and lean forward, bracing my body above hers. Our lips collide as I unleash everything I've been keeping in check, thrusting into her hard and fast, my cock pounding into her pussy.

She breaks at the exact same moment I do, and I swallow up her scream and keep kissing her, pouring myself into her as she goes tight around me like a vise. My knot swells, my cock pulsing over and over as jets of cum spill into her, and a grunt that feels like it comes all the way from my bones resonates in my chest.

In the aftermath, my arms give out, and I collapse on top of her. Her skin is damp with sweat, just like mine is, and I can feel the racing of her pulse as it trips along just as fast as my own. She wraps her arms and legs around me, and I allow myself to stay like that for a few breaths as I recover from the intensity of my climax.

But I don't want to crush her, so before she can squirm underneath me in discomfort, I roll us, switching our positions. I end up on my back with Ava draped over me, her small body resting against mine. Another few minutes pass before I finally start to catch my breath, and Ava lifts her head from my chest, pushing messy, tangled dark hair out of her face.

"That... that was..."

Words seem to fail her, which I understand. The English language is failing me at the moment as well. So instead of trying to finish her sentence for her, I just lift my head to press a kiss to her hair, letting my arms drape loosely around her. My fingertips trail down her spine, and she shivers against me, giving a contented little hum.

*There it is*, I think sleepily. *That's my favorite noise yet.*

# Chapter 35

## *Ava*

After what feels like an eternity, and yet at the same time only a single blurry day, my heat ends.

I know that actually it'll have been about three to four days, maybe longer, depending, since my heat was blocked for so long. It was something that Caleb warned us about from his research —that after all of those pent-up hormones in my body were unleashed, I might have a longer and more intense heat than most.

So I'm not actually sure how long it lasted, just that time got syrupy for me. But I do know when it's over.

I wake up, completely exhausted, and for the first time in what feels like weeks, my body isn't on fire with desire. My legs don't spread automatically, I'm not leaking slick, and I don't feel painfully empty.

When I would wake up during my heat, it was like I couldn't even think properly half the time. It was almost like being really hungry, reaching that point where you're sure that you're starving and all you can think about is food... except it wasn't food I wanted, but sex. Lots and lots of sex. I couldn't

279

even form words sometimes, just whimper and moan and grab on to whichever of my Alphas was nearest.

Or multiple of them. And god, it was amazing.

I feel like I've been baptized by fire, if the fire was the delicious heat of orgasm. I feel transformed. I might be tired, my limbs heavy and limp, but I also feel completely content. Like the way my brain gets right after a good orgasm, except longer-lasting.

I stretch and roll onto my back so I can blink up at the ceiling. As my vision clears, I feel my mind clearing as well. My limbs are feeling a bit stiff, and...

*Oh my god, I'm so hungry. Wow. I could eat an entire elephant on my own.*

I sit up, then immediately wince as I feel... *yikes*. I look down at my body, specifically at my skin.

Honestly, I don't think I've ever been this filthy in my life. It was hot as hell before, but now I really, really need a shower.

A hand lands on my thigh and I turn to see Ethan lying there, smiling sleepily up at me. "You good, sweetheart?"

I nod. "Hungry. And I need a shower."

"Don't we all," he chuckles. His thumb strokes back and forth over my skin and I see him inhale. "You smell different. Is your heat broken?"

"I think so. I can actually focus on something other than sex, for one thing." I grin.

Beside me, I feel the other three men stirring as well. Garrett groans as he stretches. "Remind me to not neglect my cardio so much."

"I'll just have to find other ways for you to do cardio," I quip, winking at him.

Dante chuckles and smiles at me proudly, like he can read

my mind and knows that if I'm this confident and flirty, it means I'm truly comfortable with them all.

Dante pushes himself to his feet. "You must be hungry. I'll get something warmed up."

I flush, embarrassed by the state I'm in. "Okay. I, uh, should really hop in the shower first."

I didn't think about it before, when I was in the throes of heat, but now I'm aware of just how messy I am, and I can't help but feel a bit self-conscious over it.

Dante leans in and kisses me like nothing is wrong. "Why don't we join you?"

Ethan sits up and kisses my shoulder, his hand on the small of my back. "You can take a shower alone if you'd like, it's up to you."

No. While my heat is finished, I do still want to savor the closeness with them, and have them touching me.

I run my fingers through Caleb's blond hair to wake him up. He opens his eyes and blinks up at me, then gifts me with a beautiful smile. I've made these four men happy, somehow, and I don't know what to do with that, other than to keep it up.

Garrett stands and scoops me up, making me gasp in surprise and then laugh. He carries me into the bathroom, the other three men following. It's the master bathroom, the one with the massive glass-walled shower, and the soaking tub.

Caleb draws the water in the tub and they help me get in. Dante washes my hair, his fingers massaging my scalp, and I feel so incredibly relaxed, with all four of my Alphas around me purring and smelling like contentment. My heart feels incredibly full.

I've heard horror stories from other Omegas, back when I was in college and thought I was a Beta. There would be stories about how after your heat, once the lust died down, you felt like a wrung-out washcloth or somehow emptied and dried out. Not empty in a sexy way like during your heat where you wanted a knot filling you, but more like you'd been drained and scraped out, hollowed.

Now, I think those horror stories came from Omegas who didn't have good Alphas providing them with the care they needed. I can easily see myself feeling just as crappy if I had to take care of myself completely on my own after such an experience.

But I don't have to. I have wonderful, loving Alphas who are still pampering me. It makes my heart swell in my chest like I'm the Grinch and it's growing three sizes.

We get out of the tub when we're finished, and I put on one of the lovely silk dressing gowns that were among the various clothes Ethan ordered for me. The men grab clothes from their rooms, and we head downstairs to eat something.

To my surprise, when Dante goes to start cooking, Ethan shoves him back into a chair at the table. "Hell no. You did all that cooking for her heat, and we ate you out of house and home. It's our turn."

"Oh, come on," Dante protests. He tries to get up again but I grab his wrist, laughing. I don't know what Ethan has planned, but I'm more than willing to go along with the shenanigans.

Besides, he's right. None of us have eaten anything other than what Dante prepared for a week, just warming up the delicious food he made. And he cooks for us the rest of the time. He deserves a break.

Dante could easily throw my hand off his wrist. He's definitely a lot stronger than I am. But he lets me keep him down at the table.

As a reward, I climb into his lap, nuzzling him.

Caleb starts to pull pots and pans out of the cupboards and Garrett snorts, grinning. "You two are cooking?"

"You're damn right we are. You say that like you think we can't."

"I think I know Dante's a reliable cook who makes me the food I want," Garrett protests.

"You're going to sit there and be a cheerleader," Ethan orders. "Gimme an 'A.'"

"Absolutely not."

Caleb and Ethan really do put their hearts and minds to it, and I realize they must've planned this at some point, probably while Dante and I were asleep from exhaustion during the heat but they had woken up and grabbed something to eat.

We were all sleeping in various combinations, so it doesn't surprise me, but it does delight me to be reminded of what playful, charming men my Alphas are.

I really do adore them.

Caleb and Ethan make us a huge spread. It starts with the crepes, filled with ham and cheese, or strawberries and Nutella, or bananas and chocolate, or spinach and eggs. Various combinations, and all of them delicious. Then there are the fluffy biscuits with thick sausage gravy, and the diced roasted potatoes that make my mouth water, sauteed with onions.

My stomach is yowling like an alley cat by the time they set the food in front of us, and I devour it like a wild animal. The Alphas are just as bad, all of us tearing into the delicious food like we haven't eaten in weeks.

Heat really does take a lot out of you.

I eat from my perch on Dante's lap, and if he minds, he

doesn't say anything about it. When I inhale, all I can pick up from their scents is happiness.

It makes me happy too.

"Not to ruin the mood..." Garrett starts.

"First time you've ever said that," Ethan quips, clearly teasing his pack mate.

Garrett rolls his eyes but continues. "I think we should check up on work. See how things are going."

Everyone glances at me, to make sure that I'm okay with it. I nod empathetically. "Yes, please."

I had completely forgotten about their work, honestly, my head full of happiness and pleasure, but the moment that Garett brings it up, it all comes crashing back down around me. Marcus. The watch.

The men pull out their phones and tablets and check in. I really hope that my heat hasn't affected anything. They were basically MIA for nearly a week. I know that they planned for it and I'm sure they told their employees how to handle things, and what they'd be up to, but what if there was some kind of disaster? I really hope that everything's going well.

Dante curses.

My heart sinks. I'm guessing things... aren't going great then. "What is it?"

Caleb sighs, and I can tell by their expressions that they're all looking at the same thing on their respective devices.

"Marcus," Garrett growls, and the way he says the name makes it sound like a curse word. "He's released a preview of his version of the watch."

"And it's exactly the same as ours." Dante turns his tablet so that I can see. "Look."

I remember what I saw on Dante's laptop when he showed

me the schematics and preview images the other day, when he was in the kitchen. In this very spot, in fact. I was even on his lap then too.

This feels like a horrible mirror image of that day. Then, my heat was building and I was horny and teasing him. I enjoyed seeing what his company was working on and how he trusted me to see all of his work.

Now, his work has been stolen, and by my abusive ex-boyfriend, of all things.

I stare at the screen, almost as if, if I stare at it long enough, it'll morph into something else. Something that's not Dante's design.

But there it is. Still there. Still Dante's.

"I'm so sorry," I whisper. "He wouldn't do this if it wasn't for me."

"You did nothing wrong," Ethan replies. "He chose to be an asshole and do this. There's literally nothing you can do to stop people like that. It's his choice to do this. You didn't provoke him."

"But you were all taking care of me during my heat," I point out.

The others all look at each other, confusion obvious on their faces.

I sigh. "It's just... if I wasn't in my heat then you would've caught this sooner. You could've been in the office this whole time taking care of the situation."

"You need to stop blaming yourself," Caleb says gently.

"First of all, baby girl, you're our Omega," Dante says. "Everyone understands how important it is to help an Omega through their heats. It's a matter of your safety and wellbeing."

"Second of all," Garrett adds, "it's on him to be a jackass.

Why should we beat ourselves up for something he did? If he stabbed someone would you blame yourself for that too?"

I laugh weakly. "Well, when you put it like that..."

Dante cuddles me close. "You have nothing to be sorry for. None of this is on you. He did this. He chose to be an asshole."

"My question," Ethan says, squinting at his screen, "is how he was able to apparently make an exact copy of our product."

A chill sweeps through me, and my stomach twists again. Dante showed me the schematics of the watch, the imagery... a whole bunch of things.

And Marcus is my ex.

"I think it's obvious," Garrett snaps at Ethan. It's clear he's not angry at Ethan, just upset in general. "Marcus has someone on the inside."

"A mole?"

"It has to be."

I feel sick. Surely they won't think...

But none of them look at me, or raise an accusing voice.

The moment of panic passes and I feel almost silly for letting myself think for a second that they'd accuse me.

I'm terrified of Marcus. I can admit that. It's not crazy to think that maybe he threatened me somehow, and I gave him information to keep him from hurting me.

But there's no time I could've done that. Marcus has no way of getting in touch with me, if he even found out where I am, and I've had one of the Alphas with me constantly, keeping me safe and keeping me from contacting anyone without them knowing.

I would never betray them. And it looks like my Alphas know that.

Dante shakes his head. He looks stricken. "The people at

this company have been working for us for years. We keep a smaller team for a reason."

"Nobody's immune to the power of money," Ethan says darkly.

Caleb looks as upset as Dante does. I'm not surprised, with how in tune to emotion Caleb is. He's an empathetic person.

Garrett looks more like he wants to commit a murder. "Whoever it is better hope that I'm not the one who finds out who they are."

I have to admit, he sounds sexy when he says that. But his hurt and anger are real, and there's nothing sexy about that. It just makes my heart hurt.

"Are you sure?" Caleb asks. "There has to be another way that he got a hold of this information, right?"

"Not that I know of," Dante admits. "He'd have to find a way to somehow beat our system and hack into it, without any of our security picking up on it. It has to be an inside job."

"While we were out of the office, it was the perfect opportunity," Garrett adds.

Guilt strikes me again, but Dante rubs my back as Ethan adds, "But he has to have been planning something like this for a bit, hasn't he? This was just a good opportunity or maybe he decided to go big or go home because of Ava. But I don't think this was out of the blue. I don't think he just walked up to someone we work with and handed them a wad of cash."

"True," Caleb says slowly. "You need to investigate, see who might be a weakness. Who has bad debts, a gambling problem, who might be dissatisfied with the company..."

That relieves me, somewhat. It might not have to do with me, at least not completely. It could be in part that Marcus is just, well, an asshole.

I shudder in relief. Dante feels it and looks at me. "What is it?"

"Nothing, I just..." I try to smile, but I know it's weak. "It just hit me how lucky I am that I got out, and that he didn't know at the time that I was an Omega. If he's bought off someone in your company..."

The sentence trails off, and I know that the others are thinking the same thing I am: how impossible it could've been for me to get away if I'd let him bond with me and claim me. He's a powerful man and it could've been bad for me.

"Well, you're not with him," Dante assures me. "You're with us, and you're safe."

I nuzzle him. "I know. Thank you."

"Okay, I'm reading through," Ethan pipes up, "and we have two problems. The first is that I think from this press release that someone was feeding him information starting weeks ago, before he knew about Ava being with us. But that does mean that he also has all of our latest innovations to the watch, like the changes we discussed the other day with the heart rate measurements."

"Oh, joy," Garrett mutters.

"The second is that unless something goes really wrong and he has to delay..." Ethan flips his tablet around so that we can all see the screen with the date on it. "His watch is definitely going to come to market first."

"Fuck," Garrett says.

I couldn't have said it better myself.

# Chapter 36

## *Ava*

I offer to clean up breakfast while the men deal with their lawyer.

At first my Alphas protest, insisting that I'm still recovering from my heat, but I put my foot down. I want to feel helpful, and it's not like there's really anything I can do with the Marcus issue.

I clean up the kitchen, while the Alphas call their lawyers first and foremost.

They stay in the kitchen while they do it, which I appreciate. I'm pretty sure they do it specifically because they know it'll help me to overhear the plans and know what next steps we can take.

"Unfortunately, boys, there's nothing we can do without proof," one of the lawyers explains.

It's odd to hear someone call my Alphas 'boys' when I know they're such men, but this lawyer is in his eighties if he's a day, and so I suppose he has a right to call just about anyone he wants 'boy' or 'girl' or anything else if he feels like it.

"You need to get proof that he got this from your company before I can pursue legal action."

"I think the fact that he has the exact schematics and designs that we have, down to a 't', proves that," Ethan points out.

"You'd think so. In a world of common sense, it does. But this isn't about common sense. The law is about proving beyond a reasonable doubt. You have to convince a court with more hard facts than you'd use to convince your neighbor. I know it sucks when you're on this end of things, but that's how it has to be so everyone is treated fairly."

I can think of quite a few things to say to that, but I keep my mouth shut. I probably shouldn't even technically be in the room for this conversation.

"What do we do, then?" Caleb asks, while Garrett and Dante silently fume.

"You'll have to do an internal investigation," another lawyer pipes in. "But as subtly as possible. If your man figures out that something is happening, he'll spook. And someone quitting on you or suddenly taking a vacation isn't enough to nail him. He'll take any proof with him and then we'll be up a creek without a paddle."

"Once we have proof that he did in fact steal from you," the first lawyer says, "you can sue him and your employee."

"All right, thank you," Dante says, ending the call. "We'll be in touch when we have something."

The call ends and the men all look at each other, frustration clear on their faces.

"Now what do we do?" I ask, drying my hands off on a kitchen towel.

They frown at me. "We need to look into everything we can

at the company to find evidence that data's been sent out to Marcus or someone on his team," Ethan says.

"Great. Where do you want me, coach?"

"Wait, you want to help?" Garrett sounds confused.

"It's not your fault," Caleb says quietly, accurately guessing the source of my discomfort.

"I know that. But I'm determined to do my part. Marcus might have already wanted to try out some corporate espionage but I think we all know that he really stepped up his game because of me. Because he wants to hurt me, and hurt you all for having me and keeping me from him."

I fold my arms, determined. "You can't leave me out of this. Put me in, coach."

Dante chuckles. "All right. If you really insist. It'll be helpful to have another pair of eyes on this thing."

I grin in relief. "Then let's get started."

Over the next few days, I spend what feels like just about every waking moment poring over records, combing through files and every email sent from one of the company servers or accounts, and double-checking finances.

It's mind-numbing at times, I admit. But I'm not going to lose focus. We need to find out who did this and who betrayed my Alphas.

Part of it is the lingering guilt and upset. Part of it is a matter of principle. But part of it, honestly, is also anger.

These are my Alphas. They're good men, and they take good care of their company. They treat their employees with respect and consideration and give them everything a boss should: time off, vacations, sick days, health care, good wages, and end-of-year bonuses.

They're good bosses who care about their employees and

treat them like family, and one of those people went and fucking betrayed them. I can't wrap my head around what kind of person would do something like that, but I almost don't care. I just care about making sure this person is found and brought to justice.

My Alphas deserve better than what's happened to them. And I know that it weighs on them.

They don't neglect me. Far from it. I'm the one who has to be pulled away from the work and reminded to do things like sleep and eat. At least one of them is always happy to distract me with lips on my neck and a hand up my shirt.

And I'm definitely happy to be distracted.

If anything, it's almost like a reverse of my heat. During those days, I needed a knot, and I needed my Alphas. Now, it's like they need me to help them stay grounded, to work off the tension and energy that fills their bodies.

I worried a bit that our bond, just intensified through my heat, would now be neglected with this new issue that we have to devote ourselves to. Instead, it's like the men have gotten into the habit of fucking me and now they can't get enough.

I love it, honestly. I'm far from complaining. Well, not seriously. I do sometimes squeal when they drag me away from my work.

"You realize that you're going to need glasses if you squint at all those lines too much," Caleb points out, his hands landing on my shoulders.

He starts to massage, and I moan a little, letting my head fall back. "I know. But we have to find this person."

"Marcus isn't going to get you if we fail in this. Sure, it'll be a disappointment, but we're going to be okay. What's most important is that you're safe."

"It's not just that." I look up at him while he keeps massaging my shoulders. "I know that it hurts you. Not Marcus. But that someone you employ... someone you trust... betrayed you like this."

Caleb sighs and pulls away so that he can sit on the table and look at me. "Yeah. That's the part that hurts us the most, I think. Garrett vets everyone thoroughly and I know Dante considers all of our employees his responsibility."

I nod. That fits. "And you like to think the best of everyone."

The corner of Caleb's mouth curls up. "You could put it that way, yeah. I know some people might say I'm too optimistic, but I really do like to hope that people will rise up to their full potential."

"You've told me that this company is like a family for you all. That it's been the most important thing in your lives."

"Until you," Caleb adds.

"Until me," I agree, smiling and blushing. Maybe someday that won't make me flush, but today really isn't that day.

"No, it's true." He shakes his head. "It's not that we haven't had crappy employees before or that we haven't run into people who've tried to screw us over. But I thought that we had a really good team this time. Just goes to show, I guess."

I look back down at all of the papers strewn around on the table in various piles. I've been combing through everything I can possibly find, trying desperately to find that single scrap of information that will lead us to the traitor.

And yet, I feel like I haven't found anything useful.

It's clear that finding the evidence we need is going to be a difficult task.

"Whoever this person is," I say with a sigh, "he's good at covering his tracks. I can't find anything."

"Further evidence that this was probably already something that was underway before you," Caleb points out.

"Or Marcus ran into someone in a coffee shop and got them to print it all out and give him the information the old-fashioned way," I mutter.

"Hey, don't rule it out. That could be what happened."

"Then we're screwed."

"No. We just have to keep being smart." Caleb takes my hand. "I know you're stressed. But we can't give up."

I take a few deep breaths, focusing on Caleb's touch and his scent, and I nod.

"Oh, there you are." Ethan pops in, grinning with something behind his back. "It's here."

Now Caleb is also grinning.

I look back and forth between the two men, my eyes narrowing into a suspicious squint. "What are you up to?"

"Nothing," Ethan says with a completely false sense of innocence. "But I did pick something out for you, for tonight."

"Tonight? What's tonight?" I scour my mind but can't quite remember anything on the schedule.

Then again, it's possible that I was told about something and then completely forgot about it, focused on my research.

Ethan grins harder. "Oh, just a little something."

"We thought it would be nice to take you out and give everyone a break," Caleb explains. "You need to get out of the house and Dante thinks the rest of us should too."

It does sound nice to go out. And with all four Alphas, I'd feel safe from Marcus if he somehow showed up wherever we go.

"This isn't just about taking a break," Dante says, startling me a little.

I stand up in surprise. He's wearing a suit, this one a rich blue color. "Where are you off to?" I ask.

"I'm off to the opening of a new exhibit at an art gallery," Dante replies. "And so are the others. And so are you."

That's when Ethan takes whatever is behind his back out and holds it up for me to see. I gasp, my hand flying to my mouth. It's an absolutely stunning dress made of soft blue fabric, with black lace applique all over the bodice and skirts, and a layer of black silk as the very base layer for the skirts. It's bold, daring, and elegant.

Garrett appears, fiddling with the cuffs of his suit. His suit is such a dark navy it's almost black, the kind of blue you can only see when he stands in the light.

"Here." I take his wrists into my hands and fix his cufflinks. "There you go."

Garett kisses me in thanks, then sees the dress. He smirks. "I see Ethan picked out something showstopping for you."

"Yes, but I'm not sure why, it's just an art gallery opening." Even as I speak, my heart races.

"It's more than that," Dante replies. "This is our first chance to take you out into society as our Omega."

"We want to start introducing you to the world as ours," Caleb says, his voice soft and aching.

My chest is aching too. "Really? That's so sweet."

"It's no less than what you deserve," Ethan says. "I'd shout it from every damn rooftop in the city if I could. I want everyone to know how I feel about you."

It is a big step, in a way. I've already gone through my heat with them, and it was amazing. I've been living with them for several weeks now.

But once we go out into society together and make it known

that I'm the Omega they're courting, it'll be really awkward and embarrassing if I change my mind and go back to the facility to try for another Alpha pack.

The men are taking a risk, bringing me out in public to a big social event like this. They're trusting that I really am committed to this, and that I won't back out and leave them feeling humiliated.

"Thank you," I whisper. I know what this means to them.

Ethan holds out the dress. "Get dressed, gorgeous. We're going to paint the town red."

"Blue," Garrett deadpans.

"The saying is red, Garrett."

"And yet, here we are."

"You think you're funny."

"He is funny." I grin and take the dress from Ethan. "Thank you. This is beautiful."

He really does seem to nail my fashion sense.

I take the dress and go get changed, admiring myself in the mirror for a moment. It's similar in cut to the dress that I wore at the Omega presentation, but it's a bit more slinky, and the skirts don't have as many layers.

After all, I'm not showing myself off in a hotel ballroom. I'm going to an art gallery show, surrounded by the rich and powerful in our city.

When I come back downstairs, ready to go, I see that Caleb and Ethan have also changed. Ethan's now in a bright blue suit, while Caleb's in a baby blue colored suit.

I love how they coordinate. It's just another way they show how they're all on the same page, individuals but united as a pack.

Dante takes my hand and leads me out to the car. I'm

already full of anticipation as we drive into the city. It really will be the first time since everything started that I'll be out properly. I was hiding in the mansion, then at the facility, and then the only place I went out to was the shopping plaza with Dante before hiding again because of Marcus.

And, well, I sure wasn't going anywhere during my heat.

But now I'm going to be out and about again and it honestly sounds really fun. Especially with my four Alphas around me keeping me safe. I never feel more loved and comforted than when I'm around them.

We get to the heart of the city and Caleb helps me out of the car. There are already other people walking up, mingling with one another as they head inside the gallery. I shrink back a little, instinctively unsure.

This is my first proper outing as an Omega, after all. Post-heat, and with all of my pack.

Dante puts a hand at the small of my back and Caleb gives me a reassuring smile. I take a deep breath and make myself relax.

This is going to be a fun evening. A break from all the work we've been doing.

We enter, and immediately people are catching sight of us and coming over. I'm introduced to so many people I can't keep track, but they all smile when they hear who I am.

"You're the Omega!" one older woman gushes. She's the wife of someone my Alphas have worked with before. "Oh, we were hoping that they'd find someone soon. It's delightful to meet you, darling."

"You're a beauty," another man says. He was introduced to me as a member of a charity board that Ethan and Caleb are on, working to provide tech scholarships to underprivileged kids.

"We all knew they were bound to wait until they could find someone really special."

As I'm complimented, I realize that I expected people to be hostile toward me. I was waiting, somewhere in the back of my mind, for people to decide that I wasn't good enough.

After all, these four men might not have entirely come from money but they've been rich for some time. They have every reason to fit in here, and their peers have every reason to look down on someone who doesn't fit it.

I guess I thought they'd realize I don't come from some family name. I'm not some person they know for being famous, or rich, or one of them... and they would judge me accordingly.

But in reality, everyone's just so happy that I'm here and that this pack finally has an Omega. It's... sweet. It's really sweet.

There are delicious snacks being passed around, and I'm given a flute of champagne. At least one of my Alphas is always with me, and the art is beautiful, creative, thought-provoking.

I'm not an expert on art by any means, so I just kind of follow along with whatever catches my eye and makes something stir in my heart. Reading the plaques is interesting, and it's nice that at a gallery presentation like this, the artists are here for us to speak to and we can learn more about their thought processes.

"This is our Omega," Dante says, pulling me away from a painting and bringing me over to introduce me to another group of people. "Ava."

Garrett is standing there too, and he puts his hand on the small of my back. I beam, hearing the pride in Dante's voice and feeling the pleasure rolling off both him and Garrett like invisible waves.

As Dante mentions that I have an affinity for animals and have dedicated my life to helping them, I can practically feel my cheeks glowing.

I've never felt anything like this before. I've never had people be so proud of me. No, more than that. Proud to have me in their lives, proud to be associated with me.

"Oh, Ava!" One of the people, a woman about the same age as my Alphas and myself, smiles. "I was wondering who would eventually be the woman to snatch these men up... I have to admit, some of us were starting to worry. It's lovely to meet you."

"It's lovely to meet you as well. I..."

My voice trails off as I notice Garrett go stiff next to me, his hand at my back shaking a little. I look over at him, frowning. Garrett might be gruff but he doesn't get nervous. Even when he's upset, he commands a room.

I follow his line of sight, and see an older couple walking over to us. Something about both of them is familiar, even though I know I've never seen either of them before. They're not anyone famous, so I'm not sure why I feel like there's something about them I recognize.

That is, until they reach us.

Garrett's not the only one tense now. Dante's tense too. Caleb and Ethan have appeared, seemingly out of nowhere, and neither of them looks happy.

The other people we were speaking to look down at the ground, too awkward to keep talking, but not wanting to move away and catch attention either.

"Garrett," the man says, and there's a tone to his voice that I know well. Marcus would use it with me when he was letting me know that I had done something wrong, something he would punish me for later, but he was maintaining a veneer of politeness since we were in public.

I bristle, wondering who thinks they can talk to one of my men like that, when Garrett says, with even less faux politeness in his voice, "Dad. Mom."

Oh my god.

These are his parents.

# Chapter 37

## *Garrett*

And the night was going so damn well too.

I can tell that Ava's been having a lot of fun, and I'm glad with how everyone's treated her. I was a little worried. I know first-hand what damn snobs rich people can be.

But nobody's tried to question her about her background and her family. Instead, they welcome her with open arms. Honestly, I'm kind of shocked to hear everyone talking about how they were waiting for us to find an Omega.

I had no damn idea that everyone was so fascinated with our dating lives, but I suppose that's how it works when you're successful and eligible. I can remember how nosy my mom was when I was growing up, and how it felt like all my parents did was get into everyone else's business and judge them for it.

Ava's not a scholar of art, but she has an eye for color, and I love watching her move through the room, taking her time with each piece. She might not know a lot of art history, but the point of art is that you shouldn't need a degree in it to be affected by it. I love watching her face as she takes it all in, as she lets each piece hit her.

She's beautiful tonight. She's always beautiful, but in her dress, wearing the same colors that we are... I'm tempted to drag her into a dark corner all night. The only reason I don't is that I'm not sure she'll appreciate me starting her first night out as our Omega with scandal, and well, she's having so much fun. I don't want to interrupt that.

If Ava thinks that we haven't noticed how she's overworking herself, she has another think coming. We can all see it. I worry that she still feels guilty about Marcus even though it's not her fault he's a scumbag.

She deserves this night out.

And besides, I want to show her off. I know that we all do. I knew everyone would be impressed by her even if I'm a bit surprised people are being so welcoming and telling us that they were waiting for us to pick an Omega. I expected a bit more wailing that they couldn't try to pair us with their young Omega kids anymore.

Point is, I'm having a good time, and Ava's having a great time, and that's what matters.

And then my damn parents have to show up.

God. I thought there wasn't a worry about running into them. Stupid of me. I should've called the gallery and asked for the guest list, or something. It's been long enough without them I got sloppy and I relaxed too much.

I should've known that they would find a way to turn up like a bad penny, right when I don't want them to.

I give them a formal nod and then look away, hoping that I've made my point clear. They might be here, but that doesn't mean that I have to interact with them. We both made our sides clear years ago.

"Garrett," Mom says. Unlike Dad, she doesn't sound like

she's disappointed in me and struggling to hide it for the sake of propriety. She sounds anguished, like I've been off at war. "It's been far too long since we last saw you."

*Yeah, I wonder why that is,* I think savagely. I don't say it out loud. I'm not going to give them ammo that they'll use to talk about how far I've fallen, how I've lost my manners from hanging out with men like my pack, on and on and fucking *on.*

"It has," I say, straining to keep my tone polite. I don't want to have a scene in public.

I've had no damn problem causing a scene in public with them before, but before, I didn't have Ava. I refuse to humiliate her by getting into it with my parents in front of everyone else.

I try to turn away from them and make it clear that I'm not continuing the conversation, but my mother then turns to Ava. "Hello. I'm Jennifer, this is Robert."

Ava smiles sweetly. Ava's just a sweet person by nature, it's easy for her. It's why I want to protect her so much. People take advantage of sweetness like that. The woman wants to run a damn animal shelter for crying out loud. How many people want to dedicate their lives to that? Not enough of them, in my opinion.

But I don't think my parents will hear that news and see it as a sign of Ava's selflessness and kindness. I've kept a distance from them and their drama for a damn good reason and I don't want myself, my pack, or my Omega pulled into it. I've built a good life for myself and for all of us. They can't come along and spoil it.

But I worry that they'll try their hardest.

"I don't think I've seen you around the art scene before?" Mom says, her tone still polite and friendly. "Are you one of the artists on display here?"

"Oh, no, I'm here to admire the art," Ava replies.

"Are you a connoisseur?"

"Very much a beginner," Ava laughs. "But I do love art. I've never had a chance to really study it and educate myself on it. But I think that's part of the beauty of the nature of art, isn't it? It doesn't matter if you know a lot or a little, it can still move you. Like music."

Dad's gaze flickers to Dante's hand at the small of Ava's back. He knows Dante, as well as Ethan and Caleb.

The very few times that my parents and my pack dealt with each other weren't pleasant ones. Dad was furious he couldn't legally do anything to stop me from using the money in the trust fund they'd set up for me to jumpstart our company and be our initial capital. None of my three pack mates come from enough of a pedigreed background for him.

He's also not a fan of entrepreneurship or science and tech. He thinks I should've gone into finance, or become a lawyer, or become a doctor. In that order.

Those are the only acceptable roles in society that one of his sons can play.

Dad's nostrils flare and he zeroes in on Ava. "You're an Omega."

Ava gets a little stiff, the way she does every time someone brings up her status. Even after her heat and how amazing that was for all of us, she's still getting used to being seen in society as an Omega.

With our love and support, I hope that she'll come to find ease and happiness in her Omega status. That it won't bother her anymore. But I know that those kinds of things take time. She spent so much of her life hiding and running, and it can't all be undone in a day.

"Yes," Ava says, her tone light and even. "Guilty as charged."

"And you're with..." Dad's voice trails off as his gaze moves to me, then back to Ava.

"You're mated?" Mom sounds surprised, but she's clearly struggling to hide it. "To my son?"

"Not mated," Dad mutters. It's just loud enough that we can hear it, but quiet enough that he can get away with acting like he didn't mean for us to overhear him. "She has no bite marks, and their scents aren't completely mingled."

"Rude, much?" I remark.

Dad shoots me a chastising glare. Yeah, right. That might have sometimes worked on me when I was eight, but I'm a damn adult now and have been for a while. He can't intimidate me into silence anymore.

"You're being courted." Mom's gaze trails up and down Ava's body, trying to find fault. She smiles. "That's a lovely dress."

"Thank you. Ethan picked it out for me, he has such wonderful fashion sense. And I love matching my Alphas. I think we make a handsome group."

Ava smiles at Dante, then at me. I can feel Ethan and Caleb hovering worriedly behind us, like they don't know if they need to leap in to shield Ava, or to drag me away before I do something stupid.

Mom's smile looks a little pained, and I know it's because she can't find fault with Ava's looks. Ava's absolutely stunning. Her thick long hair is also more traditional, from Mom's point of view, and Ava's natural curves traditionally mean that she'll be good at bearing children. I don't give a damn about that kind of thing, I just think she's damn gorgeous, but Mom does.

After all, for years an Omega was valued on their looks, and ability to have a lot of children. Mom and Dad still subscribe to that kind of thing.

"Well, you are lovely." Mom's tone is sweet, but I have to hold in a smirk knowing she's actually annoyed. "You seem a bit older than most unmated Omegas."

If she's trying to make Ava feel like she's past her prime, she's not succeeding. "Oh, yes. Well, I presented quite late, actually."

"Late? Is that a genetic thing?"

"My parents were Betas, so I really don't know."

"Your parents." Dad seizes the opportunity. Oh for fuck's sake. "What do they do?"

"I don't know," Ava replies. Her tone stays light, her smile never slipping, but I can smell a hint of agitation in her scent.

I don't know if my parents can pick up on that, though. Most people can only tell extreme emotions in someone's scent, like deep fear, or happiness, or anger. The ability to pick up on the nuances of someone's emotions through scent only comes through the bonding process.

"My parents and I haven't spoken in nearly a decade," Ava explains. "They were never really there for me. I stopped communication when I left for college. I'm not sure what they're up to now."

I'm so proud of how simply she can say it. It's not something to be ashamed of, it's not something that upsets her anymore. Or at least it's not something she'll let strangers see upsets her. She's just stating facts.

"What about when you were growing up, then?" Dad presses.

"Dad." I glare at him. "These questions are inappropriate."

"I'm just getting to know her," Dad replies.

"It's okay, Garrett," Ava says quietly. She raises her voice a little and addresses my father. "They worked multiple jobs. My mother worked at a dentist's office as a receptionist and at a grocery store on weekends. She also sometimes worked nights. My dad was a construction worker and a plumber. He had a night janitor job when there wasn't much construction hiring."

My parents both look like they need to take a bath just hearing about these blue-collar jobs. As if these very workers aren't the kind of people that the rest of us in society rely on. As if their work is without dignity and unworthy of respect.

"I... see," my dad says slowly. "And how did you meet our son?"

"Do you work with him?" Mom asks. She pauses. "For him?"

Her tone is polite, inquisitive even, but I know what she's really saying. She wants to know if I'm fucking my damn secretary or something. My parents want an excuse to say this relationship is inappropriate because of the imbalance of power, the employer-employee connection.

"Oh, no." Ava laughs. "I actually met Ethan first."

"At a club," Ethan says, because he can't ever resist needling someone.

Ava and Ethan exchange a look where they're smirking with their eyes. It's hilarious how identical that look is on their faces. I love how they're on the same wavelength like that.

My parents are less amused. "A club?"

"Were you... working there?" Mom adds, a whiff of scandal slipping into her tone.

"Just what are you implying?" I shoot back, a growl entering the edges of my voice.

I know exactly what she's implying. Mom's never liked Ethan, she thinks he's bad news. She thinks that by 'club' Ethan means 'strip club.' She thinks Ava's a stripper or a sex worker.

For the record, I wouldn't give a damn if she had been. I don't care what she does as long as it led her to us and to being our Omega. But Mom and Dad sure as hell won't see it that way.

And they're looking for any excuse to kick her to the curb.

"I was out with friends," Ava says, still keeping her tone even. I can smell it strongly on her now. Her displeasure and frustration. "I work at an animal shelter."

"You're a volunteer worker?" Dad asks.

"Well, no, I am paid."

"Not nearly as much as she's worth," Caleb says loyally.

I put my arm around Ava's waist. Dante steps back at the same moment, a fluid movement that keeps him close to us but cedes property of Ava to me, while he takes up the side so that now we're better blocked from others in the gallery.

I appreciate it. He's trying to keep anyone else from noticing this drama and gossiping about it.

"Ava's one of the most selfless people I know," I tell my parents. "She wants to help abused and abandoned animals. It's truly a noble cause."

"A noble cause to host parties and charity drives for," Mom counters. "But to actually get in there... Garrett, you're from a higher pedigree than this."

"Dogs have pedigrees," Ava says quietly. "People are just people."

I'm so fucking proud of her. I squeeze her waist gratefully.

"My dear," Mom says, in a tone she probably thinks is gentle but is really just condescending as fuck, "you don't understand our world. And that's all right. But this doesn't concern you."

"She doesn't even understand art," Dad mutters to me. "For crying out loud, Garrett. We raised you to have the best possible education."

"I don't care if Ava can talk about the rise of Cubism," I point out. "I care that she has a good heart. That she's kind and compassionate. That's the kind of values I want instilled in my kids, and that's the kind of mother I want for them."

We haven't even talked about kids yet, but I know that's something important to my parents. It's probably stupid of me to try to change their minds. I know what they're like. And yet... here I am, unable to stop myself from making the attempt.

"You are beautiful," Mom notes, looking at Ava. "I'll give you that. But Garrett, you shouldn't be choosing your Omega based on looks alone. You need someone from a good family. Someone who will give you connections. I could set you up with—"

"Don't start," I cut her off. "You know that anyone you suggest is going to be eighteen and barely legal and I'm not going to have an Omega who's a full decade younger than I am and basically still a child. I don't care what hedge fund company her dad owns."

"Well, you wouldn't be a decade older if you'd just mated an Omega when we told you to," Mom replies, sniffing.

"I wasn't ready for that."

"Yes, you had to start up your... company." Dad says the last word like it's some kind of bug.

I bristle, and Ava leans into my side, letting her scent waft over me. She's trying to calm me down.

"She says that she presented late." Mom eyes Ava. "But do

you really know that? She could have been in the facility for years waiting for the right rich Alpha to—"

"Did you seriously just call my mate a *gold digger*?" I snap.

"Garrett," Caleb says quietly, a warning. I know. I know, I'm close to causing a scene. And that's the opposite of what I want.

I take some deep breaths. While I'm trying to calm myself, Dad seizes the opportunity.

"I know that you think you two have a strong bond," he says, looking between Ava and me. "But you haven't cemented it yet. You can still change your mind and pick someone else. You'd be surprised at how quickly the love you two think you feel for each other will fade and reveal itself to be nothing but an infatuation."

Ava's mouth drops open in pure shock. Dante looks like he might hit my dad, and I wouldn't stop him if he did.

I step forward, and a little to the left, putting myself directly between Ava and my parents. Now they can't see her through the shield of my body.

"I'm an adult. And I have been for a while. This is my life, not yours. I told you that when I chose these men as my pack, and when we started our company. If you can't get that through your heads, that's on you."

Dad opens his mouth to speak, but I growl low in my throat and he shuts his mouth with an audible click.

"Ava is my choice. That's my choice to make. Not yours. And I want her. I care for her deeply, and no other Omega will be a better fit for me and my pack. I'm not leaving her and going after another Omega you think is better. That's *final*."

Nobody gets to harm my Omega or talk down to her. Not even my own parents. Ava is more than worthy to be my

Omega, or to be anyone's Omega. Frankly, I think any Alpha would be lucky to have her.

But I have her. She's mine. And I'm going to protect her from any threat, no matter where that threat comes from or who's in front of me.

Maybe that would've once upset me to have to choose between my parents and the woman I love. That was a long time ago, though. Now, I know what kind of people my parents are. And they're people that I'm ashamed to be related to. They're not the kind of people worth reasoning with.

They're callous snobs, through and through.

Mom and Dad look at me in shock for a moment. I think, in their deluded minds, they really thought that they could persuade me to give Ava up.

In a way, it's baffling to me. But in another way, it makes perfect sense. These two people were raised with silver spoons in their mouths. They both come from wealthy and well-established families. People don't usually tell them no.

In fact if someone does tell them no, they just throw money at the person until the answer changes to 'yes.'

"Stop harassing my mate," I growl at them.

I know that Ava and I aren't mated yet. But I want to mate her, and that's the plan. And whether we're technically mated or not, my parents need to know to keep their fucking snobbery to themselves. They don't own my life and I don't want their fucking opinions.

That seems to seal the deal for them. They know, just as everyone in our society knows, that you don't fuck with someone's mate. I've officially drawn the line in the sand.

If they persist after this, most people will be on my side. And my parents never like being on the wrong side of a scandal.

Mom huffs and Dad glares at me, the *I'm so disappointed in you* glare that, when I was much, much younger, would deeply upset me.

Not anymore.

They leave in a huff. I think they actually literally exit the gallery and head for the car.

Good fucking riddance.

Ava turns to me, staring up at me. She puts her hand on my chest, and I'm sure she can hear my racing heart and feel the way my chest is rapidly expanding and deflating.

My emotions are a riot, and I'm struggling to keep them from exploding in front of all these people.

I look down at her, though, and try to convey that I don't regret what I just did. I'm protective of her, yes. I'm a possessive bastard, true. But it's more than either of those things.

It's that I love her.

I've crossed a Rubicon. There's no going back now. I've made my statement, and I can't take it back. But the thing is, I don't want to.

Ava is my choice, and I'll fight for her, no matter what anyone else thinks.

# Chapter 38

## *Ava*

That certainly was an experience.

I can't deny that I'm feeling a little worked up myself. Nobody likes it when some snobs are telling them that they're not good enough. My parents might not have been the best but the things that I want to criticize about them have nothing to do with their family history or the jobs they worked.

To see such snobbery and condescension up close... it sure was something.

But as much as I'm offended at how I was just treated, I'm even more offended at how those two people just treated their son. Garrett's amazing and he's a responsible, mature man who can make his own choices in life.

To ignore all of his agency and accomplishments and act like he's a child... it burns something in the pit of my stomach.

Whatever I'm feeling, though, is nothing compared to Garrett himself.

His scent is a riot of emotions that shift the tones of it, making my nose go crazy. Even if I couldn't smell it on him, I can tell from his tone and how he's holding himself that he's on the edge. His breathing is hard and deep, and when I put my hand on his chest, I can feel his thundering heart.

I look over at Dante, seeking confirmation. I want to pull Garrett away to somewhere private so that I can give him the comfort and support that he needs, but I don't know if that's really a good idea or not.

After all, we are still in public. I don't know how many people have noticed what just happened. Ethan, Caleb, and Dante did a good job of creating a shield of human bodies to keep people from seeing our conflict directly. But people might have noticed.

I don't want to make this worse by adding to the gossip.

But Dante nods subtly, giving me the go-ahead. I just about collapse in relief.

I take Garrett's hand and pull him away from the main gallery. There are a couple of hallways that I noticed earlier, leading off into smaller gallery rooms, or to bathrooms, or storage and the back offices.

I pick one of the hallways and head toward it. There's a velvet rope at the end of the hallway cordoning off another room, but we easily duck under it. This room is smaller and bare, but with little studs in the walls for paintings and plaques. This must be another gallery that sometimes is used, but not for tonight.

The room is irregularly shaped, and there's a small alcove at one end that I lead Garret toward. Once I'm sure we're out of sight of anyone passing by, I gently press him against the wall so I can get a good look at him. Someone could still possibly come along, but it's private enough I think we'll be okay, and can talk uninterrupted.

"Garrett." I slide my hands up his chest to his shoulders, squeezing. "Talk to me. Are you okay?"

He shakes his head. "I should be asking you that. You're the one that they kept insulting. Fucking hell, little one. I know they're assholes, but I didn't expect..." He shakes his head again. "I'm sorry for how they treated you."

"Why are you apologizing? You didn't make them behave that way. You did nothing wrong."

It's funny, but this is basically what the Alphas said to me about Marcus. I understand their point of view now. It seems silly to me for Garrett to blame himself for the actions of others. Those people might have been his parents, but it's clear that their actions are their own.

There's nothing he really could've done to stop them. And, I realize, there's nothing I could do to stop Marcus from being terrible. It's what he wants to do, so he's going to do it.

Even though that weight now feels lifted from my shoulders, Garrett doesn't look very convinced about his own.

"I should've been prepared for them to be here," he tells me. "They're the kind of people who love these things. They like to think of themselves as sophisticated."

"You can't read their minds."

"Maybe not but I know my parents." He sighs. "I should know they wouldn't really give up on bringing me back into the fold and all that bullshit. I'm their eldest son, that means something to them."

I've never heard Garrett sound so tired and defeated. That's not the Garrett I know.

"Hey." I take his face in my hands. "It doesn't matter what they said to me. Okay? And it doesn't matter that you're their son. You had no control over them. They're going to do whatever shitty thing they want to do. You can't predict everything and you can't live your life paranoid about them."

Garrett smiles, a tiny, small thing, but I'll take it. "Sounds familiar."

"I know, right?" I tease him. "Look. I don't care what they think, okay? Yes, I'm... I'm still getting used to this whole Omega thing. But why would I care about the opinion of some assholes like that? It's not like I'm ever going to see them again."

"You won't," Garrett growls. "I'll make sure of it."

"I think you just did," I point out. "And that's what I'm trying to tell you. You were wonderful back there. You took care of me and protected me the way I would always hope my Alpha would. But I need to make sure *you're* okay."

I point back and forth between us. "This is a two-way street, remember? It's not just you taking care of me. I'm your Omega. But you're my Alpha. I want to take care of you too."

Garrett nods. I'm not sure how convinced he is, though. He still looks upset.

"You know I don't judge you for them, right?" I ask quietly. "I only care about you and my pack. I care what you think, and what Ethan, and Caleb, and Dante think. What we have? What exists between us? That's just for us. For nobody else."

Garrett nods. I can feel myself blush as I say my next words. "And what we have is so much better than anything I ever expected. You're one of the best and most honorable men I know."

"I..."

"I mean it. Very few people would give up their family wealth. They might disagree with their family but they would still stick around because of the money. You got rid of it. You left it behind so you could live on your own terms. I admire you for that, Garrett. I really do."

I kiss him gently on the jaw. "You're my perfect Alpha."

Garrett groans softly and pulls me close, burying his face in my hair. I wrap my arms around him tightly, inhaling his scent.

The feel of his body so close to mine and the rush of his intoxicating Alpha scent have a gush of wetness dampening my panties. I can feel it when it happens, and I squeeze my thighs together as the fabric becomes immediately soaked.

Garrett stiffens.

I know he was already affected by our embrace, the same way I was, but when he drags in a long breath through his nose, I'm certain he can smell my arousal.

*It's the best and the worst thing in the world that these men are so deeply attuned to me,* I think as my pulse quickens.

"Fuck, you smell so good, little one," he growls softly, nuzzling his nose deeper into my hair.

He inhales, and the feel of him scenting me actually makes my knees wobble.

"What do I smell like?" I whisper, unable to help myself.

It's probably not a good idea to feed the fire burning between us, not when we're in a public space only barely hidden from view of the other guests. But I can't really bring myself to care about that right now. The thick bulge of Garrett's cock is pressing against my stomach, and it's stealing my focus, narrowing my attention down to just the two of us, as if the rest of the world has ceased to exist.

"What do you smell like?" Garrett's rough chuckle teases my ear. He drags in another breath, a purr rumbling in his chest as he exhales. "You smell like strawberries. Vanilla. Lilac." He inhales again. "You smell like reckless desire." His arms band tighter around me, molding my body to his. "But most of all, you smell like *mine*."

His voice drops into a register I've never heard before as he says the last word, and I whimper softly as my legs wobble again, threatening to give out entirely.

"I'm yours, huh?" I whisper, my heart pounding in my chest as I work a hand down between us to slide my palm over his clothed cock. "Prove it."

He stiffens, hissing through his teeth, and more slick floods my panties. I haven't been this turned on since my heat ended, and the arousal I feel right now is almost strong enough to rival that.

It's not just hormones, not just the potent, all-consuming attraction I feel for this Alpha. My desire for him has gone far beyond the physical by this point. I crave him on all levels, drawn to every part of him—and this newest revelation about who this gruff, stoic Alpha is at heart only makes me crave him more.

"How do you want me to prove it?" Garrett lifts his head from my hair, gazing down at me with blazing dark eyes. "What should I do to you to prove how much you're mine, little one?"

The words *bite me* hover on the tip of my tongue, making my stomach flutter. But even though I'm tempted to say them, I know this wouldn't be the right place for that. If—*when*—I bond with these Alphas, I want to do it properly.

And hidden away in an alcove at an art gallery opening definitely doesn't fit that description.

But there are still plenty of other things we can get up to back here.

"Fuck me," I whisper, the butterflies in my stomach flapping even harder. "Right here. Let me feel your cock, Alpha. Prove that it's mine."

He groans, his features tightening with strain. "Fucking hell, Ava. When you say things like that, you make it impossible *not* to fuck you."

I grin, squeezing his cock. "Good. That's the idea."

"Do you really think you can stay quiet?" he asks, arching a dark brow. "We might be hidden from view, but if you scream, everyone in the gallery will hear you. Can you be a good girl and keep your voice down if I give you what you need?"

"Yes."

My answer comes way too quickly, and the corners of Garrett's lips twitch. It's not a full smirk, but it's clear he knows I'm bullshitting him right now.

I'll definitely do my best to stay quiet... but promising him that I'll be able pull it off is a stretch. I know what it's like to be fucked by this man, and there's an equally good chance that I'll shatter some precious piece of art with my screams as there is that I'll be able to muffle my noises.

But I still don't really care.

So I hold Garrett's gaze as I do the one thing that I'm sure will push him the rest of the way. The thing I *know* will eviscerate the last of his self-constraint. Slipping my hand down his pants, I palm his bare cock, skin to skin. My fingers wrap around the velvety warmth of his shaft, and I let out a soft, satisfied noise.

Garrett growls. He grips my chin in one hand, holding my gaze and refusing to let me look away as he walks me backward a few steps until my back hits the wall behind me.

"Panties off," he commands.

My heart skips a beat in my chest, and I use my free hand to reach under the skirt of my dress and hook the waistband of my panties. I shimmy them down over my hips, and they slide down my legs to pool at my feet.

Garrett lets me stroke his cock two more times before he steps back, and my hand slides out from his pants as he crouches down to retrieve my panties.

They're gripped in his large fist as he straightens, the small scrap of fabric looking even tinier in his hand, and when he brings them up to his face and inhales just like he did when his face was buried in my hair, I almost come on the spot. The wall at my back is the only thing keeping me upright as my clit throbs needily and my entire body shivers with anticipation.

I think for a second that Garrett is going to pocket my panties, but as he drags them away from his face, his gaze finds mine again.

"Open your mouth," he says quietly.

My eyes flare wide as I realize what he's getting at, and my pussy clenches so hard that I can feel my inner thighs getting wet.

I drop my jaw, my eyes locked on his as liquid heat burns through my veins. Garrett trails his knuckles along the line of my jaw, then grips it loosely and stuffs my panties into my mouth. The crotch is soaked through, and the distinctive flavor of my arousal hits my tongue, making me moan around the fabric.

"You like the way you taste, little one?" Garrett's dark eyes glint. "Now you see why all of us are so addicted to you. I've never sampled anything better. I could drown in your slick and die a happy man."

I whimper, unable to respond with words because of the makeshift gag in my mouth.

But Garrett doesn't seem to need to hear me beg. He tilts my chin up a little, scanning my face. "You good?"

I nod emphatically, turned on and desperate. This time, a rare smile breaks out across his face, and he releases my chin, his hands going for the button and fly of his pants. He works them open, groaning under his breath as he frees his cock. It's swollen and flushed, precum gleaming at the tip, his length so hard that it looks almost painful.

"Wrap your arms around my neck," he instructs, and as I comply, he slides his hands over my hips, gathering the fabric of my dress to get it out of the way. Then he lifts me up, bracing me against the wall. My legs instinctively go around his waist, and with my skirt pulled up, there's nothing between us to stop his cock from sliding against my slick folds.

I make a little noise in my throat, and Garrett's nostrils flare as he shifts his hips a bit, lining himself up.

The slow press of his cock as he fills me up is the most delicious kind of torture I've ever experienced. I know he's probably trying to go slow so that he can maintain some level of control, but every inch that he slides inside only makes me desperate for the next inch.

*More. More. More.*

It's my body's mantra when it comes to these Alphas, and I can't stop myself from digging my heels into Garrett's ass, urging him to take things deeper, *harder*.

The sounds of the party are a bit distant and muffled from where we are, but I can still hear them, and the reminder that we're in public, that anyone could take a wrong turn and stumble upon us at any moment, only makes me want this more.

When Garrett is finally buried all the way to the root, I squeeze my walls around him, trying to drive him as crazy as I feel.

He bites out a curse, his grip on my thighs tightening. Then, holding me in place against the wall, he draws out almost as slowly as he worked his way in. When just the tip of him is still inside me, I start to seriously consider spitting out the gag so I can beg him to stop teasing me—but before I have to resort to that, Garrett drives his hips forward, impaling me in a heavy, hard thrust that pins me between him and the wall.

My entire body stiffens, stars shooting through me as I claw at his neck and shoulders. "Mmmph! Mmhhhh…"

He chuckles, his lips finding my ear. "Sorry, I didn't quite catch that, little one. Did you say, 'I fucking love your cock, Garrett'? Because it feels like maybe you do."

I moan around the gag again, my heart thundering in anticipation as he draws out slowly and then slams back in. He keeps up the pace like that, slow withdrawals followed by thrusts that rock me to my core, and my eyes roll up in their sockets. The little alcove we're in seems to go fuzzy around me, my entire world narrowed down to Garrett's harsh breaths and the feel of his strong body holding me up, claiming me, *owning* me.

"Such a good Omega," he purrs. "So perfect and tight for me. I wish everyone here could see me fuck you. I wish they could see how beautifully you take my cock. The way you soak me with your slick, the way you clench me so tight. There's not a piece of art here that's more stunning than you are, little one."

He drops his head to suck on the delicate skin of my throat as he finishes speaking, and the sensation makes goosebumps break out all over me. His teeth scrape against the side of my neck, and my breath hitches. It's not a bite, but it's close enough that it makes my pulse race.

"I want you to come on my cock," he whispers. "With the taste of your sweet arousal on your tongue. I know you're close. I can feel the way your body is pulling me in. You want me to knot you right here, don't you? To lock our bodies together so that even if we got caught, I *couldn't* stop fucking you. Is that what you want?"

His words, and the overwhelming thrusts of his thick cock, are driving me out of my mind. I nod, my thighs cramping from how tight they're clenching around him.

He's right. As filthy and reckless as it is, I want his knot. Right here. Right now.

He picks up speed, no longer sliding out slowly, as if he can't hold back anymore. Our bodies slap together, and even with my panties wadded up in my mouth, I know we're no longer being as quiet as we meant to. The sounds of our harsh breaths and the rhythmic clapping sound aren't exactly subtle.

But then Garrett hits the perfect spot inside me, and any worries about getting caught fly out of my mind as I fall apart. My brain nearly melts out of my ears as blinding white light flashes across my vision, a burst of pleasure detonating inside me.

A scream rises up my throat, held back only by the fabric of my panties. Garrett grunts harshly, and I can feel the knot inflating at the base of his cock. It feels thicker than ever as he forces it inside me, locking us together as he swells and pulses, filling me with his cum.

My head tips back against the wall, my eyelids fluttering closed as I go limp in the aftermath, barely keeping my legs wrapped around his waist. I feel spent and worn out in the best way, and it sure as hell beats the sick, nervous feeling in my stomach as I talked to Garrett's parents earlier.

"Oh, I agree completely." The sound of someone's voice rises over the distant hum of the crowd. "Some of the pieces on display tonight are truly breathtaking. It's a triumph, certainly."

My head snaps up, my eyes going wide.

*Fuck.*

Garrett tenses up too, his dark brown eyes locked with mine as another person responds to the first speaker. They seem to be coming closer, and it occurs to me that they might be walking right toward us.

A rush of nerves floods me, along with a deviant, audacious spike of heat at the idea that we might be discovered like this.

*Hmm. Do I have an exhibitionist side that I never knew about?*

My pussy clamps tight around Garrett's knot, making him grunt softly, and he flashes me a warning look. I nod, although I can't stop my walls from fluttering around him a little.

The two of us hold our breath, still locked together, as the two patrons continue talking nearby. Their footsteps draw a bit closer, and I bite down harder on the damp fabric of my panties...

But then they change direction, heading away as the sounds of their voices grow more faint.

For a quiet, sustained moment, Garrett and I just stare at each other, waiting to make sure they're really gone.

Then, at the same time, both of us burst into laughter.

He reaches up to gently pull the panties from my mouth, and a few last chuckles spill out, but I quickly muffle them. He leans forward to kiss my lips, his chest still shaking with amusement as he brushes my hair back from my face.

"That was close," he murmurs, grinning against my mouth.

"Yeah, it was." I kiss him again. "But worth it, though."

"Oh, that was never a question." The hand still on my ass gives a little squeeze. "With you, it's always worth it."

# Chapter 39

## *Ava*

I wake up a few days later to find that I'm in the middle of an Alpha sandwich.

Caleb and Ethan are on either side of me, snuggled close. I slept amazingly well. Honestly, since I've started sleeping with the men, and I really do mean sleeping in the literal sense, I've never slept better in my life.

It's like even while I'm unconscious, my brain knows that I'm safe and protected. More than that—loved.

Not that I've said that word out loud yet. None of us have. But I feel it more and more every day. And I feel just about certain that the others feel it too.

I stretch lazily, enjoying the sensation. To my surprise, Ethan and Caleb each drape an arm over my waist, a coordinated movement that tells me they're not actually asleep like I thought.

Ethan kisses the soft skin behind my ear. "Good morning."

"Mmm, good morning."

His teeth scrape over the shell of my ear. "And happy birthday."

326

I freeze in surprise. "My birthday?"

Caleb, the one facing me, gets an adorable scrunch to his face. "You forgot?"

I shrug. "Birthdays aren't usually something I celebrate."

My parents never bothered to throw me a party, or take time off, or do anything special for my birthday. It was just another day for them. And when I got to college, I didn't know how to ask for that attention. It felt wrong, somehow, to request that people treat me a certain way on a certain day.

Once I was an Omega, sharing any personal information felt like some kind of danger. Birthdays have absolutely nothing to do with whether you're more likely to be an Alpha, a Beta, or an Omega. Some people have tried to say that star signs have something to do with it, but it's all woo-woo nonsense.

Sharing my birthday wouldn't make people suspect I was an Omega. And yet, it was personal information. That made me wary.

So really, I haven't celebrated my birthday... wow, just about ever. Never in my life have I had a proper birthday celebration.

That's depressing.

Except that my Alphas seem determined to change that.

"Well, you're celebrating them from now on," Caleb informs me.

Ethan slides his hand down my body, between my legs. "And I think we know just how to start off the celebration. Don't you, Caleb?"

Caleb's grin is wicked. "As a matter of fact..."

I moan, already wet. My body is so attuned to them now, craving even the slightest touch.

A wicked gleam enters Ethan's eyes, and he delves his hand beneath the waistband of my little sleep shorts. His thumb finds my clit, and he circles it slowly while he looks over my head at Caleb.

"What do you say? Should we show our sweet Omega what kind of pampering she should expect on her birthdays from now on?"

"Definitely."

Caleb's hand trails down my back, and when I feel his fingers slip beneath the waistband of my shorts, I half regret wearing anything to bed last night. Sandwiched between these two gorgeous Alphas makes me wish I were already naked.

Not that my clothes seem to be slowing either of them down. Ethan's thumb keeps sliding back and forth over my clit while Caleb slips a hand between my ass cheeks. His fingertip grazes over my back hole, and I drag in a breath, the muscles clenching involuntarily.

"You know, watching you get knotted in your pretty ass and your pussy at the same time was one of the hottest things I've ever seen," he whispers. "I'll never forget it. The way you took them both, so hungry for Alpha cock that it took two to satisfy you?"

I can feel him shudder softly behind me, and the idea that the memory of me getting fucked by his pack mates is affecting him so much makes warmth flood my chest.

I arch my back a little, pressing my ass into his hand, begging wordlessly for more.

"You all satisfy me," I breathe. "You more than satisfy me. Together, separately—it's all incredible. But... I did like that a lot."

"You like having all your holes filled by us," he supplies, sliding his finger into my asshole as if to demonstrate exactly what he means. The wanton moan that spills from my lips only proves him right, and when Ethan slips two fingers into my pussy, I can't decide whether to roll my hips forward or backward.

Fortunately, they don't make me choose. Both of the Alphas start to fuck me with their fingers, working them in deeper and picking up the pace of their movements. The pad of Ethan's thumb is relentless on my clit, and it only takes a few more seconds for me to go flying over the edge, moaning each of their names in turn as I come with a shuddering sigh.

"There you go." Ethan grins at me, his eyes bright. "First orgasm of your birthday, Birthday Girl."

"But not the last," Caleb promises, leaning closer to kiss the back of my neck.

And he's right about that.

They keep toying with my pussy and ass, and I come again less than a minute later, squirming between them as they trade off kissing me.

"I know you can take more," Caleb murmurs, his sky-blue eyes shining as our lips break apart. "I've seen you come until you were nothing but a puddle on the floor."

"We won't wreck you that bad this morning," Ethan adds with a chuckle, trailing his mouth up my exposed throat. "Dante and Garrett would never forgive us, because they've got plans to help you celebrate too, and it will help if you can walk for that."

I laugh, and the sound turns into a gasp as he hooks his fingers inside me, finding my g-spot.

"But give us at least one more," Ethan coaxes, his voice dropping. "I want to feel you clench around my fingers again, just the way you clench around my knot."

He brings his head a little lower, nipping at my collarbones, then ducks beneath the covers. A second later, his lips latch onto my breast, teasing my nipple through the thin fabric of the top I'm wearing. Caleb fucks my ass more forcefully, his free hand sliding around to play with my other breast.

I don't know how they do it, since there's no way either of them should be able to tell what the other is doing, but somehow, Caleb squeezes and tugs at my nipple in almost the exact same pattern Ethan is following with his teeth and tongue.

The effect is like a shot of pure heat injected straight into my veins, and I give up all semblance of trying to stay still or quiet. I writhe between them, arching and gasping, lost in the rush of sensations. One of my hands sinks into Ethan's soft brown hair, urging him to keep going, while I reach back with the other to blindly grope for Caleb. I end up finding the bulge of his cock, and he hisses out a breath, thrusting into my hand.

"I'm... I'm close," I pant. "I'll come again for you... if you give me your cocks."

"Negotiating for your orgasms." Ethan laughs from beneath the blankets. "I like that. Very savvy of you, gorgeous. You drive a hard bargain."

"Very *hard*," Caleb rasps, thrusting into my touch again.

His dick pulses as if to drive home the pun, and I want to think that I roll my eyes because it's so corny—but in reality, it's probably because that orgasm I just teased them with is a lot closer than I thought. If they don't fuck me soon, I'm going to fall over the edge again, with or without their cocks.

But I'd really rather it be *with*.

"Get inside me," I demand. "Now."

"Ooh, our pretty Omega is bossy on her birthday." Ethan bites down on my nipple, making me moan.

"We've got you, sweetheart," Caleb promises.

His fingers disappear from my ass, but before I even have

time to whine out my disappointment, he and Ethan are moving. Ethan withdraws his hand from my sleep pants, then tugs the pants and my panties down my legs. The covers are thrown off, and my top disappears so fast that I can't even track where it goes.

The two of them are naked in front of me a second later, and Ethan's green eyes gleam as he tells me, "Hands and knees. Show Caleb that pretty ass you want him to fuck so much."

I obey in a heartbeat, my thighs wet with slick and my heart thundering. I'm so close to another orgasm that even the friction from moving to get into position almost sets me off, and when Caleb grips my hips and slides into my pussy, I drop my head between my arms, too overwhelmed to hold it up.

He coats his cock in my wetness, getting himself perfectly slick, and then withdraws. The next thing I feel is the slight pressure as he starts to work his way inside my ass.

"There you go. Taking him so well," Ethan croons.

He slides into place beneath me, and Caleb helps support me so that I can adjust my position until I'm straddling his pack mate.

Ethan guides his cock to my entrance, and the two of them work together as they situate themselves inside me, thrusting in small pulses until I'm completely filled by them.

My arms are shaking with the effort of holding myself up, my entire body shaking with the effort of holding back my climax—and when Caleb whispers, "You can let go now, sweetheart," I do.

The rush of pleasure feels even better with my men connected to me, inside me, and I scream both of their names as I come hard. The sound finally gets swallowed up as I drop my head to kiss Ethan, needing his lips on mine as an anchor to survive the intensity of it all. He kisses me back like he wants to devour me, holding my hips steady as he and Caleb thrust in counterpoint to each other, fucking into me as they chase their own release.

Caleb comes first, his hips jerking as he unloads inside me. He doesn't knot me this time, though, and I have a feeling it's because of what Ethan said about the other two Alphas not wanting to miss out on celebrating my birthday with me.

Ethan finishes less than a minute later, his fingers digging into my hips as he grinds against me, pumping me full of his cum. He doesn't knot either, and even though the Omega inside me craves it, I can't deny that the feeling of these two men buried inside me is pretty damn perfect just like this.

"So..." Ethan moves his hands from my hips to my face, cupping my jaw as we break our kiss. "How has your birthday been so far, gorgeous?"

I grin down at him, so wide that my cheeks ache. "So far? Best one ever."

The two of them take their time cleaning me up, then we all get out of bed. I stand on wobbly legs, letting Ethan help me with an arm around my waist. A glint of pride enters his eyes as he watches me walk like a baby deer.

"You okay there?" he asks, lifting an eyebrow.

"I will be. Just give me a minute."

He smirks at how hoarse my voice is. That's what happens when you scream someone's name at the height of passion. "Well, I can carry you if you need me too. We've got lots more plans for the day. The fun is just beginning."

A little shiver of excitement runs up my spine. "I like the sound of that."

The door to the bedroom opens as someone knocks softly,

and Dante pokes his head in. His nostrils flare, and I know he can smell the scent of sex lingering in the air, because his eyes darken. He clears his throat, his gaze meeting mine.

"I'm glad you're all up," he says. "Come with me. It's ready for you."

"What's ready?" I ask, narrowing my eyes. But the wariness is only feigned. I trust these men, and I know that whatever they're doing, I'm going to like it.

"Throw on some clothes and find out." Dante scans my body with appreciation in his eyes, then jerks his chin to one side. "Meet us in the library."

*Okay, then.*

Ethan, Caleb and I get dressed, and then they lead me down to the library, where Garrett and Dante are eagerly whispering to each other while they set up something on the table. They stop when I enter and grin at me, gesturing to the table.

It looks like a small model of a building. Huh.

I come closer, peering down at it. It's a lovely rendering, and the building looks very well-constructed. But... "I don't understand. What is this?"

It's not a house, or a skyscraper. I can't tell what it's supposed to be for.

All four Alphas beam at me with excitement. "It's a scale model of an animal shelter that we're building for you."

My jaw drops open.

I stare from one to the other. "Are you... you're serious?"

Of course they're serious. I know that. They wouldn't lie to me about something this important. It wouldn't be a very funny or kind joke. But I find myself asking anyway.

"I asked the others if they thought it would be a good idea," Garrett tells me. "After our conversation. You'd said how difficult it can be to get the funding to run an animal shelter properly."

"And one thing we definitely have is funding," Ethan points out.

"We felt it would be best to build you a whole new building from the ground up," Dante explains. "So that we make sure it has all the room and facilities you'll need."

"It's still under construction," Caleb adds, "but we have all the plans finished and we wanted to show you what it'll look like."

Tears spring into my eyes. I'm overwhelmed by their thoughtfulness and generosity. I can honestly hardly believe what I'm hearing.

I'm going to be able to open and run my own animal shelter, a dream that I thought might not actually ever happen.

My mates did this for me.

I throw myself at them, kissing each one of them in turn, babbling out my thanks. I'm crying a little, but they don't laugh at me. They just hug me tightly.

Every time I feel like I've learned just how much my mates care about me, and how far they'll go for me, I'm proven wrong. They go above and beyond.

I'm more certain than ever that these are the men I love. The men I want to be with.

They're making all my dreams come true.

# Chapter 40

## *Ethan*

Maybe it was a bad idea to have Ava sit in my lap.

We're both focused on working together in my home office, trying to find out who this spy is. We've been talking about it, and decided that trying to find evidence wasn't going anywhere.

All of us have been working on it, of course, but Ava especially has been searching everything with a fine-toothed comb. I feel like we have to drag her away from the papers so she'll eat and sleep. I'm not complaining about distracting her with sex. Far from it. But I've worried about her being so fueled by her guilt.

Once we determined that just searching for information wasn't going to work, we decided that we're going to try a new method.

We'll set a trap.

Ava's worked with me and we've set up a sting operation. I sent a company-wide announcement that we're making a slight change to the heart-monitoring system in the watch due to an internal error.

What nobody in the company knows is that they've all gotten a slightly different pathway to access this new schematic.

It's only a minor difference in the meaningless numbers in the code at the top of the new schematic. It looks like it means something, but it's really just window dressing. We then set up an alarm system for any time someone accesses the schematics, and we're monitoring Marcus's own company announcements.

We'll know, from the difference in that coding at the top of the schematic, who exactly the mole in our company is. Marcus will include that specific sequence of numbers in his announcement, and we'll have a ping from whoever accessed the schematic.

It's a classic espionage trick the government has used a few times, usually to catch someone leaking information to the press by giving multiple people each a slightly different document. As soon as this spy makes a move, we'll know who it was.

Unfortunately, I've made the decision to have Ava in my lap while we do all this, and she's proving to be a hell of a distraction.

I'm really not looking forward to the day I'll have to be in the office all the time again. I know that Ava is going to have her own life in the shelter as well. But I love being able to have her with us all the time, getting to cuddle her and touch her constantly.

Right now, she's perched in my lap, the touching soothing both her and me. She's definitely past her heat now, but we've all gotten used to being able to be physical with her, not even in a sexual way, just in the constant touching.

Of course, there is the sexual aspect to it, as well.

Ava is perched on my lap so that she can see the laptop

screen as well, while she works on her tablet. I try to focus on monitoring the schematics for pings, but every time she shifts, her ass presses against my cock.

It's maddening.

I want to grab her hips and grind against that sweet ass of hers until I bite her shoulder and come in my pants. I can feel myself getting hard as she shifts unconsciously on my lap, the natural minute movements of her body turning into a terrible tease.

*Focus, Ethan, come on.* Sex is fun, but it isn't as important as finding out who's doing this to our company. Someone has betrayed us and is threatening all of our work and all that we stand for, and I can't allow it.

But it just. Keeps. Happening.

I wrap my arm around her waist and haul her closer to me, kissing slowly along her neck. Nothing too obscene. Just light, feathery kisses up and down her sweet-smelling skin.

At first, she tries to ignore me and keep concentrating. I can feel how hard she's working to not let me win this little game we've entered into. But her fingers tremble as she tries to hold the tablet, as she tries to use the touch screen to scroll through documents. Tiny gasps escape from between her plush lips before she can stop them.

"Ethan," she whispers, and that's when I know I've got her. "W-we need to concentrate. It could be any minute."

"You're absolutely right," I agree graciously.

I stop and rest my hand high up on her thigh. She's taken to wearing these lovely short skirts and dresses that I picked out for her. I hoped she'd like them, since they do such a great job of showing off her body.

I've noticed she started getting into them more as her heat subsided. I think that she needed the confidence boost that came from us showing her just how attractive we find her. After so long hiding who she is, including her body, now she gets to revel in it and celebrate herself.

I'm really proud of her and how far she's come. Watching Ava become more and more confident is the greatest reward I could hope for. We all want our Omega to be happy with who she is and confident in herself. She's an amazing person, and she should know it.

Of course, now the downside to this is that she's damn distracting all the time. She's cute as hell in her yellow skirt and pale blue blouse. She looks like she stepped off the cover of a magazine. But it's a bit less cute, and hell of a lot more tempting, when she's on my lap and I can push my hand up under her skirt to rest it on her bare thigh.

Ava shudders, but I focus back on the laptop. I just stay like that, letting her grow increasingly desperate from the tease of my hand so close to where she wants it.

Finally, she cracks. "Ethan... please..."

"Please what?" I ask, making myself sound as confused as possible. "I'm focusing on work like you said."

Ava deliberately grinds her ass back against me, and my cock pulses with need. Fuck I want her so fucking badly.

"Oh?" I stroke her thigh. "Is my little Omega desperate for that nice, thick Alpha knot? Is that what you want?"

Ava squirms. "Y-yes."

"Is that why you're being so naughty and distracting me during work?" I kiss her neck again. "You know it's your fault distracting me. You with that sweet ass right up against my cock. You knew exactly what you were doing to me, didn't you?"

"Yes," Ava admits in a whisper.

"What do you want, baby? I want to hear you say it."

"I—I want your cock."

"Just my cock?" I kiss up her neck to her ear, scraping my teeth over the lobe. "You don't want my nice thick knot too? You don't want me to bend you over this desk? Or, even better—I can just keep you on my lap and bounce you up and down on my cock until my knot is nice and snug inside you."

Ava moans, writhing. "Yes, yes, yes, Ethan—Ethan please—"

"I want you to say what you want. Go on, gorgeous."

"I want you to f..." Ava's voice trails off as we both jolt, my laptop and her tablet ringing with an alarm.

"Christ, who knew it would be so loud," I mutter, quickly silencing the alarm as Ava fumbles to turn hers off.

As much as I hate to be interrupted when I'm about to dirty talk my Omega to a sweet orgasm before I fuck her, all the energy I just had for lust is now immediately diverted into adrenaline as I open up the ping that just went off.

My heart is no longer racing because of desire, but for a completely different reason.

Ava and I peer together at the information. "Looks like it was someone from research and development," she notes. "They went to access fake schematic number seven."

I pull up the employee ID to see who it is. Ah, crap. "That's Tracy. Why would she do this?"

Ava looks at the photo of Tracy. Tracy's been with us for a few years. She's a Beta with delicate features and light red hair. I've always thought her a bit timid, but I liked her. She's done great work with the team.

Now she's turned around and become a spy for Marcus. For at least a few weeks, if not longer.

Ava sighs and settles back against my chest, but not like she's relaxing. More like she's seeking comfort. She feels stiff in my arms.

I wrap my arms around her and squeeze. "Hey, what's wrong?"

She gestures at the screen. "I just feel like I should've guessed it would be a woman."

*Ah.* "Ava..."

She sets her tablet aside on the table. "He's good at manipulating people and making you think he's wonderful. She's probably told him everything while they were in bed together and he just made her feel like she was the most special person in the world."

"I'm sorry, sweetheart." I take her chin in my fingers and turn her so that she's now sideways on my lap, facing me. "You know that we would do anything to erase him from your life, even your memories if we could."

Ava smiles. "You're so sweet." She kisses me gently. "I hope you know how much I appreciate you. All of you."

I squeeze her tightly, kissing her cheek. It is tragic, the idea that Marcus seduced and controlled another woman and convinced her to spy for him. But that's not our problem. Tracy can sort out her own life. She still committed corporate espionage, still stole from us and spied on us. She still broke our trust.

"Look, gorgeous." I point at the screen. "You did it. We did it. We found the mole. And now we're going to make that bastard pay for it."

Ava looks at me, her eyes luminous, and an almost disbelieving smile on her face.

"You're right," she whispers. "We did. We found the mole. We got our proof!"

I kiss her and rock her back and forth, the two of us smiling as we rest our foreheads together.

Marcus is going *down*.

# Chapter 41

## *Dante*

The first thing we have to do after Ava and Ethan find the mole is consult with our lawyers again.

I won't ever forget the looks of joy on their faces as they ran up to tell us. Ava leapt into our arms, practically glowing with excitement. I'm going to do everything I can to make sure that happiness stays and she doesn't ever have to worry about this jackass ever again.

Of course, just one sketchy log in to a new schematic alone isn't enough for us to successfully slam Marcus with proof that he's been engaging in corporate espionage. Instead, we use that as the jumping-off point.

Now that we have just one person to investigate, our employee Tracy in R&D, we can comb through everything she's done the last few months and gather more evidence to confront her.

Being a techie herself, she's done a good job of covering her tracks. I'm not surprised that Ava couldn't find anything, even with how hard she was working, although I know Ava doesn't see it that way.

She compiles everything Tracy's done, every single email sent, literally everything, including times she logged onto her work account while at home in her apartment, and goes over it all again late into the night.

We're more than happy to find ways to pull her away from her work and get her to sleep. Fucking her nice and slow and deep until she's exhausted from orgasms is my favorite way. She drops right to sleep after that and can catch up on her rest.

I tease her that this is how we're going to have to treat her when she's got her animal shelter up and running.

"Are we going to have to come into your work and fuck you to get you to leave?" I tease her while we cuddle in bed after some very athletic sex.

Ava laughs. "Honestly? Maybe." Then she adds, "But only if I can come into the office and do the same to you guys when you're neck-deep in some new invention and also forget to sleep."

What a pack we make. We're a bunch of workaholic peas in a pod. "Deal."

I love it. I love how we balance each other out and we're able to take care of each other, how we get work done but also have fun. We make a great team, the five of us.

Life truly is better since Ava came into it, and I intend to keep it that way.

Caleb goes into work and while Tracy's out, he checks her computer. We pick Caleb because he just looks so innocent. Nobody will question whatever he's doing.

From Tracy's history on her computer, it looks like she's printed out a lot of things, including blueprints and other technical information on our smart watch. There's no reason for her to print any of this, since all the work for it is done on the computer or with other equipment in one of our main development rooms.

She simply can't really get any work done on these little print-outs. Even if she were taking this all home to do some overtime, and from what I've seen of her reports to the team, she hasn't done nearly enough work for that to add up. The people who do take our work home have to get permission anyway, and log it in. She hasn't done that.

No, she's been printing this stuff up so that she can take it back to her place and give it to Marcus, who can then take it to his team and have them read it all and create an exact replica.

There's also the number of times she's logged onto her work account from her home Wi-Fi. There's no reason for her to have done that, especially since those times she's logged on also don't show any changes made or work done on the device.

It's pretty damn clear she was just logging on so that she could show Marcus, or someone from Marcus's company, the information on the watch.

We're all pretty damn sure it was Marcus himself. Ava doesn't think that he would've trusted anyone else with this mission, and besides, if he shows up at his company with all the blueprints for this new device, he gets to look like a genius to his employees and the shareholders, and nobody will be the wiser. There's no one who can rat him out.

Except for Tracy.

Our lawyers inform us that while this is all good stuff, it's entirely circumstantial. To get Marcus to cave, we need a confession from Tracy.

So that's exactly what we do.

I go into the office with Ethan. Garrett wants to come with us, but we're worried he'll intimidate Tracy a little too much and she'll clam up out of fear. Caleb's a bit too soft. She'll think she can work him over. But Ethan and I should be able to strike a good balance.

We get to my private office and call Tracy in. The moment she enters, Ethan closes and locks the door behind her. "Tracy, please." I gesture to the chair in front of me. "Sit."

She lies at first. Of course she does. She gets indignant and insists that she doesn't know what we're talking about. She says that we're out of our minds and that we're assholes for even thinking for a moment that she could engage in corporate espionage.

"We have the information from your computer, Tracy," Ethan points out. "We're not accusing you for no reason here. We know what you did. We were just hoping that we could talk to you about it instead of slapping you with legal action."

Tracy goes pale at those words, and I can feel her mentally grabbing onto Ethan's soft tone. She wavers, and holds steady in her lies for a bit longer, but finally, it all comes spilling out.

I record the conversation—and inform her it's being recorded, so Marcus can't throw it out later—as she details what happened. How Marcus ran into her and was so charming and handsome.

Yeah, I suspect he orchestrated that chance meeting. My employees at the company tend to get lunch from one of the restaurants that are on this street and they're all creatures of habit. It would be easy for Marcus to pick a pretty girl who he knows goes to the same sandwich shop every day for lunch and stage a meet-cute.

Tracy starts to cry as she explains that she didn't plan to hurt anyone. Marcus was just so charming and persuasive, and she loved him. He promised her that he'd hire her on as the head of Research and Development at his company when his version of the watch was launched, and that he would marry her.

Yeah, I know he's a big fucking liar for that, and a major asshole, but of course Tracy didn't see that. I realize, as she cries and confesses everything, that I'm looking at possibly who Ava was years ago in college.

Tracy's shy and quiet, and she's probably a bit of a wallflower in her social life. She doesn't get the attention of charming, handsome men like Marcus. They pass her over for more vibrant and confident women.

It makes my stomach churn and my blood fucking boil. This is what he did to Ava. What he's done to Tracy. What he's probably done to countless other women. He sets them up and manipulates them and then gets them to do things they never would've done. Then they get into trouble in some way or another, or just get straight-up abused, and he walks away scot-free.

Not anymore.

Ethan and I have her confession, and with her cooperation, we get all the other files that she's sent to him. She shows Ethan how she covered her tracks for anything technological so that it wouldn't show up when we went looking, and all the deletions she did, and how she would print things out so there was no digital paper trail.

"People act like technology is safer," Ethan tells me when all is said and done. "But actually, if you really want things to not be recoverable or traceable, it's better to do things the old-fashioned way."

Tracy's situation is tragic, but we'll deal with the fallout of that later. I'm not sure if we're going to prosecute her or not. She's not nearly as important as getting Marcus to stop.

And getting him to back the fuck off from Ava.

The four of us compile our file of evidence and head over to his office. There's a security guard and a check-in desk on the ground floor just like there is at our building, but we don't even break stride as we walk past them.

We step onto the elevator, glaring down anyone who looks twice at us, and take it up to the top floor of the company building.

Once the elevator comes to a stop, we march toward Marcus's office, where his secretary, another young woman, jumps up. Judging by her wide eyes and frantic expression, she recognizes us and probably knows why we're here.

"I'm sorry, but do you have an appointment?" she asks quickly.

The dark, petty part of me wants to ask if he's sleeping with her too. I want to tell her that he's using her, and that whatever promises he's made to her are empty lies.

"An appointment or not doesn't matter," Garrett growls. "We're here to see Marcus, and we're not leaving until we do."

"I'm afraid he's busy at the moment." She tries for a smile but can't quite manage it. "So if you'll please wait..."

"We're not waiting," Garrett says shortly, and then he picks her up and gently moves her out of the way so that I can storm past her and into Marcus's office.

Marcus is sitting at his desk, on the phone, and he jolts when I enter. "I'll call you back," he says into the phone. "I have to go."

"Talking to your lawyer?" Ethan says, his tone sharp and falsely sweet. "Bet you called him the second you heard us outside trying to get past your poor secretary."

"Does she know that you're fucking Tracy over at our

company?" I ask, making sure that my voice carries as Garrett steps in, so the secretary can hear me before the door closes. "Or have you made her a bunch of empty promises too?"

I think I hear a startled, upset gasp right before Garrett closes the door to the office and locks it.

Marcus looks back and forth between all of us. "I don't know what you're talking about. I have a perfectly professional relationship with my secretary, and with all of my employees. I've never heard of this Tracy person. I know what's going on here."

"Oh? You do?" Caleb asks, his voice full of acid. When even Caleb is furious with you and ready to punch you, you know you've fucked up. "By which I mean, you know why we're here, but you're going to lie and say that you think we're here for a different reason."

Marcus glares at us. "Look, I know that Ava has put you up to this." His face morphs into a mask of what he probably thinks is sympathy. "She's had a hard life, poor thing. I'm sure hiding her Omega status for so long has..."

Garrett growls and starts to move toward Marcus, but I manage to hold him back. We can't have any of us arrested. We have to work together to protect Ava and that means not looking like the bad guys, no matter how fucking annoying it is.

"Ava told us what you're like, and honestly, that doesn't even matter. We were content to live and let live so long as you stayed away from her," Ethan informs him. "But you had to go and fuck with us."

"We know that you stole everything about the Omega smart watch from us." I slam the file of evidence onto his desk. "You're not going to weasel your way out of this one. Either you give up and you back down on launching the watch, or we'll sue you into oblivion."

"And get you arrested for corporate espionage," Caleb adds.

"This is fucking ridiculous." Marcus stands up. "I've done nothing wrong. I developed my own product completely of my own design."

"Right. So when we investigate your company and we find that none of your employees came up with any work and you just did it all because you're that much of a genius, that won't look suspicious at all?" I scoff. "Face it. This is the kind of thing it takes a team working together for a while to accomplish. Nobody is going to buy that you just came up with it and handed out the blue prints."

"Everyone loves a tech genius," Marcus points out slyly.

"And everyone loves a liar they can hate even more," I shoot back.

"You won't get away with this slander," Marcus hisses. His confident, Alpha vibe falls away, and he sounds like the slimy snake that he is. "You're going to suffer for this."

"You're really not in a position to be making threats." I tap the file on his desk. "Go on. Look through it. We can wait. We have everything we need. Any threat you make toward us is empty. We know what you did."

Marcus drops his gaze down to the file, then back up to me. He goes back and forth for a second, before curiosity wins out. He snatches up the file and flips through the papers inside.

I knew he'd do it. Frankly, an innocent man wouldn't bother. If someone came into my office accusing me of shit I knew I hadn't done, I wouldn't bother to look through whatever shoddy 'evidence' he gave me, until it was time to hand it over to my lawyer if need be.

But Marcus is guilty. And he wants to know exactly what we have on him. If it's real or a bluff.

I bluff when I play poker. Not when I'm dealing with my company or the happiness and safety of my Omega.

Marcus sets the file down. He's stiff, now, and clearly pissed. I don't bother to hold in my smirk.

"I see," he says.

"Yeah, you do," Ethan snaps at him.

Marcus clears his throat and sits down. "Tracy is a spineless pushover. She was for me. I should've known she'd be the same for you."

"Don't talk about her like that," Caleb growls. Tracy might have hurt us, but we understand she was manipulated. And you just don't fucking talk about a woman that way. Full stop.

"Why, are you fucking her as well as Ava?"

"We have something called an ability to show basic respect," Ethan snarls. "Unlike you."

"Don't bother," I warn them, raising my voice. "He's not fucking worth it."

I brace my hands on the desk and lean in so that I loom over Marcus. He's about the same size as I am, physically, but I know I could take him in a fight, and I have my pack mates at my back.

"You're going to pull the watch from the market," I tell him, my voice quiet and dangerous. "You can say whatever you want. Make up some bullshit excuse. I don't care. But you're either going to pull it, or we're going to take all of our proof, and Tracy's confession, and we're going to sue your ass to kingdom come. You'll be lucky if you even have a pot to piss in by the time we're through with you. Understand?"

Marcus stares up at me with fury in his eyes, his jaw clenching and unclenching. But he knows that he's beat. We know that his product was stolen and we'll slap him silly with lawsuits before he can even get his product to market for people to try.

"Fine," he says tersely. "I'll pull the product."

"Do it today," I order. "If that product isn't gone and your statements retracted by this time tomorrow, my lawyers will be banging your door down."

Marcus nods. He looks like I just pissed in his corn flakes. Good.

I push myself up from his desk and walk out the door. The others follow, Garrett slamming the door behind him as we leave.

The secretary sits at the desk, on the phone with someone, hunched over. She glances at us fearfully and then goes back to whispering into the phone, covering her mouth so we can't hear. I think she's been crying, going by how red and puffy her eyes are.

I feel bad for her. I just hope that she gets a better job and away from that dickbag.

We leave the building and get into the car, and I grin savagely in triumph.

"We fucking did it!" Ethan crows in victory.

"Holy fuck." Caleb sounds elated and slightly disbelieving.

I grin and gun the engine. I can't wait to tell Ava.

None of the others object to my breaking several speed limits on the way home. We all want to make sure Ava knows as soon as possible. She's going to be absolutely elated.

She's been worrying herself over this even more than we have, because she blames herself for it. As if Marcus wouldn't have found some other way to be a huge asshole to someone else if he hadn't run into her.

That's just the kind of guy Marcus is. And I'm glad we got the chance to stick it to him.

I whip the car into the driveway and kill the engine, hopping out and striding up to the front door. I throw it open and immediately hear Ava's footsteps as she runs into the foyer from wherever she was.

"I heard the car," she says breathlessly. "You sounded like you were racing, is everything okay? How did—"

I don't even bother with words. I sweep her into my arms and crash my lips to hers in a passionate kiss.

# Chapter 42

## *Ava*

Dante's kiss is rough and possessive, so full of emotion that it nearly knocks me backward. My arms go around his neck automatically, my body catching up before my mind does and kissing him back.

*It's instinct,* I realize.

But not in the way I used to think, back when I was ambivalent about my Omega status and feared becoming attached to the wrong men due to pheromones and hormones I couldn't control. This isn't like that, though. Yes, the Omega side of me craves these Alphas, and their scents drive me wild. But my feelings for them? My emotions?

Those are all mine.

And they're real.

They weren't forced on me by my biology. They arose out of the hundreds of ways—large and small—that these men have shown me they care for me. Every Alpha in this pack has looked out for me, gone above and beyond to help me, and made me feel valued and respected for who I am.

And right now, with Dante kissing me as if he needs me

more than oxygen, I want to make sure he knows that I need him too.

I need all of them.

Thoughts of Marcus flee my mind, wiped away by a rush of searing heat, and my hands shove roughly at the suit jacket Dante is wearing, pushing it off his shoulders. I loosen his tie next, and he walks me backward as I do, moving us toward the living room without ever stopping our kiss.

The other three Alphas are right there with him, moving as a pack like they so often do, and as soon as we're in the living room, I find myself tossed down onto the couch. The soft cushions sink a little beneath my weight, and I look up at the four gorgeous Alphas towering over me, my heart racing in my chest.

Dante's jacket is gone, his tie loose and hanging from his neck, and his richly dark hair mussed from our frantic kiss. The other three look a little more put together, but all four of them have the same expression on their faces.

It's hard to even name what the expression is. I can see desire burning in their eyes, but it's so much more than that. So much deeper.

"Help me undress her," Dante rasps, and then all four of them move.

It only takes them a few seconds to get rid of everything I was wearing, and I shiver as they replace my clothes with kisses pressed to my bare skin, covering me practically from head to toe with their hungry mouths and hands.

"No one will ever hurt you again," Dante says gruffly, kissing my knuckles before turning my hand over to press his lips to my palm. "Never. I promise. *We* promise."

I nod, turning my head as Garrett trails his tongue down my

neck. Ethan's hand delves between my legs, his fingers sliding into me to gather my wetness before circling my clit.

With them all surrounding me like this, I feel safer than I have in a long time, as if I'm encased by a shield of their bodies. I still need to find out the details of what happened with Marcus, but for right now, all I want is more of this.

More of *them*.

By the time the Alphas finally pull back, tugging at their own clothes as shirts, ties, and pants are tossed to the floor, I'm a panting, dazed mess. My hair is mussed, my breasts are flushed, and my nipples are hard and aching. I raise a hand to my lips, which are swollen and tingling from kissing each of the men, and Dante looks down at me with such stark desire in his eyes that I sit up without thinking about it, reaching for him.

He drops his head, palming my neck with his large hand as he kisses me again. Then he sits on the couch, pulling me onto his lap—but instead of turning me around to straddle him, he settles me with my back to his chest, my legs draped over his.

His cock nestles between my ass cheeks like a brand, hard and hot and thick, and his teeth scrape my ear as he takes my chin between his thumb and forefinger, tilting my head up toward his three pack mates.

"Look at them," he murmurs gruffly. "Do you see what I see, baby girl? Because I see three Alphas who would do anything for you. Three Alphas who adore you. Who would protect you with their lives if it came down to it."

Each of his words lands in my ear and travels directly to my heart, making the overworked organ pound even harder.

"I see it," I whisper, my throat going tight. "And I adore them too. I want all of you so much."

"Fuck, I love hearing you say that." Dante nips at my ear

again, his hands gripping my waist. He lifts me up, adjusting my position before murmuring, "Put me inside you, baby girl. Let them see."

With my heart racing and my gaze locked on the three men standing in front of me, I reach down between my spread legs and find Dante's cock, guiding his thick shaft to my entrance. As soon as the tip is inside me, Dante uses his grip on my waist to lower me down onto him, and all five of us groan as he sinks into me.

Caleb, Ethan, and Garrett are all naked, their own cocks hard and ready, jutting out from their bodies as they watch Dante fuck me. They look like they'd be perfectly happy to just stay where they are and enjoy the show, but the way they're gazing at me makes me want more.

"Come here." I gesture to Caleb, biting my lip.

He steps forward immediately, his dark chocolate, caramel, and toasted hazelnut scent filling my nostrils as it rises above the other Alphas' scents for a moment. When I wrap my lips around his shaft, he lets out a low noise of approval.

"Such a good little Omega," Dante growls from behind me, holding my hips to keep me steady as he rolls his hips to thrust in and out of me. "Suck Caleb's cock while I make you feel good."

That's exactly what I was planning on doing, but the encouragement only spurs me on. I use one hand, wrapping it around his length as I start to bob my head, taking him deeper each time.

His fingers tangle loosely in my hair, and I lose myself in the pleasure of it as I ride Dante's cock and work to take Caleb farther into my throat. The other two Alphas are still watching, and that only makes it even better.

After a few minutes, Caleb grunts under his breath. His hand tightens around my hair in warning, and a second later, his knot swells. I pull back just a bit, squeezing his knot as the hot splash of his cum hits my tongue. I swallow it down greedily, clenching around Dante as I whimper. Caleb tastes so fucking good that even after he's entirely spent, I can't stop myself from dragging my tongue over his entire length, licking up any last remnants of his release and teasing his knot.

"Fuck," he whispers, looking down at me with something almost like awe on his face.

I grin up at him, darting my tongue out to lick my lips. "Yum."

He chuckles hoarsely, taking a step back—and my chest swells a little with pride as I realize that his legs are wobbling a little.

*I* did that. Me.

My gaze shifts to Garrett and Ethan just as Dante thrusts his hips upward from beneath me, hitting a spot that makes my mouth fall open on a gasp. I suddenly can't wait any longer, the need for both of them too strong to resist.

"Now you," I whisper. "Come here. Together. I want to touch you both."

They don't hesitate for even a second, and as Dante starts to fuck into me harder, I alternate between the two of them, sucking and stroking as the scents of cinnamon and sweet apple cider swirl around me.

Ethan finishes first, cursing up a storm as I squeeze his knot and hold my mouth open to catch each spurt of his cum.

When he's finally emptied himself onto my tongue, he gives me a crooked smile, trailing his knuckles down the side of my face. Then he steps back, allowing Garrett to have my full attention.

It's a good thing I'm not trying to multitask between the two of them anymore, because with the way Dante's fucking me, I feel like my mind is about to explode into a thousand pieces. He's released his grip on my hip with one hand and slipped it between my legs instead, toying with my clit as he slides in and out with shallow thrusts.

There's not as much friction from his cock in this position, but I love the way he stays mostly buried inside me the whole time, making me feel full and perfectly connected to him.

My clit pulses beneath his fingertips, and I know I'm close. So I pour everything I'm feeling into making Garrett feel good too, sliding my mouth up and down his shaft. Every time the head of his cock hits the back of my throat, I swallow around him, squeezing and massaging his crown.

"Goddamn, that feels incredible," he grits out. "I'm gonna come soon, little one. Can you take my knot in your mouth?"

My eyes flare wide, my gaze darting up to his face as my pulse spikes. With the other two Alphas, I fisted their knots with my hand while they came, but what Garrett's asking for is a little terrifying... and also thrilling.

My body responds immediately, a wave of heat rushing through me, and I gush all over Dante's cock, making a purr rumble in his chest.

Without taking my mouth off Garrett's cock, I nod.

His nostrils flare, and I can smell how turned on he is by this. He and Dante work in tandem, fucking my mouth and my pussy, and I try to keep my eyelids from drooping closed as the sensations build higher and higher.

"Fuck, I'm close," Garrett warns, his knot swelling. "Fuck. Fuck!"

His knot inflates fully just as he presses deeper inside my mouth, burying his cock down my throat as jets of cum spill from him. I feel intensely full, my jaw open wide as his knot lodges between my teeth, locking my mouth around. My heart flutters like a hummingbird's wings, and I can feel more slick coating Dante's cock as fire seems to fill my veins.

I'm coming, I realize. It's so intense and blinding that it nearly makes me black out, every atom in my body bursting with pleasure. It seems to trigger Dante's own orgasm, because he lets out a rough growl and pulls me down hard on his shaft, burying his knot deep inside me.

I'm stuck between the two of them, completely rooted in place, knotted in both my pussy and my mouth. My nostrils flare wide as I struggle to breathe, the orgasm still rolling through me like an endless tide, and Garrett's strong hand pets my hair soothingly.

"You've got this," he murmurs, his gruff voice pitched low. "You're doing so fucking beautifully, little one. There you go. Just relax."

The Alpha command in his voice affects me immediately, my heart rate calming as he continues stroking my hair.

His knot starts to loosen only a few moments later, and he carefully withdraws from my mouth. The second he does, he bends down to kiss me, replacing his cock with his tongue as it slides gently inside my mouth. I kiss him back, reaching up to cling to his shoulders, and when we break apart, I slump back against Dante's chest.

"That was..." Dante's voice vibrates in his chest, and I can feel it in my torso where we're pressed together. "That was one of the hottest damn things I've ever seen." He chuckles. "You might kill all of us, baby girl. But what a way to go."

I grin, looking at the other three Alphas as they slowly settle onto the couch beside us. Dante's knot begins to deflate, but he makes no move to pull me off his cock for several long moments as we all rest in comfortable silence.

When he finally does pull out, it's only so that he can adjust me on his lap, turning me so that I'm sitting sideways across his muscled thighs. He nuzzles my ear, and I moan contentedly as I tilt my head. I'm pretty sure I know the answer to my earlier question by now, but I ask him anyway.

"I take it that things went well with Marcus?"

"He caved," Dante tells me, his voice laced with satisfaction and power. It makes me shiver.

"Tracy confessed everything," Ethan says. "Marcus tried to bluff his way out of it but we knew the truth and we kept at it."

"Having Tracy's confession and the evidence she provided helped," Caleb adds, trying as always to see the best in people.

Garrett scoffs, like he's not so willing to give Tracy even an inch of grace. I understand. She was manipulated by Marcus, used by him, and I understand what that's like. But it doesn't change the fact that she betrayed Garrett and the others, people who had trusted her and looked after her as their employee.

I reach out and run my fingers through his hair, soothing him. It's all over and done now. "And he agreed to back off?" I ask.

"Yes," Dante confirms. "No legal action necessary. He's going to pull the watch from the market."

I grin in relief, that cold sick knot in my stomach that's sat there like a lump for days finally loosening and dissipating.

We're okay. We're finally okay.

Joy wells up in my chest, and I find myself wanting to say the things that I've kept back. The emotions that I've known for days to be true, but haven't been able to voice.

I love these men. I'm in love with them. I was already falling for them before I was taken by the ORD and they had to court me, and it's only become stronger since then. I know they're the ones for me. They're my pack.

I clear my throat. "For a long time I was really scared. It feels like I've forgotten how not to be."

Four pairs of eyes turn toward me. I take a deep breath.

After all this time I thought that saying this would take a lot out of me. But instead, I find the words are there, and easy, tripping off the tip of my tongue.

"I don't think I've ever known what it's like to be loved. But you showed me how that feels. With you, I feel safe. I feel loved. It's more than I ever thought I'd get."

Four soft smiles greet me. I smile back. "So... I've decided."

I take a deep breath. "I love you all. I want your bite. I want the bond. I want you to be my mates."

These are words I didn't ever think I would say. Ever since I presented as an Omega I've been scared of a bonding bite. I thought it would mean that my agency and free will were taken away, and that I would be under the control of my Alpha from then on out, never truly free again.

But my Alphas would never do that to me. With them, the bite would be a symbol of what we already have. It would just show the rest of the world what the five of us already know, and make sure everybody understands that I'm off the market.

I'll never be bothered by handsy Alphas again. I'll never be alone again. I'll always be loved, supported, and protected.

Joy enters the faces of all four Alphas. Dante sits up

straighter and kisses me again, and I laugh into his mouth. All four of them look like they're literally going to vibrate to pieces with happiness.

My heart feels like it's too big for my chest. I can't remember the last time I was this elated. Actually, I don't know if I ever have been.

Heat and desire fill their faces, and I know that they want to do the bonding, the bite, right now.

I'm far from objecting to that.

I open my mouth to say something about it, to invite them, or possibly to ask how this will work specifically—when there's a knock at the door.

"Ignore it," Dante growls, not taking his eyes off me.

He leans in to kiss me again, but before he can, another knock comes, more forceful this time.

The men all frown. "You expecting a package?" Caleb asks Ethan.

Ethan shakes his head, scowling. "Fuck. We'd better deal with whatever it is." He shoots me a hungry look. "If we're gonna do this, I want to do it right. I don't want anything to interrupt us."

Another demanding knock has us all getting up, throwing clothes back on so that Garrett can go see who it is. He strides out of the living room, and a second later, I can hear low voices as he answers the front door.

An odd silence follows the voices, and I bite my lip, a spark of worry lighting in my chest.

Dante must feel the same thing, because he follows after Garrett, his brows drawn together. Caleb, Ethan, and I trail after him, and as we enter the foyer, my heart skips.

I might not be officially bonded with Garrett yet, but I'm so attuned to his scent now that I can catch the faint hint of his emotions. I can sense his anger. His unhappiness.

His fear.

He's standing at the front door, a murderous expression on his face. And in the doorway, facing off with him, are several people who look far more intimidating than ORD agents.

It's the police.

# Chapter 43

## *Ava*

My heart lurches in my chest and my stomach twists sickly.

"Ava Charleston?" one of the officers asks me, looking past Garrett.

Dante puts a hand on my shoulder as I nod. "That's me," I say meekly.

I feel like I might throw up. The officers look stoic and unwavering. I don't know why they're here or what they want from me, I haven't done anything wrong, but judging by the looks on their faces, this isn't anything good.

"Miss Charleston." One of the officers starts to step forward, but Garrett growls threateningly in the back of his throat, baring his teeth.

The other three Alphas close ranks around me, so that I can't be seen by the officers.

I can hear the officer sigh. "Please let us do our jobs. Ma'am, we need to place you under arrest for the theft of one hundred thousand dollars."

"What?" I push past Dante to stare the officers down. "What the hell are you talking about?"

I've never stolen anything in my life, much less thousands of dollars. I have no idea who I could have even stolen it from. My old boss at the animal shelter didn't have that much money on him for me to take, and there's nobody else. The only rich people I know are the four men whose foyer I'm standing in.

"We're talking about a report filed with us a few hours ago," the second officer says. "From a Marcus Travers."

"And you just arrest people based on what others tell you, huh?" Ethan demands. "Just on fucking hearsay?"

The officers bristle. "No," the second one says, glaring. "We come to arrest people when the accuser provides proof that what they're saying is true."

My mind races. The 'proof' that Marcus has given them must be false. It has to be. I know that I'm innocent. I never stole anything from him.

"He alleges, and the documents show," the first officer says, "that you and Mr. Travers were in a relationship a few years ago, and that during that time you fled with a hundred grand of his money and have been on the lam ever since."

Well, the running away part is true. But that's only because I was fleeing his abuse.

"She didn't do that," Caleb says. "She ran away from him because he's a piece of shit. She never stole any money and if you go and do a proper damn investigation, you'll see that we're telling the truth. He's a fucking liar."

"Sir, if you want to take legal action of your own against Mr. Travers, you're welcome to do that. But in the meantime, what we have from him is sufficient evidence for us to press charges on his behalf."

"So, what, she's supposed to just go with you because you

say that?" Dante challenges. "Where's the evidence? Where's the proof, I want to see it for myself."

"The court will lay everything out in due time, but first, we have to book her. We will set her a bail, and if you want to pay it, you're welcome to. But she has to go through our system first so that we can set her court date and get the ball rolling. Including in appointing her an attorney."

"Don't bother, we'll get her one," Garrett snarls. "In fact, we'll get her one while she stays right here, because this is a fucking miscarriage of justice. I hope that you two aren't fond of your jobs because you're about to lose them."

"You can't be serious," one of the officers mutters.

"Sir, please. We don't want there to be any trouble."

All four of my Alphas look like they would like nothing more than to cause a whole lot of trouble. I feel sick to my stomach.

On the one hand, I did nothing wrong, and I refuse to go to prison or be arrested for something that I know I didn't do. In fact it's preposterous to think that I did. I would love to know exactly what Marcus did to lay these false charges down on me.

I wonder if he paid someone off. Bribed someone? He got to Tracy after all. Maybe he was able to convince someone in law enforcement to cook something up against me for a fat enough paycheck.

"You can't take her," Dante says stubbornly. "We know these are trumped-up charges and we're not going to stand for them."

"Can you prove right now that those are trumped-up charges?"

"Don't get fresh with me," Dante snarls, striding toward the guy.

"Don't!" I cry out, grabbing his arm. I know that I can't really hold him back physically. He's far stronger than I am. But my touch will control him. He'll listen to me. "We don't want to make this any worse than it already is."

Dante looks at me. "Baby girl, you didn't do anything wrong."

The others all nod, and I know that they're prepared to literally fight for me to keep me safe, just as they were with the ORD agents.

No, it's even more so this time, because this time they know they're in love with me, and that I'm in love with them.

And that makes this so much harder.

"I know that." I try to keep my voice calm. I'm shaking, and my stomach feels like it's completely in knots, but I know I have to stay strong now. If I don't stay calm and take care of this, it could go really, really badly for everyone.

I won't let my Alphas, the men I love, get hurt or go to jail because of me.

"You know I'm innocent," I insist. "That means that there'll be a way to prove it. All right? They'll set my bail quickly and you can get me out. It won't take long. And then you can call the lawyers and we'll get me acquitted. It'll be fine."

"You might want to listen to her," the second officer says.

Garrett gives a growl that makes it clear he'd like nothing better than to rip the man's throat out. The officer shrinks back a little and I feel a bit of pride at how strong and confident my Alpha is.

I squeeze Dante's hand and look at the other three. "It's okay," I promise them. "I know you'll get me out quickly. It'll all be okay."

None of them look happy. Their scents have turned dark

and smoky with their anger and I know that they're all seething with rage. It's plain on their faces and in their clenched fists.

To be honest, I'm terrified. The last thing I want to do is go with these police officers. But I know it's what I have to do to keep my Alphas safe. I might be an Omega, but that doesn't mean I can't do my part to take care of my pack.

I let go of Dante's hand, but he grabs me and pulls me back in for a last kiss. Ethan and Caleb each kiss me, and then I pull away, walking to the front door.

When I get there, I kiss Garrett. I know that this is killing them. I hate that I'm contributing to their pain, even though I know it's the right thing to do.

I look over at the officers and nod. "Okay, I'm coming."

I kind of wish I'd thought to put on something a little sturdier than just the first t-shirt and pair of shorts I could find, but it's too late for that now. I doubt the police are going to let me spend another ten minutes debating my perfect jail outfit.

They put me in handcuffs and each grabs my elbow, leading me down the front steps to their waiting patrol car. I feel like I'm in a nightmare. Like any second now I'll wake up, and I'll actually be in bed with my Alphas, a little disoriented but safe.

This isn't really a nightmare, though, as much as it feels like it. It's just the worst day of my life. I knew that there was a reason to be nervous over Marcus. I never should have relaxed. I should've known that he would find another way to get at me and hurt me.

I can feel the eyes of my Alphas on me as I'm forced away from them. Knowing how much this hurts them and how concerned and protective they are makes me feel a little stronger. If it was just about me, I would probably be crying right now, but I have to be strong for my Alphas. I have to show them that I'm okay, so that they don't do something we'll all regret.

The officers help me into the back seat of the car and I keep my head high, but I don't let myself look back at my pack.

These are the men that, just a short time ago, I wanted to bite me and officially bond with me. I want them to be my mates.

Now I'm being taken away from them.

I know if I look back I'll burst into tears, and we can't have that. I don't want them to know or they'll probably try to rip the car apart to comfort me, and I sure don't want to cry in front of these police officers.

I keep looking forward as I'm driven away from my home. From safety.

From my pack.

# Chapter 44

## *Ava*

When they show people going to jail and such in movies and on television they really don't go through how all the booking process and minutiae work. It's terrifying in how mundane it is. You feel like you're just a number in the system. Like they're trying to take away your personhood.

I've never been so scared in my life before. The officers are silent when they drive me to the jail, as if the moment they put me in the backseat I stopped being a human to them. When we get there, they don't talk at me, they talk *about* me, over my head, like I can't understand them or speak for myself.

A sob wells up in my throat and I swallow it down. I'm not going to panic in front of these people. I'm not. I refuse to be called a stereotypical 'hysterical Omega', as if it's my designation or being a woman that makes me upset and not how they're treating me.

"What's she in for?" the officer at the front desk asks as she signs me in.

"Grand larceny."

*Grand larceny.* It sounds oddly fancy for the crime I'm

accused of committing—stealing a pitiful hundred thousand dollars. Okay, so that's definitely not a pitiful amount of money. In fact it's a life-changing amount for most people.

But I can remember what Marcus was like. He threw money around like it was nothing. I can't say that he's not smart, or accomplished, but he comes from money like Garrett does, and he was happy to brag about it and show it off while we were dating.

At the time, of course, I'd liked the idea of a man who could take care of me, after growing up poor and having parents who never took care of me at all in any way that mattered.

Now, though, I understand it was another way for him to wield power. Some people like having money because it allows them to spoil themselves. Other people like money because it means they can be lazy. But some men, like Marcus, like it because of what it can buy for them, the leverage it allows them to have.

They can rewrite the rules in their favor all the time.

If I'd actually stolen a hundred thousand dollars from him way back in the day, there's no way that he would've noticed. The fact that he's taken until now to 'accuse' me of this crime only reminds me of how fake it is.

I want to scream at these police officers booking me into this horrible place that if they would think about it for two seconds, they'd realize it doesn't make any sense for Marcus to only come out with evidence and an accusation now.

Even if he couldn't find me before, he still would've reported it stolen. The case would've been open all these years with no lead. He's only opening it now with his so-called evidence because he wants to punish me.

And he knows that hurting me is not only the best way to

cause me pain directly, but also the best way to hurt my Alphas. They wounded his pride when they got Tracy to confess and stormed into his office.

I wonder if his office is full of people gossiping now. If people there know the truth. Surely someone was eavesdropping. I doubt any of my men were subtle and polite about it. And gossip spreads like wildfire through an office.

Once he immediately went out and told them all he was withdrawing the watch from the market, they have to know that something's up, and that my Alphas had something to do with Marcus's change in plans.

He must feel humiliated right now.

It's a small, cold comfort to me as I'm taken from the two officers who brought me in and I'm duly sorted into the jail system.

All of my personal effects are taken from me and I'm put in front of a desk where another officer writes a bunch of things down on a piece of paper, without looking at me even once. Then I'm taken to put on the classic orange outfit, and my fingerprints and all the rest are taken.

I'm not told anything about my bail, or how long I'll be in here, but I am told that a public defense attorney will be appointed to my case, and that I can speak with them tomorrow.

That doesn't give me much comfort.

I spend the night in a chilly cell with a bunch of other women. This isn't a prison, so we don't get the small rooms with the two-person bunk bed. Instead, we're in one large cell with a bunch of cots and we have to make do.

Everyone here looks as miserable as I feel. I'm in a room with all Omegas, while the Alphas and Betas each get their own rooms. It's theoretically to stop any fights from breaking out, but it just reminds me of all the ways that people look at me differently now that my status is known.

Being an Omega became something wonderful and special when I was with my Alphas. But now I feel scared about it again. I feel alone, and empty, and vulnerable.

There are a couple Omegas crying in one corner, and when I ask another woman about them, she shakes her head sadly. "They tried to run from the facility," she says. "And stay unregistered. They were caught, obviously, so they're here overnight until the ORD agents can come and get them in the morning."

I want to tell these women about my experience, and how it turned out, but I know what they'll say, because I know exactly what I would've said in their shoes a few months ago.

*You just got lucky. What if I'm courted by a bunch of asshole Alphas? What if they bite me before I'm ready, and I'm stuck with them? What if my agent at the facility isn't as good as yours?*

There's nothing I can do to make them feel better. All it does is make me grateful that I didn't run. That Ethan found me and took care of me, brought me to the others, and that when the ORD agents came for me, I didn't let the men try to fight for me while I ran for it.

I can't even imagine how out of my mind with fear I would've been in jail for that. And I wouldn't ever get to see my Alphas again. They wouldn't be allowed to court me. They broke the law for me and I don't think the ORD would see that as a good thing. I never would've gotten to be with them.

At least I had them, for a little while.

*You still have them,* I tell myself as I lie down in my cot to sleep. *They're going to get you out of here. They won't abandon you.*

My hope keeps me warm as I fall asleep.

The next day, sure enough, I get to see them in the afternoon. I'm taken to a room where I get to talk to them, similar to an interrogation room in movies. I'm glad it's not one of those telephone rooms with the plexiglass. At least this way, I can touch them, even if the guards say we can't do more than just hold hands.

All four of my Alphas stand when I enter the room, worry etched clear on their faces. Garrett growls when he takes in my outfit. I can see them straining not to rush across the room and hold me.

It makes me want to cry. All I want is to be enveloped in their arms, and I can't. We have to keep our distance.

I sit down on the other end of the table, and my four Alphas sit. Ethan lurches his arm across the table and grabs my hand. He looks pale, with circles under his eyes. They all do.

"Please tell me you slept," I plead with them.

"I mean, we can lie if that'll help you feel better," Ethan replies, trying for a joke. It doesn't quite work.

I've never seen them all look so worried and upset before. My heart squeezes in my chest. It's sweet that they love me so much, and that they're so worried for me, but I want them to take care of themselves.

"Please." I squeeze Ethan's hand. "I'm not there to do it for you, so I need you to look after yourselves for me while I'm gone. You have to promise me that."

"You won't be gone long," Dante insists. "We're working with our lawyers. We'll get you out of here and we'll get the charges dropped.'

"Have they not set the bail yet?"

"Not yet. Rumor has it the judge is trying to decide if you're scamming us too, so he's hesitant to place you on bail. He thinks you might take our money and run next."

"That's ridiculous," I blurt out, appalled.

"That's what I said," Garrett mutters.

"To be fair," Caleb says, sighing heavily, "that's exactly what a scheming thief *would* say if she was seducing us to get our money. And we know you won't do that, ever, but this judge hasn't met you."

"He just has Marcus's lies," Ethan snarls.

"Do you think Marcus paid him off?" I ask. Ethan's thumb strokes back and forth over my knuckles. It's not nearly as much touch as I want, but even that little gesture helps to soothe me.

"We don't know," Dante says. "But we're working on it."

"Marcus has to know that these charges won't stick," Caleb explains. "The moment a proper attorney looks into this, they're going to see all the holes in logic and that the evidence was fabricated."

"We think he's doing this just to humiliate you and distract us while he does something else, like maybe put a slightly modified version of the watch on the market," Garrett says. "Or delay our launch of the watch so that even if he doesn't win, we still lose."

"You can't let that happen." I reach out and take his hand in both of mine, squeezing hard. "You can't let your company suffer because of me. We can't let him win like that. You have to launch the watch like you planned, even if I'm still in here."

Dante smiles proudly. "That's our girl."

I smile softly back at him. "Really. I don't want him to win. If you're right and he's just trying to hurt me, and you, then it's just some... I don't know."

"Psychological warfare?" Ethan hazards.

I crack a smile. "Yeah. That. We can't let him know that he's getting to us. I know that... this isn't fun for any of us. I can't say I'm enjoying my time here. But I know that you'll get me out. I know I'm innocent. And you know I'm innocent. We'll make this work. But if we let the watch be delayed, or let him see how upset we are, then he wins. I can't have that."

Caleb takes my hand and raises it to his lips, kissing my knuckles. "I hope you know how brave you are, sweetheart."

"I don't feel very brave," I admit.

"Doing this even though you're scared is what makes you brave."

"And you won't be in here long, I promise," Dante adds. "We're going to have our lawyers talk to the judge tomorrow, and make sure that he gets you out of here. Even if that means paying a bail, we'll pay whatever it takes."

I try so hard to keep the tears in, but a few of them well up in my eyes anyway. I wipe them away quickly. The distress I see on the faces of my Alphas, knowing they want to hold me and nuzzle me but can't, only makes me want to cry harder.

"I hate that you don't smell like us anymore," Caleb admits, his voice soft. "Usually I can smell all of us on you. It's been getting stronger the past few days. And I can smell you on myself, and the others. But now..."

Garrett nods in agreement. I realize, with a horrible sick jolt, that they're right. I don't smell like my Alphas anymore. I smell like the stale air of the jail and the plain unscented soap that we use in the bathrooms.

"I'll smell like you soon enough when I'm out," I promise, even though my voice wavers. "Like you said, it's going to be okay."

They all nod solemnly.

"We're going to be with you every step of the way," Dante states. "You're not alone in this, baby girl. We're all here for you. We're not going to stop until you're back with us and you're safe."

"It'll be sooner than you know it," Ethan agrees.

"It doesn't matter what we have to do," Garrett adds quietly. "Even if that means a prison break."

"Please tell me you're joking," I say, giggling.

"Only partly." Garrett winks at me.

"You're the strongest woman we know," Caleb says. "You've already overcome so much. I know that you're going to overcome this."

I wish I could kiss him. I wish I could kiss all of them. I nod. "Thank you," I tell them all. "You really don't have to do this."

"Of course we do." Dante sounds incredulous. "You're our Omega. We might not be officially mated to you yet, but you're still ours. We know that. We'll do anything for our Omega, like any good Alpha should."

Someday I'm going to have to get it through their heads that while they see themselves as simply doing the basic, decent thing, in actuality they're the most amazing men I've ever met "You're my Alphas," I promise them. "I know that it might not say that on paper yet. Or on my neck."

My neck, in fact, feels rather bare without their bites. I can't quite believe that something I once feared and hated the idea of is now something I wish for. If I had their bite, then even if the guards took everything else from me, they couldn't take that. It would still mark me as belonging to someone even in these stupid orange clothes.

"But I know what we are," I conclude. "And I trust you."

"I'm glad you do," Ethan says. "We want to be worthy of your trust."

There's a rap at the door, and then it opens, a guard stepping in. I know what that means. Our time together is up.

I hold both of my hands out, and my Alphas grab on to them, holding on tightly. I squeeze as best I can. It's a physical ache in my chest, the need to touch them more, but I hold myself back. I know it won't do us any favors if I get in trouble for launching myself over the table to nuzzle them.

"Come on, you four," the guard says, sounding weary.

Garrett shoots the man a glare, and I nearly do too. I suppose working in a place like this must drain you of your humanity, because how else do you sound so completely bored with the fact that five people are in agony over having to be separated? I don't understand it, and I don't want to.

I stand from the table, and clasp my hands in front of me, holding my own fingers tightly so that my Alphas won't see them tremble as one by one, they file out of the room.

Then they're gone again.

The guard returns a moment later. "May I use the restroom?" I ask.

He nods, and escorts me to the bathroom. I go inside, and immediately burst into tears.

I grip the sink hard and sob everything out, my knuckles white and my vision blurring. I don't want anyone else to see me like this. I refuse to let them know how upset I am, these cold, unyielding, uncaring jailers.

When I'm finished, I wash my face and take a few deep breaths, staring at myself in the mirror. "You've got this," I whisper to myself. "It's okay. You're brave. You can do this."

I carry the memory of my Alphas' scent and their touch

with me throughout the day, trying to hold on to it as I sit in my cell, eat the flavorless dinner they set out for us, and finally tuck into bed to sleep.

Seeing my Alphas has made me a little more hopeful. I know that they'll do anything to set me free. Marcus might have bought people off or temporarily convinced them of my guilt, but I know that he's nothing against my mates. They'll find a way.

Sure enough, when we're woken up in the morning for breakfast, one of the guards stops me as I file out.

"Not you," she says. "The charges against you were dropped. You're free to go."

I stare at her for a moment in shock, my jaw slack. I can't have possibly heard her correctly. "What?"

The guard looks like she wants to roll her eyes. "I said that we're taking you out of here. The charges against you were dropped. Come on."

She sounds impatient. I'm sure she's glad to be rid of me. I'm sure all the guards are. One more prisoner gone is one less person to keep track of for them.

I'm led down the hall through the maze of oppressive cinderblock until I'm back in the front office area. I'm put in front of a desk again with that same dispassionate man who fills out paperwork once more, without looking at me, just like last time.

Then I have to sign a bunch of paperwork myself at the front desk before I'm given my personal affects, which mostly just includes the clothes I was brought here in.

"May I change?" I ask, trying to keep my voice soft and meek. I hate asking for permission for something like this, but there's still this weird, primal terror in me that suggests that if I do anything to upset them, if I ask for too much, they'll change their minds and put me back in a cell.

The guard nods toward a bathroom at the other end of the room. Nobody accompanies me this time as I go and change. I'm no longer a prisoner, so they don't care. Before, I couldn't so much as wash my hands without a guard following me to make sure I didn't do something like try to escape. Now they don't even care enough to keep an eye on me.

It's all very dehumanizing and scary. My skin itches for me to get out of here.

As I change, I feel more and more like myself, and it feels like my brain is coming back to life after being dormant, shutting down in self-defense. Like everything around me was dulled and my brain refused to process it all or take it in as a way to keep me from truly realizing how bad my situation was.

Now, though, as I finger-comb my hair and braid it to try to look somewhat presentable, I can't help but wonder how this happened. My Alphas made it sound like it might take longer, but maybe they did something to truly intimidate Marcus. Maybe they presented the judge or others with their evidence of Marcus's corporate sabotage and that was enough for them to doubt his case against me.

However it happened, I'm filled to the brim with relief. I knew that my mates would help me get out of here, even if I didn't think it would be quite so soon.

I finish putting on my clothes and freshening up, double-checking myself in the mirror. I wish I looked nicer to meet my mates, but it still feels so good to be in my own clothes again, and to feel like myself. I can't wait to take a nice hot shower or a bath when we get back, and to eat one of Dante's home-cooked meals. I'm going to cuddle and nuzzle my mates shamelessly.

It's crazy how life changes. Here I am, excited to see them and to get cuddles and be pampered, when once I would have shied away from something like that, sure that it couldn't be real.

I exit the restroom and finish signing myself out, and then I'm told the door is that way, and suddenly, it's like I don't exist.

"Did anyone say they would be here to pick me up?" I ask the desk clerk.

He shrugs, eyes on his computer. "Probably. Go outside and check."

For crying out loud. I roll my eyes but manage to bite my tongue so I don't say anything rude. I don't want to get in trouble when I'm so close to freedom.

I exit the building, blinking and squinting in the morning sunlight. I hadn't realized how much I'd been inside and how dim it all was until now.

I walk farther down the large concrete area that's used as a parking lot and driveway, squinting and searching for my Alphas. I don't see Ethan's sports car or Dante's sensible luxury sedan.

*Maybe they're in a car I don't—*

My thoughts are cut off as a white van speeds up from seemingly out of nowhere and slams to a halt in front of me. The side door slides open and a pair of hands lunge for me.

I scream in surprise, caught off-guard. I'm not fast enough to jump back in time, and I'm hauled inside. I scream again, but a hand is over my mouth, and the door is kicked closed. I feel the van take off, and I scream through the hand, terror filling my veins like ice.

I'm shoved down to the floor of the van on my face, my arms yanked back even as I try to struggle and fight off my attacker.

It's dark in here and I can't see anything, and whoever this is, they're stronger than I am.

My wrists are grabbed, and then zip-ties are placed around them, forcing them together and biting painfully into my skin.

"Let me go!" I scream. "Get off me! Get off me! Let me go!"

The person grabs my hair, yanking painfully and craning my head up, bending close—and that's when I smell it.

That horrible, off-putting scent. The one that I hadn't smelled in years until I was out shopping with Dante. The one that's burned into my brain whether I want it to be or not.

*Marcus.*

I stifle a whimper as he draws close, inhaling deeply.

"Mmm. I missed that sugary scent," he growls.

He releases me, and my head falls hard back onto the floor of the van. I try to curl up, to protect my body a bit, trembling in fear.

"You and I have a lot to talk about," Marcus tells me. "*Omega.*"

My body shakes with uncontrollable fear. Marcus has me, and nobody knows that he took me, or where I am.

And I have no idea what he plans to do with me.

# Chapter 45

## *Garrett*

I pace in the living room, my hands clenched into fists at my sides.

Ethan's pacing too. We keep crossing back and forth from each other, moving across the length of the room. We've turned it into a sort of command center as we work around the clock to get Ava free.

She said that she wanted us to get rest and take care of ourselves, but I know that none of us can do that. It's practically unthinkable. Taking care of ourselves means getting her free. Then we'll be able to sleep again.

Dante's been trying to enforce some kind of rest on us, but when I tried, I slept fitfully and couldn't really manage anything past a doze. My body knows that Ava's not safe, and it won't let me relax until she's back here with us.

We might not have officially finished mating with her. We might not have bitten her. But in every way that matters, she is our mate, our Omega, and our instincts know that.

My mind can't stop coming up with every single horror story I've ever read or heard about Omegas or women in prison, about corrupt officials and guards, about brutal fights and hazing among the inmates.

Even without Marcus, I don't feel that Ava's safe in prison, and I can't stop thinking about it.

Dante and Caleb work the computers we've set up, trying to find out information on what Marcus did and the people he has in his pocket. We all look like messes. We've barely eaten. But it'll all be worth it when we have Ava safe in our arms again.

"I think we should consider releasing our evidence about the watch," Ethan says as he paces. "It's proof that Marcus was stealing our ideas. He'll be disgraced."

"And then what?" Dante asks. "He'll just keep hitting Ava harder to retaliate."

"So we play softball?" Ethan snaps. "We need to hit the man where it hurts!"

I'm all for hitting Marcus. In fact I'm all for hitting him with my fist. But I also don't want Ava to suffer or be punished because of what we do.

"I can't find evidence that the judge is corrupt," Caleb says from his computer. "But that doesn't mean that he didn't take some kind of bribe."

"I think at this stage it's more likely that he believed whatever evidence Marcus brought him," Dante replies. "He knows that this charge can't stick."

"That doesn't make sense to me," I admit, continuing to pace. "If he knows the charges won't stick then why not go through with a bribe to make sure that Ava's put away for a good few years?"

"We caught him last time he tried something. Maybe he's not trying to put Ava behind bars for good. Maybe he's just trying to scare us and distract us. Remind us of how much power he supposedly has."

I snort derisively. I can't see Marcus settling for anything less than total victory. But guys like him do enjoy playing mind games. He could be toying with us like a cat with a mouse.

I'm not a mouse. I'm a goddamn Alpha. And that man is going to know it before this whole thing is over.

Caleb scrubs a hand across his face and then runs his fingers through his hair. It makes the blond strands stick up every which way, like he stuck his finger in a light socket. "Well..."

The phone rings.

We all dive for it, but Dante's closest and picks it up first, hitting the speaker button. "Hello?"

"Dante, hi." It's one of our lawyers that we put on the case. I'm sure our legal team is pretty sick of us bugging them for updates on Ava's case, but I don't care. We pay them the big bucks to go above and beyond and we need them to deliver on this more than we've ever needed them to deliver on anything else for us before.

"You have news?" I ask, bracing my hand on Dante's shoulder to hover over him and the phone.

"Yes. Surprisingly good news. Ava's been released."

We all blink at that. My brow furrows. "What?"

"She was released this morning. The charges against her were dropped."

"They were—what do you mean, dropped?" Ethan asks.

"I mean that Mr. Travers dropped the charges. If he's dropped them, then unless the DA's office wants to go ahead with prosecuting anyway, there's no reason for her to stay in prison. The DA declined to prosecute. An Omega supposedly stealing a hundred grand years ago isn't exactly the big political case that makes the DA look good."

The noise of papers rustling filters in from the background. "Besides, I think the DA knew that there was something odd about this case. It took Mr. Travers years to file a report about the stolen money."

"*Thank* you," Caleb mutters under his breath. "If the money was really stolen then why the hell didn't he report it back then? Why wait until now? There's no damn reason for it. You don't decide to forgive and forget and then change your mind years later."

"Especially now," Dante adds. "He's even richer now than he was when she theoretically took the money, so it's not like he's down on his luck and needs that cash."

"All good points," our lawyer replies. "My point is that you should be all right now. I can't say that Mr. Travers might not decide to harass you in some other manner, but he's dropped the charges and Ava is free."

A suspicion makes my gut tighten, but before I can say anything, Ethan adds, "What if he tries to bring this up again at a later date? Can you keep looking into the case anyway, just so that if he tries, we have evidence that he faked it?"

"I can do that," our lawyer promises. "I'll talk to you soon."

"Thank you," Dante says, and hangs up.

"She was freed hours ago?" Caleb asks. "That doesn't sound right."

"No, it doesn't," I agree. "Call the prison."

If Ava was freed, then surely we would've heard from her by now asking us to pick her up. Or even showing up on our doorstep having been dropped off by a taxi or the police, or *someone*.

The phone rings, and rings, and rings, and finally someone picks up. The person sounds like a very bored guard, lazily reciting the prison and ending with a 'how can I help you' that sounds so fake it might as well be sarcasm.

"Hi," Dante says, putting on his most calm and charming voice, the kind he uses to convince skittish shareholders. "I'm looking for information on an inmate who was released today. Ava Charleston?"

I pick up the sound of typing on an old, clunky computer keyboard, and then the guard says, "What about her? She was released hours ago, so if you want to talk to her, she isn't here anymore."

"Hours ago?" I demand. "How many hours ago?"

"I don't know." More typing comes from his end. "Four."

And we haven't heard anything from her. "Why didn't you notify us that she was being released? We're listed as her contact information."

"All contact is up to the prisoner. It's on them to secure a ride and other necessities out of prison unless they are registered with our halfway home rehabilitation program."

Oh for fuck's sake, are you fucking kidding me? "So you just let her walk out of there," I say. "And you don't care what happens after that."

"She's no longer in our custody. She's a free woman. She can do what she wants."

I'm going to strangle this man to death. "So you have no idea where she is."

"No."

"And no one's seen her."

"Not since she walked out four hours ago."

"Thanks for nothing." I hang up the phone, wishing I could throw it against the wall or slam it against something.

We all look at each other. The suspicion in my gut is now deep, sick fear.

Caleb speaks up. "Marcus. Marcus tricked us."

I look over at him.

Caleb stands up, running his hand through his hair again. "He never planned to actually take Ava to court. This wasn't to intimidate us into dropping the watch business, or to just scare us. It was to separate her from us."

Holy fuck. It all clicks in my head. He's absolutely right.

"Think about it," Caleb goes on. "We would never let Ava out of our sight or presence long enough for him to get to her. So he has to force us to be separated. Accusing her of theft and providing some trumped up evidence..."

"He knew it wouldn't stick," Ethan says. "But he didn't care."

Caleb nods. "He only needed it to create chaos and convince the police long enough to get her locked up in jail for a day or two. That way she'd be away from us. Then he drops the charges, she's set free, and he alone knows that's happened. He knows she'll be released the moment he drops the charges. So he's already there when he makes the call. Ava walks out..."

"And he takes her," I growl, fury choking me.

Caleb nods, looking the most distraught I've ever seen him. "He wanted to get her away from us so we couldn't protect her."

He's right. I know he's right. Fuck. I feel sick.

"Then there's no time to waste." Dante stands. "I'm calling the police."

"I'll grab the car," Ethan says, rushing out of the room.

I crack my knuckles. "I'm driving."

Dante and Caleb exchange a look. I'm what's been called an 'aggressive driver' so usually they don't let me drive, which ordinarily, I don't mind. But I think some damn aggressive driving is called for right now.

"All right," Dante agrees. "You're driving."

Caleb's already on his phone as we head out the door. "Okay, so Marcus has two places. One's a penthouse here in the city but the other is a family estate somewhere upstate."

"That's where he'll take her," Dante agrees. "Plenty of quiet and privacy. And it's far away from us. Can you get the address?"

"You bet your ass I can."

Ethan brings the car around, and I go over to the driver's side. "Out. I'm driving."

Ethan gets out and moves into the back seat. Caleb takes the front passenger so he can give me directions, so Dante slides into the back with Ethan.

I gun the engine and tear out of the driveway. If any police end up on our trail, then let them chase us. I'll lead them right to Marcus, and they'll help us fucking arrest the guy before I do something incredibly stupid like kill him with my bare hands.

My mind is filled with images of Ava being hurt and in danger. I can barely see the road in front of me through my rage, operating on autopilot.

I can't bear the thought of losing her. She's too important to me. She's in our lives, in our hearts, in our blood.

I'm going to do whatever it takes to save her.

# Chapter 46

## *Ava*

My mind is consumed by fear as I lie in the back of the van.

Marcus immediately wraps a gag around me so I can't scream or yell anymore, and then after a few minutes the van pulls off to the side of the road. Marcus exits, closing the door behind him, but I can hear him walk around to the driver's door. It opens, and I hear quiet talking.

"Help!" I scream at the driver. "You can't do this! Please! Please help me, please you can't do this, please!"

My words come out muffled and garbled. I'm not even sure the man can hear me.

There's the sound of something like paper shuffling, and my blood goes cold as I realize it's someone counting out cash. Marcus has paid this man to be the getaway driver.

I scream again, sobbing, trying to get this man to hear me and invoke some kind of sympathy or mercy in his heart. But if my pleas are heard, he ignores them. I can hear his footstep going around the side of the van, and then the sound of Marcus getting into the driver's seat.

The car door slams shut, and the van lurches as it pulls out onto the road again.

I cry, curling in on myself as best I can with my hands zip-tied behind my back.

This is the thing that I feared would happen to me when I presented as an Omega. This is the nightmare scenario. This is what I lay awake in bed at night imagining if I'd had presented as Omega while still in the clutches of my relationship with Marcus.

However much he controlled me then, however much he scared me and intimidated me, it's so much worse now. Then, I was a Beta to him. Now... well, I know what he thinks about Omegas. He would tell me plenty of times while we were together.

He's going to treat me like a prisoner, and use me however he wants.

I can't let him take me to wherever his end destination is. I'm not sure where he'll bring me. Back when we were together, we were in college, so he had an apartment just off campus. I'm sure he has an entirely different place now. But wherever it is, it'll be a place where he can easily control me and keep me under lock and key.

There's no way I can let that happen. I have to find a way out of here before then, if that's even possible.

My stomach is so sick with fear, and between that and the jostling of the van as it races down a highway, I think that I might throw up. I breathe slowly and carefully through my nose. Throwing up with a gag in my mouth sounds like the worst possible experience.

Marcus's horrible, sick scent fills my nose, and I close my

eyes. I can't focus on that. I have to think of something else, and clear my mind of fear. I have to overcome this.

I just wish my Alphas could save me.

My Alphas.

I picture in my head their scents, the smells that I know so well at this point they feel like they're a part of me, like they're in my blood and my bones, intertwined with my DNA.

Dante, the first Alpha that I smelled, the way that spicy clover and warm bourbon with honey made me feel a way I never had before. He makes me feel on fire in a slow, sensual way, his scent making me feel safe and sexy at the same time.

Ethan, whose scent comforted me even when I was in the middle of the club and terrified out of my mind. He was a stranger, and I was unsure if I could trust him, but his scent called to me. The cinnamon, freshly baked cookies, and hint of toasted marshmallows reminds me of being a kid around a campfire, taking me back to a simpler time, full of laughter and playfulness, just like how Ethan is. It makes me feel relaxed and a little flirtatious.

Caleb, who immediately understands me. His scent makes me think of home and comfort, with its rich dark chocolate, smooth caramel, and toasted hazelnut notes. If Ethan's a summer campfire then Caleb is a winter fire in the fireplace, when it's snowing outside and you can curl up with a good book and a mug of hot chocolate. I'm always safe with Caleb.

And finally, Garrett. His scent is like that of a classic lumberjack, all male but also gentle and protective, not aggressive or overbearing. He smells to me like a freshly baked pie, a wood-burning fireplace, and sweet apple cider. It's like the home-cooked meal that your man makes for you, the firewood he chopped for you, the wine he mulled for you. Alpha male as service and care, not posturing or anger.

I hold those scents in my mind and picture my four Alphas. They think I'm brave. They think I'm strong. And for them, I want to be.

I'm not just fighting for myself, after all. I'm fighting to come home to them. I know they'll be devastated if they lose me. They love me and they care about me. If they'll fight for me, then I need to fight for them. I need to come home to them.

Maybe it's just my imagination, or maybe our bond is already stronger than I think, even without the claiming bite, because I swear I can smell their scents in my nose. I breathe in and out deeply, taking those scents into me, and keep myself calm.

Slowly, my heart rate slows, and I feel less like I'm about to have a heart attack from panic.

*Okay. Think, Ava. What can you do here to escape?*

I look around me as the van rolls along the highway. There's nothing in here, it's entirely bare. I test my zip ties. They're tight, and unlike rope I don't think I can find a way to wriggle out of them, or easily cut them on something.

I close my eyes again and pay attention to the road we're driving on. Just on the bare floor of the van like this I can feel every bump and dip in it. The road seems well-maintained. That's good. It means that he's not taking me out completely in the middle of nowhere, where it's only dirt roads. There's a possibility I can find someone and get help.

There aren't a lot of stops or sounds of traffic, so he's not heading into the city. Okay, where else would he take me?

Marcus has family money. I don't think his parents are alive anymore. If they are, he never mentioned them to me, and I never met them. But he probably has some kind of old-money house around the area. A lot of rich kids do.

That's probably where he's taking me. It's not too far away, and it's probably still near anything he might have to go and get stuff from like a grocery store, but it's still not in the heart of everything like a city.

There will be neighbors nearby, though. And possibly some large backyards, or gardens, or even some woods that I can try to lose him in. I just need to time it carefully.

If he gets me inside the house, or wherever he's taking me, it'll be too late. My chances of getting out will drop to near zero. I need to make a break for it when he parks but before he gets me inside.

I can't get out of these zip ties, so I'll just have to make do and run for it anyway. If I can find someone to help me, then they can get the zip ties off me. Or, possibly, I can find a sharp enough rock or something similar to cut them off, although I'm not hoping too hard on that one.

The possibility of this failing has me frozen in fear, but I breathe through it. As I remember how happy I am with my Alphas, and how much I want to get back at them, something else takes hold in my stomach.

Anger.

Because you know what? I'm actually sick of being scared.

I was so scared of Marcus that I dropped all of my friends and ran away. I was so scared of an Alpha like him finding me that I used blockers and suppressants for years, keeping my distance from everyone. I had no friends, no one to care about me, until my Alphas came along.

And now, Marcus wants to take this happiness away from me? Now that I've finally found people that I love and I'm building a life for myself? Not just any life, but the life I've always dreamed about, the life I've wanted for years?

Hell no.

I'm not going to let him.

I'm angry at how scared he's made me feel and at how his shadow has controlled my life and my thoughts for so long. And I'm angry that he's coming after me and my pack. My mates. Nobody comes after my mates.

I may be an Omega, not an Alpha, but that doesn't mean that I can't be protective and angry too. That doesn't mean that I can't fight in my own way.

And you know what, my fear is what he wants. He wants me to be scared. He wants that power over me. That's why people like him behave the way that they do.

It's kind of sad, actually. Marcus is an Alpha, looked at with respect by society. He comes from money and owns a company. He's handsome, and he knows how to be charming. He should be set for life.

And yet there's something inside him that's so insecure that he has to abuse and manipulate people in order to feel happy. He has to amass even more power.

Well, that's not my damn problem. And I'm not going to give him any power over me anymore. He doesn't get my fear.

I keep that anger burning in my stomach as I'm driven off the highway and onto paved roads. They seem to be empty, from how few stops Marcus has to make. I try to sit up and get my back to the door so I can open the door handle with my bound hands and roll out while he's at a stop, but I can't quite manage to get my balance.

I have to wait until he brings the van to a full stop and opens the door himself.

Finally, after what feels like hours, I feel him slow down and make a turn, then another, rolling to a stop.

This must be some kind of driveway.

My heart is pounding, but it's no longer from fear. It's from adrenaline and anticipation.

The van stays stopped for a few moments, then I hear him kill the engine. He opens the door, his footsteps echoing in my ears as he walks around to me.

The van door opens.

Now's my moment.

"All right," Marcus says, grabbing me by the arm and hauling me up onto my knees. "Time—"

I headbutt him as hard as I can, right in his sternum, throwing all of my weight forward. I nearly topple over onto my face, but luckily manage to keep my balance as he stumbles back, wheezing, stunned.

I've fallen hard onto my back before, and I remember what it was like to have the wind that badly knocked out of me, and how much it made my ribs hurt. I felt almost paralyzed, in too much pain and shock to move.

This is my only chance.

I lean back and swing my legs around so that I'm sitting with my feet dangling in front of me. Then I jump out of the van, landing on my feet. My hands are bound, so my balance isn't nearly as good as it should be, but I can't take any more time.

I have just a few seconds to get an impression of where I am. It's a large house, something like a manor, but old-fashioned, the kind of house that was built a few generations ago and maintained by the family.

There's a massive driveway, which is where we currently

are, and then the front lawn, and a side path around to presumably the back of the house—and most importantly, there's a thickly wooded area to the right.

I can't see any other houses around. As I suspected, this is one of those places where they build the houses far enough apart each obscenely rich person can pretend that they're the only house in the area, unable to see any neighbors—or have their loud parties overheard.

The woods are my best chance. I have no idea where the other houses are, and I'll be too exposed on the road. It's too quiet, I have no idea if any other car will come along and see me and stop to help.

I have to hide.

I take off running as fast as I can while Marcus is still stunned. I'm panting around the gag, sucking in ragged breaths around the fabric, and it's difficult to stay upright while going at top speed with my hands behind my back.

The zip ties cut into my wrists, and the gag hurts the edges of my mouth. I feel like a moron, like anyone would laugh if they saw me trying to sprint like this. But I don't stop. I don't care. I have to keep going.

I don't look back as I sprint through the trees. I have to stay focused, and if I look back I could trip and fall and all will be lost. I'm not sure I could get back up again if I fell, or if I'd even have time before Marcus got to me first.

"You fucking bitch!" Marcus's voice carries and I shiver.

I remember that angry tone so well from all those years ago, when I would do something he decided was disrespectful. It wasn't just the few times I stood up to him either. It could be for not laughing hard enough at his joke, or laughing too hard and having him decide that I was faking it and mocking him.

Marcus could find any excuse to scream at me. Any reason to tell me I wasn't good enough, and that I had to fix myself.

That familiar, furious tone cuts through my pounding heart like a knife, but the remembered terror just spurs me onward. I can't let him catch me. I won't let him catch me. He's never going to hurt me again. I don't care what it takes to earn my freedom, I'm going to do it.

What I told Ethan in the car when we first met still holds. He asked me what I wanted, and I told him.

*Freedom.*

I still mean that.

But now I understand what true freedom means. What I had before... sure, I was technically free in the sense that I wasn't registered, and I wasn't bound to any Alpha. But I was living in terror and hiding myself.

Now, I'm truly free. I get to be the best version of myself, supported and protected by my Alphas.

I refuse to give that up. I'm not letting Marcus take my happiness from me. I don't care what it takes or what I have to do.

My mind is clouded with adrenaline as I dash through the trees. I have no idea where I am, or if I'm moving toward safety or away from it. I just know that I have to put as much distance as possible between Marcus and me.

Behind me, distantly, I can hear him coming after me. I can hope to lose him, but I also know that my scent is strong, and he's going to try to track it down. He's not bonded to me the way my mates are, even without their bite on me, so he won't be able to track me quite as well. But I still can't take the chance. I have to get far enough away that he can't trace my scent.

I have no idea how long I've been running for when I realize

I can't hear his footsteps anymore, but I don't stop. I have to keep going. I'm not safe yet.

He could be moving stealthily to sneak up on me, or he could be circling around. If I stop, rest, for even a minute, I could give him the chance to catch up with me.

My body aches, and my breaths start to come in short, sharp gasps. Breathing through the gag is hard, and I feel like I must be disgusting, constantly trying to swallow down drool and breathe hard at the same time.

But I don't stop.

The idea of Marcus getting his hands on me again is too much to bear. I will literally die before I let that happen. If that means my damn heart gives out from pushing my body too far as I run, then so be it.

That fear and anger keep my mind focused on my goal. My single objective.

*Escape Marcus.*

# Chapter 47

## *Caleb*

Dante gets the police on the phone while Garrett drives like a maniac.

Usually, when Garrett drives like a maniac, I tell him that I'm going to call the highway patrol on him, but right now, I've never been so damn grateful that he's such an aggressive driver. I don't care how much trouble we get in so long as we avoid a collision and get to Ava in time.

"Yes, we have a missing person," Dante insists. "Yes, Ava Charleston. Five foot two, long dark hair, and brown eyes. She was released from—yes, you have her file. No, nobody's heard from her. We have reason to believe that her ex-boyfriend Marcus—yes, the one who brought the charges against her—yes, damn it, this is an emergency, start treating it like one!"

I don't think anyone would be quick to call me aggressive or someone who's prone to anger. I leave the Alpha posturing to Dante and Garrett. There are times when a quieter strength is what's called for.

But right now? I could yell at some fucking police myself.

Hell, I'll yell at anyone. I'll do whatever it takes to make sure we get to Ava before Marcus can do anything to her.

I keep my eyes on the maps application on my phone, giving Garrett directions as he weaves in and out of traffic on the highway. We quickly leave any other cars behind and get past the usual commuters, ending up on the part of the freeway that is used by people coming up to their fancy house for the weekend when they know it's worth the long drive.

The idea of Ava stuck with that monster for a long drive like this makes my blood boil. I don't think I've ever wanted to kill anyone before, but Marcus is sure coming in close on being my first.

Behind me, I hear Dante finally managing to convince the police this is an issue and getting information.

"He says that security footage on the cameras outside of the prison shows a white van pulling up and a man matching Marcus's description grabbing Ava and yanking her inside before it takes off," he tell us. "They were able to get a partial license plate and they're checking through the database now."

"Watch," Ethan says darkly. "Marcus will have bought it with a fucking credit card or something."

"Don't underestimate him," I say darkly.

Marcus completely fucking played us. We thought that he was trying to put Ava in prison, or at the least drag her through a long and painful court process. Even if his 'evidence' against her ended up being proven as false, it would still be a lot of heartache and headache on our parts. Especially Ava.

I thought he wanted to drag her through the mud and make her relive their relationship. Maybe even try to make some kind of legal claim on her since he was in a relationship with her while she was technically an Omega, even if she hadn't presented yet.

Sure, that charge wouldn't stick because an Omega's consent is important, and if Ava didn't consent to this, then it would all fall to pieces. But he could still very well try.

But I was thinking too small. Too *legal*. I should've known that a man like Marcus, one who made Ava that goddamn scared, would pull an even bigger piece of bullshit like this.

Ava may look delicate in her features, it's part of why she's so beautiful in my opinion, but she's not delicate in spirit. She's strong and determined. To have her afraid of someone like that says a lot about what kind of person they are and it's nothing good.

Now Marcus is determined to make her his, legal or not.

Terror boils in my stomach as my mind races, my thoughts full of all the worst possibilities. I struggle not to tell Garrett to drive faster. This is one of Ethan's sports cars, so it's built for speed, but there are limits to how fast any vehicle can go.

Garrett's going as fast as he can. I just wish we could fucking teleport.

What if Marcus manages to give her the bite while she's with him? What if he forces himself on her like that? It makes me want to scream and rip things apart with rage. Preferably Marcus himself.

"They're treating this as an abduction," Dante says, sounding annoyed and weary as he hangs up the phone. "They know the address of Marcus's residences so they're headed there now. Both the penthouse in the city and this one."

"We'll get there first," Ethan notes, sounding savagely triumphant.

I'm with him. I'm glad we're going to be there before the

police. I want to have some time just the four of us with this piece of shit.

We keep driving, and I give Garrett instructions to take the next exit off the highway.

We're almost there.

"Hang on," Garrett informs us. "I'm ignoring red lights."

"Good," I tell him, but I brace my feet anyway.

There aren't any other cars around, thank fuck, so we don't have to swerve to avoid T-boning anyone. Garrett's as good as his word and blasts through every red light, obeying no laws of traffic except the directions I give him.

Finally, we end up on one of those streets where the houses are divided by the remains of the forest that once conquered this land. It keeps all the houses apart and private, so that people can enjoy their parties or solitude as they wish.

"Up ahead," I tell him. "On the right, two more down."

Garrett skids the car to a halt as he turns sharply into the driveway, all of us jolting from the sudden stop.

I don't waste a second. Garrett throws on the parking brake and we all rip our seatbelts off, rushing out of the car.

There in the driveway ahead of us is a goddamn white van. I don't bother asking Dante if the license plate matches the partial that the police were able to get off the security footage. What are the chances this white van is sitting in Marcus's driveway for perfectly innocent and coincidental reasons? Practically fucking none, that's what.

As if my thoughts have summoned him, out of the woods emerges a figure, cursing loudly. "Dumb fucking..." he growls.

My rage completely takes me over, and before I even know what I'm doing, I'm rushing him.

Alpha rages aren't really a thing the way that fantasy stories and others like to portray them. They're greatly exaggerated for dramatic purpose in those stories, especially the ones that make it a big plot device, like a prince going into an Alpha rage and causing a major diplomatic incident, or killing an ally he didn't recognize in the moment. High drama stuff.

But right now, I feel like I'm in the grip of something primordial, some deep instinct from back when we were literally out surviving in the wild, taking on saber-toothed cats and woolly mammoths and all other manner of animal that was three times our size.

I literally leap at Marcus, catching the surprised look on his face right as I slam into him and knock him onto his back on the ground. I grab him by the arms and pin him, snarling in his face.

"Where is she!" I demand, my voice a low, thunderous growl I've never heard come out of my own mouth before.

A small, distant part of me is detached, observing this behavior and marveling at how Ava could bring this out in me.

The rest of me is too busy being fucking furious to care. I'm in the grip of righteous rage, and nothing is going to stop me.

Marcus whines and tries to get out from under me, twisting this way and that like a snake. "I don't know what you're talking about! Get off me! You people need to stop fucking harassing me. This is assault, and trespassing. I'll call the damn police on you."

The fact that he's trying to weasel out of it just makes me angrier. "You kidnap a woman so you can't even find the stomach to admit to it?" I snarl. "You have to pretend that you didn't do anything? You can't even find the goddamn balls to stand up and say that you took her and you want her for yourself?"

I'm almost stunned at the cowardliness on display in front of me. I know that most people who are abusive are actually quite cowardly when people stand up to them properly. They're usually deeply insecure and that's why they feel they have to manipulate people, to get the power and attention they crave.

They can't actually face up to someone when they know that person has the power here. When they know that admitting to their crimes will get them in trouble.

Knowing and seeing, however, are two different things, and I find myself furious all over again at this piece of shit.

"Come here," Garrett snarls, grabbing one of Marcus's arms.

Dante grabs another, and they haul him up as I back off, turning him and slamming him against the side of the van. Dante grabs the back of Marcus's head and pins it harder against the van. I hear the satisfying crunch of his nose breaking and see blood sliding down his face and the side of the vehicle.

"You son of a bitch," Dante snaps.

"Where is she!?" Ethan demands. He slams his fist against the side of the van by Marcus's head, making it clear what he'll do to Marcus himself if Marcus doesn't give us what we want. "Where is Ava!?"

The sound of sirens cuts through the air. Dante and Garrett don't let up their grip, but we all turn our heads to see several police cars racing down the street. They pull up the driveway and stop, with multiple officers getting out, hands on the weapons at their hips.

The four of us step back and put our hands in the air. I realize belatedly that I'm growling, but I don't care if it makes me look like a knothead. This man kidnapped our Omega and I don't want the police dealing with him. I want us to deal with him. Ava's pack.

It's our goddamn right. It's justice.

"Officers!" Marcus puts his hands up too. "Officers, you have to help me, look at what they're doing to me. They're trespassing, and assaulting me—"

"You're Marcus Travers?" one of the officers asks.

"Yes, yes, this is my house." Marcus indicates the house behind him. He sounds relieved.

I can't help my smirk when the officer replies, "Then, sir, we're placing you under arrest for abduction."

Marcus's jaw drops open. "You can't be serious."

"Very. Please turn around." The officer pulls out a pair of cuffs.

"I don't know what you're talking about!" Marcus pleads.

"You abducted Ava Charleston from outside of the correctional facility where she was released six hours ago," the officer replies. "Using this van."

"Look, I don't know where the bitch is, all right?"

Garrett and Dante drop their weight, clearly ready to attack him, but I hold up my hand to get them to wait.

Marcus just came out of the woods, and he was angry. He didn't come from the house, or the van, which I can now see is open on the other side, empty and dark.

The woods...

"He's telling the truth," I tell them. "Kind of. He abducted her, but she fled into the woods. I saw him come out of there furious. She must've lost him in there."

The officers all exchange looks, like they're not sure what to do with this information.

Screw it. We'll let the police deal with Marcus. As much as I want to beat him into a pulp, I know that Ava's more important. She could be hurt out there.

"Then let's go," Dante says.

I nod, and we all take off running into the woods.

We're quickly enveloped by the trees, and I realize how easy it is to get lost in here. That's a good thing for Ava when it comes to running away from Marcus. She could easily lose him among all these trees.

But it's a bad thing when it comes to getting her to safety.

The woods here used to cover a massive area, and the houses were carved out of it piecemeal. The woods still exist, in between each house and surrounding them, interconnected like Everglades snaking through the houses down in Florida.

It doesn't look like much when you're out on the road. You think it's just a large patch of trees. But then you get into it, and you realize it's all bigger and wilder than you thought.

"Ava!" I yell. "Ava! It's us! We're here!"

I can hear the others fanning out, yelling for Ava as well. We're going in separate directions, by silent agreement covering as much area as possible by splitting up. I'm glad, not for the first time, that I'm on the same wavelength as the rest of my pack and we can all read each other so well. There's no stopping to huddle and waste time planning or questioning. We know what we're doing.

I try to strike a balance between moving fast and being thorough. I don't want to accidentally pass Ava by because I ran too fast and didn't see her, but I also want to cover as much ground as I can.

At first, I'm sure she has to be nearby. She can't have gone all that far.

But then minutes pass. And then one hour. And then two.

Night falls.

A light rain begins to pour down. Normally, it wouldn't bother me at all, but right now, it just adds to my fear. There are far too many things that could've happened to Ava out here. She could've hit her head and died or gotten a bad concussion. She could have broken her leg or twisted her ankle badly.

Hell, she could've been attacked by a deer. They can be surprisingly aggressive if they feel threatened and they have young to protect.

Marcus could have been so angry because he accidentally killed her while she fought back. We could be looking for her body somewhere.

*No. Don't think like that.* Ava has to be alive. She has to be. I feel like if she wasn't, I'd know, somewhere deep in my chest.

"Ava!" I keep yelling her name. I can't even hear the others anymore, we've spread so far apart. I tell myself that's a good thing. It means that we're covering more ground.

Maybe one of them has found her, and I just don't know it yet.

Maybe she's already okay.

I comfort myself with that, but I don't stop looking anyway. Until I hear from one of my pack mates that Ava is found and safe, I'm going to keep going.

I yell and yell for her into the darkness until it feels like I'm going to lose my voice. Like her name is the only word I know how to say anymore.

My fear and desperation are at a fever pitch. I don't know what I'll do, what any of us will do, if Ava doesn't turn out okay.

And then.

"Ava!" I yell. "Ava!"

Very faintly, I hear a muffled word. A word that just might be my name.

My heart lurches in my chest. I can't see her in the damned dark, but if I close my eyes... and inhale...

It's faint, but I can trace it, that sweet scent I now know so well. I follow it through the trees as it grows stronger and stronger, until finally, I see her.

She's curled up and shivering at the base of a large tree in a clearing. The moment I see her, my heart stutters with anger.

She's got her hands behind her back, zip-tied, the skin raw and cut, bleeding. And there's a gag in her mouth. That's why she couldn't say my name properly.

"Ava." I rush over to her and work the gag out of her mouth.

Ava bursts into tears. She's shivering uncontrollably, and she's soaked, covered in dirt and leaves. I pull out my pocket knife.

"Hold still, sweetheart, I know."

I cut through the zip ties, and then pull her into my arms. Ava clings to me, hissing as she moves her arms properly for the first time in what must be hours.

"Yeah, I know. I know." I massage her arms to get the feeling back into them, and check her hands.

It doesn't look like any blood flow was cut off, no permanent damage, but the zip ties cut through her skin, bruising her wrists and making them bleed. We'll have to dress her wounds and take care of some things for her for a bit while she heals.

Far be it from me to complain. I'm more than happy to have an excuse to pamper her after this, even though I'm shaking with fury over what Marcus did to her.

Ava sobs in my arms, and once I've gotten the feeling back into her, I hold her tightly, rocking her.

"I've got you, sweetheart," I breathe. "I've got you. You're safe now."

"I tried so hard," she hiccups. "To be brave. To be strong. I wasn't... I wasn't going to let... I'm going to be free. I'm free with all of you."

Her words are pouring out in a broken rush, and I'm not quite sure I follow what she's saying. I place the back of my hand on her forehead to check, and sure enough, she's got a fever. Must be from the cold. And I have no idea when she last ate or got water. My poor sweet Omega.

"Guys!" I yell at the top of my lungs. I haul Ava into my arms and stand up. "Guys! I found her! I've got her!"

Ava loops her arms around my neck and rests her head on my shoulder, still shivering and crying.

I hear shouts and gruff voices in the distance, and soon, the other three emerge from the trees, barreling toward me. They crash into us, grabbing Ava and holding her tightly, the four of us now enveloping her in a group hug.

She clings to us, and the relief I feel is palpable—as strong as the love I feel for her.

"I'm never going to let anything like this happen to you again," I promise fervently.

*Never.*

# Chapter 48

## *Ava*

I'm not really sure what happened to me in the woods past a certain point, and so I'm not sure when it is that Caleb finds me.

One moment, I'm shivering and in pain, and I can't find it in me to be brave anymore. I just want to die. Everything hurts, and I'm cold and hungry, and I can't even think properly.

The next moment, Caleb's calling to me. He's picking me up and cradling me close, freeing me from my bonds and easing my pain. And then all four of my Alphas are around me, promising me that I'm safe now, and that nothing bad will ever happen to me again.

I wonder for a moment if this is a hallucination. If maybe, I have a fever, or I'm dying, and this is what my mind is coming up with to comfort me in my last moments.

But hallucinations don't feel this real, and they don't last for this long. This is real. I've been found. I've been saved.

My four Alphas hold me tightly for a long, long time, and I bask in their scents. As I breathe them in, I feel alive again. No, more than that. Like I'm no longer a scared animal operating purely on instinct, but a real live person again.

After however long, the other three reluctantly pull away so that Caleb can carry me out of the woods. That's when it gets fuzzy again. My vision and consciousness fade in and out.

Sometimes I feel like I'm seeing things, but I'm not really awake. I'm not processing any of it. It feels like trees and trees and more trees. Like we're walking for days.

Other times, my eyes are closed and I can't see anything, but I can hear the men talking in low voices. They discuss therapy, and a doctor, and one of them says he's going to "pamper the fuck out of me."

I'm so out of it that I can't tell who says what. It all sounds the same to me, a chorus of soothing voices. But I know that all four of them mean safety. They mean home.

I can't seem to stop shivering, even with Caleb carrying me and letting me leech off his body heat. At some point, there are other voices, and strange bright lights that I feel should be familiar, but I can't place them. Red and blue, and red and blue, and red and blue.

I watch them until I can't watch them anymore, and when I can pay attention to anything again, I'm inside somewhere enclosed and close.

This place smells even more like my mates, and I burrow even deeper into Caleb's embrace. A leather jacket is draped over me, and I know it's Garrett's from how it smells.

"You're driving this time," someone says. "So Garrett doesn't kill us."

"Hey, now."

"We have precious cargo this time."

"Fair enough."

"I'm still speeding."

Their soft teasing washes over me. I try not to move too

much, despite my shivering. My mouth hurts, my ankle hurts, and especially my wrists hurt.

We drive for a long time. Like in the woods, sometimes it feels like I've been in this space for days. Caleb keeps holding me, and someone else is stroking my hair. It takes me a moment to realize it's Dante. I know that scent, the spicy clove. The bourbon and honey.

At some point I must drift off properly, because it's all black and I don't think or feel anything at all.

I wake up when we stop moving.

Immediately my body starts shivering again, uncontrollable. I can't even speak with how my teeth are chattering.

"I've got the bath," someone—Ethan?—says, and then I'm being passed from Caleb's arms to someone else.

"Here you go," Garrett rumbles, and I realize he's the one carrying me. He purrs soothingly as I'm carried somewhere.

I can't seem to open my eyes, so I'm not sure where I am. I just know that Garrett is carrying me, so I'm safe, and that he's purring because he's trying to heal and comfort me.

Eventually, I'm brought somewhere that's dimly lit. I hear and feel Garrett snort. "Candles?"

"I think it'll help her feel safe," Caleb says. "No harsh lighting."

I'm lowered into deliciously hot liquid, and I gasp, my eyes flying open.

Everything's blurry for a second, as I sink into the tub. That's where I am. I'm at home, in the bathtub.

Dante strips and climbs in with me, holding me close. "Careful."

He dips my wrists into the water and I hiss at the pain. Dante purrs quietly, the sound vibrating against me. "I know, I know, but we have to clean them so we can bandage them, there we go."

Garrett and Ethan climb in next, and although it's a big tub, it's still a bit of a tight fit for all four of us. Not that I'm complaining. I want all of my Alphas as close as possible.

I'm not sure how many minutes go by, but Caleb appears with some first aid supplies a short while later. He sits on the edge of the tub and bandages my wrists. Something about my wrists, and why they're hurting, pierces through the fog and fever in my brain.

*Danger. There's danger.*

"Marcus," I manage to get out.

"Shh, it's okay."

"No." I try to grab at them, tugging my wrists away from Caleb. "No, he—"

"We know," Ethan promises me. "We know it was him. We know he's the one who kidnapped you. The police arrested him. It's okay."

In a way, I'm not sure what his words mean, and yet at the same time, they hit something in my brain, some button that turns everything off and lets me know that I'm safe. It's okay. My mates will handle it.

I sink back against Dante's chest and let Caleb finish bandaging my wrists.

"Good girl," Garrett murmurs. "You're being such a good Omega for us, letting us take care of you."

"We'll take care of everything," Dante promises me. "You don't have to worry about anything. We'll watch over you."

We stay in the tub for a little bit, the hot water and their bodies warming me up, until I stop shivering. Caleb feeds me a spoonful of what I presume is medicine. It has a crappy artificial fruity taste, but I swallow it down, along with the water he makes me drink.

Then Dante gets out, and I must doze off, because when I open my eyes again, Ethan is holding me and Dante is wearing clothes and has a bowl of something delicious in his lap.

"Here," he says quietly. "Eat up."

He feeds me, spoonful by spoonful, delicious soup. It's hot and clear and tastes delicious without being too much for my body, and goes down easy.

When I finish, my eyelids are drooping again.

"Okay," Ethan says. "Bedtime."

Caleb and Dante each take one of my hands from outside the tub and lead me out, wrapping me in a warm towel that they must have heated up. The other two men get out and quickly dry off and drain the tub, then wrap me in a big, fluffy bathrobe.

Dante picks me up, and the four of them carry me to bed, where they strip so that I can have as much skin-to-skin contact as possible.

I burst into exhausted tears when I'm placed into my nest. My lovely, lovely nest, my nest that I spent so much time working on, my nest where I sleep safely with my wonderful mates.

The four of them crowd around me, all of them holding me in some way or another. As my head hits the pillow, it's like the last part of my consciousness finally accepts that I'm safe, and that there's nothing to worry about anymore.

I can completely let go, so I do, and let the darkness of sleep claim me.

∼

It takes days for me to recover.

My fever lasts for a couple of them. I'm not quite sure how long exactly, since I'm out of it, but I know that it's at least two. I'm in bed with at least one of my mates the entire time, but most often it's all of them.

The only time one of them seems to leave is to use the bathroom or to grab food to bring up to the rest of us. It's almost like my heat, except more solemn, and with a lot more sleeping. I'm not sure what my mates get up to while I'm resting, but whether they're watching a movie or just resting or chatting, they're at my side.

I'm fed the basics, like chicken noodle soup and toast, and given plenty of water. I sleep with my head on one of their laps or shoulders, intertwined with them as much as possible, and let myself doze. I don't think I've ever slept so much in my life.

Sometimes I toss and I turn, the fever too much for me, and nameless monsters chasing me in my nightmares. I wake fitfully to find all four of my mates staring at me with concern, like they would reach into my mind and take the pain away from me if they could.

I wish I could tell them that they're already doing perfect just the way they are, but I can't find words. It's like I've forgotten what they are.

But finally, finally, I wake up from a deep sleep feeling refreshed.

I'm no longer shivering, and I actually feel properly hungry and thirsty. My head isn't pounding, and I can think straight.

I sit up, nearly bursting into tears with relief at how good it feels to be *thinking*. To know where I am, and who I am, and what's going on. I don't feel like I'm half-awake in some kind of dream state.

Garrett was spooning me from behind, but now that I've sat up against the pillows, his arm is over my waist. Caleb is on my other side, and Ethan and Dante are at the foot of the bed, talking quietly.

They both turn when I sit up and smile with relief. "How're you feeing?" Ethan asks softly.

"Much better," I admit. "Starving."

Dante jumps to his feet. "I have food."

He hurries out of the room while Garrett yawns and sits up, and Caleb blinks his eyes open. "You okay?"

I nod at them both. "Yes. I'm okay."

Dante returns with a bowl of delicious spicy noodles with chicken. "This will perk your senses right up," he teases gently, setting the tray down in front of me.

I chuckle and dig in, wolfing down the food. All four Alphas beam at me. I can't quite remember everything that I saw and felt during my fever. I'm not sure which of the vague memories I have are dreams, and which are based on reality.

But seeing how relieved and happy they are now tells me just how concerned they were while I was in the grip of my fever. I'm relieved that they're relieved, and that I'm not worrying them anymore.

I finish eating, and then take some vitamins that Dante hands me, along with drinking a lot of water. It's only when I finish all of that, that I think to look down at my wrists, and wiggle my ankle.

"How am I doing?" I ask them quietly.

"Your ankle wasn't that bad," Caleb promises me. "It must've been what sent you to the ground, but it's just a bit swollen. We've tried to keep it on ice but you tossed and turned a lot. You just have to take it easy while it finishes healing."

"We had a doctor do a house call," Garrett says.

I must've been really out of it, because I don't remember this doctor at all, or any ice on my ankle.

"He said that you were going to recover just fine, and that there shouldn't be any major scarring, but he gave a salve to help with that healing process just in case. You need to keep the bandages on for a little while longer."

"Mostly because of the bruising," Dante adds. "Similar to your ankle. They're kind of swollen right now."

I nod, looking down at my wrists. I recall the pain of the zip ties, but I also remember how it kind of just... became something I didn't feel anymore. It didn't matter.

I'm pretty sure that must've been when the fever set in.

The idea of what could've happened to me if my Alphas hadn't found me in time is haunting, but I know that they did find me in time, and that's what matters.

"Are you feeling okay to tell us what happened?" Caleb asks gently.

"Marcus apparently is refusing to talk, on the advice of his lawyers," Garrett says, his voice sharp.

"It makes sense," Ethan grumbles. "It's what I'd suggest if I was a lawyer. There's nothing he can say that won't incriminate him so might as well keep this mouth shut."

"We'd like to hear what happened, from you," Dante says. "But only if you want to. You don't ever have to tell anyone. Although we thought maybe getting you some therapy might help too, if you're up for that. It would be entirely confidential."

"You don't owe us any information."

I nod. I appreciate that they want me to be taken care of and to process my trauma without pressuring me to tell them anything. I know in my heart that if I told them I didn't want to ever talk about what happened, they would respect my wishes and never ask again.

But I don't want any secrets between us, and I don't want them thinking that something worse happened than what actually did. And I think it will help me to get it off my chest, to remind myself that it's in the past and that I'm safe now.

"The prison guards didn't do anything once I was released, they just processed my paperwork, and gave me my things, and then... I was on my own."

Garrett gives Dante a sharp look that Dante returns. I have the feeling that a call to some fairly high-up people will be happening soon.

"I assumed that you guys had gotten the charges dropped, so you'd be out there waiting for me when I left. The guards didn't tell me anything. I went out, and a white van pulled up, with someone yanking me inside. He tied me up and gagged me and I..."

The memory of that horrible moment hits me. The way that Marcus yanked me inside so fast I had no hope of escape. How nobody saw anything and didn't care. How quickly he overpowered me. And his horrible, terrifying smell.

I take a deep breath. I made a decision in that van not to let my fear of Marcus rule me anymore, and I plan to stick by that rule. I need to talk about this out loud so I can purge it from myself and move on.

"He smelled awful," I admit. "I've thought for a long time his smell was discomforting. Unsettling. But smell is so strong for us. I didn't get it when I was on blockers and suppressants, but once I was free of them..."

"As an Omega, you'd be especially sensitive to the scents of Alphas," Caleb agrees.

I nod. "Yes. His smell was so much worse then. I tried to fight back, but he overpowered me. After a short bit of driving, I think to make sure nobody was following them, the van pulled over and the driver left."

"We found him," Ethan says. "The guy is one of the workers in a production factory that Marcus owns in the city. He was a foreman and would give Marcus tours when he came down to check on the work."

"The guy was hard up on cash," Dante says. "And Marcus promised him a lot of it."

"I thought so," I replied. "I could hear what sounded like cash being counted. And then the man walked away, and Marcus got into the driver's seat. I was alone in the van."

"That would explain the other bruises," Caleb says.

"Other bruises?"

"On your back and upper legs. We thought maybe he hit you."

I shake my head. "He didn't. He threatened to do a lot of things to me, but he never hit me. Not that time, anyway. I think he wanted to wait until I'd... earned it."

The four men around me look like they're debating if they can get away with breaking into the prison and killing Marcus with their bare hands. Knowing how protective they are of me makes me feel overwhelmingly safe.

It helps to banish the nightmares and let me talk about what happened.

"Well, I'm sure you can imagine what happened next, because you were there. We drove to Marcus's place. I think it's his family home. He was never close with his parents. I didn't meet them. But I knew he came from money so when we were driving for a while I figured he was taking me upstate, since a lot of rich families have homes there."

Garrett snorts. "Yeah. My damn family is one of them."

I squeeze his hand fondly and he kisses my shoulder.

"When we got there, I admit I was terrified. I knew what would happen and how he would treat me. But I was sick and tired of being afraid, you know?"

I look around at my four Alphas, making sure that I make eye contact with each of them for a moment before I speak again. "You four showed me just how rich of a life is out there for me. Just how much I can be loved and be joyful."

I gesture at myself. "For all those years I thought I was living on my own terms, but really, I wasn't living much at all. I was terrified of people knowing my true status so I never made friends. I never took any risks, I never got to relax. I was scared all the time."

I smile at Ethan. "And then the best accident of my life happened, and I met all of you. And I realized the kind of life I really could have. I experienced what true freedom was."

"We're proud of you, baby girl," Dante assures me, reaching out and squeezing my knee.

"I didn't want to lose that. And it made me so angry, what those years of being scared had stolen from me. What Marcus had stolen from me by being so terrible that I ran away and abandoned all my friends. So I decided to fight back."

"That's our girl," Ethan says proudly.

"When he opened the van, I head-butted him..."

I have to pause because all of my Alphas start laughing. I'm confused for a second, because I know they're not laughing at me, and it's not necessarily a funny story that I'm telling.

But then Garrett wheezes out, "I would've fucking *paid* to

see that knothead get fucking body slammed. Oh my god. I bet his face was priceless."

They're laughing at Marcus, I realize. I grin. "I wish I could've stopped to drink it in. The glimpse I did get was pretty funny. But I knew he'd recover quickly so I ran into the woods."

The others nod, serious again.

"I just wanted to lose him. I thought, that since there were other houses around even though I couldn't see them, that I could just run fast enough to get him off my trail and find one of those houses and get help." I shrug. "Maybe nobody would be in one but I could hide out somewhere on the property."

"Smart thinking," Caleb says.

I make a face. "Yeah, except the woods turned out to be way bigger than I had expected and I got lost."

"Marcus gave up trying to find you, at least for a bit," Dante says. "That's when we showed up. Luckily Caleb saw him coming out of the woods and cursing you, otherwise we might not have found you as quickly."

"He refused to tell us where you were," Ethan says.

"We would've made him talk," Garrett says. "Police or no police."

"The police showed up," Caleb explains.

Oh. That explains a scrap of memory, the red and blue lights. I didn't understand it at the time, clearly out of it all with fever, but it makes sense now. "What were the police doing there?"

"We called it in as a kidnapping," Dante says. "The police took a minute to take it seriously but once they figured out that we were right, they were on it like flies on honey."

"That's why Marcus is in custody," Ethan adds. "The police

were on-site to arrest him. We didn't have to subdue him and then call the police and then find you."

Garrett sighs. "As much as I wish the police had been just a minute later so we could've roughed him up a bit, I'm glad they came. It meant they could deal with Marcus and we could focus on finding you."

I shake my head. "I feel kind of stupid. I twisted my ankle, busted myself up, and got a major fever."

"You got hypothermia, to be exact," Caleb says.

"Exactly."

"Babe." Ethan gives me a fond smile. "You were kidnapped. You were tied up and you couldn't get help. What the hell were you supposed to do? You did the best you could, and you succeeded in getting away from Marcus. That's the most important thing."

"That's why you're not alone anymore," Dante points out. "You're never alone. You always have us. You do your part, and we'll take care of the rest."

"I hope that we never have to do something like that all together again," I admit. "I'd rather we stuck to being a team on things like chores."

The men all chuckle. "Deal," Dante agrees.

"Marcus is going away for a long time for what he did," Garrett says with an air of deep satisfaction. "Abducting anyone is bad enough but an Omega? Trying to force her to be his mate? The prosecutor is going to have a damn field day with this."

"There's more than just the abduction charge, though," Ethan says with glee.

"Oh?" I ask, playful.

Knowing that Marcus is in jail and is going to stay there for what he did makes me feel that much more relaxed, and I sink back against the chests of my Alphas.

Prison was a terrible place. I hated it there. And maybe this makes me less of a good person, but I'm glad that Marcus will be there. He tried to make me an object, to make me less than a full person, to own me.

Now he'll be in a place where the guards treat him the way he wanted to treat me. They don't care about him. They look right through him. He'll finally feel as small, insignificant, and powerless as he wanted me to feel.

Good. It's what he deserves.

"Tracy, the employee of ours that he got to be the mole in our company," Ethan says, "she's come forward and wants to give evidence. She gave us a call."

"Oh, that's really good for her." I'm glad. I hope that this means she's able to move forward. I understand how charming Marcus can be, and I know he manipulated her. I hope she can be better than that now.

"Well, it's not just that she's testifying about his corporate espionage at our company," Dante says. "It's that she suspects we weren't the only company that Marcus would do this to."

"After we confronted her, she started to realize that she was being used, and she decided to look into other products that Prodigy Corp has put out," Caleb continues. "And she noticed in her research that the products were coming out right around the time other tech companies would start acting like they were about to make a new product announcement."

"But Marcus would make his announcement first," I guess. "So the companies would have to cancel their product."

"Or, in some cases, try to release their product anyway with slight changes," Ethan says. "But they'd be accused to stealing

Marcus's ideas. And of course, they couldn't ever prove that he had stolen theirs."

"We got our lawyers on the case," Dante says. "And they interviewed some former Prodigy Corp employees. Turns out, Marcus has a suspicious habit of showing up with all the schematics and information for a new piece of tech, like he came up with all of it himself."

"At the time, they all believed in his charisma and thought he was a genius." Garrett sounds offended, like he can't believe that people ever fell for that schtick.

"But of course, these people left for a reason," Caleb concludes. "It looks suspicious that this one guy's showing up out of the blue with hit after hit invention."

"Almost everybody shows their work," Dante says. "Even Steve Jobs. Marcus would refuse to show anyone any works in progress, wouldn't let people into his studio... he was way too secretive."

"And nobody ever saw him actually do any tech work," Ethan adds.

"Are these people willing to testify?" I ask. "And can you find evidence other than their testimony? Because you know that a case built entirely on witnesses and no hard evidence is shaky."

The four men beam at me with pride and I can feel my face flushing. "You're so fucking smart," Ethan says, delighted. "I hope you realize how smart you are."

"Yes," Garrett assures me. "They're all willing to testify and to provide whatever evidence they can from their time working at Prodigy. But we're also having our lawyers subpoena him for company information."

"We've contacted the other companies that Tracy suspected

had been stolen from," Dante says. "And we're letting them know what happened to us. We expect they'll be slapping Marcus with their own lawsuits before long."

"We're going to take down his entire damn company," Ethan says, that signature gleam in his eye. "It won't just be Marcus. It'll be Prodigy Corp too."

"He won't be able to use his wealth in shady under-the-table ways to be the king of jail," Garrett says, "because he won't have any wealth to do it with."

"And if, for some reason, he's able to get out early, like for good behavior or, I don't know, overcrowding," Caleb rolls his eyes, "he won't have a company waiting for him. He'll have absolutely nothing."

Dante takes my hand. "You might have to testify. It depends on how the case goes. Are you okay with that?"

I think about it. Being up in court, in front of a couple dozen people trying to figure out if I'm lying, while Marcus stares me down, doesn't sound like my idea of a good time.

But I decided I wasn't going to live in fear of him and I'm sticking to that. I'm going to do whatever it takes to make sure he pays for what he did to me, and if that means testifying, then so be it.

"Yes," I promise Dante, and the others. I squeeze his hand. "I can handle it."

"You're amazing," he promises me.

Listening to them talk about Marcus, and how they're going to make sure he never hurts me ever again, makes me feel a sense of safety and comfort that I've never experienced before.

Ever since I met these men, they've taught me what it is to have a family and a home. What it is to be loved. I feel surrounded by that love and by their protectiveness.

I know without a doubt that I want to be with these men forever.

"Can I... talk about something else, real quick?" I ask.

The men all nod, listening attentively.

"I know that I said it before, but that was before everything happened, and so I want to say it again so you know I haven't changed my mind." I smile at them all. "I want to be bonded to you. I want you four to be my mates. Officially. The way you already are in my heart."

The reaction is immediate. I see all four pairs of eyes darken, and I smell how their scents shift. I brace myself in the best way, certain I'm about to be deliciously devoured, when Dante takes a deep, steadying breath and holds up a hand.

"Baby girl, you're still recovering. As much as we really... *really*... want that for all of us... you're not up for it right now."

The others nod, the heat subsiding from their scents.

"You just woke up," Caleb points out. "And you were asleep for a bit."

"We were really worried," Ethan admits.

I pout. "But I'm clearly fine," I point out slyly.

The idea of getting to seal my bond with my mates, after what Marcus tried to do to me, is beyond appealing. I want them, and I want to know for sure that nobody will ever be able to do that to me again, because I'll already have a bite and be claimed.

But even as I pout, I see the other four exchange looks that I know means I'm not going to get what I want... yet.

"We're not taking any chances," Garrett says. "We'll bond with you when you're fully recovered."

"And trust me," Dante purrs. "We'll make it worth the wait."

"Well, if you promise," I tease.

"We do," Caleb says solemnly.

My heart melts all over again for these men, these wonderful men who would clearly do anything for me. I've never felt so happy before in my life.

The four of them cuddle me close. "We'll stay by your side until it's the right moment," Ethan promises.

"And then we'll make you ours forever." Garrett's voice is full of promise.

There's no second-guessing. No worry. No fear.

I just trust them, and believe them.

# Chapter 49

## *Ava*

Several days go by while I recuperate.

As much as I'm desperate for us to seal our bond, once I actually get out of bed, I realize that my Alphas are right. I'm really in no shape for it yet.

On top of the ankle and my wrists, I'm pretty stiff and sore from being bounced around in the back of a van and then running for a while, and my body is weak from the fever. I really have to take it easy for the next few days, so I do.

My Alphas make good on their promise to stay by my side, but they're not idle. Far from it. They've got a case against Marcus and the Prodigy Corp to pursue.

I'm busy as well. The doctor checks on me regularly, and even though I'm healing fine, I let him keep checking up because I know it's not so much for me as it is to reassure my Alphas.

I can't even imagine how much what happened to me scared them. I was pretty terrified myself, but at least I knew what was going on, and I knew that my Alphas would stop at nothing to save me. I was able to find comfort in that.

My Alphas, on the other hand... they had no idea if I was even alive. I picture what it would feel like for me the other way around, wondering if one of them was hurt or even alive, and it makes me sick to my stomach. I couldn't possibly bear to lose any of them.

So I let them fuss, and have a doctor over to check up on me. They also set me up with a therapist so that I can talk to someone about what happened, and make sure that I'm okay emotionally. Especially with the possibility of a trial.

Their lawyers are working with them on suing Prodigy Corp as a group with the other companies and inventors who have been hurt. We also heard a rumor that some of the current and former employees will be suing as well, citing wrongful termination, being made unwitting accessories in corporate espionage, that kind of thing.

There's no way that Marcus can get out of this, or at least I don't think so, but the lawyers want to be thorough. And I might have to testify.

It'll depend on if Marcus wants to try to protest his innocence or not. If he just pleads guilty to the kidnapping, my statement might not be needed, although there's a chance the judge will want to hear it anyway, perhaps in writing or in person.

But if Marcus wants to fight it, I might have to take the stand in court, and my men want me to be as emotionally prepared for that as possible.

It's an exciting and tense few days, but the possibility of getting to put Marcus behind bars and wipe his company off the map helps me heal faster, I swear it does. I feel like I finally have power again. Like I no longer have to ever be afraid.

"How do you feel if you end up having to testify in front of him?" my therapist, Rachel, asks kindly halfway through one of our sessions.

I like her. I think I'll keep seeing her when this is done, so I can work on dealing with my parents and my childhood, and the daunting task of reconnecting with the friends in college I left behind when I fled Marcus.

I think about the question. "When it was first brought up, I was scared," I admit. "But now that I've had time to think about it and prepare, I'm not worried anymore. It might be good for me, to have a chance to tell people what he did and what he's really like."

"You've never told anyone besides your Alphas?"

I shake my head. "I didn't know how to talk about it. But my Alphas believed me and supported me. Thanks to them, I feel confident. I don't think it would be scary. I think it would be... good to share my story. And I know it would put him behind bars. I have confidence in that."

Rachel smiles. "I'm really proud of you, Ava. And I'm glad you have such a good support system."

I really, really do. And they're proud of me, as well. In fact, I'm proud of myself.

And what a support system it is. While my mates have made good on their promise to not officially claim me until my body is all healed up and they know I'm in the right headspace, they aren't letting this court case against Marcus keep them from showering me in affection.

Honestly, if anything, they're showing me even more love and attention than ever before. I appreciate how they're making sure that I know I'm loved and cared for, even though they're in the middle of this tough situation.

On the one hand, preparing to kick Marcus's ass and make

sure he never sees the light of day again is fun. On the other hand, it is a lot of work with lawyers, a lot of paperwork, a lot of minutiae. I try to look after my men as well as they look after me, making sure they take breaks, that they're fed and drink water, that they relax when they need to.

Dante, who's on the phone with one of their lawyers, smiles at me as I come into the kitchen. He's been smiling more and more as we draw the net tighter around Marcus. All of my men have been.

It's another reminder to me that those dark days of fear really are over. That I'm finally free of that man and his influence.

I crawl into his lap and let him cuddle me. I've been adoring all of their cuddles, getting to nest with them and have them close. I'm so happy that I get to have this. I'm out of my heat, so I can truly enjoy all the touch and closeness without being blinded by my lust, and I haven't been snatched away from them.

It's really sinking in for me that I can have this. I can have them. Nobody will ever take me from my pack, my Alphas, ever again.

And that's why as I sit in Dante's lap, I try very hard not to ask him again for the one thing that I'm craving. The one thing that I know I'm missing.

Their bites.

I want it so badly, but I haven't gotten it yet. I understand that I need to heal, but my ankle is fine now, and my bruises are just about gone, and my wrists are all better. I've been doing well with my therapist and we're moving me to once-a-week sessions instead of every other day.

It's time.

Dante hangs up the phone. "That was the lawyer. He said that Marcus is still trying to beat the charges of corporate espionage, but our team knows he'll have to cave eventually. There are just too many lawsuits now. But he had even better news. Marcus is pleading guilty for your kidnapping and endangerment."

I suck in a breath. "Does that mean I don't have to testify?"

"The judge will want a statement from you, but you don't have to make anything verbally, and damn well not in front of Marcus. You're free, darling." He kisses the top of my head.

I nuzzle him, my heart feeling so full it could burst. "I'm so glad."

I meant what I said to Rachel, my therapist. I'm okay if I end up having to testify in front of Marcus. But knowing that he's given up on this fight with the abduction and endangerment of an Omega charge means that he's more likely to also give in on all the lawsuits.

We're going to win. I can feel it.

"That charge alone will put him behind bars for ten years," Dante informs me proudly. He kisses my neck. "You did it. He's going to be punished for what he did to you. He'll never lay a damn hand on you again."

"I know someone I wish would lay a hand on me," I point out, dropping any pretense at subtlety.

Dante laughs. "We'll see."

I don't hear anything more for the rest of the day, and I don't want to push too far. I know that this isn't really just about me. It's also about my Alphas feeling comfortable with this. They'd never forgive themselves if they accidentally hurt me in any way or if we started, got halfway, and I had to stop from fatigue or just not having my heart in the right place.

But I'm more than ready.

The next day, I wake up to find that my alarm has been turned off, allowing me to sleep in. I head downstairs, and Caleb treats me to a foot massage while I eat breakfast. Then, Ethan takes me out to a spa day, waiting in the lobby with a book while a masseuse makes me feel absolutely boneless and completely relaxed, and my skin is smoothed over with lovely smelling hot oils and my face is given a mud bath.

When we get back, I take a nice long bath, and Garrett climbs into the huge tub too, joining me to wash my hair and cuddle me.

Then he leads me downstairs, where I find an incredible dinner laid out for us. Dante's putting the finishing touches on the table, and I smile so hard my face hurts. It's linguine di mare, with shrimp and mussels and my favorite sauce, and delicious freshly made crab cakes, and buttered lobster steaming on plates.

I couldn't possibly feel more pampered. My heart is so incredibly full.

Dante pulls out a chair for me and we all sit down to eat. The food is exquisite, not that I'm surprised. I've come to expect restaurant-quality food from Dante. But it's clear from the pricey food and how carefully he's plated everything, making it all look beautiful and even putting candles on the table, that tonight is something special.

"What's the occasion?" I ask as I mop up the last of my pasta sauce with a slice of warm, homemade bread. "Did Marcus finally roll over on the other court cases?"

The four men look at each other, smiling, and Dante shakes his head. "No, not that, although things are going well and we know that we'll have him all wrapped up before long."

I finish eating and push my plate aside. "What is it, then?"

Dante looks me in the eye, and I can see the heat in his gaze. "Why don't we have dessert first?"

I shiver, feeling like I'm the dessert that's about to be devoured.

Dante brings out some warm chocolate souffles, delicate and decadent, and we dig in. The chocolate explodes in my mouth, but it's not just chocolate. There's a hint of spice to it, and a tang like alcohol, and a smoky aftertaste...

It's the flavor versions of the smells that I get from the scent of my mates. This dessert is my mates.

I finish my dessert and look at Dante in astonishment, impressed with his skills. He smiles knowingly. "Ava. How are you feeling?"

"Amazing," I tell him honestly. "I feel amazing. And so loved. Thank you all for today."

"Are you feeling strong enough?"

The breath catches in my throat as I realize what he means.

Instead of nodding or answering him, I push back my chair and stand up, the taste of chocolate and my mates' scents still heavy on my tongue. I walk down the table to Dante, crawl right into his lap, grab him by the front of his shirt, and kiss him.

I pour every bit of my hunger into that kiss, and I hope that he's gotten the message.

I want them to claim me. *Now.*

Dante's arms tighten around me, his scent spiking in the air as he pulls me close. I can feel the bulge of his cock, already hard between us, and I can't help grinding against it, rolling my hips so that my clit drags over the hot bulge.

We both groan, and the sound is echoed by the other three Alphas around us.

Suddenly, dessert is the last thing on anyone's mind—or at least, what we all want for dessert has changed.

"I feel perfect," I whisper against Dante's lips. "I'm totally healed up, and I'm ready. So ready. I want your bite. *Please.*"

My voice turns to a plaintive whimper on the last word, and he purrs deeply, his tongue delving into my mouth in a fierce, claiming kiss.

I lose myself in it for a long moment, our lips moving together as if they've perfected this dance. When we finally break apart, Dante moves his mouth over to my jaw, kissing along the line of it before trailing downward to press his lips to the pulse throbbing in my neck.

A shiver runs down my spine, wetness gushing from me and soaking my panties as he scrapes his teeth lightly over my skin. It's a gentle touch, not hard enough to even leave a scratch, but it still affects me all the way to my core—because I know it's just a precursor to what's coming. To the bite I've been craving for so long.

"Take me upstairs," I whimper. "Now."

"Anything our beautiful Omega wants."

Dante's chair scrapes against the floor as he stands up, bringing me with him. My legs wind around his waist, and his large hands cup my ass as he turns away from the table and heads out of the room. The other Alphas flank us on either side as he carries me upstairs, and when I look over Dante's shoulder at them, the heat and emotion in their eyes makes my heart flutter.

This is real.

We're doing it.

I whimper again, feeling more desperate for their knots than I ever have before. It feels even more intense than when I was at the height of my heat, although I don't know how that's possible. I'm filled with the strongest urge to have all of them inside me, to find some way to take all of them at the same time... but another part of me wants to fuck each of them separately, to be able to focus on each Alpha in turn.

"There will never be enough time for all the ways I want you to claim me," I breathe, catching Ethan's gaze.

He chuckles hoarsely, reaching down to palm his cock as we hit the top of the stairs.

"Walk faster, Dante," he tells his pack mate, his voice strained.

Dante laughs, but I can smell the arousal in his scent, and he does pick up the pace, his long strides eating up the hallway as he carries me toward my room. Warmth fills me as I realize where he's heading. He could've taken me anywhere in the house, but he chose my room, the place where I first nested and was knotted by them during my heat.

As soon as we step inside, I feel an overwhelming sense of calm, of *rightness*, fill me.

This is how it was always meant to be. From the very beginning.

Dante lays me on the bed gently, and for a moment, I find myself staring up at all four of the Alphas as they gaze down at me. They're all so fucking gorgeous, muscled and tall and breathtakingly handsome in their own unique ways. My nipples peak, heat sliding through my veins as I reach for the hem of my shirt and tug it off.

All four men react to that, their gaze snapping to my exposed breasts. My bra is still covering the best bits, so I reach back behind me and undo the clasp, then slide my bra down my arms and toss it away.

"Fuck," Caleb murmurs. "So damn beautiful."

Dante is breathing harder, his chest rising and falling as he watches me, but he stays where he is for the moment, even though I can tell it's taking some effort.

"Keep going," he tells me.

So I do.

Under the heavy gaze of my Alphas, I continue to strip, and each article of clothing I remove feels like a promise. A vow. A declaration of what I want—what I *need*.

When I'm finally completely naked, I run my hands down my body, shivering at my own touch. I'm so keyed up already that even though it's nowhere near as good as having them touch me, it still affects me. One hand stops at my breast, squeezing and molding the soft flesh, and the other continues even lower, ending up between my legs.

I spread my thighs a little, and I can tell that the movement allows more of my scent to fill the air, because the men's eyes dilate, their nostrils flaring.

"I'm ready for your cocks," I whisper. "For your knots." I spread my pussy lips with my fingers, allowing them to see how wet and swollen I am for them at the same time my other hand moves up to my neck, grazing over the curve where it meets my shoulder. "For your bites."

Dante lets out a quiet growl, shucking his shirt and then his pants before crawling up onto the bed to join me. He grabs the hand that's been playing with my pussy, bringing my fingers to his mouth and sucking on them.

He bites my fingertips gently, and I squirm as my clit throbs in response.

"We'll give you all of those things, baby girl," he promises. "You already have our hearts. I love you so much."

Unexpected tears sting my eyes at his words, emotions threatening to overwhelm me, and I reach for him, pulling him down to kiss me.

"I love you too," I breathe.

My hands thread through his dark hair, and I can feel the heat of his body on my skin as he settles between my legs. His cock nudges my entrance, and I hook my legs around his waist, pulling him closer.

He presses slowly inside, stretching and filling me, and I kiss him harder, panting against his lips.

"Yes," I whisper. "Yes, yes. Oh fuck—*yes*."

The last word is forced from my lungs on a sharp cry as he pitches his hips forward, burying himself the rest of the way. He fucks me with firm, steady strokes, rocking our bodies on the bed as he kisses me over and over, and it's everything I ever needed.

"So slick for me," he praises, grabbing one of my legs and pressing my knee to my chest, opening me up wider for him. "So fucking tight. So good."

The stretch in my hips is only outdone by the stretch in my pussy as he manages to get deeper than he ever has before. My jaw falls open as I forget how to breathe for a second. My pulse is hammering in my throat, and I can feel the beginnings of an orgasm creeping through me, making my limbs tingle.

His hips snap forward again and again, claiming me with each thrust, and I gasp for breath as if I'm about to be hit by a tidal wave.

"Oh god, keep going," I beg. "Please, Dante, please, oh..."

He lifts my other leg, nearly folding me in half as he presses my knees to my chest, the weight of his body keeping them pinned in place, and I fall apart. He slams in one more time, and pleasure explodes through me, making my back arch.

"Fuck. *Fuck.*"

His knot swells, and at the exact moment he shoves it inside me, he leans down and sinks his teeth into the side of my neck.

Something I've never felt before explodes inside me, sending my climax spiraling to new heights, and I cling to him as he holds the bite, his teeth clamped down around my delicate flesh. There's a bite of pain, but it's the best kind of pain I've ever felt, making me gush all over his cock. The fluid of my slick seeps out from the place where we're connected, soaking us and the bed, and I cling to him with shaking arms as all of the sensations wash over me.

It takes a long time for me to come down from the intensity of it, and after a while, Dante shifts our positions, wrapping my legs around his waist instead of pressing them to my chest. My hip flexors breathe a sigh of relief, and I vaguely wonder how he knew I needed that when I didn't even know it myself. But I'm too lost in the moment to ask, held in a perfect bubble where nothing matters but the intense, unbreakable connection between us.

When Dante finally loosens his jaw and pulls back a little, I whimper at the loss. But he grins, dropping his head to lick at the tender spot.

*Oh fuck.* The feel of his tongue sliding over his bite mark is almost better than his tongue on my clit.

"Aahh..." I turn my head a little, shivering from head to toe. My pussy squeezes around his cock as I come again, another rush of pleasure hitting me so hard that little sparkly lights dance in my vision.

"Mine," he breathes, licking me again.

The possessiveness in his voice just about makes me melt into a puddle, and I nod, my voice a whisper as I reply, "Yours."

We stay like that until his knot slowly begins to deflate, murmuring to each other quietly, sharing kisses and soft words. I'm aware of the other three Alphas watching us, aware of their scents filling the room—but instead of making this moment feel *less* intimate, it only makes it feel more so. I'm glad they're here to witness this, and I'm even more glad that I'm going to have their bites too.

Dante slips out of me after several more minutes, and I sigh at the feeling of emptiness.

Luckily, I know it won't last long.

He gives me another deep, long kiss, then draws back. His thumb brushes over my lower lip, adoration shining in his slate-gray eyes.

"I'm so glad you found us, baby girl," he murmurs. "My life was incomplete without you in it. All of our lives were."

As he speaks, he turns to look over his shoulder at his pack mates, and each of them nods. I bite my lower lip, blinking back tears. I'm not sure I'll be able to keep from crying at some point tonight, with my emotions so high, but I don't want them to blur my vision. I don't want to miss a second of this.

"Ethan," I whisper, gesturing to the tall Alpha with the crooked smile who came to my rescue that night at the club. "Come here."

He does, tugging off his clothes and then switching places with Dante. He kneels between my legs, his fingers skimming along my inner thighs and leaving goosebumps in their wake.

"Can I tell you something?" he murmurs quietly.

"What?"

"I've wanted to do this ever since the first night I met you."

I blink, my heart skipping a beat. "Really? But you didn't even know me then. I could've been anyone."

"But you weren't just anyone," he says with a smile. "You were *you*. Ava. The most beautiful woman I've ever known, inside and out. I was drawn to you so much that night. And sure, it's gotten stronger every moment that I've spent with you, as I've gotten to know you. But the seed of it was planted that night. Even then, some part of me knew that I had found the Omega who would make us whole."

"I was so scared that night," I admit, reaching for him. He comes willingly, leaning over me so that our faces are only inches apart. "But I think part of what scared me was how *safe* I felt with you, right from the beginning. I wasn't used to that, and I wasn't expecting it."

"You'll always be safe with us," he promises, his cock finding my entrance.

He presses inside, and with our faces so close, I can see the way his eyes spark with heat at the feel of my pussy stretching around him. I squeeze my inner walls just to make those sparks flare brighter, and Ethan lets out a hoarse chuckle.

"Such a little vixen, you are," he breathes. "You're asking to get fucked hard and bitten even harder."

My heart trips over itself, skipping a beat as my breath catches. Then I nod, clenching around him as tightly as I can. "Hell yes, I am."

Ethan's nostrils flare, and despite the teasing tone of his voice earlier, I know he absolutely meant it. Keeping one hand braced by my head, he grips my hip with the other, holding me steady as he draws out and drives back in. He angles his hips in a way that makes every hard thrust send an explosion of sensation through me, and I wrap my arms around him, digging my fingernails into his back a little.

That only seems to drive him into more of a rut, and he nearly knocks the breath out of me as he fucks me harder and faster. It's wild, intense... and so fucking perfect.

Pleasure ripples through me, and I'm mewling and panting, making noises I'm sure I've never made before. I turn my head, offering my neck up to him, and the movement makes Dante's bite mark ache pleasantly.

"Fuck," I whimper. "Need you... need your bite. Ethan, please."

"Not yet," he grits out, although I can tell it's difficult for him. "Not until you come. I want to feel you fall apart on my cock while my teeth sink into you."

*God, if he keeps talking like that, he won't have to wait long.*

I nod fervently, focusing on breathing as my body becomes an inferno of pleasure. I keep forgetting to exhale, the breath getting trapped in my lungs as Ethan's snaps his hips forward again and again, burying himself deep each time.

And then, suddenly, it all breaks. The tension coiling inside me explodes, and I scream raggedly, bucking beneath Ethan as I palm the back of his head and pull is face down toward my neck.

He doesn't need any more urging than that. The warmth of his breath gusts over my fevered skin, and then his teeth are there. As my orgasm crashes through me, I brace myself for the burst of pleasure and pain—but it still shocks me when it comes.

Ethan bites down hard, and I can feel the vibration of his grunt against my skin as his own orgasm hits. His knot swells inside me, binding us together and filling me up, until all I can think about is him. This.

I have no idea what the bite feels like from the Alpha side, but it must be pretty incredible, because Ethan keeps coming for what feels like forever, pulse after pulse of his cock matching the clenching of my pussy. I can feel each spurt of his cum, and the thought of being so full of his release makes me shiver.

By the time it ends, I feel like someone took all the bones out of my body, leaving me a limp, sated puddle.

Ethan keeps his teeth clamped down on my neck for a while longer, and when he finally releases the bite, he peppers kisses to the spots where he broke the skin. It's soothing and arousing at the same time, and each press of his lips makes my body jerk slightly.

"You're mine now too," he whispers. "Just like you're Dante's. Just like you'll be Caleb's and Garrett's."

I smile at the warmth in his voice, sliding my fingers through his sweat-dampened hair as I murmur back, "I was always yours. This just makes it official."

# Chapter 50

## *Ava*

Ethan lifts his head, grinning down at me like I just told him he won the lottery.

Actually, he looks more happy than he probably would if I told him he'd won the lottery. These men are already insanely wealthy, and although I know they all have a lot of ambition and big plans for their company, I also know that none of them care as much about money as they do about each other—and me.

"I love you," I tell him, and it feels so damn good to say it out loud.

I swear I can feel the bite mark on my neck pulse, as if it's somehow sealing those words, locking them in and entwining them with our bond.

"Good." Ethan beams. "Because I love you so much that it would be really fucking awkward if you didn't love me back."

His words draw a laugh out of me, because it's just such an *Ethan* way of saying it. I kiss him again and then bury my face against his neck, breathing him in.

When we finally disentangle from each other, I see the other three Alphas watching us with smiles on their faces. Even

Garrett, who's usually less prone to displays of emotion than the others, is grinning like an idiot.

"What?" I ask, flushing a little.

"Nothing." Caleb's warm blue eyes dance. "It's just... you two are so fucking cute."

Ethan rolls his eyes, lifting a hand to flip off his pack mate as he drops his head and gives me a kiss that feels more *filthy* than *cute*. I'm gasping for breath by the time our lips separate, and he draws back, gazing down at me with satisfaction.

That kiss revved up all of my Omega instincts, and I don't even have the mental capacity to try to banter with Caleb right now. So instead, I just shift my focus toward him, spreading my legs wider as I lick my lips.

I know what I must look like, my pussy swollen and dripping with cum, my skin flushed from exertion, and marks on my body from his pack mates. I'm a mess—but in a good way, hopefully.

His gaze travels over me, his eyes shifting subtly back and forth as he takes in every inch of my small frame. Then he tugs off his shirt, baring the lean muscles of his chest. He discards the rest of his clothes without ever looking away from me, and when he joins me on the bed, the intensity of his gaze makes my skin prickle with goosebumps.

Caleb has always been a bit quieter than the other three Alphas, the one who made his way into my heart with his softness and warmth. From the very beginning, I've always felt so *seen* by him, as if he can almost read my thoughts sometimes.

And just like always, it seems as if he can sense what I'm thinking, because one corner of his mouth curves upward in a smile.

"So beautiful," he murmurs. "You look like you've been properly fucked, sweetheart. Have you?"

"Yes." I nod. "But that doesn't mean I'm done."

Warmth bleeds across his features, and his smile widens. He slides two fingers inside me, fucking his pack mates' cum back into me, and my eyes roll back at the feel of it. His fingers glisten when he withdraws them, and even before he starts to move them upward, my mouth is already falling open.

"Hungry?"

I nod again, and he brushes my bottom lip with his index finger, smearing a mixture of Dante's and Ethan's cum there. I lick it up, then lift my head suddenly, capturing his fingers and sucking hard on them.

All four of the Alphas groan, and Caleb swallows hard, the corded muscles in his neck tensing a little.

"Come here," he whispers, kneeling between my legs and slipping his fingers out of my mouth. He lifts me onto his lap, as he sits back on his heels, his cock jutting up between us. "Ride me, sweetheart. Show me how much you want this."

I don't hesitate, lifting up as I wrap my hand around his shaft, then guiding him to my core as I sink back down. He glances down to watch my body accept him, and I do too, entranced by the sight for a moment.

He lets me set the pace, and I start off slow, letting my body recover from the overwhelming pleasure of being fucked by two Alphas already. My clit is so sensitive that every little brush against it makes me shiver, and I roll my hips as I slide up and down his cock, chasing what feels best.

"I can never look away from you," Caleb whispers, adoration in his voice. "You look like a goddess right now."

I smile, my heart thumping as our gazes meet. Then,

because I *feel* like a goddess with the way he's gazing at me, I wrap my arms around his neck and start to ride him harder, showing him just how much I like having his cock inside me.

Over his shoulder, I'm aware of the other three Alphas watching us. Garrett is undressed already, his fist wrapped around his thick length as if waiting to claim me is almost more than he can take. Ethan's and Dante's expressions are a little less strained than Garrett's, but I can see the raw desire in their eyes.

They like watching, and I love that.

I love that I never feel like I have to choose between these men, that they're happy to share me with each other, even in this.

My attention moves back to Caleb, his dark chocolate scent mixing with caramel and making my mouth water. I kiss him, and when I press gently on his chest, he follows my urging and lies back, adjusting our positions so that I'm straddling him.

I have more range of motion this way, and I brace my hands on his muscled pecs and fuck him so hard that my breasts bounce.

"Fuck," he breathes. "You're gonna make me come, sweetheart. You feel too good."

"Uh huh," I whisper back, as breathless as he is. Pleasure is rising inside me again, filling me up to the brim, and I bite my lower lip in concentration as I push toward my release.

The slapping sound of our bodies fills the room, rising up over our soft moans and grunts. Caleb's abs contract every time he bottoms out inside me, meeting me halfway as he thrusts his hips up. His knot starts to swell, not fully inflated yet, and I force myself down on it over and over, the pressure so incredible that I feel like I might pass out.

"Ava!"

He grunts my name, grabbing me suddenly and flipping me over so fast that everything becomes a blur for a moment. I land on my back on the soft bedding, and Caleb ruts into me like a mad man, his teeth bared as he pistons his hips one last time. He drives his knot deep inside me as it pulses and grows, lodging behind my pubic bone and joining our bodies as one.

Then he's biting me, his teeth finding the spot just above Ethan's bite and sinking into soft flesh. I wrap my arms and legs around him, squeezing him like I'll never let go. A soft wail pours out of me, every inch of my body tingling with sensation.

With his teeth still buried in my skin, Caleb sucks lightly, and the feel of it makes me shudder in his arms.

"I love you," I whisper. "I always will."

He can't respond with his mouth occupied the way it is, but he hums against my flesh, and I can sense the change in his scent—pure happiness.

I grin up at the ceiling, the room seeming to spin around us a little as I regain my bearings. Caleb soothes his bite with his tongue after releasing it, lapping at Ethan's mark too, and I whimper.

"Is it always going to be like that? Will it always feel so good when you touch your marks?"

Caleb chuckles. "I don't know for sure, but from what I've heard, it's possible."

I purse my lips, tightening my thighs around him. "That's no fair. You guys are basically giving me four extra clits—and on my neck, of all places! I'm holding you responsible for what happens if you kiss one of them in public and I have a screaming orgasm in front of a bunch of strangers."

He laughs again, teasing the sensitive bite marks with his tongue, almost as if he's testing my theory that they're as sensitive as my clit. "I think we'd all be more than happy to take responsibility for that."

"Definitely," Ethan echoes, and I can hear the hunger and amusement in his voice.

If I wasn't so ridiculously happy and sex-drunk, I'd probably regret giving him all the ideas I know must be running through his head right now. But that's a problem for future me to deal with... and to be honest, I don't think she'll really mind that much.

Caleb laps at my neck one more time, then sighs softly. "I'd stay inside you all day if I could, sweetheart. But I think Garrett would actually kill me if he doesn't get a chance to knot you soon."

"He's right about that," Garrett growls, and even though it's clear he's joking, I can hear the edge in his voice.

He's been patient long enough. He needs me.

And I need him too.

Caleb slips out of me as his knot loosens, joining the other Alphas who surround me on the bed, and Garrett climbs up onto the mattress too. It's a bit crowded with all of us here, but much like when we all fucked in my nest, it doesn't get in the way. If anything, having everyone else so close just makes it better—a reminder that this bond is shared between all of us, stronger because of each link in the chain.

Garrett's pupils are dilated, the deep brown of his eyes almost obscured by blackness, and he gives his cock another firm squeeze. The crown is swollen and flushed, slick with precum and tinged purple from the rush of blood. It looks like it's almost painful, and it plucks at my Omega instincts, making my exhausted body respond instantly.

I was made for that cock. My Alpha's cock.

"You know I love you, right?" Garrett rasps, leaning over me to run the pads of his fingers down my cheek. He brackets my jaw with his hand, and I nod.

"Yes," I whisper, because I do. "I love you too."

"Good." A muscle in his jaw pops. "Because I need you so much that I don't know if I can..."

He trails off, but I understand what he's getting at. It makes me smile, even as my stomach flutters and my pussy clenches, already anticipating the feel of his cock.

"It's okay. I don't need you to be gentle. I don't need you to fuck me like you love me right now. I just need you to fuck me like I'm yours."

Relief and heat flare in Garrett's eyes, and he surges down to press a hard kiss to my lips. Then he flips me, lifting me up like I weigh nothing and depositing me on my hands and knees. I barely have time to get all my limbs under me before he grips my hips and drives into me from behind.

He fucks me hard and deep, grunting each time his hips slap against my ass. My fingers claw at the bedding as my body rocks, and I end up giving up the fight against gravity and letting my arms buckle. My cheek presses against the sheets, my back arching as Garrett's fingers tighten around my hips.

"So good," he groans. "Such a good little Omega. You smell so perfect. Look perfect. Gonna take all of our cum. All of our bites."

"Yes," I moan. "Yes, yes, yes, yes."

This is exactly what I needed, exactly what my body and soul were craving from him, and I can't seem to stop babbling the word *yes* over and over as he pounds into me.

His strokes are rough and choppy, and I know he's holding out for as long as he can, staving off the orgasm that wants to come in order to make this last just a little longer. That makes me love him even more, and I try to do the same, pushing back against the rising tide of pleasure.

But neither of us can stop the inevitable.

After a few more deep, almost brutal strokes, Garrett buries himself inside me, his knot bulging and tying us together. His cum floods my womb, branding my insides, and he loops an arm around my waist, lifting my upper body to press against his chest. One of his large hands palms my breast, squeezing it, while the other slips between my legs and pinches my clit.

And that's it. It's all over for me.

The sharp sting of pain unleashes all the pleasure that's been building, and I squirm in his embrace as I bear down on his cock, coming all over him. He doesn't let up, rubbing harsh circles over my clit as he drops his head, mouthing at my neck.

When he bites down right next to Dante's mark, I come undone completely. I think I scream, but to be honest, I don't even hear it. All I can hear is the rushing in my ears as blood surges through my veins. It goes on and on, sending me floating through a sort of subspace that I've never experienced before—as if I'm both in and out of my body.

"...a good girl. You did so well..."

"That's our sweet Omega."

"...perfect..."

"We love you so much. You're..."

My eyelids flutter, and I realize I closed them at some point. All four of my Alphas are surrounding me, Dante in front of me, Ethan and Caleb on either side, and Garrett still behind me, his knot buried in my pussy. They stroke my skin, pressing soft kisses in the wake of their fingers as Garrett finally loosens his teeth from the place where he bit me.

He rests his head against mine, and I can feel his chest rise and fall behind me with a heavy breath.

"Are you all right?" he murmurs.

I'm so exhausted that it almost feels like it takes too much energy even to smile, but I manage it somehow, my lips curling upward.

"I'm so much better than all right that there isn't even a word for it," I promise.

He huffs a laugh. "Good."

I can tell that his knot is starting to loosen a bit, but he doesn't pull out. He keeps his cock inside me as he carefully lays me down on the bed, spooning me from behind. The other Alphas surround us, and I breathe in the air that smells like sex, cum, and their unique scents.

My neck throbs, each of the four bites on my skin reminding me of their presence, and as I fall into an exhausted doze, I realize that I don't just feel safe with these four Alphas.

I feel like I'm home.

# Chapter 51

## *Ava*

I stir in my sleep, feeling the warmth of my Alphas surrounding me.

It's that warmth, and knowing who's providing it, that slowly pulls me from my slumber. I feel so completely safe, I can take my time waking up. My body feels heavy, but content. I actually don't think I've ever felt so happy in my life.

When I read romance novels, the feeling of being in love was often described as something that made you feel light and bubbly, like you could float. For me, waking up like this, I feel the opposite. Not heavy in a bad way, but rather grounded. Secure. My feet firmly planted on ground that will not give way beneath me, but will instead lift me up to new heights.

I open my eyes, and find Dante watching me.

His gaze is heavy, but not with the heat from last night. It's warm and soft, like a blanket on a cold night.

When he sees that I'm awake he moves closer, nuzzling his face into my hair. I feel him take a deep breath, inhaling my scent, and I close my eyes and smile, feeling utterly content. His closeness comforts me.

The idea of needing an Alpha, or multiple Alphas, close to me as much as possible scared me once upon a time, but now I know that my Alphas will always do everything to take care of me. I never have to worry about missing them or feeling like I'm alone and adrift. They'll always be there.

"How do you feel?" he asks, wrapping his arms around me and nuzzling me.

"I feel happy," I tell him.

Those simple words would've been so hard to say once upon a time. I never would've wanted to admit to them, to give up so much of myself. How could I trust the feeling, I would reason. What would happen, I asked myself, if I admitted to such a thing and it was taken away from me, or the person took advantage?

But I don't have to ask myself those questions anymore. I trust my Alphas completely.

"I never expected this," I admit to him, as Dante gently kisses my neck. "I didn't think I wanted this. But now... I wouldn't give this up, I wouldn't give any of *you* up, for anything in the world."

I take his face into my hands, my thumbs brushing back and forth over his cheeks. "I never knew that Alphas like you existed. But you're perfect for me."

Dante smiles at me, looking so very pleased with my words, as if somehow he still doubted after everything that he could make me happy.

"Thank you for loving me," I whisper.

Dante's brow furrows. "Ava. You don't have to thank me. Loving you is as natural as breathing. My pack and I will treasure our perfect little Omega." He kisses me softly. "Always."

I feel the others stir, and warm lips drop a kiss to my shoulder.

"What he said," Ethan says, his voice rumbling against my back from where his chest is pressed against it. "You're incredibly easy to love, gorgeous. We're happy to do it."

"Honestly," Caleb notes, "I don't think we could stop even if we tried. But we're not going to try. Loving you is natural. It's just who we are."

"Well, I think loving you is who I am," I reply, smiling. "I don't know how people know the moment they fall in love. I feel like I was in love with you for ages before I realized it was happening."

"Good," Garrett says. "Because we're going to love you for the rest of our lives. You're stuck with us."

He winks at me, and it warms my heart. I love that I can bring out his playful side. I know that not many people can.

I smile, basking in the glow of their love. I feel so incredibly lucky, to have my Alphas who love me so much, and to be able to love them so much in return. I had no idea how amazing it would feel to love someone the way that I love them. People talk about how great it is to have someone love you, but what about the other way around? I feel like I have a purpose now, like I'm made up of more than just myself. I'm part of a bigger whole.

I'm part of my darling pack.

Everything that I do now feels like it has more meaning, more life, more joy in it. I feel incredibly special, and I'm so glad that I have these men who gave my life the many things it was missing. I have a family again, and I can love them the way I didn't get to love the last one.

"Oh, almost forgot." Ethan drops another kiss to my

shoulder and nudges me playfully, grinning. "We have a surprise for you."

I frown at him. "A surprise? But it's not my birthday."

The others all laugh fondly.

"You need to get used to being spoiled more often than on your birthday," Ethan teases me. "A surprise could come for you at any moment."

"We love to do things for you," Dante points out. "And why bother waiting for a special occasion?"

I laugh. I really am going to have to get used to this attention. "All right. What's the surprise?"

"We've renamed our latest product in your honor," Garrett says. "We're calling it the AVA Watch. It was already a product for Omegas, so it felt like this was fate."

"It's the kind of thing that we think you would've wanted, back when you first presented," Caleb adds. "We hope that if someone else is scared the way you once were, this device will help them to feel more in control of their lives and be less afraid."

"We never want any Omega to feel the way you did," Dante says. "Like being an Omega is anything less than a gift."

Tears well up in my eyes. "Guys... you really don't have to..."

"Of course we do," Ethan says. "You're our inspiration. Our reason for everything. You're the person we were waiting for our entire lives, the hole in our pack we could never fill."

I start crying properly, overwhelmed by my love and by their gesture. I'm so grateful for these men and for having them in my life. They're my Alphas, my protectors, and my mates, and I know that I will always be loved and treasured by them.

"Thank you," I whisper, pulling them into me and kissing

them. I'm thanking them for so many things, for so many reasons, but I can't quite get anymore words out. I'm too overwhelmed.

Given the way that they all kiss me back, I think they understand anyway.

# Chapter 52

## *Ava*

It's time for the big release celebration.

The AVA Watch has had the last finishing touches put on it and is ready to go. It's actually been ready for a few weeks now, but the lawyers advised that we wait until we were finished getting through everything with Marcus to debut it.

I haven't minded, and I don't think my Alphas have either. Not just because of the satisfaction of putting Marcus behind bars, but also because we've been busy adjusting to our new life together.

Plans for the shelter are moving along nicely. It's a bit overwhelming, being a business owner and in charge of so much, but I love the challenge. And it's my dream come true, so no matter how daunting some days might feel, every morning I wake up feeling grateful and happy that this is what I get to work on.

I've worked to incorporate my taste and style into the rest of our home too, so that every bit of it feels like it belongs to me as well as my Alphas. The whole building feels like it's a part of our pack now, and not like I just have a set of rooms separate from everyone else.

Despite how busy we've been, we're all glad that the product is finally launching. My Alphas are so proud of it, and I'm so proud of them.

They're amazing Alphas to care about the needs and concerns of people so unlike them, and to work tirelessly to put a product on the market that's affordable and will help so many Omegas who are just like me.

If there are other young, scared Omegas out there, or Omegas who were on suppressants for a while and now worry about bearing children or how their heat will go, or Omegas whose blockers are messing with their heats—any Omega, who for any reason is having a hard time—I really hope that they're all able to get help through this product.

And I hope they know that they deserve the help and support. Just like I do.

I admit, sometimes it still takes a bit to get used to being pampered. After so much of my life feeling neglected, and then being taught by Marcus that the only attention was bad attention, and it was best to be ignored even if that didn't fulfill me... it's still a shock sometimes to be shown just how much my Alphas adore me.

They do little things for me every day. Whether it's coming home to flowers picked out just for me, or a new book or piece of jewelry that one of them saw and made them think of me, or fresh-baked cookies that I love, I'm shown in a million ways what it is to be truly loved and adored. To be the center of someone's attention and have it be a good thing.

In a way, I hope I never get used to it. I hope that I keep being surprised and delighted by my Alphas. My mates.

Now, however, Marcus is finally in prison and his company, Prodigy Corp, has declared bankruptcy. We've gotten everything we could possibly want, and I have the justice that I deserve.

But beyond that, it means that we can wrap up our legal proceedings and go ahead and release our product: the AVA Watch.

I get ready in front of the mirror, double-checking myself. Ethan helped me pick out my dress, a sparkling red dress with flowing skirts that looks like it's made entirely of scarlet stars. It has a low back, showing off a daring amount of skin.

Looking at myself in the mirror, I hardly recognize myself. The old Ava would never have worn such an eye-catching dress. She would've wanted to fade into the background and be a wallflower.

I adjust my hair, elaborate waves falling down my back and framing my face. My eyes are framed by dramatic black winged eyeliner and dark red eyeshadow, and my lips are smeared with a bright red lipstick to match. I never would've put on such bold makeup either.

The woman I see in the mirror is a woman full of confidence. She's a woman who knows what she wants, and more than that, she already has it. She's happy and fulfilled.

She's beautiful.

I twirl in the mirror, smiling, watching my skirts spin around me. I'm so happy, and it shows on my face. I never thought of myself as beautiful before. I didn't think I was ugly either. But my face was just my face.

Now, it's different. Everything's different. I've changed so much from the woman I was before I found my mates.

I never wanted to be an Omega. I was scared of it, and angry about it. But that was because I could only see the negatives. I could only imagine being bound to someone like Marcus.

Never in my wildest dreams could I have imagined someone like my wonderful, amazing mates coming into my life. And it wasn't just one person. It was four people. Four men who give me everything I could ever need. Four men who have shown me the incredible, beautiful parts of the mating bond.

The door opens behind me and in the mirror I see Ethan enter. He looks fantastic in his bright, bold purple suit. Caleb's in lilac, Dante's in a rich royal purple, and Garrett's in a dark, sultry purple shade that almost looks black until you catch it in the light.

Ethan wraps his arms around me from behind and kisses my neck. His gaze meets mine in the mirror. "You look beautiful."

His hands slide over my body. "Whoever helped you pick this dress out has good taste."

"I'll be sure to tell him," I reply, tipping my head back to expose my throat to his hungry mouth. "But I have to warn you, sir, I'm mated."

"Mm, are you?"

"Mm-hm. To four men who'll beat you up for trying to get fresh with me."

Ethan chuckles against my skin, playfully nipping at my throat. "Good to know." He locks gazes with me in the mirror again. "I hope those four men treat you right later."

There's a heavy promise in his voice, and I shiver. "Oh, I'm sure they will." I'm looking forward to it.

As much as I'd love for him to take me right now, bend me over and have his way with me, I get the feeling he's not here just to fuck me. Sure enough, Ethan pulls back, his hands at my hips. "We have to go, or we'll be late."

I sigh. "I suppose we should make an appearance."

"Seeing as it's our product and you're the guest of honor?" Ethan chuckles. "I'd say so, yeah."

I grin at him, and we exit the bathroom where I've been getting ready. I slip my heels on and we go downstairs to where the other three are waiting for us.

They all look so very handsome. The three waiting men smile at me as I descend the staircase, Ethan taking my hand and then using it to give me a twirl when I reach the bottom of the stairs, showing me off. I blush.

"You look stunning," Dante informs me. Garrett hums in appreciative agreement, and Caleb offers me his arm to escort me to the car.

It makes me feel like a princess, which I know is probably their intention. My mates never miss an opportunity to make me feel like royalty.

Even all these months later, it still feels like something new and special to say, even in my head: my mates. My mates. *My mates*.

We get to the car and Ethan drives us neatly through the darkening streets to the city, where we're hosting the party in one of the beautiful conference rooms at the historic hotel. All four men look like they're about to vibrate with excitement.

I'm excited for them. This is the culmination of so much of their work. It was nearly taken from them, but they persevered, and now they get to show it to the world.

We pull up in front of the hotel, where Ethan tosses the keys to the valet, and Dante and Garrett each take one of my arms. Together, the five of us go up the steps into the hotel and down the hall to the ballroom we've rented.

As the guests of honor and the presenters, we get to be slightly fashionably late. Pretty much everyone else is already here, and I can feel myself flushing at all the attention we're getting as we walk through the ballroom.

I might be getting used to the love and attention from my Alphas, but from strangers, it's a whole other matter. I struggle not to turn away from all the eyes on me.

"Be proud," Dante whispers. "You're the most beautiful woman in the room."

"According to you."

"According to objective truth."

The men lead me to the small platform that's been set up, and everyone takes their seats at the various round tables that are scattered strategically throughout the room. Dinner is served to them, a menu that Dante himself put together, and I go up the steps to sit on a chair at the back of the platform while my mates approach the podium at the front of the stage.

"Ladies, gentlemen, and reporters," Ethan says, smiling out at the crowd and earning himself a few chuckles. "It's an honor to be here with you all tonight. They say if you do what you love, you never work a day in your life. I've found that if you do things with the people you love, you never work a day in your life. Please allow me to present my esteemed business partners and pack mates to unveil our latest creation."

He gestures to Dante, Caleb, and Garrett, and the crowd enthusiastically applauds. I applaud too, grinning.

Caleb speaks next. "As you know, this product has been in development for some time. We've been very excited to bring it to you, but stronger than our excitement was our desire to make it the best it could possibly be. We took extra time to make sure that every piece worked perfectly."

Garrett speaks next. "But while working on this product, we

met someone very special. Our inspiration and joy, the love of our lives, our Omega."

He gestures to me, and I find myself blushing as everyone looks at me. I wave, trying not to feel too self-conscious. Everyone applauds politely.

"It hasn't always been an easy road as we've gone through a lot of challenges," Garrett continues. "But our original determination in creating this product was to help Omegas, and since meeting and falling for our Omega, that determination only grew."

"We asked Ava, if she was all right with us briefly sharing some information," Dante says, taking his turn, "and she agreed. So to be brief, Ava showed us the struggles that Omegas sometimes go through. Her first heat was unpredictable, and a bit scary for her. She shared with us stories of Omegas who had gone through tough times."

I can feel people still looking at me, but I do my best to ignore them, to let the crowd melt away and just focus on my Alphas. They're the only people who matter anyway, so they're the only people that I should pay attention to.

"As a society, we do our best to take care of Omegas. But we can always do better, and there are times when we all could use a little help. That's why we wanted to create this product. To help continue our mission to make life easier for Omegas. To help them have control over their bodies, and know how they work so they can live their lives to the fullest, no matter what curveballs are thrown at them."

"And that," Ethan adds, "is also why we named the product the way that we did. Ava showed us so much more about being an Omega than any actual research could, and she's the reason why we get up in the mornings."

"So, without further ado," Caleb says, wrapping things up. "We'd like to present the AVA Watch: a smartwatch to help Omegas track their bio signals."

"It will help them know when their heat is coming, how long it will last, how intense it will be, when they're most fertile, and..." Garrett trails off. "Wait, we have a PowerPoint and pamphlets for this."

The crowd chuckles and Garrett waves his hand to indicate to the person running the projector to start the PowerPoint presentation.

In the back of the room, a few of the servers are now setting up sample AVA Watches on fancy stands, with colorful spotlights turning on beneath them to show them off. It'll be ready to go when the presentation finishes so that when people turn around, they're met with a beautiful display that's appeared as if out of nowhere.

The four men step back to the edge of the stage near me, and we sit through the smooth and soothing presentation on the AVA Watch's various abilities.

There are customizable settings for Alphas and Betas as well, since we wanted the watch to be inclusive, but it's a product designed with Omegas in mind first and foremost, and that's what makes it stand out.

I smile, watching with pride as everyone takes in the work my Alphas have done. Marcus tried to take all of this from us. He tried to take this product from my Alphas, and then tried to take me from them.

But it didn't work. He's behind bars for good now, and not even his company will survive. For the first time since I fled from him all those years ago, I have nothing to fear from him. I never will ever again.

The future is bright, and full of possibilities, but one thing is certain: I'll have my mates by my side the entire time.

The presentation finishes and everyone claps loudly and enthusiastically. I join in, applauding until my hands hurt. Once it all dies down, Dante asks everyone to please enjoy the food, and sample the product for themselves.

The band comes onto the stage to replace us, and a bit of room is cleared so that people can dance after dinner if they feel like it.

I certainly take a turn dancing with each of my four Alphas, enjoying the light music and the way that everyone loves the food and the watch. I hear nothing but compliments as I'm led around the dance floor.

"You're the belle of the ball," Dante promises me. "Everyone's staring at you and they think you're beautiful."

I blush. My therapist, Rachel, tells me that I need to start accepting compliments instead of deflecting them, especially from my Alphas who love me. "I feel beautiful," I admit.

And I really do mean it. I don't see how I couldn't feel beautiful when I'm so loved and cherished by my Alphas. They make me feel beautiful every day.

The three men I'm not dancing with at the time are constantly in demand by the rest of the attendees, and I can see that they're so happy and proud to be showing off their product.

In our invitations, we encouraged people to bring their Omegas, or if they themselves weren't mated, to bring an Omega friend or family member with them. That way we could demonstrate for their Omegas the features of the watch.

Sure enough, as I dance with each of my mates in turn, I watch as various Omegas try the watch while their friends, family, or mates assist them. A few Betas and Alphas also try it out, testing the modification features.

Everyone seems incredibly impressed. I'm not surprised, since I knew the watch would work well. My Alphas settle for nothing less than perfection. But I am delighted.

To my surprise, however, I'm pulled aside by Dante before long.

"I think it's time that we got out of here, don't you?" he purrs.

I frown up at him. "But everything's still in full swing. People haven't even finished dinner yet. Are you sure you don't need to stay longer?"

"We're sure." He smirks. "We've gotten the party started. Made an appearance, given our speech, let people meet us and feel like they got the personal touch from the inventors and owners of the company... and now we can disappear."

"And we're just going to abandon everyone." I raise a teasing eyebrow.

"No, we have our managers who will take care of the rest of the party, whether it's the party planners for the actual food and dancing and entertainment, or our company managers who will sell and explain the product, demonstrate it for people."

"But..." I slide my hands up his chest. "Dante, isn't that skipping out? What could be so important that you need to leave your own party early?"

He growls a little, grabbing me by the hips and pulling me into him. "You," he informs me. "Our sexy little Omega is going to be taken home and shown just how much her pack needs her."

I shiver as his lips ghost over my jaw. "Is that so?"

"Uh huh. It is. So I hope you're ready to be taken for a ride."

"More than ready," I promise him.

The other three men move through the room to join us, operating on that level where it's almost like we can read one another's minds. I swear that we've all gotten even more in tune with one another since my Alphas gave me the bonding bite.

All four of them now wear almost identical looks of dark promise on their faces. I shiver again, and smile, tilting my head toward the door.

Together, we leave the party.

Even though it doesn't take us long to get to the car, it feels like it might as well be hours. My body is already burning with anticipation, and I crawl into the back seat with Dante and Garrett as Caleb gets behind the wheel and Ethan takes the front passenger seat.

As soon as the car doors close, it becomes insanely obvious how turned on we all are. Someone might as well have dropped a pheromone bomb in the small space, because I can smell the way their unique scents deepen and shift with their arousal.

Ethan flips on the radio, and music drifts through the speakers as Caleb pulls onto the street. Almost in unison, Garrett and Dante each rest a hand on one of my thighs, and I spread my legs wider, letting my head fall back against the seat.

"Dammit," Ethan groans, looking over his shoulder. "I should've sat in the back."

"That's what you get for always calling shotgun," Garrett shoots back with a deep chuckle, his hand sliding higher up my leg until his fingers brush my damp panties.

"Is she wet?" Ethan wants to know, his gaze dropping between my legs.

Garrett's fingers slip past my panties, delving inside me and making me squirm. "Fucking soaked."

"Shit." Caleb adjusts his grip on the wheel, his eyes darting to the rearview mirror.

"You're driving them crazy." Dante leans over to murmur in my ear. "Should we make them even crazier?"

I grin, unable to help myself. "I think so."

"What do you think would do it? What would drive them wild?"

Heat floods my veins as Garrett curls his fingers inside me, teasing me with them.

"If you both fucked me, right here on the back seat," I whisper.

Garrett's fingers still, and he lets out a strangled noise. He and Dante share a look over my shoulder, and then Garrett is peeling my panties down, discarding them somewhere. I'm suddenly very grateful I'm wearing a dress, because it's easy enough for them to work the fabric up to my waist, bunching it up and leaving my lower half bare.

"Damn, gorgeous." Ethan curses. "I can *smell* you."

"So can I," Dante growls hungrily, working at the button and fly of his pants before shoving them down. His cock juts out as it's freed, and he pulls me onto his lap so that I'm straddling him.

"Ride my Alpha cock, baby girl," he purrs, and the words go right to my clit as I sink down onto him.

I moan as he fills me up, and I can hear both of the men in the front seat groan in response.

"Such a good girl," Dante praises. "You ride me so damn well."

"Yeah," I breathe, rocking against him. "Yeah."

"But you didn't just want to fuck *me*, did you?" His palm cracks across my ass, not hard but sharp enough to make me gasps. My slick coats his cock, sliding down between us as I whimper. "You want Garrett too, isn't that right?"

"Yes." I nod fervently, already losing myself in the pleasure these men give me.

"It'll be a little awkward back here, but we can do it," Dante promises. He glances over at Garrett. "Right?"

"Fuck, yes," Garrett grates.

He shifts on the seat beside us, and Dante adjusts our position so that we're horizontal across the seat with Garrett behind me. It is a bit of a tight fit, and there's not a lot of room for my knee on the side where the seat back rises up, but I don't care. I'd twist myself into a damn pretzel right now if it meant I could get what I want: both of my Alphas' cocks railing me while my other two Alphas watch.

"There you go, just like that. That's perfect," Dante murmurs, gripping my ass in his big hands and pulling me a little higher. My upper body collapses against his, one hand braced on the seat and one hand resting on his chest. In this position, my ass is exposed fully to Garrett.

I hear the rasp of a zipper as Garrett gets his pants out of the way, and I shiver as Dante pulses up into me with shallow thrusts. Dante's fingers start to creep toward my back hole, and I know he's planning to help warm me up for Garrett.

But I shake my head. "No."

"No?" He freezes immediately, so attuned to me that all it takes is a single word to make him stop. "You don't want this, baby girl?"

"I don't want him there," I whisper, my pulse picking up a little as I speak. "I want him in my pussy... with you."

"Holy fucking shit." Ethan sounds like he's dying. "I'm *never* sitting in the front seat again."

Dante laughs, and I can feel it rumble in his chest beneath my palm as he gazes up at me. The car is dark, but street lights outside illuminate his face, making his gray eyes glint like steel.

"You think you can take us both in this tight little pussy? You want to feel us both claim you like this? You want us both to knot you at the same time?"

I gush all over him in response, and Garrett's purr is almost louder than the car engine as he moves in closer behind me.

"Use your words," the massive Alpha growls, dropping his head as he leans over me. "Tell us exactly what you want."

"I want you to fuck my pussy at the same time. I want your knots. Together."

He inhales sharply, one hand wrapping around my hair and the other going to my waist. "Tell us if it's too much, okay? We can stop anytime."

I nod, a little flutter of nerves rising up to join the need rampaging through me. What I'm asking for is a lot, but I *do* want it.

I rest my cheek against Dante's chest, the fabric of his shirt feeling rough against my burning skin. With my head turned toward the front of the car, I can see the way Caleb's eyes flick up to look into the rearview mirror every few seconds, intent and focused as he glances back at us.

Ethan doesn't have to worry about keeping his eyes on the road, so he's watching us over his shoulder as if nothing could make him look away. My eyes meet his as I feel the head of Garrett's cock nudge at my entrance, and I bite my lip at the foreign sensation.

Being fucked by these Alphas is nothing new for me—but taking one of them in a hole that's already filled is something

I've never done before, and I hiss out a breath at the intense stretch as he starts to work his way inside.

Dante tenses beneath me, and although I have no idea what this feels like for him, I know it's doing something. My pussy clenches hard, and I force myself to drag in a breath and relax, opening myself up as Garrett wedges the head of his cock inside me.

"That's it, gorgeous," Ethan murmurs, shifting his gaze from my face to my core and back again. "You've got this. You can do it. I know you can."

I nod, my fingers digging into the soft leather of the seat as I push back against the intrusion, taking Garrett just a few millimeters deeper.

It takes a while for him to work his way inside, and he goes slow enough that my body has time to adjust to each incremental change, my pussy stretching so tight it's slightly painful as the two men sandwich me between them.

"Almost there. Can you take more?" Garrett asks, his voice like sandpaper.

I nod, beyond the power of speech at this point. He draws out just a little, and when he pushes deeper again, I whine softly at the sensation. His hips press against my ass, and I realize with a shock that he's all the way inside. I'm taking both of their cocks.

"How does she feel?" Caleb's eyes are on us again in the rearview mirror, and his voice is a low rasp.

"So. Fucking. *Tight*," Garrett grunts.

"So good," Dante adds. "Like she's trying to drag us both deeper."

He's right. My pussy keeps clenching around them, my body so overwhelmed by the sensations that all I can do is lean into them, squeezing tightly around the two massive cocks buried inside me.

"I need you to..." My voice gives out, and I have to remind my lungs how to take in oxygen properly before I can speak again. "Please," I whisper. "*Move.*"

Dante's hands go to my hips, and Garrett keeps one hand on my hair while the other braces against the seat for leverage. They start slowly and carefully at first, always gentle with me, sliding out a little and then pressing back in. It's almost as intense as it was when Garrett was working his way in, and I squirm between them, grinding my clit against the base of Dante's cock as they both bottom out.

"More," I beg. "Keep going. I want to feel you come inside me."

"That's not gonna be a problem," Garrett says, half laughing and half groaning. "It's so fucking much, I'm not gonna last long, little one."

"Same." Dante's voice rumbles in my ear. "Can you come for us first, baby girl? I want to make you feel good. I want to feel you milk us both."

I nod, then whimper as Caleb takes a turn and we all shift a little on the seat, bringing me down harder on their cocks.

Garrett's hand leaves my hair, and he manages to wedge it between me and Dante, finding my clit and circling it. He can't get a lot of motion, but it doesn't matter. I'm so close to falling apart anyway, and this is just the icing on the cake. I writhe between them, my toes curling. Both of my shoes are gone, although I have no idea at what point they fell off.

"Oh shit, she likes that." Dante's fingers flex around my hips. "Keep going. She's close."

I'm spiraling, higher, higher, higher...

And then suddenly, I'm falling, crashing into an orgasm that swallows me up like an ocean.

I stiffen and jerk, my body barely able to contain the rush of pleasure that surges through me, and Garrett lets out a jumbled string of curses. His knot starts to swell, and Dante curses, gripping my hips so tightly that I'm pretty sure I'll have a reminder of this written on my body tomorrow. Dante's knot inflates too, and I let out a shuddering moan at the feeling of fullness.

They're both locked inside me, their knots pressed together and bound inside my body, and I can feel the hot pressure of their cum as they explode, one after the other.

"Fuck. Fuck!"

Garrett's head drops, his hips jerking as he empties himself inside me, and Dante pulses his hips up from beneath, wedging himself even deeper inside.

I'm shaking all over, and the intense stretch keeps my orgasm rolling for what feels like forever. Garrett collapses over me, crushing me between him and his pack mate—although he must still be bracing himself on the seat, because his weight isn't so heavy that I can't breathe.

It's a good thing too, because I'm gasping as it is. My pulse is a frantic beat in my chest, slowing only gradually as their knots slowly start to soften.

"Fucking hell, gorgeous," Ethan breathes. "That was amazing."

I blink at him blearily, realizing as I do that the car is no longer moving. I don't know when that happened, but sometime in the middle of everything, we got home.

I crane my neck a little to find Caleb's gaze in the rearview mirror, and his eyes crinkle a little in the corners as he smiles and adds, *"You're* amazing."

Warmth blooms in my chest at his words.

The scent of sex in the car mixes with the scents of content-ment, adoration, and love.

I smile back at Caleb as Dante strokes my side and Garrett presses a kiss to my hair, and something tells me that my Alphas are far from finished with me tonight.

# Epilogue

## Ava

It's taken several months, but at last, my dream has come true: I am running my own animal shelter.

No longer do I have to worry about trying to make things work for my beloved pets while on a tight budget from a struggling owner. Thanks to the financial success of my Alphas, I never have to worry about financing the shelter.

In fact, since the release of the AVA Watch, NexusTech and my Alphas have been doing better than ever. People are calling it revolutionary for Omegas, and the value and profits of the company have skyrocketed.

I don't really feel it in my day to day. My Alphas continue to be down to earth, and I sure don't plan on living like some kind of celebrity anytime soon. I like to focus on my goal of making the world a better place for animals, one rescued fur baby at a time.

My mates do love to keep surprising me, whether it's with small things like a new dress, or big things like a vacation to the Caribbean. But they did those things before, so really, the shift in our wealth hasn't really affected us. I do love to go around with cash in my pocket to give to homeless people, and I've started recently to expand my work to helping out at various charity events.

Ethan teases me that I'm going to be a community leader before I know it. I don't know about that. I'm not sure I have the leadership skills for it. I like animals first and foremost, still.

But on the other hand, I've already ended up doing things in this life that I never expected to want or be able to do. I'm so much happier and more confident than I was before. Who's to say I won't end up doing what Ethan says as well?

But most importantly to me, above all else besides the happiness of my Alphas, is that my shelter is ideal for the animals. They need to be comfortable and cared for, and given all the medical needs and training from our workers so they'll be ready for adoption.

I'm determined to house as many as I can, and to spend as much time hands-on as I can with them. My boss back at the old shelter was rarely there. He was only concerned with the finances. I'm there almost every day, helping to take care of the animals myself, showing my volunteers and paid workers through example.

Today, for instance, I'm taking one of the dogs out for a walk. Lucky is a rambunctious poodle, and very intelligent. He's also due for a haircut, I note idly.

I blame my thoughts about Lucky's fur on why I don't see the man walking toward me, but his scent warns me for sure. I stop in the middle of the sidewalk and stare up at him.

Dante grins down at me. "You should probably watch where you're going."

"At least I didn't drop the leash this time," I tease him, holding up the aforementioned leash still in my hand.

It's only because his scent is so ingrained in me that I knew he was there, though. I definitely would've run into him again otherwise. It's almost exactly like the first time we met. Except then, Dante was a stranger.

Now, he's my Alpha, and one of the loves of my life.

Dante's eyes are dark and heady. "No, you didn't drop the leash," he murmurs.

I step closer, letting myself feel the heat of his body, and letting him feel mine. "So, what's a busy business-running Alpha like you doing wandering around in the middle of the afternoon?" I ask.

"I came to see if you needed any help. I finished up work at NexusTech a little early, and..." His arm slides around my waist. "I wanted to spend time with you."

I smile, my free hand landing on his chest. "I like that idea. First things first, though. Lucky needs his walk."

We go on a nice stroll together with the dog, holding hands, just like any other Alpha and Omega couple that we might pass along the way. Except that we're not. Maybe it's smug of me, but I feel like we're special.

When we get back to the shelter, I set Dante to work helping me feed the dogs their afternoon dinner, and then hand-feeding with the eye dropper the baby kittens we got last week who still need us to feed them like their mother would.

"I was really worried about them when we first got them in," I tell Dante in hushed tones as we feed them. "They don't often survive if they're this young without their mother. But I think now that they're going to be okay."

Dante smiles down at the tiny furry kitten, which looks even smaller in his large hand. "Yeah, I think so too."

My heart flutters as I look at him and how gentle and caring he is with the baby. He's going to be an amazing father.

We've just finished feeding the kittens when I hear the front door to the shelter open. "The poop cleaning brigade is here!" Ethan announces.

"Please stop saying that," Garrett says, and even though I can't see it, I can hear him rolling his eyes.

I pop my head out. "What are you three doing here?"

"We finished work and came to help," Caleb says, smiling at Jade, one of my employees who's currently manning the front desk, as he scoots on by her.

"That's very sweet of you," I tell them. "If you really want to, some of the cages could do with rinsing, and the dogs would love a little playtime with you in the yard before they have to go down to their kennels for the night."

Ethan salutes, and the three of them are on it.

I smile, watching as my four Alphas take care of my animals for me. They might be going on to different homes, but right now, they're my animals, and they deserve all the love and care I can possibly give them.

And they're getting as much love and care as my Alphas can spare too. I know that my mates would find a way to help people no matter what. That's just the kind of men they are. But they're here, at the shelter, whenever they can because they know it matters to me. They care about it because I care about it.

Nerves flutter in my belly as I watch them finish playing with the dogs and taking them all into their kennels for the night.

I was going to tell them at dinner, but they're all here now... and I admit it's been difficult to keep this secret from them. I didn't want to tell them until I went to the doctor and was absolutely sure. At first, I thought it might just be exhaustion from busting my ass getting this shelter opened.

But now I know what it is, and I want to tell them.

The four men approach me, waiting for my next orders. Dante frowns when he sees my face. "What's up?"

"Nothing's wrong," I promise them quickly.

"All right," Caleb says, trusting me. "What is it?"

I take a deep breath and smile. "I wanted to tell you over a special dinner or something, but..." I put my hands on my stomach. "I'm pregnant."

For a moment, all four Alphas look stunned.

Then they swoop in on me, hugging me and holding me tightly, rocking me, kissing my face all over. I laugh, smiling so hard my face hurts.

I knew they would be happy, so I'm not sure why I was even so nervous, but now I'm nothing but elated.

Garrett purrs, clearly pleased. "You need to tell your employees that they're going to close up, because we're going to take you home now... and celebrate."

His tone leaves absolutely no question as to what 'celebrate' means.

I laugh. "I can't just foist the work off to my employees! What kind of example would I be setting?"

"Oh my god," Jade says, laughing from the doorway. I look over at her as she waves her hands at me. "Go home! We can close up. I'm happy to do it. You guys need to go and celebrate. Congratulations, boss!"

I smile gratefully. "Thank you, Jade."

"Of course."

She gives me a little salute, and I look over at my Alphas. "Well, I suppose just this once, that does mean I'm free to go."

"Damn right it does," Dante says.

He nods decisively, and as my four Alphas hustle me out of my animal shelter to take me home, I can already feel the heat and anticipation building between us. I smile, a giddy feeling of joy overtaking me for a moment.

This isn't just the beginning of an incredible night.

It's the beginning of an incredible life.

# Also by Sadie Moss

**Magic Awakened**
Kissed by Shadows (prequel novella)
Bound by Magic
Game of Lies
Consort of Rebels

**The Vampires' Fae**
Saved by Blood
Seduced by Blood
Ruined by Blood

**The Last Shifter**
Wolf Hunted
Wolf Called
Wolf Claimed
Wolf Freed

**Academy of Unpredictable Magic**

Spark
Trials
Thief
Threat
Hunt
Clash

## Hidden World Academy
Magic Swap
Magic Chase
Magic Gambit

## Her Soulkeepers
Sacrifice
Defiance
Ascension

## Feathers and Fate
Dark Kings
Wicked Game
Wanted Angel

## Claimed by Monsters
Bound to the Dark
Captive of the Dark
Queen of the Dark